Unbuttoned by the Boss

NATALIE ANDERSON
ROBYN DONALD
KIRA SINCLAIR

D1181041

80003378929

All rights reserved including the right of reproduction in whole or in part in any form. This edition is published by arrangement with Harlequin Books S.A.

This is a work of fiction. Names, characters, places, locations and incidents are purely fictional and bear no relationship to any real life individuals, living or dead, or to any actual places, business establishments, locations, events or incidents. Any resemblance is entirely coincidental.

This book is sold subject to the condition that it shall not, by way of trade or otherwise, be lent, resold, hired out or otherwise circulated without the prior consent of the publisher in any form of binding or cover other than that in which it is published and without a similar condition including this condition being imposed on the subsequent purchaser.

® and ™ are trademarks owned and used by the trademark owner and/or its licensee. Trademarks marked with ® are registered with the United Kingdom Patent Office and/or the Office for Harmonisation in the Internal Market and in other countries.

Published in Great Britain 2015
by Mills & Boon, an imprint of Harlequin (UK) Limited,
Eton House, 18-24 Paradise Road, Richmond, Surrey, TW9 1SR

UNBUTTONED BY THE BOSS © 2015 Harlequin Books S.A.

Unbuttoned by Her Maverick Boss, The Far Side of Paradise and *Rub It In* were first published in Great Britain by Harlequin (UK) Limited.

Unbuttoned by Her Maverick Boss © 2010 Natalie Anderson
The Far Side of Paradise © 2011 Robyn Donald
Rub It In © 2012 Kira Bazzel

ISBN: 978-0-263-25216-3
eBook ISBN: 978-1-474-00395-7

05-0615

Harlequin (UK) Limited's policy is to use papers that are natural, renewable and recyclable products and made from wood grown in sustainable forests. The logging and manufacturing processes conform to the legal environmental regulations of the country of origin.

Printed and bound in Spain
by CPI, Barcelona

UNBUTTONED BY HER MAVERICK BOSS

BY
NATALIE ANDERSON

Northamptonshire Libraries & Information Services DD	
Askews & Holts	

Possibly the only librarian who got told off herself for talking too much, **Natalie Anderson** decided writing books might be more fun than shelving them—and, boy, is it that! Especially writing romance—it's the realisation of a lifetime dream kick-started by many an afternoon spent devouring Grandma's Mills & Boon® novels...

She lives in New Zealand, with her husband and four gorgeous-but-exhausting children. Swing by her website any time—she'd love to hear from you: www.natalie-anderson.com.

Kathleen Anderson, Kath Hadfield, Grandma.
Twenty years have passed since you left us, but you
know I still have your library of M&B—and I'm
adding my own to it now. Wish you were here so I
could show you. But I know you know, and you know
you live on in our hearts. Always will. Thank you for
giving me the belief in everlasting love.

CHAPTER ONE

TIME stood still for no man. And Sophy Braithwaite didn't stand still either.

She tapped her toes on the concrete floor. Slowly at first, just releasing a smidge of the energy pushing under her skin, but after a while the small rapping sound sped up.

The receptionist had directed her straight up the stairs to the office—the sign on the door ensured she'd found the one the woman meant. So she was in the right place at the right time.

Waiting.

She turned and studied the pictures on the wall beside her. Picturesque scenes of Italian countryside—she figured they were Cara's choice. Her assessment and appreciation took less than a minute. Then she looked again at the monstrosity masquerading as the desk. Good thing she wasn't into corporate espionage or fraud. She'd had ample time to rifle through files for sensitive info. Mind you, given the mess it was in, she wouldn't even find anything as useful as a pen in there. The papers were piled high in dangerously unstable towers. The unopened mail had long since filled the in-tray and now cascaded across the computer keyboard. Cara hadn't been exaggerating when she'd said she'd left it in a mess. If anything she'd been understating the case.

'I've just not had my head there and it all got away from me. I feel so terrible now with this happening,' she'd said.

'This' was the early arrival of her baby. Six weeks premature, the tiny sweetie was still in hospital and Cara was hollow-eyed and anxious. The last thing she needed was to be worrying about the part-time admin job she did for a local charity.

Sophy's irritation with the situation spiked. Where was he, then? This Lorenzo Hall—supposed hotshot of the wine industry and darling of the fundraising divas—the CEO of this chaos?

'Lorenzo's so busy at the moment. With Alex and Dani away he's dealing with everything on his own.' Cara had sounded so concerned for him when Sophy's sister, Victoria, had handed the phone to her. 'It would be just brilliant if you could go in there and stop him worrying about the Whistle Fund at least.'

Well, Sophy wasn't here to stop Lorenzo Hall from worrying, she was here to stop Cara worrying.

She realised she'd been subconsciously tapping in time to a rhythmic thunking sound coming from a distance. As if someone were using a hammer or something but speeding up, then stopping, then starting again. She shook her head free of the annoyance and looked around at the chaos again. It would take a bit of time to sort through. She wished she could say no. But then, she never said no. Not when someone asked for help like this. And didn't they all know it. She'd arrived back in New Zealand less than a month ago, yet her family had managed to fill her schedule to bursting already. But she'd let them, passively agreeing to it all. So much for becoming more assertive and ring fencing even just *some* time for her own work.

She knew they saw no change, and wasn't she acting as if there weren't—with her 'yes, of course' here and 'sure' there? Tacitly acknowledging she had nothing better to do. Or, at least, nothing as important as what they were asking.

But she did.

While she loved to help them out, there was something else she loved to do. Her heart beat faster as she thought of it as 'work'. She badly wanted to prove it could be just that. But to make a go of it, she needed time.

So she really didn't want to be standing here waiting for anybody—certainly not some guy who couldn't even seem to organise his own temp. The same boss who had Cara calling her from her hospital bed asking if she could help out. If her help really was needed, then okay, but she wasn't going to wait here for another twenty minutes. She glanced at her watch again. Ordinarily looking at it brought a tingle of pleasure—fine little vintage piece that it was. She'd found it in a flea market in South London one day. With a new old strap she'd found at another market and a trip to the watch doctor, it worked beautifully. It was definitely not running fast.

The thudding impinged into her brain again, stirring a dormant memory from school days.

No. Surely not?

She stood, walked across the office and right round behind the desk to the window. Looked straight down to the asphalt yard at the back of the warehouse. She inhaled some much-needed cool air into her lungs.

But *yes.* Basketball.

Lorenzo Hall—she just knew it was him—out there having himself some fun. If he'd been playing with even one other person she might have understood it—that he'd wanted to finish the game before seeing her. But there was no opponent to beat. He was playing alone—while she was waiting for a scheduled meeting with him. Long minutes up in his office—and it was for *his* benefit.

The irritation rose to a rolling boil. How come no one realised her time was precious too? She walked out of the office, her high heels clipping quickly down the stairs. She passed the receptionist, who was running in the other direction with the cord of her phone headset trailing after her.

'Will Mr Hall be long, do you think?' Sophy asked with extreme politeness.

The receptionist stopped, but looked harassed. 'He's not up there?'

Sophy gave the woman a cool stare. She didn't know? Wasn't she his receptionist? Where was the efficiency in this place—off on a holiday to Mars? She inhaled and crisped up even more. 'Obviously not.'

The frown on the receptionist's face deepened. 'I'm sure I saw him earlier. You could look and see if he's up on the third floor or try out the back.' With that she was gone, hurrying to do whatever it was that was so urgent.

Sophy continued down the stairs and went through the doorway behind Reception. This was a meeting that had been arranged two days ago. He might be the newly crowned king of the wine exporters, but for the life of her she couldn't figure out how he'd managed it. Not when he couldn't even make it to a meeting on time. She found what had to be the door leading out to the yard. She paused for a second, squared her shoulders and then turned the handle, pulling the heavy wood back.

From what she'd seen at the window upstairs she'd known what she was about to face—but she hadn't accounted for the effect it would have on her up close. She swallowed, momentarily speechless.

He had his back to her—a mightily broad back it was too, and very bronzed. Well, it would be from all the time he obviously spent out here—*shirtless*.

The fire that blazed through her was surely all due to anger.

The baseboard and basket were on a stand on the far side of the asphalt square. He had the ball in hand, feet apart, his knees slightly bent as he readied to take the shot.

Sophy waited for the exact moment. Just as his body moved to shoot the ball, she called—raising her normal volume more than a fraction, and using what her speech and drama teacher had referred to as 'the tone'.

'Lorenzo Hall?'

Needless to say, he didn't make the basket. Sophy smiled. But then, in an instant, it died on her lips.

Even with the three or so metres between them she could feel the scorching heat of him. He turned his head, looked her over—a quick, slicing glance with the darkest eyes she'd ever seen. Then he turned back to the wretched basket.

That had been all he needed to sum her up? Sophy wasn't used to being dismissed so quickly. She might not have lived up to her family's stellar success in the legal fraternity, but she did okay in the appearance stakes. Always immaculate. Always appropriate. Presentation had been drilled into her for so long it was second nature now. So she knew she looked more than acceptable in her baby-blue linen skirt and pressed white shirt. Her lipstick was muted but smooth and her face wasn't shiny. Her one-style-only hair would be in place—she didn't even have to try for that to happen.

The ball had bounced a couple of times. He barely had to move to retrieve it. Once it was back in his broad hands he turned and gave her another look—even more pointed.

Then he turned back to face the baseboard, took careful aim and replayed the shot—landing it this time.

Sophy would have turned and walked if she wasn't too angry to move. So that was the way of it, huh? His little game of by-myself-basketball was more important than a meeting scheduled with her. She'd heard nothing but positives about this guy's charitable organisation. Had heard the rumours about his own background and his meteoric rise—marvellous, wasn't it, people said, that someone with a background like that could become such a success?

Well, Sophy wasn't about to patronise the selfish jerk. 'Are we meeting any time soon?' She *refused* to offer to come back at another time—bit back the conciliatory words by pushing her jaws together. She wasn't going to put herself out at all for him.

The ball had bounced back to him again. He tossed it to the side and walked towards her. His jeans sat low on his hips. He wore them with no belt and she saw a glimpse of a waistband—briefs or boxers? She shouldn't be wondering. But she couldn't stop looking.

There was no fat beneath his skin, just lithe muscles that rippled as he walked. She managed to force her gaze a fraction higher, skimming over the dusting of masculine hair, the dark nipples. He had straight, broad shoulders. Sleek curving muscles stretched down his arms. And all over was the sheen of sweat—burnishing the smooth, sun bronzed skin.

She found she was mirroring his slight breathlessness. His chest was rising and falling that bit quickly, that bit jerkily, and her own felt tight as she studied him. He had an amazing torso—the strength, the undeniable masculinity had her spellbound. Her gaze coasted downwards again.

He took two more steps—bringing him too close.

Startled, she looked up as he loomed over her. Realised that with a narrowed, keen gaze he was watching the way she was looking him up and down.

She met his stare, matched it, refusing to let her embarrassment at being caught ogling burn her skin red. But then, when he knew he had her attention, he let his gaze strip down every inch of her body. She actually *felt* the way his attention lit on her neck, on the small V of exposed skin on her chest, on the curve of her breasts...

She fought harder to stop the blush and felt her anger resurge. But she probably deserved it. Hadn't she just done this to him? But not intentionally—not *provocatively*. She just hadn't realised quite how obvious she'd been or how long she'd been staring—her brain had gone AWOL while her eyes feasted.

But his was a deliberate, blatantly sexual action.

Her toes curled in the tips of her heeled pumps. The rest of her wanted to shrivel too—so she could disappear. And she used the anger to block that other message striving to move from brain to body—the desire that wanted to unfurl and scurry through her veins.

'You must be Sophy.' He gestured back to his mini basketball court. 'I was thinking. Lost track of time.'

Well, that fell way too short for an apology.

'My time is valuable to me,' she asserted vocally for the first time in her life. 'I don't like it being wasted.'

Certainly not by a half naked man. Not like this anyway.

Those black, bottomless eyes met hers. The colour rose a little higher on his cheekbones. She wasn't sure if it was from exertion, embarrassment or anger. She suspected the latter.

'Of course,' he said smoothly—too quietly. 'I won't do it again.'

Something had kindled in his eyes as he'd added that. Something she didn't care to define. As it was she felt herself flushing—unable to stop it now—as if she were the one in the wrong. She shifted her weight from one foot to the other. Stole another quick glance at his torso and then aimed to concentrate on the concrete.

'You never seen a man sweat before, Sophy?' His soft question hit her in the gut.

The crisp spring morning suddenly got a whole lot hotter. She tried to say something. Couldn't. The dry irony in his voice just devastated her.

He turned away from her. 'Want to play a little one on one?' he asked. 'I find it helps me focus. You might find it helps you too.'

Oh, so she needed help with focus? Heaven help her she did.

'It's also good for burning excess energy.'

Now *that* was said with deliberate innuendo. He was trying to tip her balance—as if he weren't doing it already with his sheer physicality which was on display. With considerable effort she pulled herself together. Well, she could do a little innuendo too. His few words could flame, but her cool delivery would crush. 'I'm obviously over-dressed.'

His eyes widened fractionally, before he replied calmly, 'Easily fixed.'

She lifted her brows very slowly, determined to stay cool. 'You want me to strip?'

He laughed then, his whole face breaking into an absolute charmer of a smile. Sophy lifted her fingers to her mouth to stop her jaw from gaping in surprise. His whole demeanour changed—like quicksilver—from seriously brooding to sparkling good humour. The flash was utterly intriguing and devastatingly attractive.

'It would be fair, don't you think?' he said. 'I mean, you have me at a disadvantage.'

'You put yourself at a disadvantage.' She was even more breathless now. And privately she thought his semi-nudity a huge benefit to him—how to fuzzle the minds of your business opponents in one easy step. She angled away from him—trying to recover her equilibrium. She got a clear view of the fence and saw one section was covered with a huge bit of graffiti. The colours leapt out, almost 3D, in bold blocks. An image of a man—like an ancient statue—with vibrant shades of blue leaping out from behind and an indecipherable word shooting up from one side. She'd never have expected it; the reception area she'd walked through had been incredibly slick—it was only the office upstairs that had been a total mess. Now there was this—what many people would consider an eyesore.

He walked in front of her line of vision and picked up the ball again, spinning it in his hands. 'We can talk through the details at the same time.'

He was still smiling but there was an edge back now—a deliberate challenge. But it was one she just had to turn down. No way was she playing ball with him. This wouldn't be like some Hollywood movie where she scored a hoop first shot. She'd miss it by a mile and totally embarrass herself. She hadn't played in years—to land baskets you needed to practise. She had no hope of relying on muscle memory now.

'Perhaps it would be best if we reschedule this meeting,' she ducked it.

The smile tugged harder on one corner of his mouth.

'You might want to take a shower now,' she added coldly.

His brows lifted then. 'You really don't like sweat?' He

laughed as he looked over her pale blue suit. 'No. You wouldn't, would you?'

She went silent—refusing to rise to that one. Truth was, she was feeling utterly human right now and starting to sweat herself just from looking at him. Cara hadn't mentioned that her boss was completely gorgeous.

She looked at the graffiti again, eyes narrowed as she tried to work out one of the letters in that word.

'Damn kids.' He'd followed the direction of her gaze.

'It could be worse,' she said. Not wanting to find anything to agree on with him.

'You think?'

'Yeah, it could just be a tag—you know, initials, a name or something. But that's actually quite a cool picture.'

He coughed. It started as a clear-your-throat kind of cough, but rapidly turned into a hacking one that sounded as if he were in danger of losing a lung. Anyone else and she'd ask if he was okay. But she wasn't going anywhere nearer the personal with him. As it was they'd crossed some polite lines already and she was finding it way too unsettling.

'It must have taken a while.' She commented more on the graffiti just to cover the moment until he breathed freely at last. There actually was a lot of depth to the design. It couldn't possibly be a three-minute spray and run number. 'But it's bad to do it to someone else's property.'

'You're so right.'

She gave him a quick look. Was that a touch of laughter in his voice? His expression was back to brooding, even so, she suspected him.

'So you're desperate for an administrator, is that right?' Finally she snapped back on track.

'For the Whistle Fund, yes.' He too suddenly went professional. 'Kat, my receptionist here, has been too busy to be able to help much since Cara left. We've got a lot on right now so I need someone who can stay on board for at least a month. I need the mess sorted and then help with training a new recruit. I haven't even got to advertise yet. Can you commit to it?' He looked serious. 'You'll be paid of course. I wouldn't expect anyone to take on this level of work voluntarily.'

'I don't need to be paid. I like to work voluntarily.'

'You'll be paid,' he clipped. 'You can donate it back to the charity if you like, but you'll be paid.'

So he didn't want to be beholden to her? But she didn't need the money, the income from her trust fund was more than enough for her to get by. She'd always needed something to give her a sense of dignity—had never sat around doing nothing but shopping and socialising. It wasn't the way she'd been raised. Yes, they had money, but they still had to do something worthwhile with their time. Only she hadn't managed to follow in the family footsteps and pursue a law based career. Her mother, brother and sister were all super successful lawyers. All the true save-the-oppressed kind, not corporate massive-fee-billing sharks. Worse was her father, who was a retired judge. He still worked—publishing research, heading reviews of the system. Sophy's surname was synonymous with excellence in the field. Not one of them had failed or even deviated from that path.

Only Sophy.

So she'd tried to gain her credibility by being the yes-person. Doing all the voluntary stuff, being the consummate organiser of everything they asked for—mainly their own lives. She might not have their legal brains, but she was practical. Yet in trying to keep up with them she'd made one stupid, massive mistake—she'd mistaken her personal value. So she'd gone away. While overseas she'd finally found her own passion, her own calling. And as soon as she got the time she was going to build her business and prove her skill to the family.

'Cara's office is in the building here.' He seemed to take her silence for acquiescence. 'It's all yours. I thought we could cover her okay but with her baby coming so soon and with Dani away with Alex, I need someone who can concentrate wholly on it.'

'Full time?' Sophy's heart was sinking. She just wasn't going to be able to say no.

'Maybe for the first week to catch up.' His grin was touchingly rueful. 'After that just the mornings should be enough. And I'd need you to be present at whatever evening meetings there are and the functions. Actually, you need to finalise the details for the next one.'

Yes. The Whistle Fund was famous for its functions—fabulous evenings of entertainment that drew the rich and famous out, and got them to open their wallets too. The presence of the 'stars' meant the presence of Joe Public was huge too—everybody liked to be a VIP for a night.

'You can't find anyone else?' Sophy tried one last avenue. 'Maybe from a temp agency?'

'Cara wanted to be sure the office was in good hands. She doesn't trust that a stranger will be able to come in and fix it. I don't want to stress her any more than she already is. And she told me you're the only one who can get this job done. I promised her I'd give you a shot.'

Sophy's ears pricked at the slight hint of sarcasm—did he think she couldn't get it done? Her spine stiffened—why, she could sort that lot upstairs in her sleep.

Cara had pleaded for her to come. Because Sophy's sister, Victoria, was one of Cara's best friends. And Victoria had talked to Cara—assured her Sophy was the one to do it: she was available, she was capable. Now it seemed she was all Cara could accept.

Sophy might as well have never gone away. Since landing back she'd stepped straight back into the overcommitted, overscheduled life she'd left two years before. No one had stopped to think she might have other things she wanted to do. And why should they? Hadn't she been saying yes—as she always had?

So she should say no now. Say sorry, but that she had other priorities and couldn't give him that much time. She looked at him, tried really hard not to let her gaze slip down his body again. There was a hard look in his eyes— as if he didn't really believe what Cara had told him about her, and that he expected her to say no. That he'd just as soon phone for some anonymous temp and be done with it. Suddenly she sensed that he didn't like having to ask her at all. That made her stand up even straighter.

And there was Cara herself, wasn't there? Hovering over her tiny daughter in the incubator—with enough on her mind without needlessly worrying about her boss being so stressed out. What a crock. If Cara had seen him today, she'd have known she had no cause for concern— he was so relaxed he was out wasting time playing ball. But Sophy couldn't let her sister's friend down—just as she'd never let her sister down.

'I'll be back tomorrow to start,' she said briskly.

'I'll be here to show you the ropes.'

'Nine a.m.' She let her gaze rake him one last time. 'Sharp.'

She turned and walked. His words came just as the door closed behind her. Whether she was meant to hear the low suggestively spoken reply she didn't know, but she did—and it almost incinerated her.

'*Yes, ma'am.*'

CHAPTER TWO

NINE a.m. came and went. Sophy sat in the office that looked as if it had been hit by a cyclone and checked her watch every thirty seconds or so. Unbelievable. No wonder this place was in such a mess. He certainly needed help. But he was so going the wrong way about getting it.

She filled in five minutes by moving some of the mail to find the keyboard. Decided to start opening and sorting it. Forty minutes later a portion of the desk was clear, the recycling bin was full of envelopes and half the letters were neatly stacked in classified piles. At that point she decided she shouldn't go further without consulting him. She went downstairs to the receptionist.

'Kat? I'm Sophy. Here to work on the Whistle Fund admin. Do you know where Mr Hall is?'

The receptionist blinked at her. 'I thought he was up with you. I've been taking messages because he's not picking up the phone.'

'Well, he's not with me.'

'He's not out the back?'

No. Naturally out of the window had been the first place she'd looked. Sophy heard the front doors slide open and turned expectantly. A courier driver walked in with a parcel under his arm.

'Can you see if he's on the third floor?' Kat asked. 'I need to deal with this.'

'Of course,' Sophy answered automatically.

The third floor—was that where Lorenzo's office was? She climbed the stairs. Stopped at the second floor and checked the other two offices there once more—both were in a far better state than Cara's. They actually looked as if people worked in them—several people even—but there was no one present. Further along the corridor there was a massive room that was almost totally empty. Was the place run by ghosts? The communication was appalling. Sophy swallowed the flutter of nerves as she climbed up the next flight of stairs. There was no corridor off them this time—just the one door marked 'private'.

She knocked. No answer.

She knocked again. Still no answer.

Without thinking about it she tried the handle. The door swung open and she stepped inside.

The space was huge—and much brighter than the dimly lit stairwell. Sunlight shone through the skylight windows in the roof. She blinked rapidly and took in the scene. This wasn't office space. This was an apartment—*Lorenzo's* apartment.

And if she wasn't mistaken, the sofa was occupied.

'What's wrong?' Pure instinct drove her forward to where he was sprawled back on the wide sweep of leather.

It was hard dragging her eyes up his chest to his face but once she did she was able to focus better. Beneath the tan he was pale, but dark shadows hung under his eyes. Hell, if this was a hangover she'd be so mad with him.

'Sore throat.' A total croak, not the slight rasp of yesterday.

Sore throat and then some, Sophy reckoned. He looked dreadful. Actually he didn't, he looked one shade less than magnificent. So that meant he really must be sick. She couldn't help give him the once over again. Just impossible not to when he had the most amazing body she'd ever seen up close.

He was in boxers—nothing but boxers. Not the loose fitting pure cotton kind, but the knit type that clung to his slim hips, muscled thighs—and other intriguing bits.

So that was that question answered. And a few others too.

Sophy stopped her gaping. She needed to pull herself together and deal with him.

'You have a temperature.' It was obvious from his glistening skin. She marched to the kitchen area in the open-plan space. Poured a glass of water. Wished she could snatch a moment to drink one herself, but she was too concerned about how feverish he looked.

'I'm fine.' He coughed, totally hacking up that lung.

'Of course you are,' Sophy said smartly. 'That's why you missed our meeting.' She held out the glass to him. His hand shook as he reached for it. She took his fingers and wrapped them round the glass herself. Only when certain he had it did she let him go.

Their eyes met when she looked up from the glass. She saw the raw anger in his—impotent anger.

'I'm fine,' he repeated, grinding the words through his teeth.

Yeah, right. He was shivering. He ditched the water on the coffee table in front of the sofa after only the tiniest sip. His laptop was on the table too, the faintest hum coming from it. Did he really think he was capable of work?

'When did you last eat?' she asked, her practical nature asserting itself.

He winced.

'I need to take your temperature.'

'Rot.'

She gingerly placed her palm on his forehead. Snatched it away at the same time that he jerked back.

'Quit it,' he said hoarsely.

She curled her tingling fingers. 'You're burning up. You need to see a doctor.'

'Rubbish.'

'Not negotiable.' Sophy pulled her mobile from her pocket and flipped it open. 'I can get someone to come here.'

'Don't you dare.' It would have sounded good if his voice hadn't cracked in the middle. He tried to move, evidently thought better of it and just rasped bitterly, 'Sophy, back off. I'm fine. I have work I need to get on with.'

She ignored him, spoke to the receptionist at the clinic she'd been to all her life. Two minutes later she hung up. 'A locum will be here in ten.'

'Too bad. I'm not seeing him. I have to do this—'

'Your social networking will have to wait.' Sophy closed the laptop. Picked it up and put it far, far away on the kitchen bench.

'Bring that back here—I was working.'

She went close and looked down at him. 'I really wish I had one of those old-fashioned mercury thermometers. I know where I'd stick it.'

'Don't.' His hand shot out and gripped her wrist—hard. 'You're right. I'm not feeling well. And if you keep provoking me I'll snap.'

Really? And do what?

She stared into dark eyes, saw the tiredness, the strain, the frustration—and even deeper she saw the unhappiness. At that she relented. 'Okay. But you have to stop fighting me too. You're sick, you need to see a doctor and you need taking care of.'

He shifted on the sofa.

'Look, it's happening whether you agree or not, Lorenzo. Why not make it that bit more pleasant?'

He breathed in—she could see the effort hurting him. He closed his eyes and she knew she'd won. 'Okay, but you've done your thing. You can go now. Kat can send the doctor up.' Another tremor shook him.

But she didn't think she could go now. She couldn't leave anyone alone in this state. And oddly enough she felt that even more strongly about him—he'd never admit it, but he was vulnerable. He was alone.

He shook his head slightly and looked cheesed again. 'At least bring my laptop back.'

'What's the point, Lorenzo?' she said quietly. 'Staring at the screen isn't going to get it done. You're better off getting some sleep and getting well. Then you'll do the work in a quarter of the time.'

His head fell back against the sofa cushions. Round two to her.

The doctor stayed only ten minutes. Sophy waited on the top of the stairs, put her phone in action some more. Then, after exchanging a few words with the doctor on her way out, she went back in to face the grumpy patient.

'I'm getting you a rug,' she said, heading towards the doors at the back of the room, refusing to be embarrassed about the idea of going into his bedroom.

'There's one on the end of the sofa.'

She stopped. So there was. She'd not noticed it. Hard to notice anything else in the room when he was mostly naked. 'Well—' she tried not to stare at him as she reached down and picked it up '—I think perhaps you'd better put it on. You don't want to get a chill.'

He was well enough to send her an ironic glance. But he leaned back on the sofa and pulled the rug over his waist and down his legs. 'Happy now, nursie?'

His chest was still bare, so, no, she wasn't. But he was obviously feeling a touch better. The doctor said she'd given him some pain relief—must be fast acting stuff.

'So it's tonsillitis?' Sophy asked carefully, not wanting to intrude too much, yet unable to stop.

'Stupid, isn't it?' Lorenzo said.

No. Like anyone, Sophy knew how painful a sore throat could be. 'Did you get it as a child?'

'A bit.' He nodded. 'Haven't had it in years, though.'

'They didn't take them out for you?' While it might not be a regular practice any more, she knew that for the most recurrent cases they still did tonsillectomies.

He repositioned his head on the sofa cushions again. 'I was on the waiting list for a while. But it never happened. When I got to boarding school the episodes seemed to stop.'

Sophy poured the electrolyte drink the doctor had given her into a glass. 'It was a good school, wasn't it?'

'Better than all the others I went to.'

She knew he'd been at school with Alex Carlisle—his partner in setting up the Whistle Fund. It was the school her elder brother had gone to too—years before. Private, exclusive, incredibly academic and with superior sporting results as well. It was a tough place to shine—and she just knew Lorenzo had shone. Her sister had gone to the girls' equivalent. But by the time Sophy had come along their parents were happy for her to just go to the local—they'd said they didn't want to send her away to board. But Sophy knew it was because she hadn't had the off-the-charts grades her siblings had had. It wasn't that she was below average, she just wasn't brilliant. 'The antibiotics will have you better in no time. Then maybe you should have a holiday.'

His brows shot up.

'Cara says you've been working too hard,' Sophy said

blandly, ignoring his mounting outrage. 'Perhaps you've gotten run down.' At that she sent him a look from under her lashes—unable to resist the temptation to let a hint of flirt out.

'Honey, I'm hardly run down.' His muscles rippled as he stretched out his arms in an unabashed display of male preening.

Oh, he was definitely feeling better. And she just couldn't resist teasing him some more.

'The muscles might look good, Lorenzo,' the devil made her whisper, 'but you wouldn't be up to it. You'd be spent just trying to stand.'

'You want to move closer and we'll test that out?' Sick or not, he didn't miss a beat.

She turned and paced away. Enough channelling of Rosanna—Sophy just wasn't as practised a flirt as her best friend. 'I'm not in the mood for more disappointments.'

'You were disappointed I wasn't there to meet you?'

She spun and caught his amused, *satisfied* look. She inhaled. 'You should be lying down. Hurry up and finish that drink.'

'Sophy—' his eyes glittered '—I don't need a mother.' It was a slicing rejection of any sort of kindness.

'No,' she agreed curtly. 'You need a nurse. I've arranged for one to come from an agency.'

Lorenzo was so shocked he couldn't speak for a full minute. He repeated her words in his head several times. Still didn't believe it. 'You've *what*?'

'I've got a nurse coming. I've got work to get on with, so does Kat, and you can't be left alone.'

Can't be left alone? What did she think he'd been all his life? 'You can tell your nurse she's not necessary.'

'No. Too late for that.' She moved back to the table and took away the empty glass. 'She's on her way.'

Oh, she thought she was so damn competent, didn't she? 'She'll have a mobile. Call it.' Wasn't getting a doctor around enough for this woman? Another tremor shook him from the bones out. Blow the fever—he was boiling mad.

'Don't bother trying, Lorenzo,' she said coolly, cutting him off before he'd even got started. 'She's on her way and she's staying.'

He gritted his teeth and glared at her. He'd never felt this frustration—hadn't felt this useless since he was a kid being shunted from place to place with no say in it.

He closed his eyes as a wave of utter weariness hit him. Okay, he had been working hard—even harder than usual recently. He didn't know when his hunger for success would be filled. Always he was chased by the feeling that it could be whisked away from him, that he'd wake up one day and find himself with nothing. So he worked, worked, worked—building the base bigger. He could never have enough of the security he needed.

But investing in Vance's bar idea might have been one project too many. He'd sent all his staff and resources there for the last week. Helping him get ready for the big opening night—which Lorenzo was going to miss at this rate. As a result his own offices had been sadly neglected. The Whistle Fund in particular. It wouldn't take too much to get it right again, but it needed time that he simply didn't have right now. He'd been working twenty-hour days in the last fortnight as it was. So Cara's office was a mess. It was stupid, but there was a big part of him that hated this woman seeing it like that.

Sophy—the supremely interfering piece of efficiency. And how could he be finding her remotely attractive? She was so damn quick and proper and *right* it was nauseating. Had she ever made a mistake in her life? He so didn't think so. And if she had, he bet she'd never admit to it.

Utterly perfect, wasn't she?

He shifted under the rug. She *was* perfect—like a porcelain doll. Creamy skin and a blonde bob that sprang into neat curls at the ends—how long did it take her to get it to sit just so? Then there was that little nose and the lips that had a sweet cupid's bow that begged to be kissed. And big blue eyes that went even bigger when she looked at him—a blend of intense interest and reserve. She looked as if she wanted but was wary. She half teased and then withdrew again. It made him want to pounce all the more. He saw her gaze flick over him again. Damn the weakness in his bones. Because that look in her eyes made him want to strip her bare   inch by beautiful inch—and find out whether the hint of the fire he could see really was just the glow from an inferno beneath. He sure as hell was fantasising it was.

Only he was so damn helpless.

That one last part of his body refused to acknowledge the sickness. He raised his knees, lifting the rug to hide the evidence, and mentally berated himself. So inappropriate. It must be the fever putting these kinds of thoughts into his head.

He looked at her, she was speaking briskly into her phone again. Some other poor soul was at the mercy of her efficiency. He was beyond even trying to listen. All he wanted was to rip the gadget from her and press his mouth to hers—just to shut her up. Just to slake the lust. So damn irresistible. So damn impossible. For one thing he was harbouring a million nasty bugs in his throat, for another she just wasn't his type. Not at all. Not when he was on form.

But he felt an almost feral need to touch her—had done since the second he'd first seen her looking so snippy out the back of the warehouse. He wanted to muss her up so bad he wanted to growl.

Sick. He really was sick.

'Okay, that's everything settled, then.'

'You're going?' Oh, man. He grimaced. Where had that sound of disappointment come from?

She paused. 'You didn't think I was going to stay, did you? I've got other things to do. And you said it yourself, Lorenzo—you don't need a mother, or any kind of sympathy.'

'So you're going to leave me here at the mercy of some stranger?' He opted to try to wheedle. Thinking on it, he'd rather have her here than some nurse—even if she was a little too efficient for his liking. Did she never stop and slow down? She should slow down— he'd make her. Give it to her really, really slow. Bend her back and lick all the way up her gorgeous length until she... *Hell*, his eyes were probably glazing over. He shut them tight. It made the fantasy worse. It made the aching in his gut worse.

On seconds thoughts, the sooner Sophy left, the better.

'She's very well qualified and has great references,' Sophy said—oblivious to the base nature of his thoughts. 'She'll get you right again.'

'I do not need a damn nursemaid.' What was she going to do all day? He'd had the pills, now he just needed to sleep until it was time to take more. The last thing he wanted was some woman poking round his apartment. He never let women poke around. He liked his privacy—the peace in isolation.

'Your temperature is sky-high. Until it's down and the antibiotics have kicked in, then you are not being left alone. We're talking twenty-four hours or less, Lorenzo. Get over it.'

He opened his mouth. Shut it again. He hadn't been given orders quite like that in *years*.

'Now you need to rest. The nurse will be here in twenty. She's bringing more medicine with her.'

Enough was enough. He wasn't putting up with this for a moment longer. He put his feet on the ground and hauled himself up.

'Lorenzo.' Sophy's heart lurched. She moved fast.

His eyes were closed and the frown on his face was heightened by his extreme pallor. His whole body was covered in a film of sweat but he shivered again. She wrapped her arm around him—felt every single muscle in his body go tense. Sophy bit her lip. The sooner the nurse got here, the better.

'I'm fine.' The anger surged in his voice. Directed at both her and himself. He was furious with his weakness.

'And I'm the Queen of Atlantis.'

'This is ridiculous. I'm hardly at death's door. It's a sore throat.' But he sat back down all the same, put his feet up this time and scrunched more into the sofa, lying shivering beneath the rug. His teeth were tightly clenched—to stop them chattering or because he was so mad? Probably both.

Sophy was definitely staying 'til the nurse arrived now. She sat in the chair across from the sofa. Keeping a wary eye on him and sneaking interested glances round his apartment. The space was gorgeous—huge and light. The kitchen was modern—had all the lovely stainless steel appliances a gourmet home cook could ever want. There was a massive shelving system on one wall—filled with books, CDs, DVDs. She leaned close to look at the titles, even though she knew she was being nosy.

She glanced at her watch. Shouldn't be long now 'til the nurse arrived. He'd gone very quiet. Was he asleep? Quietly she moved back to the sofa, bent so she could see his face.

His jet-black hair was just slightly too long—as if he'd missed his last appointment with the barber—and right now it was a tousled mess. It was gorgeous—just begging for fingers to tunnel into it. And his features were beautiful. His eyelashes were annoyingly long while the shadow on his angular cheek tempted her to touch. And then there was his mouth. In the heart of his chiselled jaw were the most sensual lips she'd ever seen. Full, gently curved, slightly parted as he slept. The shivering seemed to have eased. Had his temperature dropped? She put her palm on his forehead again.

His hand moved fast, clamping round her wrist as his eyes shot open. The brown so deep as to be black, filled with a fire she wasn't sure was purely fever.

She was caught, crouched half over him, unable to move. His eyes burned into her. 'I told you to quit it.'

But he wasn't holding her hand away from him, instead he pressed her fingers harder to his skin. Afterwards she never knew from where she'd got the audacity, but she spread her fingers, gently stroking them over his damp brow. Smoothing the frown lines, stretching higher to reach into his hair, rumpling it ever so gently.

Her fingertips felt so sensitive—never had she felt something so strong inside from just touching someone. The strangest kind of electricity surged into her. Thrilling yet relaxing at the same time. It felt right to be touching him. It felt good. Okay, more than good. Sexual energy strummed through her, just like that. She wanted to move, to touch more, to shift her hips—tease the ache that had woken deep within.

His eyes didn't leave hers, filled with a look so full of…something. Was it anger or desire or something deeper and darker still?

The buzzing made her jump. Made him grip her even harder—so hard she winced.

'That'll be the nurse,' she muttered.

Despite the illness he had fearsome strength when he wanted to use it.

She finally broke away from his deepening gaze, and pointedly looked at his hand. 'You need to let me go.'

His fingers loosened and she pulled her hand free. Her heart was beating so fast she felt dizzy. Maybe it wasn't tonsillitis that he had. Maybe it was the flu and she'd caught it just like that. She felt as hot as he looked.

She caught a glimpse of herself in a mirror hanging on the wall as she hurried to the door. Yes, the colour in her cheeks was definitely more than the usual. And her eyes looked huge.

The nurse was at least fifty and looked like a total grandma with her specs and cardigan and knitting needles poking out of her bag. She talked like a grandma too—incessant, interested and caring but with an underlying thread of steel.

Sophy smothered her smile as the woman began her no nonsense fussing over Lorenzo. Definitely time to make a move. She needed some space to examine that moment again too.

'I'll phone later,' she said to the nurse.

'Aren't you going to talk to me?' A growl from the sofa.

'You're going to be asleep.' Sophy went even warmer inside when she saw the put out look flash on his face.

But then he started shivering again and the nurse turned to him. 'We need to get you into bed, don't we? I'll go and put some nice fresh sheets on it. No, don't worry, I can find them. You just lie back and relax. Medicine, some painkillers, something nice and warm to drink. We'll have you better in no time.'

Sophy watched the woman bustle off, finding her way around the place by some kind of special nursing sixth sense. She looked back at Lorenzo; he was looking at the nurse with such loathing that Sophy had to clap her hand over her mouth to stop herself laughing. At her movement his head whipped round and he glared at her. Oh, boy, definitely time to go.

'Sophy.'

Halfway across the room she hesitated.

'Come here.'

Sick as he was, it was a command. And Sophy felt a scarily overwhelming urge to do as he bid. How pathetic—it wasn't as if he could do much if she refused.

'Come here.' Softly spoken again, but it wasn't just a thread of steel in there—it was a whole core. And his magnetism wasn't something she could ignore.

She walked over to him. Even though he was the one lying down, even though she was the one who could leave, somehow the balance of power had changed. In those few minutes when she'd been crouched next to him, stroking him, something had changed completely.

She stopped a little distance away, met the deep, dark gaze a little nervously.

'I want to thank you,' he said quietly.

'It's not necessary.' She felt the blush rising in her cheeks. Sorting out others was her speciality. She had a family of geniuses who could barely organise what they wanted to make for dinner every night. This was nothing.

He was still looking at her so intensely she wondered what it was he was trying to read. His focus dropped, to her mouth. She swallowed—determined not to give herself away by licking her suddenly desperately dry lips. Her pulse thumped in her ears.

'I'm kissing you. Can you feel it?'

Sophy blinked. Had she just dreamed that? Was that a fantasy moment? Had he really just said that? Like *that*— a purring whisper?

Mind sex. Was that what this was? Because she had to admit she was feeling it—and was desperate to feel more. Okay, *she* was delirious. She really was. Definitely burning up. She licked her lips, not realising she was 'til she was done and they were still tingling with the need for touch—*his* touch. His kiss.

Suddenly he was smiling—that absolutely brilliant smile that had disarmed her so completely yesterday.

She snatched in a breath—her lungs felt as if they were eating fire. 'Get better soon.' And she ran, his low chuckle hard on her heels.

Every time Sophy thought of the expression on his face as she'd left she blushed bodily. And it wasn't without a few nerves that she walked up to the second floor three days later. Lorenzo was back on deck—Kat told her as soon as she arrived. And he was waiting for her in his office. She was to see him as soon as she got there.

Sophy had the feeling it was going to be interesting. He hadn't liked her seeing him so vulnerable. Certainly hadn't liked the way she'd handled it. If she'd learned anything about him from their brief meetings so far, he liked to be the boss. Only she'd overruled him. She suspected he was going to make her pay for that—only the burning question was *how*? In the devastatingly direct way that he'd reclaimed the power in his apartment? By using his way-too-potent sensuality? She totally shouldn't be hoping so. Lorenzo Hall had playboy commitment-phobe stamped all over him—in permanent ink. She took a breath and knocked on his door.

'Just a moment.'

She waited, her nerves stretching tauter with every tiny tick of her watch. What was this pause about—did he want to force her to break point? Because he knew, didn't he? Was all too aware of his effect on her—and on any woman. Why, he'd used it to his advantage in his apartment—a look, a very few words and she was practically in a puddle at his feet. Then she heard him.

'Okay, you can come in now.'

She opened the door and stopped on the threshold. Gaped.

He was standing by the window, had turned to watch as she came in. He was in jeans. But still no shirt. From behind him the light touched his body like an aura giving it a golden glow. It didn't need the emphasis. It was blindingly gorgeous already.

It was as if she were two feet from a launch tower that had just sent a rocket into space—the heat from the blast nearly eviscerating her.

His torso was bronzed, no sheen from sweat this time, but she wanted to see it wet again. Her fingers wanted to slide through the slickness, they wanted to torment him to slickness.

She squeezed her eyes shut. Since when did she have rabid sexual fantasies about a virtual stranger? Such uncontrollable, lusty urges? She blamed it on the sight of all that beautiful skin.

'The first time was a mistake,' she muttered. 'The second you couldn't help.' She opened her eyes and stared some more, watching as he slowly walked until he stood ten inches too far within her personal space. 'This time—'

'Was entirely deliberate.'

CHAPTER THREE

ALL Sophy could hear was the thud, thud, thud of her heart. 'Deliberate?'

He smiled. Such a slow, amused smile she wondered whether the word had actually emerged from her mouth or whether it had just been some sort of scared-animal squeak.

'You seemed to like it,' he said quietly, tiny twin lights dancing in his otherwise incredibly dark eyes.

Like it? Oh, that was the understatement of the century.

She blinked at him. He was so calm. So at ease in his gorgeous skin. So sure of his effect on her—the effect he *definitely* had on any woman—he was that confident. It was enough to slap sense back into her. 'You're definitely feeling better, aren't you?'

'One hundred per cent.'

'Great.' Sophy took a step back into the corridor. 'Then perhaps you'd like to see what I've been doing with sorting out the admin in there.'

'I've seen it. It's looking good. It's very easy to understand the system you're setting up.'

'Oh.' She was deflated—he'd stolen the ball back just like that.

'But we do need to talk about the function coming up.'

He walked out to the corridor after her. 'And I need to show you some of the stuff to update the website. I understand Kat's been helping you a bit when she can?'

'Yes, she's been great.' Sophy tried really hard to keep her concentration on the conversation but it kept sliding down to where his flat abs hit his jeans. *Unbelievable*— both his body and her reaction to it.

'The rest of the team will be back in later today. They've been helping on another project.'

'The bar.' Kat had told her about it. Lorenzo was the backer behind some guy opening up a new bar in the heart of cooldom. And she could totally be professional in the face of this provocation. Sure she could.

'Yes.' He was sounding all serious but his eyes were dancing. 'Shall we go into your office and get on with it?'

She stopped only three paces along. Nope. She couldn't be professional—not like this. 'Do you possibly think that you could put a shirt on?'

A deep, totally pure sound of amusement rumbled out of him. 'It really bothers you.'

'It's inappropriate.' Sophy felt her temperature rising. She wasn't a prude—really she wasn't. But this was just before nine a.m. and they were at *work*. Hell, yes, it bothered her.

'No more inappropriate than you bursting into my apartment and ordering a nurse for me.'

Sophy smiled, feeling a sense of power return. 'Now *that* really bothered *you*, didn't it? Me seeing you like that—in such a weakened state. Did it wound your male pride? Is that why you're showing your muscles again now? Proving your masculine strength?'

'You really think I was weak?' He turned, his big frame took up half the space in the corridor. And then he moved. Instinctively she retreated—backing up against the wall.

But he followed, totally hemming her in. She stuck her chin in the air trying not to feel anxious—or, worse, the lick of anticipation.

Sparks seemed to be coming from his eyes. 'I don't think I'm the one who needs to prove anything. I think that's for you to do.'

'What exactly do you think I need to prove? That you don't bother me?' Altitude sickness on the second floor—that was her problem. She must be the world's first case but she'd swear the air was thinner here because she could hardly get her words higher than a whisper.

His brows flickered. 'Don't I?'

'Of course you do.'

His brows shot higher. What, he hadn't expected honesty?

'You're half naked. *All* the time,' she explained the obvious. 'But it's the inappropriateness that bothers me. Not your actual body.' Oh, great, now she sounded prissy. And not at all honest.

His smile was back showing off his even white teeth. And he was playing with her the way a cat did a mouse. She needed to talk to Rosanna—really badly. She needed advice from a pro. Because there was no way she was letting Lorenzo Hall win this with such one-sided ease. She wasn't going to roll over and be the latest in what she was certain was a very long line—at least not without scoring some points of her own. For nor was she going to cut off her nose to spite her face. She wasn't going to deny herself a moment of pure pleasure should the opportunity arise. Yes, he bothered her—like that. Yes, she wanted him.

But she'd make like Rosanna and have him on her terms. For once in her life she was going to turn her back on responsibility; she'd take a risk and go for something she wanted. She just had to figure out how.

* * *

Lorenzo knew he was being naughty. But there was that bit in him that had always derived pleasure from taking risks. From doing exactly what society said he shouldn't—stretching the boundaries as far as he could and stopping only just before they broke.

He had matured—his transgressions were nothing near the edge he'd veered towards all those years ago. He stayed on the right side of the law now. But this oh-so-perfect Miss made him push it. Even just this little bit, to risqué, to rude, when really he wanted to ravish—really, really badly.

The look on her face had been worth the dodgy removal of his shirt. So worth it—even if he was struggling to contain his wayward hormones now. He just wanted to reach out and pull her against him—hard. His skin was on fire—had been since she'd touched him in his apartment the other day. Her small, cool hand hadn't soothed him at all—had only stirred the desire he'd already been battling to control. In those first twenty-four hours when the sickness was at its worst, he'd done nothing but dream of her. He was still dreaming of her and where he wanted that hand.

He'd been working too hard, round the clock with no room for fun. But it should ease up soon. Once the bar was open he'd be able to take a step back. And have some fun. Then again, there was no reason why he couldn't have some fun right now.

Her eyes had narrowed. He could just about see the cogs turning and whirring in her brain. The vixen-with-training-wheels looked as if she was plotting.

A phone rang—hers. Her hand went to her bag. He was disappointed to see her move. But he didn't move away. Took too much pleasure in watching her shrink back an awkward inch as she answered. But felt the pleasure turn to

ash when he heard the male tones. He listened as she organised.

'Yes, don't worry, Ted. I'm picking it up on my way
home. I'll drop it round before six.'

Who the hell was Ted? Lorenzo waited 'til she said
goodbye. Then let the power of silence work its magic.

'That was my brother. Sorry,' she finally said.

He took the phone from her hand and switched it off.
'When you're with me, all your attention is with me.'

Her eyes widened. He watched her swallow.

'On work,' he added, way too late.

He held out her phone for her to take back. Smiling
inside as he saw her jerky movements. Yeah, he liked the
way he could bother her. Because she really bothered him.
He took a careful step away—right now they both needed
a minute. 'I'll go get my shirt and then we'll go through
the stuff for Whistle, right?'

Sophy poured the entire contents of the ice tray into her
glass—not caring that half the blocks fell out onto the
bench and skidded onto the floor. She was unbearably
hot—Lorenzo putting his shirt on had made no difference. For over an hour she'd suffered—sitting at the desk
while he hovered beside her, behind her. Filling in the
holes that had appeared in the days when she'd been
working without the information only he or Cara could
provide. She'd had the rest of the day to recover—but she
hadn't succeeded. She gulped down half the glass of water,
sagged against the bench, she was so out of her depth.

'Where have you been? I'm only home for half a day
and I wanted us to go for a pedicure and—'

Sophy turned, dropping the glass in the sink. 'You're
back!' Thrilled, she ran across the room and hugged her
elusive flatmate.

'Okay, you've missed me too.' Rosanna's arms came round her and tightened. Then pushed her away. 'Shirts, doll, we can't crush our shirts.'

Sophy laughed. In the sentence of life, Sophy figured she was like a verb—the action, the one who got things done. Not very exciting perhaps, but necessary. Rosanna, however, was the exclamation mark. The rare beauty that could fill a whole paragraph—a whole room—with excitement. She even looked like one. Always dressed in black, she was a thin streak of long limbs, her glossy dark hair swept in a high ponytail that swung halfway down her back. She was full of vitality, and sheer outrageousness.

'Now where have you been? I landed hours ago and have been lonely ever since and now the taxi to take me back to the airport will be here in ten. What's up with your mobile?'

Sophy walked back to the bench to find and refill her glass. How was she going to explain this one? Rosanna was not going to be impressed. 'I'm doing some admin work.'

Rosanna frowned. 'You've got a job?'

'Only for a few weeks. Their usual administrator's baby arrived sooner than expected.'

'Baby okay?'

'Baby's fine.'

'So why couldn't they get a temp? Why did it have to be you?' Rosanna rolled her eyes. 'Who asked you?'

'Cara, the new mother, is a good friend of Victoria's.'

'Of course she is. Of course you couldn't say no.' Rosanna gave a theatrical sigh as she went to the pantry and pulled out a bottle of wine. 'So where's the job?'

'You heard of the Whistle Fund?'

Rosanna wolf-whistled as she unscrewed the cap of the bottle. 'Alex Carlisle and Lorenzo Hall. Who hasn't heard of them? Alex got married recently and Lorenzo's someone you don't forget. Ever.'

Well, that was true. His image was burned on Sophy's brain, every inch of skin, muscle and pure man.

'Every bit as good as he looks, apparently,' Rosanna drawled.

'You've hooked him?' A hot flash of envy sliced through Sophy.

'No,' Rosanna said, pausing as she poured the crimson wine. 'Not that I'd turn him down. But the one time our paths crossed I didn't even score a second glance.'

'I'm sure that's not true.' Sophy was able to smile again. 'Every man gives you at least four glances.'

'Sweetie-pie.' Rosanna flopped into a chair, giant wine glass in hand. 'No, I've heard he's impossible to catch. Tangles in the nets now and then but always swims free.'

Sophy was quite sure he tangled and then ripped free. 'I think he's a shark.'

'Do you now?' Rosanna giggled—half choking on her wine.

'Absolutely,' Sophy said. 'I think he's far too used to seeing any fish he wants and getting the kill.'

Rosanna held her glass up to the light and with a flick of her wrist let the liquid swirl inside it. 'At the very least you might score some wine.'

Sophy shook her head. 'I don't know that we'll be getting on well enough for that.'

Rosanna tilted her head on the side and appraised Sophy, a sly smile on her lips. 'You're interested.'

'No I'm not.' Sophy lied. And then immediately started to laugh.

Rosanna laughed too. 'Of course you are. We all are. But—' her nose wrinkled '—I don't think he's your type.'

'No?' Sophy felt irrationally put out.

'He *is* a shark,' Rosanna said. 'You need a dolphin.'

'Oh, great. Someone with a big nose.'

'And with a habit of rescuing rather than destroying. It's true.' Rosanna sat up. 'You need a good guy, Soph, someone safe and cuddly, not some dangerous type you couldn't handle.'

'You don't think I could handle him?'

'I know you couldn't.'

'So you've no advice for me?'

Rosanna looked up sharply. 'I'm the last person you should take advice from.'

How did she figure that? She was the one who had them all eating out of her palm.

'You were wearing that when you saw him?' Rosanna's expression clouded.

'What? What's wrong with it?' Had she committed some terrible fashion faux pas? She couldn't think what.

'Nothing. But if he has a Grace Kelly fantasy, then you're in trouble.'

Sophy snorted. 'Now who's the sweetie-pie?'

'He'd gobble a kitten like you.' Rosanna frowned. 'Don't say I didn't warn you. Anyway, I'm grumpy, we don't have time for a pedicure now. I've had to sit here all day doing nothing.'

Kitten? She thought she was a *kitten*? 'Poor you.' Now Sophy had zero sympathy. 'It's about time you stopped and did nothing for half a day.'

Rosanna cupped her hand round her mouth, making a pretend megaphone. 'Pot calling kettle, come in, kettle.' She stood. 'At least I'm busy pushing my career. You're just busy doing everything for everyone else.'

'You're going to miss your next flight. Go have a good trip.' Rosanna was a buyer for one of the major fashion chains. Knowledgeable, chic, damn good at her job and away more nights than she was at home.

Rosanna picked up the handle of her chic trolley case. 'I love Wellington.'

'The boys are going to miss you.'

'It'll be good for them.' Rosanna bent and flicked an invisible speck of fluff from her black trousers.

Sophy watched the studied indifference with a smile. 'Are you ever going to make a decision?'

Rosanna appeared to think on it for a moment, then smiled shamelessly. 'I don't think so, no.'

Rosanna had been dating two men for the last month. They knew about each other. Hell, they all went clubbing together, the boys' rivalry half jest, half serious. Rosanna, the black widow, liked to have as many in her web as possible to play with. And once they were caught, they were never freed. She had carcasses all over the globe. Emmet and Jay were her latest victims yet somehow she pulled it off with such charm they didn't seem to mind— in fact they salivated over her.

Sophy knew there was a heart of gold underneath the glam. It was just that Rosanna wouldn't admit to it, certainly wouldn't let anyone near it. She spent her life fencing, flirting on a superficial—if somewhat bitchy— plane. Sophy knew why; Rosanna's heart had been broken and she wasn't letting any man near it again. She was only about having light, harmless, fun and keeping any seriousness at a distance.

Sophy's heart had also been broken. Frankly she wanted some of the fun now too—and she knew who with. She walked with Rosanna to the door, waited for the taxi to arrive and tried to absorb some of her friend's zest for life.

Rosanna did all the things Sophy was too 'responsible'

to do: she had crazy flings, she went to far flung destinations, she was impulsive and a risk-taker. She did danger—she'd do dangerous like Lorenzo Hall kind of dangerous.

But Sophy had always had more than herself to consider. She loved her parents and had never wanted to embarrass them. As she was the judge's daughter it would have made the perfect salacious storyline—if she'd gone off the rails, been a teen drinker, teen pregnant, or got into drugs. But she'd done none of those things. She'd tried to be the perfect kid—even when she knew she was a disappointment in not following them into the law. She'd even tried to find the perfect boyfriend. If she couldn't live up to the family name she'd marry someone who would. She'd been so naïve—her ex had only wanted her for what he could get out of it—the connection to her family. She supposed it served her right.

She was the boring, goody two-shoes who'd been embarrassingly naïve. Now she was in the habit of playing safe. Not playing at all. Not taking risks.

She never discussed her family with anyone at all now. Privacy had been important anyway, discretion a must. People were put off just as much as they were intrigued, as if they thought she'd run to her father if they mentioned anything even slightly shady. It was as if they expected her to be a pillar of morality, never once veering from doing right.

And in truth she was.

'Is this job full-time?' Rosanna asked.

'Initially.'

'You know your problem, Soph?'

'Go on, enlighten me.'

'You're too sweet. Why don't you ever say no to them? Why don't you ever say no to me?'

'How can I?' Sophy argued. 'You let me move in.' She hadn't wanted to stay with her parents. But hadn't wanted to live alone either—at least, not all the time.

Rosanna shrugged. 'I'm hardly here. It's a selfish move on my part—you're a good house-sitter.'

'Yes.' Sophy laughed, not in the least offended, knowing Rosanna didn't mean it.

'But when are you going to get those pieces finished?'

Sophy bit her lip. She'd known Ro would bring it up eventually. 'I don't know that I can.'

'You're doing it, Sophy. This is such a great opportunity.'

'You've just told me to learn to say no.'

'Only to the things you don't really want. This is something you do want, isn't it? This is something to push for. Put your ambition first for once.'

'I will.' Sophy groaned, but Rosanna was right of course. 'When are you back?'

'Later in the week. Another flying visit home and then off again.'

'You don't get tired of it?'

'No.'

And perhaps if they saw each other more they'd drive each other nuts. The taxi finally pulled up and Rosanna strutted down to get it, her ponytail swinging, her ultra-high heels tapping and her trolley rattling along the concrete path.

'Don't say yes to anything else while I'm away,' she called as she got into the cab. 'I mean it.' She stopped and opened the door again to holler, 'Especially not Lorenzo Hall!'

'Kittens have claws, you know.'

'Not enough to make a mark on a man like him.'

Laughing, Sophy shut the front door. Rested against it

for a moment, listening to the vast silence Rosanna had left behind her. She'd been right. Lorenzo was out of her league. And probably not genuinely interested anyway—he was just amusing himself by making her squirm.

Rosanna was right about something else too. Sophy needed to finish up her pieces and prepare for the exhibition. It was a fantastic opportunity and she shouldn't blow it. Inspired, she went into her room and got to work on them—kept working late into the night. Once she got into it the excitement flowed and she decided to make the most of her lunch break—she had no time to waste if she wanted to get enough made.

She got to work early the next day to get ahead. She opened the window in the office to let the fresh spring air in. Looking down, she saw Lorenzo was out the back. Wide brush in hand, he was covering the graffiti with black paint—to match the rest of the fence. So it bothered him enough at last? Sophy thought it was a bit of a shame. But, unable to resist, she watched. His jeans hung that little bit low on his hips, an old tee was stretched across his broad shoulders. His feet were bare. He had his phone trapped between ear and shoulder and his voice carried across the still yard. As did his laughter.

She should probably close the window.

Instead she switched on her computer. She'd concentrate on the work. Not listen to every word winging through the window.

'So what's the castle like?' Lorenzo asked.

Alex had taken Dani to Italy on a belated but extended honeymoon. They were staying in some castle for a few weeks.

'Amazing. As it should be for the price. How's Cara?'

'Shattered but holding her own, I think.' He swirled the

brush through the paint. 'She loved the flowers. She said the baby is tiny but she's doing well.'

'You've not been to see her yet?'

'No.' Lorenzo winced.

'Renz—'

'Not my scene, Alex, you know that.' Happy families weren't him. He was concerned for Cara, of course he was, and he'd sent over a ton of presents, asked if there was anything he could do. Of course there wasn't, she and her husband and their entire extended families had it together. So he didn't have to go and feel awkward around them.

'What about the Whistle Fund? Did you find someone to help out?' Alex moved on.

'Yeah,' Lorenzo sighed. 'Cara did—a friend's younger sister or something. One of those socialites who likes to be involved.' Lorenzo jabbed a fence paling with the brush. 'She's so damn efficient. Organised. Officious. She looks like a frigid girl scout.'

Alex laughed. 'So many adjectives, Renz—she bothering you?'

'No.' If only he knew.

Alex laughed even harder—okay, so he knew he was lying. 'So she's a babe?'

Lorenzo slapped some paint on even thicker. Yes, she was a babe. In more ways than one. All big blue eyes and blonde hair that begged to be ruffled. Hot-looking but with an air of innocence that Lorenzo wasn't at all sure that he should taint. 'She's doing the job. That's all that matters.'

The job would be done—brilliantly—and he'd find a permanent replacement very soon. Because he had too much else to do to be fixating on her all the time like this.

He ended the call to Alex, finished up the fence. Picking up the can, he swung round, glanced up to the first floor.

The window to her office was open but he couldn't see anyone sitting at the desk. Kat must have opened it.

He jogged up to his apartment—scrubbed the paint off in the shower. But he had an itch that just had to be scratched. He had to go have another look, see if he could make her spark again. It was like she'd put some kind of homing device in him, drawing him near. He went down to Reception and stole the mail from Kat's tray. Then his feet just went to where she was.

Irresistible.

'You going out with your boyfriend tonight?' he asked. So lame. So unsubtle.

She froze where she was bent over a pile of papers.

'You should come to the bar. It's the opening night.'

'You're that desperate for customers?' She looked up, all frost. Touchy this morning.

'Actually no. We're confident it'll do the business. I just thought you might like to see it.' He leaned his frame against the door. 'It's a nice little place, intimate. You can cuddle on a sofa in the corner.' Would she be the type to cuddle in public? Somehow he didn't think so—she had that aloof thing going. 'Or you can work up a sweat on the dance floor. Oh…' he paused deliberately '…you'll be on the sofa, then, won't you?'

'I like to dance.'

His muscles tightened at the unexpected tinge of boldness in her tone, he looked harder at her.

'But I already have plans for tonight.' Oh, she was *ultra* cool—it made him suspect she was even hotter beneath.

'With your boyfriend?' Yeah, again, real subtle. But he really needed to know. Now.

Sophy gave up pretending to look at the file in front of her. 'No,' she said as calmly as she could—tricky given the anger zooming round and round her veins, searching for a way out. 'I don't have a boyfriend.'

'No?' Annoyingly he didn't sound that surprised. Worse, he looked pleased about it.

'I don't want one.' Damn, she'd tacked that on too quickly, sounded too vehement. And they both knew it.

His brows lifted. 'Why's that?' He put the mail on her desk, the action bringing him even closer to her. 'Did some twerp break your heart?'

She took a moment to draw breath—so she could answer with icy precision. 'What makes you think I have a heart?' She bit the words out with the experience of seven years' elocution lessons behind her. 'We frigid girl scouts don't bother with them. We find machinery to be more efficient.'

Slowly, deliberately, she lifted her gaze—it clashed with his for a long, long time. His own eyes revealed nothing, yet seemed to penetrate her façade—delving into her secrets. She felt the blush rising—stupidly—when he was the one who'd been so rude. He'd said it. She'd only overheard it by mistake. So why was she the one feeling so uncomfortable now?

'Struck a nerve, did I?' Without breaking the stare he walked around her desk. 'I only said you look like that, not that you actually are.'

'Same difference.' All her nerves were prickling now.

His smile sharpened. 'But I already know you're quite capable of feeling something.'

She just stared at him, fighting to slow her pulse.

'Anger.' He grabbed her arms and pulled her out of the chair. 'Are you very angry with me, Sophy?'

He was inappropriately close—again—holding her tight, yet she didn't fight to step back. She refused to let him intimidate her, or to play with her.

'Do you want me to make it better?' His arms looped around her, hands warm and firm on her waist.

'How are you planning to do that?' She took a quick breath, shaking inside, but stabbed him with some sarcasm. 'With a kiss?'

'Isn't that how it works?' He leaned closer, spearing her with his dark, unreadable eyes. 'Isn't that what you want?'

'No.' Now she was even more angry. Because he was right. It was what she wanted. What she'd been wanting since she first laid eyes on him, and especially since she'd been in his apartment and touched him. But she didn't want it like this. 'I don't think it would make it better.'

'No?'

'I think it would make it worse.' She flashed at him. 'Don't *patronise* me, Lorenzo. You think you're better than me? You think I'm some robot? Some spoilt, bored socialite? Spending all my time doing this and that for everyone else? You think I don't have ambition of my own? Dreams of my own? Desires of my own?'

She shut up, suddenly aware she was verbally vomiting an ancient bitterness that she'd never wanted to talk about to anyone, certainly not to him.

His hold on her tightened. 'I don't think that. But obviously you think some people do.'

Yeah, a little bubbling mass of resentment, that was her.

'Why didn't you say no to working here, if you had other things you wanted to do?' He made it sound so simple.

But she never said no—not to that kind of request. And she did have some time to help. She *liked* to help. It make her feel useful, needed. Except now it felt as if Lorenzo had been laughing at her willingness and her diligence. Were they all laughing at her? Was she valued at all or were her efforts just taken for granted?

Tired. That was her problem. Tired and frustrated and overwhelmed. And he wasn't helping—towering over her like this, tormenting her all the time. She looked straight down to the floor as tears sprang in her eyes. 'Forget it.'

'No.' He took her chin in firm fingers and tilted her head back up so he could see her face. A half-swallowed growl sounded. 'You're really upset.'

'My wounded pride will get over it,' she snapped, cross with her stupid weakness. 'I don't care what you think. I'm here to do a job. Now I'm going to get on with it.'

'Not until I apologise.'

'I didn't think you'd be the type to say sorry.'

'And you think I'm the one making assumptions?' His eyes glinted but the smallest of smiles appeared. 'Okay, I don't say it often. But when I do, I mean it.' He stroked her jaw. 'I'm sorry.'

'It's fine.' She shrugged, too crushed to accept it with good grace and determined not to let that smile have its usual disabling effect. 'I don't care what you think about me.'

His smile deepened just a touch. Okay, so she was protesting too much.

She sighed as a flicker of good humour returned to her. 'Don't get big-headed about it. I care too much what everyone thinks about me.'

'What you think matters to me too.'

Okay, so now his niceness was making it worse. Embarrassed, she shifted. 'Look, just forget it.'

'No.' His grip tightened. 'I'm going to make it better. I'm going to do it anyway. It's been on the cards for days. You know that.'

She froze, her body rendered immobile with anticipation overload. All she could do was gaze up at him—drowning in his eyes, yearning for that beautiful mouth to touch her.

And then it did.

A butterfly-light brush of lips on skin—a shade too close to her mouth to be a safe kiss on the cheek. And he lingered too long for it to be safe too.

'Better?' His question almost inaudible, but she heard it, *felt* it as his lips grazed her as he asked.

'No.'

The smallest of pauses as they stood—intent hovering. Only a couple of inches separated their bodies, only a millimetre separated their lips. She could feel his heat, and smell his fresh soapy scent. A tremor ran through her as anticipation almost broke her nerve. Suddenly he moved—that merest fraction, the littlest drop to her mouth. His lips were warm, and they clung.

Her eyes closed, her body blanking everything so it could focus only on the touch. His gentleness so unexpected, the rush of sensation pierced through her.

A moan—was it her? The softness, the slowness, the sweetness overwhelmed her. She trembled again and his hands tightened. This wasn't enough.

And then it was over.

She couldn't breathe. She saw his eyes zooming in on her. Jet black now. Intense. Beautiful. Time and motion stopped for a moment that felt like infinity. Her every nerve was wired, waiting, wanting. Would he come back—would he kiss her again?

'No,' he said roughly, stepping back. His hands dropped—leaving her suddenly cold. 'You were right. I was wrong.' He walked out of the door. 'I really am sorry.'

CHAPTER FOUR

SOPHY managed to stay standing 'til Lorenzo was out of sight, then collapsed into the chair. Fisting her hands over her eyes, shoulders rising—blocking all sensation. Just for a second. Just to stay sane. Her whole body tingled, as if she'd been zapped by some kind of extra-terrestrial ray-gun making all her cells jiggle.

The disappointment was devastating.

Why had he stopped? She *knew* he'd felt it—she'd seen it in his eyes, heard it in his voice. But he'd practically run away.

If she was Rosanna she'd have been the one to move that second time. It would have taken nothing—the slightest tilt of her chin to resume the contact. She'd had it on a platter. Yet she hadn't taken the chance.

Now she was mad with herself for wishing she had, even madder for having been so damn passive. Why hadn't she had the guts to take the risk? But she'd been knocked—first by his words, second by the kiss and the emotion that had flooded through her.

And now he was sorry? Not just for what she'd over-heard, but for kissing her. She understood. But she couldn't understand how he could regret it. He'd felt it as she had; that kind of chemistry couldn't be one-sided.

And she wanted more. She *really* wanted more. A fire had been lit in her belly and it needed feeding. Except it looked as if she was going to be left starving.

Well, she was taking her lunch break today. She was working to rule and jolly well going to work on her own project. Spurred on by what she'd said to him—she *did* have her own ambition. And now, more than ever, she was determined to make it. She'd do this exhibition and show them all she had more to her than great organisational skills. She had dreams—and she'd make them real.

That had been a mistake. Oh, man, had that been a mistake. Lorenzo's body hurt as he moved— every cell rebelling as he made himself walk away.

Yeah, she had emotions all right—her want for him so hot and sweet. He wanted to bury himself completely in the delectable softness she offered.

She'd stared at him. Just waiting with her eyes so huge. It was like corrupting an innocent. She really was a good girl, wasn't she? And Lorenzo never messed with good girls. Ever. Things got too messy. And it was obvious things with Sophy would get nuclear messy. Hell, she'd been crushed by that stupid comment he'd made to Alex. Her big eyes brimming with hurt—from just a few silly words. And he felt bad for it—an absolute heel. Because she hadn't deserved it. He didn't like feeling guilty.

And now he knew for sure there was no way in hell she was frigid. She wasn't just warm either. She had volcanic qualities. Like a snow-capped mountain, she was capable of blasting fire when you least expected it, able to melt granite with her heat.

That just made it fifty times worse because he *ached* to make her tremble again and again. Being with her, in her, would be more than explosive, it would be some kind of divine experience. But if she was hurt by just a few words, no way could she handle a short-term fling. And that was all he ever did. She was a relationship woman. Ms Monogamous.

She was far too good for him—literally. He just wasn't crossing that line. It didn't matter how hot he was for her, it wasn't going to happen. Because Mr Monogamous he wasn't. He'd tried it once when he'd been young and naïve enough to think the past wouldn't matter. He'd been shot down and wasn't taking a hit like that again. Sure, he liked women—lots of women—for the physical fun of sex. No more than three times with a partner—preferably in the same night. That wasn't a kind of deal straight, sweet Sophy could handle.

But he couldn't stay away, not all day. He told himself he couldn't be rude and ignore her after what had happened. Somehow he had to get them back to a purely professional footing. Going to be tricky given he was the one who'd been flashing skin the whole time.

She was at the desk, her head bent as she concentrated on the stuff in front of her—piles of tiny objects. She had a bag open on the edge of the desk, small sharp-looking tools to one side while she made her decisions. It was the first time he'd seen her actually sitting still and not busily typing while filing and talking to someone on the phone all at the same time. Now she was so concentrated, so quiet, looking so intently at the stuff on the table in front of her. He leaned his shoulder against the door jamb and said nothing. Just waited for her to realise he was there, enjoying the time he had to observe.

It was several minutes until she glanced up, did a double take and squeaked.

'Oh, sorry.' The tempting colour rose under her skin. 'I didn't hear you.'

'What are you doing?' He'd figured it out already but didn't want to admit just how long he'd been standing watching her like some stalker.

Her hands moved, as if to hide it from him, her serenity broken as she started packing it all away. A velvet covered board with grooves in it into which she was arranging small semi-precious stones or beads or other bits.

'It's okay,' he said, wishing he hadn't shattered her moment of calm so completely. It was as if he'd tripped the switch and now the efficient automaton was back. 'You're allowed a lunch break.' Except lunch had been hours ago. Had the goody two-shoes abandoned her job all afternoon?

She looked guilty.

Yep, he'd caught her out. He couldn't stop his mile wide smile. 'What are you making?'

She blinked at him, hurriedly looked away. 'A necklace.'

'A hobby of yours?' He saw her tension spike.

Then she nodded. All back to brisk. 'Yes.'

He watched as the guilt gave her an all-over-body sweep of red.

'Sorry,' she muttered. 'I lost track of time.'

She was just never going to be a cheat, was she? Never going to be someone who could do something she shouldn't and not own up about it. He bet she'd never done anything remotely dodgy in her whole life. Jeez, they were poles apart.

'Don't worry about it.' He didn't care. She'd done an amazing job clearing up the mess that was the Whistle Fund office. Everything was running on schedule again. Even the opening of the bar looked as if it was going to go off okay. The chaos of the last couple of weeks seemed to be at an end. In no small part thanks to Sophy. She was allowed an afternoon to slack off. 'Just go home early. You've done heaps already.'

She lifted her head, the cool look back. 'Okay. Thanks.'

He lingered for a half second too long, tempted to say or do something more. Finally he made himself turn and walk along to his own office. It had just been a kiss. Nothing more than that. He could forget it. He could ignore the tantalising prospect of seducing her. Sure he could.

At least try to do the right thing, Lorenzo—for once in your life.

Sophy hadn't had any sleep. She'd sat up late again, working on her pieces. Unhappy with the necklace she'd made the night before. Her jewellery had to be something really special—couldn't be something anyone could make in their own home if they had the time and the inclination. It was all about the eye, the detail and the little spark of difference. She had the resources—had been collecting vintage bits and bobs for years. Had gathered a lot while in Europe and had got invaluable experience when she'd worked on the floor of a jewellery shop in France. She'd spent her lunch breaks sitting in the workshop with the jewellers learning some of the finer points. She'd done a few courses too, so she had a reasonably solid technique now. But she didn't have so much time to make the amount she needed for the show. And she wasn't sure she had them exactly how she wanted them.

But on top of everything she was distracted. Wished Rosanna were on hand to help her out—with Vamp 101 classes.

She didn't see Lorenzo all morning. But early afternoon, as the sun was hitting its zenith, she heard that familiar sound. She looked out of the open window. He was on his makeshift basketball court, wearing jeans of course. But his torso was covered this time—with a loose NBA style singlet.

He glanced up to the window, saw she was watching. She pulled her head back in but she saw his grin. He bounced the ball a few times. Executed some fancy run up to the board and jumped high—landing the shot.

He glanced back up to her. Yeah, okay, she was still watching and he knew it. Too slowly he lifted the hem of his singlet, used it to wipe the sweat from his brow— revealing his abs in the process. Deliberately. Provocatively.

He lifted his head and looked up at her. He wanted a reaction? Impossible— she couldn't move, just stared at him.

His smile appeared and both his hands moved to the hem of his singlet. In a flash he'd whipped it over his head—tossing it to the side.

Oh God, she just couldn't take it any more. She slammed her window shut. Heard his laugh anyway. That tore it. She stood and marched downstairs, opened the back door, let it slam behind her. He turned, she saw his surprise. So he was just winding her up? He'd pay.

She walked past him and went to where the ball was rolling towards the fence, scooped it up. It was bigger than the netball she used to play with. She prayed to the sporting gods for some kind of benevolence. It had been years since she last played netball, but she had been Goal Attack—responsible for shooting through the hoops. She rolled the ball against her palms, pulling it in tight to her chest, getting the feel for it. She was too steamed to care much anyway. Really she felt like throwing the thing at his head rather than the hoop.

She turned. He was too close behind her. She gave him

a pointed look and he took a step to the side. Neither said anything. She looked up at the basket. So damn high. Still, she had energy in her muscles that needed to be expended.

She aimed and threw. The net swished as the ball slid through. Confidence from her success swamped her and she turned to stare hotly at him.

'Been keeping secrets?' His voice was low. 'You want to play with me, Sophy?'

'I want to beat you.'

His whole body tensed. She saw the electricity surge in him.

'No one beats me.'

'Not afraid, are you, Lorenzo?'

The briefest pause and then that smile curled. 'What are we playing for?' He quietly walked closer.

Yeah, she'd hoped she could bring out his wicked side. She just hadn't realised quite how easy it would be. 'What do you want to play for?'

Was this her? Leaning provocatively close to him, practically purring?

His amusement deepened but it didn't bother her, for she saw the fire too. 'You're the one suggesting the game; you come up with the prize.'

She just stared at him, letting her eyes say it all.

'Really?' He dropped the basketball. It rolled away, coming to a rest against the newly painted fence.

'Don't you think?'

He'd gone very still. 'I'm not sure either of us is thinking.'

'Isn't it going to happen anyway? Hasn't it been on the cards for days?' She angled her head and studied him, half dying inside now with her boldness. He was so silent. Too silent. 'Do you really want to stop it?'

His hands were on his hips, his biceps flexing. 'We probably should.'

'Why?' She could see his chest rising and falling faster than before. She knew he felt it too.

Angry fingers suddenly gripped her upper arms. 'Why are you chasing this?'

She flinched. Chasing? Like some infatuated teen stalking her first prey? Shocked, she blurted the truth. 'I've never done this before. I've never had a fling. Never had a one night stand. I've always been "good", always watched out for my reputation, always gone out with "safe" guys.' She'd had a couple of steady boyfriends, then that engagement. She shut her mind to the memory, turned back to the heat of the moment. 'Just for once I want the freedom to do what I want to do, take what I want, have what I want.'

'And *I'm* what you want?' His jaw was rigid, the strength in his fingers not easing an iota.

She glanced down his body. 'You're very fit.'

'What is it that's really turning you on? Going with someone outside your select social circle? Someone from the wrong side of the tracks, someone rougher? Is that what I am to you?'

Her senses flared at the word rougher. She could do with some rough right now. 'I don't care about your background.' She didn't actually care about *him*—did she? 'Like I said, you're just very fit.' She sighed, frustrated. 'And every time I see you, you're half naked. What do you expect? I'm only human.'

A short laugh was shaken from him. 'So you just want physical, Sophy?'

'Really physical.'

The breath whistled out between his teeth. She held her breath, frozen as she watched him decide.

'I don't do relationships, Sophy.'

'You think I don't know that?'

His fingers relaxed but didn't let her go and his smile returned. 'This is not going to get out of hand.'

She stepped closer, anticipation twisting with satisfaction and spiralling higher. She'd won. For once she'd been bold and it had worked. 'Of course not. You're going to be very much in hand.' She smiled. Really, dirty flirty talk was easy. She could so be the queen of it here.

'I think you're confused about who's going to be dominant.' His hands tightened again, drawing her closer still. 'I'll be in control, Sophy—you don't want to be.'

That was exactly it. She didn't want to be in control any more. She just wanted to feel. Not think. Just experience it, release the tension from her system. 'Okay.'

His expression flared. His hands moved, looping round her back, imprisoning her. 'So what did you have in mind?'

'What about my office?'

'Now?' He laughed freely. 'A late afternoon lay? Just before you leave?'

'It has a certain appeal.' Her eyelids were heavy, her cheeks flushed. She'd wanted him for days, of course she wanted him now.

'Aren't you getting ahead of yourself?' His voice dropped to a carnal whisper, but his eyes were like polished stones. 'We've barely kissed. We might not be that good.'

Barely kissed? Oh, he was full of it. Her lips curved into a lush, lazy smile. 'You don't believe that. Besides…' she skated the tips of her fingers over his jaw, shivering with the pleasure of being able to touch '…you do everything to a brilliant standard.'

'So do you.'

Not quite true, but she was happy to skip it. 'Then we'll be brilliant together, won't we?' She was wholly leaning against him now, feeling the heat of him through her linen shirt. 'Let's try it out.'

'Oh, Sophy,' he muttered, his face even more angular. 'You'd better know what you're doing.'

In answer she lifted her face, inviting it all.

In a fast movement he caught her mouth with his. It wasn't anything like the gentle kiss of the day before. This was brazenly sexual—branding her with its heat. She gasped, held back for a scrap of a second beneath the bruising, blazing invasion. Then threw herself headlong into the eye of the storm, locking her hands behind his neck, letting her breasts press against him. His hands pushed her tighter against his hardness. And he was hard all over.

His heated skin melted her. His tongue swept between her lips, she parted to let him in as deep as he wanted. Twirled her tongue around his and felt his grip tighten even harder on her.

Yes.

Her neck muscles strained as she pushed up into his kiss, not wanting the searing assault to ease even a smidge. She rocked her hips. Rising onto tiptoe to feel that bulging ridge nearer to where she really wanted it, rubbed closer again, desperate to relieve the agony that now flared deep within. She felt rather than heard his grunt. His hand cupped her butt, fingers firm on her flesh, holding her as he rocked back against her—his thrusting slow, devastating, while his mouth was still sealed to hers. His tongue teased into her the way she really wanted that other part of him to. Her moan reverberated between them then. Oh, yes. That was what she wanted. All the strength of him ripping into her.

His kiss altered, breaking but quickly returning. Nipping at her mouth he pushed her harder against his straining erection. She shifted her feet to part her legs that fraction more, rotating the half centimetre she could against him, torturing them both. She cursed the clothes that were scrunching between them. He bent her back to force her body closer still, until all she could do was cling to his shoulders and accept his demands. She didn't want to stand any more anyway. She wanted to lie down. She wanted him to pin her with his weight and pound into her. Fast, hard, now.

All her desire unleashed with just the one kiss.

He took the weight of one breast in his hand and her body buckled with the sensation. 'Yes.' Her high cry, half whispered.

So there was such a thing as pure, carnal lust. An attraction to a body, where nothing else mattered but touching it, feeling it and making its beauty come alive. There could be a free, physical joy. She'd been missing out for years—had always taken everything too seriously, been too cautious. She swept her hand hard across his shoulder, up his neck and into his hair, clutching to his deliciously dangerous heat. It was time to play catch-up.

Lorenzo fought hard with his raging lust, and hers, easing them out of the kiss, forcing his hands to slow and then to stop their exploration of her skin. It hurt.

He lifted his mouth a millimetre away from hers. Saw that passion had made her blue eyes glow more vividly than ever before. He couldn't resist another brushing kiss, nor could he resist the way her nipple was pressing into his palm. His fingers mirrored the action of his mouth—brushing the sensitive nub just as his lips did hers.

Very, very lightly.

Her shudder nearly had him on his knees. He'd wanted to test her—to see if she really meant it. So he'd kissed her hard. No gentle beginning, no tenderness, just the brunt of his raw, blistering passion.

And she'd met him, matched him. Almost *beaten* him.

Now he wanted to strip her, to kiss her, to make the whole of her wet with want. He wanted her drenched with desire—and him too—for their bodies to slide together, fighting for that furious, physical release. He hadn't wanted sex so badly in ages.

Instead he pushed away, made himself take a whole step. Forced his feet to move another. 'I'm not going to take you now,' he said breathlessly. Telling himself as much as her. 'Not like this.'

'Why not?' She didn't seem to realise the extent to which she was giving herself away.

His body tightened, the animal part of him so keen to take up her unguarded offer. To topple her here and now and be done with it. But he couldn't. She needed some breathing space to be sure. He needed her to be sure. The lust was hot enough to make them both brainless. Do something she yet might regret. Lorenzo couldn't bear those regrets—not his, not hers either.

Stupid. Since when did he care? Since when did he let any kind of second thoughts stop him from having a good time?

Because she'd told him—she didn't usually do this. He'd known that already but having her actually say it made it worse. She needed to be certain. He didn't want any uncomfortable ramifications. 'Are you sure you can handle it?'

She turned away. He saw the chill descend, the stiffening in her shoulders. 'Don't treat me like an idiot. Of course I can. We're only talking one night, Lorenzo.'

He ruffled his hair, needing to get his conflicting emotions under control. Hell, it was one p.m. and he was this close to having her in a quickie session at the back of the warehouse. He wanted more than a quickie. He wanted a bed. He wanted the whole night.

One night—her suggestion.

His body chafed—eager to take the offer up now. But no way was he taking her upstairs to his apartment. Inviting her in there might lead to mixed messages. He'd have to take her out. Damn, a date meant more too—or might to her. He shook his head, could she really keep it uncomplicated? But he wanted it too much to say no. The burning need forced him to take the risk. 'I'll take you out tonight.'

'That's not necessary.'

Oh, she was cool, wasn't she? His edgy feeling sharpened. Had he underestimated her entirely? 'You don't want to go out?'

She looked evasive. 'You could come over to my place.'

It was probably a good idea. He didn't like that it had come from her, but she was right. Better not for them to go out together—looking like lovers, feeling like lovers. But ironically nor did he want some sordid assignation. Just for him to knock on the door and her let him in—literally. The warring feelings frustrated him. 'For dinner?'

'If you like,' she answered carelessly, giving him an address, a time.

He stared at her as she spoke, tried to figure out what the hell she was thinking. Failed. But she'd come to him. She was asking him. If she wanted to go through with it, who was he to say no? He'd never been one to turn down an opportunity. 'Okay.'

She smiled, and walked back inside.

He glanced up to the window and waited. Soon saw her swinging into her role as the perfect administrator again. It should please him, not annoy him—given she was on the payroll and all. But for some reason he found it incredibly irritating. She could go back and concentrate on boring work just like that?

Man, he wanted to see her out of control. He wanted the perfect clothes crushed and the never-out-of-place hair messy. He wanted her eyes wide and wild and her mouth parted as she panted. He wanted her both laughing and crying with pleasure so intense that she was no longer in charge of anything. He wanted her to writhe for him.

And he wanted it now.

CHAPTER FIVE

LORENZO had been fantasising about this for too long.
That was why he was so edgy. Had Sophy known the
XXX rating of his dreams, she'd never have offered him
this kind of access. The things he wanted to do…

He took a deep breath. Her home was as he'd expected.
A cute little villa in the heart of poshville. Just the place
for a young Auckland socialite. He walked up the path
with the fatalistic feeling growing inside him. He hadn't
brought flowers, not even a bottle of wine. Just himself.
His body was what she wanted—and it was all she was
getting. He shook off the clanging bell of doom—stupid.
This was just going to be some hot sex—nothing more.

She answered the door swiftly. Delicate colour sat high
in her cheeks. She'd changed her clothes. Wearing a different blouse, a casual skirt that flared out, emphasising
her little waist. Sandals on her feet. Pink polish gleaming
on her toenails. Her hair was styled in that nineteen-fifties
Hollywood-starlet style.

'I didn't cook. Sorry. Been busy.'

Getting ready for him? He liked that idea a little too
much.

She turned and led him down the polished wooden
hallway.

'It's okay.' He wasn't that hungry anyway. Not for food.

'I cheated and picked up some stuff from the deli.' She led him to the dining area. 'Thought we could snack.'

'Sure.' He looked at the table. She'd unloaded the deli pots into pretty little dishes. Floral. Heaven help him. Fragile fine bone china. That was her all over.

She was watching him, a knowing look in her eyes that unsettled him more. 'You're not having regrets already?'

'I don't do regrets. Why, do you?'

She shook her head. 'New Year's resolution not to.'

Yeah, right. 'You've never done anything to regret, have you?' He couldn't hold back the bitter note of accusation.

'You think?' She stepped up to him. 'I'm no angel, Lorenzo.' She leaned forward and whispered, 'And I'm no virgin. You're not going to hurt me.'

He swallowed. For someone who'd said she'd never done this before, she was holding her own. So the snacking could wait a while. There was something far more pressing to be done. He lifted a hand and stroked her hair, gathered a lock and ran his finger and thumb along the length of it. He tugged gently, straightening the curl at the bottom. When he let it go it bounced right back. 'So you're sure.'

A look of irritation crossed her face. 'You know I am. You're here, I'm here. End of conversation.'

He laughed inwardly. It seemed he wasn't the only one to have been dreaming of this for too long. He watched her, waited and soon saw the slight nervousness steal into her eyes, despite her words. She'd taken a smidge of her lower lip between her teeth, he could see her biting hard on it. And she was staying very, very still—waiting.

He leaned forward and so slowly, so gently caught that lower lip between his own teeth. She gasped, freeing it so it was his. He sucked on it, let his tongue run over the swell of soft flesh. She opened for him completely—and they hurtled straight back into the red-hot kiss of earlier. Her hands lifted to his shoulders; he liked the feel of them, he liked the feel of her hips digging into him too. It was as if everywhere they touched the power surged, pulsing between them.

He broke free, determined to slow it down. 'You don't want to eat first?'

'Can't you just shut up and get on with it?' She thrust against him again. 'Anyone would think you're stalling.'

He looked at the gleam in her eyes. The nerves had gone. She was enjoying being provocative now. And she wanted it fast. Too bad. She'd told him the truth earlier. She wasn't a one-night-only girl. Not before now.

'What's wrong?' he asked bluntly. 'Why do you want it to be over so quick?' Did she want it done and then him leave inside the hour? Like some naughty fantasy that she could tell herself wasn't really real?

Not happening. If she wanted it, then she was getting it—one *whole* night. And one night didn't mean once only. And it certainly didn't mean quick.

She didn't answer, had fallen silent, breathless as she leaned her lower belly against him. He understood—even just that simple closeness turned him on too. He traced her collarbones with the tips of his fingers. Watched for the reaction. Yeah, there it was. The widening of her pupils and the increase in her breathing. Her response so quick, so gorgeous. Impulsively he leaned forward and kissed her cheek.

She turned her head but he didn't take the mouth she offered. Instead he kissed her ear, let his tongue lightly trace the whorls, let his teeth gently bite on the soft lobe.

Then he kissed the skin just below—she shivered. Yes, she was sensitive there, vulnerable.

He liked to touch her where she was vulnerable.

The constraint fell from him. Too late to pull back now. Inside he knew it had always been too late—from the moment he'd seen her looking so crossly at him at the back of the warehouse he'd wanted her. And he was going to get what he wanted—now.

She moved restlessly. He saw the flicker in her eyes but he refused to kiss her again. Not yet—he needed to regain his control so he could play with her the way he wanted. He undid each button on her blouse, so slowly, until it fell open. He pushed it back on her shoulders, took in the pretty bra. White, floral lace. Very pretty—but the soft globes it encased were even prettier. He could see her lush nipples pressing against the lace and nearly groaned aloud.

He had to kiss her again, not her mouth—not yet—but the soft creamy column of her throat. He brushed his lips against it, felt her pulse beating beneath him, breathed in the subtle scent that he found so sexy. Her head fell back, giving him greater access to that sensitive area. He traversed down, seeking to anoint more of the sweet skin with his tongue, his lips, eventually crossing over her collarbones and to the rising slope of her breasts.

Her hands lifted to his waist, pulling on the belt loops of his jeans, trying to draw him closer. He refused to move. So she did. Rising to tiptoe, bumping against him. He smiled as he hit the lace edging of her bra.

'Lorenzo.' The need made her voice sound raw.

He slid his hands up her thighs, soothing the ache he knew she was feeling with the promise of that intimate caress. Soon. Very soon. He was so glad she was wearing a skirt.

'Lorenzo, please.' She swirled harder against him.

He felt her hands on his back, on his skin as she went

beneath his tee shirt. He tensed. He couldn't handle her touch just yet. He lifted his fingers higher against her, swept them across the front of her panties.

She jumped. Stepped back from him.

He froze.

She wasn't looking at him. 'Like the good little girl scout I am, I'm prepared,' she gabbled, fumbling with her skirt. He watched narrow-eyed. Finally she pulled a condom out of her pocket with shaking fingers. But she dropped it as soon as she had it. She groaned with frustration.

He spared a quick glance down to where it had fallen and then stepped forward and slid his hand round the back of her neck, pulling her to him. 'We don't need it.' He bent and resumed his savouring of her skin.

'We don't?' She sounded startled.

He bit back the laugh—barely succeeded. 'Not yet.'

'No?' She was panting now, her hips circling again, pushing into his in that way that was slowly driving him out of his mind.

He gripped her butt, stopped her. 'No. Not yet.'

He was determined to have his slow discovery of her, but he'd give her a taste of what was to come. He kissed his way across her breast, moving up the gentle slope, finally taking the nub deep into his mouth, his tongue raking over the tip—pretty lace and all.

She cried out. He felt the satisfaction burning into him. Couldn't resist sucking harder, letting her feel the edge of his teeth. She jerked, and he clutched her closer, stopping her from slipping to the floor.

Her hands clasped his shoulders. He lifted away from her so he could see into her eyes and tease the hell out of her. 'You're not that well prepared, are you?'

Looking dazed, confused, she said nothing.

'Don't you think we might need more than one?' He straightened and set her right on her feet again, dug one hand into his back pocket and pulled out the stash he'd stuffed in there earlier. Holding his hand in front of her, he uncurled his fingers and half a dozen condoms scattered on the floor between them.

He caught her round the waist as he felt her soften. 'Now stop trying to control me.' He pushed her into the dining chair, and went down in front of her. Placed his palms on the inside of her knees and pushed them apart.

'What are you doing?'

'Maximising pleasure,' he muttered, hands sliding up her thighs. 'It's like making wine, Sophy—producing the best takes time. Patience. A gentle touch.'

'But I like to get things done.'

'I know you do. And this is one thing we're going to do very thoroughly.' He slid his hands back down to her knees, skimmed them down to her ankles.

This wasn't going to be quick. He'd wanted too long. He was going to touch every sweet part of her—and make her mindless.

Sophy looked down as he knelt between her legs. His eyes jet black, his face concentrated as he watched his fingers trace over her soft skin. He bent and she closed her eyes. Yes. There it was. That sensual mouth, those full lips brushing against her—setting every tiny spot he touched on fire. Someone had to help her—*he* did. She just couldn't take this kind of torture.

'Lorenzo.' But there was no point—he wasn't in any hurry as he kissed across her thighs. She tilted her hips towards him in an ancient rhythm, mentally begging him to go higher, to where she needed him. Finally his hands glided to her hips, his fingers grasping the elastic. She pressed her heels into the floor, lifted her butt from the chair so he could slide her knickers down. In seconds his hands were back at her knees, pushing them wide again. She screwed her eyes shut tighter.

But the kiss she expected didn't come. It was her breasts that he touched, nuzzling through the lace, his hands pushing her skirt up higher around her waist.

She could feel the heat of his torso so close, she wanted it closer. She honestly thought she was going to die, she wanted him so badly. 'Please, Lorenzo. Please.'

'No.' His half-laugh was unbearably wicked.

'I can't wait any longer.' The touch of his lips to her nipples sent an SOS to her cervix—starting the contractions, the searing need of her sex to have his.

'Yes, you can.'

'But if I come now, I won't…' How could she make him understand? She didn't want the edge taken off her hunger, she wanted all of him inside her when she had the release. She wanted it to be the best she'd ever had—she could almost taste it. 'I want it *all*.' All at once. Immediately. She was reduced to basic instinct now—to demand his possession.

He laughed. 'You'll have me. Again and again. I promise. Why not just enjoy this moment?'

She was going to go insane, that was why. The volcano inside her threatened to erupt. He moved—but not how she'd wanted—not to pull her to the floor so he could thrust into her in the way she was so desperate for.

No. It was only a slight change in hold but it was enough to bring her firmly under his control. He spread one hand wide on the inside of her thigh, placed his other much higher, cupping her breast, his fingers caressing her painfully taut nipple. But she could no longer move, her body bound by his, utterly enthralled by the simplest of touches: he licked her.

She gasped as his tongue swirled, tasting, teasing her most intimate, most sensitive part.

And it killed her.

She pushed back against the hard chair, unashamedly thrusting her pelvis into him. The waves of pleasure lapping at her, as he lapped her. Oh he knew what to do, how she wanted him to do it. The waves rose higher, starting to wash over her—every muscle tensed, tingled.

'Don't stop, please don't stop,' she begged him, shaking as she felt it surging. She wanted it, but she wanted more. She didn't know what to do with her hands, with her heart, with the heat burning her inside out. In the end she reached out and drove them into his hair. Thick and vibrant beneath her fingertips, the texture rough and all male. Her head hit the back of the chair as she arched higher to meet his kiss—tension locking her body in an endless moment of stillness. His hand went from her thigh to support her beneath—holding her to his hungry mouth so he could go deeper, suck and stroke harder. And he didn't stop. The slow, rhythmic, divine touches intensified. Her fingers curled into claws as she shook, her cry high and harsh. And as she buckled he still didn't stop, not giving her any respite, forcing every last ripple of response from her— until neither her body nor mind could take any more and the world went black.

Sophy was no longer a sentient being. She couldn't think, couldn't move, couldn't speak. Couldn't even open her eyes. His hands traced over her. Gentle kisses followed their path. It was as if he was worshipping her skin, her scent, her sex.

Her pulse slowed, steadied and then started to leisurely rise again as she heard him murmuring her name. She opened her eyes then. He lifted his head from her skin, met her gaze, his smile almost boyish with pleasure. He knew, he knew just how well he'd thrilled her and how ready she was for him to do it again. Like now.

'You still want it all?'

'More than ever,' she answered honestly.

His smile faded as his hand cupped her jaw. 'You humble me.'

He twisted away, grabbed a few of the condoms. Once on his feet he lifted her into his arms and walked, instinctively stopping at the door to the master bedroom.

'Not that one.' She was in the smaller of the two rooms.

He placed her in the middle of her bed. Stood back and whipped his tee shirt from his head. 'I think you'd better take off your bra and skirt.'

She was too busy enjoying watching him strip to bother with that. He took a moment with his jeans, taking care with the zip.

When finally, jaw-droppingly naked, he ripped open a little pack and rolled the condom over his erection, his teeth clenched for the few seconds it took.

Then he looked up at her. Frowned. 'Bra and skirt Sophy? I'll lose it if I do it.'

Maybe she wanted him to lose it.

'If you want me inside you then you have to do it.'

She smiled, thrilled to see him so tense. But she knelt up on the bed and twisted her arms behind her back to undo her bra clasp.

He stood at the foot of her bed, looking like some ancient Greek athlete—no, some ancient Greek *god*.

And the look on his face made her feel like a goddess. She stood on the bed then, unzipped her skirt, and with a shimmy of her hips let it fall.

He stood stiller than a statue.

Legs apart, she put her hands on her hips, filled with a

new confidence—just from the way he was watching her. 'What are you waiting for?'

He answered slowly, through clenched teeth. 'Some degree of control.'

She dropped to her knees and crawled to the end of the bed. Straightened up and put her hand on his chest— watching it rise and fall. Then she looked up into his searing black gaze.

His fingers tangled in her hair, twisting in her curls, and he pulled. She didn't resist, let her head fall back so her mouth was his to plunder. And he did.

But then she ran both hands through his hair, holding him to her as she let herself fall back onto the mattress. As she intended, he overbalanced and came down hard on top of her.

'Sophy,' he grunted, automatically bracing a hand on either side of her, lifting his weight off her. 'You okay?'

She hooked her legs around him, arched up to stop him moving too far away. 'No. I'm tired of waiting for you.'

'I can't wait any more.'

She smiled and rippled beneath him. 'Good.'

He stayed braced above her for a long moment, gazing into her eyes. She lifted her hips, trying to hurry him. He just smiled—that heart-meltingly brilliant smile. Then he lowered his weight half onto her again. Her heartbeat rocketed. Anticipation made breathing difficult. At last he moved, a smooth powerful stroke forward, filling her in the one hit.

She gasped, expelled an even harsher breath as she shook.

'You okay?' He moved again.

'Yes,' she panted. 'Yes. Yes. Yes.' But her breathing pitched wildly, the blackness threatening again as she gasped, struggling to cope with the blissful sensations. Too much, it was too much.

'Easy honey.' He pressed into her once more—slow, deliberate—and held there until she steadied. The weight of him and his careful hold anchored her, but his power had the potential to pull her apart. After a wavering moment, she began to breathe more deeply, softening, increasingly able to handle the intensity.

He kissed her, a soothing kiss. 'Stay with me,' he muttered.

She nodded, feeling his slow rhythm begin again, and she started to move with him this time. She ran her hands over his back, feeling the strength he had to offer her. She smiled as she felt it surge beneath her fingers. In her most secret fantasies she'd never imagined it would be like this.

'Yeah.' He kissed her properly then.

She took his face in her hands and kissed him back—as deeply as she possibly could. As the feelings ratcheted she felt him grow more tense. Until he wrenched his mouth from hers and bored a burning look into her, the smile gone, *his* breathing ragged and uneven now.

He rose higher above her, working them both harder, until she started to lose it again. Then he kissed her jaw, her ears, her brow, her neck, while his hips moved in that maddening, magical way. All at once the sensations rushed at her from every direction. She was half panting, half crying, mostly screaming. And just like that, too soon, not soon enough, she shattered. Her body convulsed in ecstasy, clamping hard—forcing utter capitulation from him too.

The tips of his fingers touched her damp skin. 'So you do sweat.'

'Contrary to popular opinion, I am actually human,' she answered with her eyes closed.

'And do you like it when I make you sweat?'

She didn't answer. He'd had enough from her already. He'd had everything.

'Your hair is still perfect.' He ran his fingers through it. 'What do you do to it?'

She made herself answer this time—keep the conversation on this light level. Even though she felt as if she were on shakier ground than if she were standing on the rim of an active volcano. Really she didn't want to talk at all. She just wanted to absorb herself again. Right now she felt all that was precious in her was hanging up in the air, able to be seen—and shot down. She wanted to suck it back up. 'Nothing. It's just the way it is.' She knew he didn't believe her. But it was true—she could only have the one style. Boring as anything.

'I don't think I've ever seen you so still.'

She turned her head and looked at him. 'What do you mean?'

He lay on his side, facing her, watching her with an impudent grin. 'You're usually doing a million things, ever so efficiently, never stopping.'

'I only work fast because I want to get the job done. There are other things I want to be doing.'

He levered up higher on his arm, glanced around her room. At the table. 'Making the necklaces?'

She was such an open book, wasn't she? 'Yes. And other pieces.' She watched him closely. If he dared laugh she'd brain him one. She'd hidden it from her parents. Her brother and sister had teased her one too many times about never getting over the toddler threading beads phase. She was just the child who'd been unable to live up to their achievements, was only useful as the errand girl.

And the silly thing was she *was* like a child—eager for their acceptance. But she couldn't help that craving. She'd never been one to disrespect her parents, always had been dutiful. But she wanted more than that; she wanted to make them proud. She wanted them to value her contribution to the world as much as they valued her brother and sister's and their own. Trouble was, she was hardly off saving people as they were.

He'd hopped off the bed and was looking at the pieces on the desk. 'They're pretty good.'

'And you're an expert?'

He whirled, looked all wolf. 'I've seen a few necklaces in my time.'

Of course he had. He'd seen a few necks, hadn't he? And he knew how to make love to a woman's neck, that was for sure. The niggle she felt about that was shamefully fleeting. She just wanted him to do it again.

He looked at the tray of beads and glass and trinkets. 'They're different.'

'Thank you.'

'You've got a few done.'

Sophy hesitated. Then the small burst of pride beat over her usual reticence. She wanted to impress him—just a little. 'I'm putting them in a show.'

As soon as she'd said it she regretted it. The nerves flared—what if no one liked them? What if she sold none?

'What show?'

'There's a film festival coming up at the academy. My jewellery is going to be showcased in the foyer.'

'Cool.' He nodded. 'That'll be great.'

Sophy's bubble of excitement popped. 'I just have to finish enough to mount a decent display.'

He looked at the table. 'This is where you work?'

'Sometimes I use the dining table, but it's easier in here.' Less mess for Rosanna.

His brows flickered, but then he looked at her. She

knew the subject had gone from his mind and something else was in its place. It was obvious—his body gave him away.

Lorenzo hadn't snuck out of a girl's room in years. Usually he could manage breakfast. He'd mastered the art of a sweet departure—a kiss, a smile, some lush words. But final. Always final.

But he didn't want to touch Sophy again. If he did, he knew he wouldn't be able to stop. And he refused to mess with her any more—although the reality was, she'd messed with *him*. He'd known it would be wild, but he hadn't thought he'd be filled with such awe. Be so moved by her. In truth, she scared him. How she made him feel scared him. She was so soft, so abandoned, so delicious.

She made him want more.

He carefully eased from her bed. She was lying in a sweet curve, her blonde curls spilling over the pillow. He resisted the urge to kiss her goodbye. He was hard again anyway. He didn't need to make it worse.

It was more nerve-racking then when he'd been trying to sneak out of the school dormitory with Alex crashing round behind him. It was all right for Alex—if he'd been caught it would have been a figurative rap on the knuckles. For Lorenzo it would have meant expulsion. He was always on that last chance. But then, as now, he made it.

He stood on the footpath outside her house and stretched, feeling the adrenalin surge through his muscles as he thought of their night together. He watched the dark sky start to lighten. Oh, yeah, as fantastic as it had been, he shouldn't have done it. Never, ever should have done it. And he sure as hell wasn't doing it again.

CHAPTER SIX

Sophy opened her eyes when she heard the front door shut. She lay still a few moments longer just in case. Lorenzo had wanted to escape, she hadn't wanted to stop him. She figured he didn't want the awkward morning after either.

Had he even left a note? She rolled over, closing her mind to the slight tenderness of her body. No note—not on the pillow anyway. She lay on her back and looked up at the ceiling. Waited until she was sure he'd have driven away, then got up and walked into the lounge. The food was still on the table—all untouched. The only thing they'd eaten last night was each other. He'd had to come back out to the lounge at one point in the wee small hours to find the last couple of condoms that were hiding on the floor. And she was no girl scout—she *hadn't* been prepared for him. And she certainly wasn't prepared for this now. No regrets, but a nasty case of uncertainty.

She scraped the food into the bin, looked about as she worked. But there was no note anywhere else either.

And she had to face him at work in four hours' time.

She didn't bother going back to bed to try to get any more sleep. Instead she found her favourite navy trouser suit and made sure the shirt to wear beneath was pressed.

She refused to let him ruffle her—not any more. But her heart thudded.

So they'd had their one night. And while she felt as if she'd died and gone to heaven, he obviously hadn't. He couldn't wait to get away—and hadn't wanted to deal with her. Okay, she'd get over that.

She really wished Rosanna were home. It wasn't her advice on how to get it that Sophy had needed. It was her advice on how to achieve a painless aftermath now. How did Rosanna keep on such good terms with all her old flames? And, even more importantly, how did she keep them all burning for her? Sophy shook her head—no, she didn't have either the secret or the skill for that.

Well, at the very least she'd try to borrow some Rosanna cool. She handled the boys with charm and smiles, right? Just made it easy for everyone. She winced. Sophy had made it easy for him all right. But he'd wanted her too, hadn't he? It hadn't been totally one-sided. She'd felt him shaking when he'd moved in her, she'd heard him growl with pleasure.

The balm from that reflection didn't last anywhere near long enough.

He just liked sex. It was obvious. It wasn't her he'd wanted, just the physical pleasure that she'd offered on a plate. What had she been thinking?

Okay, so the regrets were coming now—and the hurt that he hadn't felt anything special when she so totally had.

He wasn't in when she got there. Kat the receptionist said he'd be out most of the morning. Sophy was sure it was on purpose.

Fine.

She sat at the desk and did what she was famed for—

getting on with the job. Organising everything. Victoria phoned, asking her to pick up some supplies from the deli for the dinner at their parents' place, and she had some meals to drop to Cara's house too—could Sophy do it?

Of course she could.

And in the end her nervous energy was wasted—he didn't show up at all. Sophy decided to leave early too. She'd cleared the backlog—there was no reason for her to be working full time hours any more. She'd stick with what she was good at. She did the errands for Victoria, then went to her parents' place for the catch-up. While there she did more, making herself feel useful—wanted by someone for something.

When she got to work the next day he was out again. Sophy bristled inside—really, wasn't he taking it a bit far? What was he afraid of? That she'd throw herself at him—*again*?

She winced. She *had* thrown herself at him. Not making that mistake again. Not ever. Hours later she hung up from her millionth call and looked up at a small sound.

He stood in the doorway, his face half in shadow. 'Everything okay?'

'Yes.' Sophy smiled. 'Of course.' She looked at the piles of paper in front of her. 'It's been a busy morning but I think I've got just about everything sorted now. Including all the details for the fundraising gig at the bar tomorrow night.'

'Great.' He hesitated.

She waited.

But he said nothing. So it was true that men never did want to talk about it. Well, she didn't want to either. What was the point? It was done. It was finished. She wasn't going to go all cold and wounded on him. But not flirty and desperate either. She'd aim for friendly professional.

She flashed him a smile—just the right touch of warmth but not overly so. 'I'm off in a minute. I'll drop to part-time hours as we discussed now the backlog is cleared.'

He annoyed her completely by walking further into her office instead of hoofing off to his own as she'd hoped. She looked out of the window so she didn't have to look at him.

'The vandals have been back.' She'd noticed it this morning. The graffiti was huge—stunning, if Sophy dared offer her opinion, which she didn't because now he had that really brooding look on his face. 'You didn't hear them?' It had to have been more than one kid to spray a piece that big in a short time.

'I'm a deep sleeper,' he said dryly.

She shifted a letter unnecessarily. That was dangerous territory. 'What a pain for you to have to paint over it again.'

He shrugged. 'I'll leave it for a bit.'

'Fair enough.' She was quite pleased. She liked the colours, the whole fence looked on fire with the crimson reds and burnt gold coils.

She logged off the computer, gathered a couple of items to put back in the cabinet. It only took a moment. Then she reached for her favourite shiny handbag. Definitely time to make her exit.

Lorenzo leaned against the window frame and watched. Wow, she really was efficient, wasn't she? Had filed him away as if he were one of those pieces of paper. Checked him off her list and moved on. Forgotten about him.

And he shouldn't give a damn.

And he didn't—it was just his cock making things complicated. Leaping to attention when he merely walked the corridor—before he'd even seen her, let alone caught her fresh scent on the gentle breeze. The desire gnawed at him—had ruined his sleep last night. He'd lain awake, the noise of the city at night loud in his ears. So often it had soothed him. He'd spent so many nights listening to the traffic, imagining he was in one of those cars and just driving, driving, driving away.

And the restlessness had driven him outside—to the cover of darkness where he could create. Despite it being his property, it still thrilled him—helped release the anger that had burned in him since he could remember. Making his mark—he was there and they couldn't get rid of him, no matter how much they wanted to.

Alex had had a bit of bitterness with the mess his parents had made. Lorenzo was filled with it.

He'd chuckled as he worked on the fence. What would the do-good miss say if she knew it was him? He'd spent hours on it—switched all the lights in the warehouse on to cast a glow out to the yard. But in the end it hadn't done its job. Nor had the five-mile run he'd taken after. He was still angry. He was still frustrated.

He still burned inside.

But he'd discovered something that offered the softest respite from the old torment.

Sophy.

Unfortunately she was also the cause of half his trouble. Somehow just being around her—and her perfect looks, her proper manner—brought those old feelings back.

'You are coming to the fundraiser tomorrow night, aren't you?' he struggled to ask casually.

'You really need me to?'

'Yes.' Hell, yes. 'It would be good to have you on hand to make sure the information side of things goes smoothly.' He totally made it up. There was no information side of things.

'Then I'll be there.' She paused by the door on her way out, turned back to look at him, an irritatingly benign smile on her face. 'I assume it's all right to bring a date?'

Every muscle locked onto red alert. A date? He had to force his jaw apart to answer. 'Of course.'

Rosanna flew back late Saturday afternoon. Sophy gave her an hour to relax in the bath then asked her as she lay on the sofa flicking through a magazine. 'You have to come out with me tonight.'

'And you're so desperate for my presence because?'

'I need your support.'

Rosanna tossed the magazine to the floor. 'What's happened?'

'Nothing. But I don't feel like walking into a crowded bar all by myself.'

'What bar?'

'Wildfire. Only opened this week. There's a fundraiser tonight for the Whistle Fund there. I have to go. But I don't want to go alone.'

'How is our favourite shark?'

Sophy shrugged. 'I hardly see him. He's very busy. He's the money behind this bar.'

'I'll text the boys. Spread the word. It should be fun. And it's for a good cause.' Rosanna leapt up into action. 'Well, we'd better find ourselves something suitable to wear, then, huh?'

Sophy grinned. Yeah, there was no holding Rosanna back from a party—or an excuse to get dressed to the nines. But two hours later she stared at her reflection in horror. 'I'm not wearing this.'

'Why not? You look hot.'

She looked like a wannabe catwoman, in Rosanna's favourite black—skin-tight satin pants and a sleek, sheer top. It smacked of trying too hard, too out of character—as if she were going out of her way to draw his attention. Which she wasn't. Not again. 'It's more you than me.'

'Keep the trousers, change the top.' Rosanna was working on her eyes.

Okay, that she could handle. Sophy went back to her own wardrobe and found one of her pretty silk tops—that flowed, less in your face figure-hugging. She picked up one of her necklaces.

Rosanna appeared in her doorway. 'Can I borrow one?'

'Absolutely.'

The bar was already packed when they got there. There was no formal aspect to the fundraiser. It was just that the charity was getting a percentage of the ticket sales—so, really, she didn't think she had to be there. But she couldn't not.

Yeah, the place was an instant success. Lorenzo had the Midas touch, didn't he? Knew the investments to pick, always had his finger on the new big thing.

Sophy let Rosanna lead the way to the bar, she had a way about her that parted crowds. They ordered—classic cocktails—and waited for them to be mixed. Rosanna flipped so her back was against the bar and surveyed the room. 'Looks good.'

Sophy nodded, trying not to look anywhere. She didn't want to see him. Didn't want to have to admit she had no date.

'Oh, my.' Rosanna sighed, fanning herself.

'What?'

'I just saw Lorenzo.'

'Oh.'

Rosanna spun back and leaned into Sophy. 'I just saw the way he was looking at you.'

'Oh?' Sophy's skin felt as if it were about to blister.

'Kitten you are going to be gobbled. One bite.' Rosanna laughed. 'Lucky kitty.'

'The jet lag is getting to you,' Sophy muttered, lifting the glass to her lips.

'Going to introduce me to your date, Sophy?'

She gulped, the liquid burning. Oh, there he was. Right behind her. She turned. In the crush of bodies at the bar he was too close.

'Of course.' She summoned some social skills. 'This is my very special friend Rosanna. Rosanna, this is Lorenzo.'

'Pleasure.' Lorenzo was purring like the cat who'd not just got the cream, but the bird too. 'Vance wanted to meet you too. He's my co-owner and manager of the bar.'

Lorenzo moved slightly closer to Sophy so the man behind him could be seen. Sophy felt Rosanna stiffen.

'Hi, Vance.' Sophy smiled, breaking the short silence.

But the newcomer wasn't looking at her. He was staring—hard—at Rosanna. And she was positively glaring back. They were squaring off like ancient enemies.

'Aren't you too old to still be dressing like a skateboard punk?' Rosanna was all snark.

'Aren't you too old to still have an eating disorder?' Vance answered ten degrees too coolly.

Sophy's jaw hit the floor. Rosanna was sleek, utterly sleek and stylish. But she wasn't sick. At least, Sophy didn't *think* so. And this guy so wasn't her type—she liked them with as much style as her own. Sophisticated style, not street wear. Although Vance had his strengths, to be sure.

'Do you two know each other already?' Sophy asked, despite the obviousness of the answer. It wasn't normal to be trading insults so soon in an acquaintance.

Rosanna didn't even glance at her. 'We met a few years ago.'

'Come and dance, Sophy.' Lorenzo grabbed her hand in a death grip, took the glass from her other and ditched it on the bar, marching her away despite her protests.

'Hey, I'd hardly had any of that.'

'I'll get you another later.'

She pulled to slow him, twisted back to catch another glimpse of Rosanna. 'Do you think they're okay? They look like they might kill each other.'

'I think they'll be okay. She's all grown-up.'

Sophy really wasn't so sure. She tugged her arm again. 'She's not as tough as she makes out.'

Lorenzo laughed, the glint in his eyes too dangerous for comfort. 'She'll be fine. Forget about it.'

Well, she wasn't going to do that. 'She's my friend.'

'Just give them five minutes.' He looked at her, the darkness in him piercing now. 'Or is it that you don't want to dance with me?'

She went cool, despite the thudding in her heart. 'I like dancing.'

'Right.'

The music was loud—if they were to hear each other they'd have to lean close. Sophy opted for silence. But he was too close anyway, moving closer. And she couldn't cope with the way his big body moved—with surprising grace—or the way he absorbed the beat so naturally.

She felt increasingly stilted, her pulse skipping—too fast for the rhythm of the music. She couldn't relax—tried not to look at him at all. Until he grasped her by the upper arms and pulled her to him.

She gasped as their bodies collided.

'You're mad with me for leaving like that,' he roughly muttered in her ear.

'No, I'm not.' She shook head and glared at him. 'It was good you did, actually.'

'Oh?' His eyes glittered in the lights. It looked as if his temper was off the leash now.

'Saved us from any awkwardness,' she snapped.

'And you're not awkward now?'

'No.' She tossed her head, refusing to admit she was basically dying of discomfort. 'But my shoes are killing me so I've had enough dancing, thanks. You don't need me for anything tonight anyway, right? For the Whistle, I mean.'

'No.' His reply was frigid. Hard eyes raked her. 'Not at all.' He pushed her away and stalked through the crowd.

Sophy felt her own anger grow. What did he want—for her to fall at his feet again? To act the desperate female? Never.

She pushed her way back to the bar where Rosanna was standing alone—a fresh cocktail in hand. She handed it out and Sophy gladly took a deep sip and handed it back.

'Why don't you just do him and be done with it?' Rosanna asked as if it were the most logical thing in the world. 'Honestly, the tension between you two is electric.'

Sophy didn't inform her that she already had done him. And that instead of making the tension go away it had only made it worse. Much, *much* worse.

'I should have known you'd have it in you. You never give yourself enough credit, as a result no one else does,' Rosanna commented. 'Our mistake.'

Have what in her? The ability to attract a shark like Lorenzo? Big deal. Rosanna had been right first time round—she couldn't handle him. 'What's with you and the Vance guy?' Sophy asked, wanting to think about something else. 'I mean, that was rude, even for you.'

Rosanna shrugged. 'Unfinished business, you know?'

Um, well, yes. Sophy knew Rosanna was angry, but she had her own frustrations too—and she needed space to deal with them. 'I've had enough. I'm going home. You coming?'

Rosanna had the huntress look in her eye. 'No. I'm finishing the business. Tonight.'

'Are you sure?' Sophy didn't think it was such a good idea. Rosanna rarely allowed her emotions to bubble close to the surface and right now they were clearly on show.

'Deadly.'

Sophy hesitated, wondered if she should stay—convince her friend to let it go. But she felt the presence at her back—the surge in awareness. She turned. Lorenzo—standing a millimetre away but looking totally remote. And she just knew he'd been listening in.

'Stuck for a ride?' he asked bluntly.

'I can get a cab.'

'No need. I'll run you home.'

'You're not staying?'

'Obviously not.'

She hesitated. It would be churlish to refuse. And she was handling this like a sophisticate, wasn't she? 'That would be great. Thanks.'

They walked from the bar. Not awkward at all? Ha.

'It's a real success,' she said for the sake of saying something.

'Yeah. Vance had the vision. It was a good one.'

But it was Lorenzo who had backed him on it. Kat had told her some of the background—turned out Lorenzo was the only one who would back Vance, when the banks wouldn't.

'I wonder how Rosanna knows him.'

'You'll have to ask her.'

Quite the clam, wasn't he? She gave up on the small talk and simply watched him drive. The powerful machine purred under his hands, responding to his slightest touch.

Just as she had. She started to sweat again, clenched her muscles to stop the softening. She still wanted him, *badly*. But she wasn't going to make the mistake of asking him again—she didn't want to hear him say no. He pulled over outside Rosanna's villa. She undid her belt and had her door open in a split second. The sooner she got away from him, the more likely she was to escape with the little dignity she had left. But her deeply ingrained politeness made her bend and glance back into the car—right at him. 'Thanks for the ride.'

'My pleasure.' His hard gaze bored into her.

Utterly still, she took in the intensity in his face. Why so angry? Burning with confusion, with embarrassment as she suddenly thought of an alternative to the 'ride' they were talking about, she slammed the door.

Lorenzo swore. Forced himself to wait until she was inside the door of her home and then put his foot to the floor. What the hell was he doing hovering around her? She was determined not to be bothered, that their night truly was all over. She couldn't have made that clearer. And wasn't that what he wanted?

No. He'd wanted her to admit she was feeling as out of sorts as he was—as unfulfilled, as hungry.

He gripped the wheel tighter and knew he'd better head back to the warehouse pronto before he did something stupid. He could feel it surging within him, the energy seeking to burst out of his skin. He hadn't felt it this bad in a long time—the anger and the desire to destroy. The darkness deep within him was awake. Maybe it was a result of the illness last week. His control had been weakened. But it was the thought of Sophy that threatened it the most.

He'd just stay up all night. He'd get it back under control.

CHAPTER SEVEN

ROSANNA didn't return that night but sent a safe-status text in the morning. Sophy grumped her way through breakfast, telling herself she desperately needed to Get Over Lorenzo.

She stayed at home all Sunday but went to work her usual ten minutes early on Monday. Tried to keep her pulse at a vaguely normal rate as she climbed the stairs up to her little domain. Not awkward. Not awkward at all.

She heard the voices as she neared the top. Stopped on the threshold of her office door. The girl was very pretty. Already seated in *Sophy's* chair. Kat, the receptionist, was showing her the damn computer system already.

'Hello.' Sophy smiled, ultra bright and polite. She was not going to get evil over this.

'Hi, Sophy.' Kat looked up and beamed. 'This is Jemma, who's here to help you out.'

Oh, right. Help her out. Like she needed helping out? Like she needed a pretty, petite thing to do the work for her? Oh, please. After she'd just spent the last week giving the place a complete overhaul? She didn't need help *now*. No, it was more like now the hard stuff was done she wasn't needed any more.

Now he'd slept with her he didn't want her around at all.

It wouldn't be awkward at all then, would it?

The jealousy kicked in, the resentment swirling around, the energy building in her until she had enough fuel inside to launch a rocket to the moon.

'Are you okay showing her some stuff for a while longer, Kat?' she barely managed to ask nicely.

Kat nodded.

'Great.' Yes, she wasn't needed at all. She gripped her bag all the more tightly. 'I've just got to see Lorenzo.'

Kat nodded. 'He's about. I saw him earlier.'

Oh, good. Sophy briskly walked the few metres along the corridor to his office—it was empty. She checked the other office—the other staff were back now, having done their bit for Vance. But Lorenzo wasn't in with them either. She walked faster—she refused to let him avoid this one.

She went downstairs but he wasn't out in the yard. She went into one of the darkened rooms where they stored the cases of wine—all on pallets ready to be shipped. He was bending down by one, checking the dispatch label by the looks of things. He straightened when he saw her. Watched as she walked towards him, the heels of her shoes rapidly clicking on the concrete floor.

'You've got a temp in,' she said briskly.

'Yeah.'

Even though she knew already, she had to take a second to absorb the hit from the casual dismissal in his tone.

'I thought you were all about keeping Cara happy and not getting some clueless temp in?' Sophy cringed even as she bitched at him; she was quite sure Jemma wasn't clueless, but it had been his point originally. 'Do you have any idea how hard I've worked here? I've fixed the whole mess.'

'I know you have. A five-year-old could work the filing system you've put in place. It's perfect for a temp now.'

She reeled. Was that supposed to be a compliment? To make her feel okay about it? 'You mean it's the perfect time to get rid of me.'

He walked towards her. 'What are you so mad about? I thought there were other things you wanted to be doing anyway?'

That wasn't the point. The point was his shabby treatment of her. 'You just don't want me to be here any more? You're embarrassed. You're the one who's feeling awkward.'

'That's not why I got a temp in.'

'Yeah, right. Can't handle it, can you? Anything remotely personal going on in your precious little domain.'

'What happened with us is not why she's here.'

'That's rubbish, Lorenzo. At least be honest and admit it. You want me gone.'

He swore right back at her—only worse. 'Quite the opposite. Come with me.'

Given he now had hold of her wrist in a clench that threatened to break the smallest bones in there, she didn't have much choice.

'Lorenzo!'

He didn't listen. Didn't stop. Stormed out of the store room and up the stairs, past the offices until he got to the empty room at the back.

He let her go and she was still moving so fast from being dragged along with him she half ran into the middle of the room. He strode back to the door and slammed it shut, whirled to face her, his arms flung out. 'This is why.'

She stared around the big empty room. There was a large table in the middle, a few chairs around it. 'I don't follow.'

Clearly fuming, he enlightened her. 'You can set up in here. Work the rest of the day, half the night if you need to. To get your jewellery done for the show. This can be your workroom.'

She stared at him. 'You're kidding.'

'No.' He walked further into the room, turned his back to her so she couldn't read his expression. 'I'm vaguely useful. If you need to use power tools or something, I can help.'

'You mean you can plug them in?'

He grunted then—almost a laugh. 'Yeah.' He faced her, his hands on his hips, still looking like a warrior about to launch an offensive any minute. 'I just thought you could work here in the afternoons. You'd be around if the temp needed help but you'd have the time to work on your own stuff. You can stay later. You don't have to pack it up at the end of the day, just spread out and get it done.'

Calm descended over her, her earlier anger soothed by a new suspicion. 'Why didn't you tell me?'

He looked even grumpier. 'It was supposed to be a surprise.'

She blinked. Well, it had been a surprise. But he'd meant it as a *nice* surprise. 'Why did you want to surprise me?'

He looked away. 'I don't know.'

Yes, he did. She waited.

'You've done a lot for the fund,' he muttered. 'I thought it was a way of saying thanks.'

And that was all it was? She didn't think so. She walked right into his personal space, her heart hurtling inside but trying to keep her efficient cool look on the outside.

He stiffened but didn't move away.

'Did you want to do something nice for me, Lorenzo?'

He looked to the side but still didn't step back.

She smiled and took another pace closer. And closer still.

His hands were suddenly on her arms. 'What are you doing?'

'I thought I'd say thank you,' she breathed oh-so-innocently.

His gaze dropped to her lips. His fingers tightened that extra notch but the rest of him stayed rigid.

Bingo.

The guy still wanted.

Well, the guy would get.

But not yet.

She reached up on tiptoe, brushed her lips ever so gently against his jaw—that inch too close to his lips to be purely platonic as he had once done to her. She stayed there a second longer, whispered in a way she'd only ever fantasised about, 'Thank you, Lorenzo.'

She tried to move back but his hands were keeping her there now. 'Sophy.'

Part warning, part what? Sophy couldn't decide. But the whisper seemed to have gone down quite well.

He sighed—part groan—and his fingers softened, smoothing over her skin. 'You smell good.'

'Do I?'

He nodded. 'I smell you everywhere.'

'Cheap shampoo. Everyone uses it.'

'No,' he half laughed. 'It's you. Only you. And you don't use cheap shampoo.'

Oh, that was nice. She let her weight rest against him a little more.

'If we do this again, and I mean *if*, then no one knows,' he said firmly.

'What, it's our "little secret"?' She pulled back to look at him. She wouldn't have thought he'd be one to care.

'I'm not having gossip on site. No one is to know.'

'So we remain professional through the day and meet up for rabid sex at night? Is that it?'

His whole body tensed.

She stepped closer, her confidence blossoming despite his obviously conflicted feelings. At least it meant he had feelings. 'Let's get one other thing straight, Lorenzo. If we do this again, and I mean *if*, then it's for more than one night.'

He swallowed.

'We're not done until it's finished,' she told him quietly. She was not having another couple of days like this. She'd work him right out of her system. She'd had a taste of danger and she wanted to take it all until there was no danger left.

'But it will finish.'

'Sure.' She nodded. It was serious physical chemistry, that was all. She'd get her stuff done for the exhibition and be able to walk away. A week or so would be enough to neutralise it. 'Deal?'

He nodded. 'Come upstairs with me now.' His hands were seeking already, sliding beneath the hem of her clothing, hunting for bare skin.

'I thought you didn't want to have sex here?' What about gossip onsite? Hell if any of them came looking for either of them now they'd be in trouble.

'I've changed my mind.'

As his hot gaze drank her in she could read his thoughts and she struggled to stay calm.

She put her palm on his flushed cheek. 'What about Kat? And Jemma and the others?'

He closed his eyes. 'Sophy.' He sounded so tormented.

She reached up. 'I want you.' She kissed him. His arms tightened and he didn't let her free of the kiss. But his tension eased, his hands stroking with care now. So that had been what he needed. How surprising—so the neediness wasn't all her? She could feel his heart pounding against her. Maybe they could go upstairs—sneak up there now just quickly.

Her phone rang. And rang and rang.

Sophy broke the kiss. 'I have to get that,' she muttered.

He looked at her, bitterness flashing on his face. 'Of course you do.'

She scrabbled in her bag to find the phone at the bottom, smoothed her hair behind her ears, quickly inhaled to cover her breathlessness and put a smile on her face so her greeting would sound friendly. 'Sophy speaking.'

He watched her, his face as readable as a stone. She flashed a wider smile at him.

'Hi, Ted, what's up?' She swung away as she listened. 'And you need me to pick it up? Sure. No problem. Give me the address.' She dug back into the bag for a pen—no point asking her brother to text the details; he would say he didn't have the time. Sophy repeated the address back to him, glanced up in time to see Lorenzo walking out of the room. Two minutes later the call was dealt with. Sophy stared at the door, wondering why he'd gone.

She went back into her office—found Kat had left Jemma figuring out stuff on her own.

'It's great you're here.' Sophy smiled, meaning it this time.

But Jemma's attention wasn't on her. She was looking out of the window.

Thud, thud, thud.

Sophy didn't need to look to know what it was but she did anyway. He was back out there already bouncing his damn ball. Well, she wasn't going to go running after him, not this time. She looked across and frowned at the fence. It was covered in even more graffiti now.

She didn't see him the rest of the day, didn't expect to see him until the next. But when her doorbell rang she wasn't surprised.

'Have you eaten?' she asked as she opened it to let him in.

He was leaning against the door jamb. Dressed entirely in dark clothes—black trousers, a charcoal V-neck tee. 'That's not why I'm here.'

She deliberately leaned against the opposite side of the door frame. 'No? Then why are you here?'

'Don't play games.' His glare blistered. So he was still brooding.

'You'd better come in.'

He crossed the threshold into the hall, stopped as he saw the black-clad sylph standing at the other end of the hall.

'Lorenzo, you met Rosanna the other night. Rosanna, this is Lorenzo, my boss.'

His frown super-sized up.

Rosanna moved swiftly down the hall, her case rolling behind her. 'I'm off, darling. Back in a few days. Be good.' She grinned wickedly.

'You too,' Sophy tried to coo, but it was a squeak.

She heard Rosanna's chuckle.

Lorenzo was still frowning long after the door had closed behind Rosanna.

'She's very discreet,' Sophy said to reassure him. 'She won't say anything.'

He jerked his head to the side. 'I'm not your boss.'

Oh, was that the problem? She smiled. 'Yes you are.'

'Not really.'

She knew what he meant and this was different from the usual office affair. In truth she was doing him a favour working for Whistle. The balance of power wasn't so weighted towards him—at least not in respect of that. Sophy wanted to smooth it even more. 'Tell you what, why don't you let me be the boss in the bedroom—that'll even us out.'

'Never.' The fire in his eyes burned from ice-cold to hot.

'But it's my bedroom.'

He shook his head, chasing off the last of the threatening storm clouds.

'You just see if you can stay in charge, then. *Boss*.' She threw down the challenge. Knew she didn't have a hope in winning at all—but shrieked with laughter as she turned and ran as fast as she could to her room.

He caught her before she got there and went completely caveman. And she was quite happy to be his woman of the moment.

The days couldn't pass fast enough. He was on her doorstep before she even got home some nights. But he didn't suggest she ride home with him and nor did she offer to take him. The boundaries might be invisible but they were there.

But as the evenings lengthened and their physical need was temporarily tamed she turned and talked to him. About nothing. About everything. But never about anything personal. She didn't want to talk about her family, sensed he never would talk about his. But one night she got some courage and steered the conversation slightly towards him. 'Why the Whistle Fund?'

He lifted his head off the pillow. 'Why at all?'

'No, why the name?'

'Because that's what you do when you need help. You whistle.' He pursed his lips and gave a short whistle.

'And you whistle so you're not afraid—there's a song about that.'

'Yeah, and when you're doing something you shouldn't, you have a mate keeping lookout—who'll whistle if you need to make a run for it.'

She laughed at that. 'Did you need to make a run for it often?'

'All the time.' He grinned.

She laughed with him but wasn't at all sure how much he meant it as a joke. 'And you whistle at pretty women, right?'

'Oh, no,' he said mock soberly. 'That's not pc.'

'You're not pc.' She rolled onto her tummy. 'Have there been many women Lorenzo?'

'Are you sure this is a conversation you want to have?'

The coolness was almost visible. Damn it, why shouldn't they talk about their pasts? Couldn't they have a laugh about the mistakes they'd made before? Why was he blocking her from getting to know anything more about him? She'd heard the little there was to hear. So his childhood hadn't been a picnic, okay, she'd gathered that. But he'd gone to that great school hadn't he? Someone had cared enough to pay for that. And he'd become amazingly successful.

'Why not? Tell me about your first and worst, I'll tell you about mine.'

'Look, we're meeting up for the *occasional* screw. That doesn't mean we're going to swap life secrets or play twenty questions.'

Sophy flinched. Every night wasn't exactly occasional. Jerk. Her temper flared. 'Touchy, aren't you? What happened? Did you fall in love once? Did she reject you— did she say you weren't good enough for her? The poor boy from the wrong side of the tracks?' Sarcasm flavoured every mean little word.

He sat up and pushed the sheet from him. 'Actually I rejected her.'

'Oh,' Sophy said. 'Of course. Silly me. You like to do that, don't you? And why did you? Did she want too much from you?'

He swung his legs off the bed, turned his back to her. This time she had it right. The anger rippled through his muscles.

'Poor Lorenzo, someone actually wanting emotional commitment? Support, honesty, love?'

'Nothing so devastating,' he denied. 'She no longer turned me on.'

Sophy blinked. Ouch. There was a warning. She got out of bed too, pulled a shirt over her cold arms. She didn't want him to be with her all night now. Not tonight.

'You know, I have lots of work to do.' She let her gaze slide over her desk—it was covered with designs and half-finished pieces that she'd decided weren't going to go in the show. But he didn't know that.

He looked at the table, then at her. 'You want me to leave?'

Sophy forced a shrug. 'Rosanna's back in town, she'll probably be home soon.'

'And you don't want her to know how loud I can make you come.'

She coloured. She supposed she deserved it. She was being rude chucking him out. 'I wouldn't be able to come with anyone right next door.'

'Really.' His sarcasm practically splashed on the floor. He pulled on his tee shirt and jeans.

He was angry—the way he moved totally gave it away. Well, so was she.

He didn't kiss her goodbye. Just strode out. She didn't speak—just slipped into the lounge and watched from the window as he jogged down to his car. But to her surprise he didn't get into it and drive off. Instead he kept on jogging, his pace picking up to a hard-out run. In the darkened room she kept an eye on the street. It was a good forty minutes later before he returned. His tee shirt sweat darkened in patches. He didn't look at the house, stayed too focused on his car for it to be natural as he unlocked and slid into it. The engine roared. He was at the speed limit in a second.

Sophy usually spent an hour each morning working with Jemma making sure the girl had a good grasp of the processes. She did—she certainly wasn't clueless. Then Sophy left and went into her mini workshop. Her heart sank as she saw the volume of work she still had to do. Her confidence had dipped—none of it was good enough to go on display. She was totally fooling herself. She was going to embarrass herself completely. Her mobile went and she answered right away—glad of the excuse to turn her back on the mess. She listened. 'Sure, I'll come right away.'

She met him on the stairs on the way out.

'Where are you going?' His super-size frown was back.

'I've promised my mother I'd meet her to help with something at lunch.'

'But you're supposed to be making your jewellery. You've still got several pieces unfinished.' He climbed to the stair just below hers.

'I know,' she said, pausing for a second to wonder how *he* knew—had he been poking around in her room up there? 'But I promised.'

He looked angrier than he had when he'd left last night. He stretched his hands out to the rails either side of the stairs so he made a wall she somehow had to get past. 'But you've only got a week 'til the show.'

She knew that too. 'I'll work on them later.'

His eyes narrowed. 'You don't want to do it, do you? The exhibition.'

'What? Of course I do.'

'If you did you'd be prioritising it.'

She stiffened at the implied criticism. 'Things other than work have priority in my life, Lorenzo. *People* have priority.' Which was more than could be said for him. As far as she could tell he lived for work and work alone. People—*relationships*—didn't feature in the equation at all. 'My mother has asked for help. I'm pleased to be able to.'

'No, she could get someone else. It's just that you can't say no when someone asks you. It wouldn't matter if it was her or anyone.'

'And that's a bad thing?' She glared at him.

'It is when it stops you from achieving your own dreams.'

'Like I said, people come first for me, Lorenzo. Always.'

'Aren't you a person? Isn't what you want just as valid as what others want? Surely if you explained how busy you were, she'd find someone else to do whatever it is. A paid assistant, perhaps?'

She stiffened—but not because of the little jibe.

His eyes narrowed. 'She doesn't know, does she?' With scary precision he zoomed in on the problem.

No, and Sophy didn't want her to—didn't want any of them to. 'The sooner I go and do this, the sooner I can get back upstairs.'

'But you were out yesterday afternoon too. For three hours.'

What was he, her timesheet? She wasn't accountable to him. Not on this.

'You can't let this opportunity go, Sophy. Your work is too good.'

That made her even more tense—she felt pressure enough without him making sweet comments like that. 'I really have to go, Lorenzo.' She looked past him down the stairs. 'And it really isn't any of your business.' He wouldn't open up to her at all, so why should he have the right to comment on her life?

'Sophy,' he said quietly, leaning forward and branding her lips with the heat of his. 'At least be quick.'

CHAPTER EIGHT

'SOPHY, can you come with me, please?' Lorenzo met her as she walked into the building.

She glanced at Kat behind the reception desk, hoping the girl hadn't picked up on the chill in his words. 'Of course.'

Was he mad with her? She hadn't returned to the warehouse yesterday—had got held up completely until the early evening. Her sister had come round and it had turned into a whole family gathering. She'd made excuses and gone after a while—but she needn't have hurried. Lorenzo hadn't come round, had left no message on her phone. It was the first night they hadn't had sex all week. And stupidly she'd had less sleep than ever. So she really wasn't in the mood to have a hard time from him.

He led her out the back and gestured for her to get into his car.

'Where are we going?' She fixed her seat belt—he already had the engine running.

'You'll see.' He fiddled with the stereo and put the music up loud. What, he didn't want conversation?

'I had a nice night, thanks.' She chit chatted really loudly just to annoy him. He didn't want to talk personal? Tough. 'Big dinner with my parents and Victoria and Ted. It's my niece's birthday this weekend so we were celebrating early. Rosanna sent a text. She's in Sydney for a few days.'

He gave her a sideways look but said nothing.

Yeah, she loved having conversations by herself. So she gave up. They drove through half of Auckland and she relaxed into the comfortable seat. Suddenly she sat up. 'Lorenzo, this is the airport.'

'And we're right on time.'

On time for what? 'Where are we going?'

'Have you ever gotten on a plane and not known the destination?'

She shook her head.

'Now's your chance.'

'Lorenzo—'

'Have you ever taken a risk? Gone with an impulse?'

'Maybe,' she said cautiously. Like the time she'd come on to him with the basketball.

He parked the car, crossed his arms and called her on it. 'What are you going to do, Sophy? Play it safe or walk on the wild side? Come on an adventure.'

'How wild an adventure?'

'Totally legal.' He rolled his eyes. 'Honestly, don't make a big deal about it, you'll end up disappointed.'

She didn't think so. She didn't think she'd ever be disappointed when he was offering adventure.

He got out of the car. 'Are you coming or what?'

As if she could say no. He loaded a surprisingly heavy-looking suitcase onto a trolley and headed to the check-in. She wasn't worried. It wasn't as if they were going to go overseas—he didn't have her passport, this was the domestic terminal.

'We're flying back tonight, right?' She'd better check on that though.

'No.'

'Then when?'

'Sunday.'

Sunday? 'Lorenzo, I can't. I promised my brother I'd organise the cupcakes for my niece's party.'

'Were you going to bake them?'

'They're not that hard.' She nibbled her lower lip. 'Oh, I can't, Lorenzo. I can't let him down. I can't let her down.' But she was disappointed for herself more than anything.

'Do you have to be at the party?'

'No. It's for her little friends. I was just making the cakes. She likes the icing I do.'

'Someone else can do icing.'

Who? Baking wasn't something anyone else in her family did.

'Phone a bakery and get them to deliver,' Lorenzo said, as if he were instructing a small child. He was right, of course. It would be so easy.

'It's short notice.'

'Just offer to pay double and they'll do it.'

She laughed. 'Is that how you get what you want? Offer to pay?'

'No. That wouldn't work with you. I have to come up with other alternatives.' He grinned. 'Like abduction.'

She chomped on her lip some more. So tempted.

'Phone up and get it done.' He gave her a sideways look. 'What else did you have scheduled for the weekend?'

'A few things.' Sophy dug out her phone and her diary. 'What am I going to tell them?'

'The truth.'

'I don't want to.'

'You don't want to say you're running off for a dirty long weekend?'

Oh, she couldn't hesitate now. 'We're a secret, remember?'

She got on and made the calls. It took the whole twenty minutes they had left on the ground to rearrange everything she'd agreed to do in the weekend.

She put the phone away but her practical-oriented brain presented her with the next set of problems.

He lifted her face to his. 'What's wrong now?'

'I don't have any clothes with me.'

'You don't need any.'

'Oh, we're going to a naturist colony? Awesome.' She aimed for sarcastic but was burning inside with the naughty promise of his words. 'They don't mind furry teeth either?'

He laughed. 'There are shops where we're going. We can get you a toothbrush, okay?'

'Fabulous.'

The flight was only just over an hour. Christchurch. She knew the destination now, of course—the signs and the pilot's message had given that one away. She was fine with it. Christchurch was a nice city and she hadn't been there in ages.

But when they got into the rental car he headed straight onto the bypass and the motorway north.

'Where are we going?'

'I told you, you'll see.'

After forty minutes or so she thought she had it figured. The rows and rows of vines in the fields gave it away. Waipara—part of the wine region.

'We're staying on a vineyard?'

'No.' He kept driving.

It was another hour, passing alongside a river and the weird shaped cabbage trees that looked like something Dr Seuss would have drawn. A few sheep were scattered in the fields. And then they got there—to Hanmer Springs, an Alpine spa town in the heart of a geo-thermal area. He slowed down as they drove through the main street of the village.

'Look, swimsuit shop on the right,' he pointed out. 'Leopard print number in the window gets my vote.'

Oh, please.

'Superette on the left for toothpaste and other essentials.' He pointed with his hand. 'Bakery for the best pies in the country.'

She chuckled. 'Everything one could possibly need.'

'That's right. Now I'm going back to Waipara for some meetings.' Halfway up the hill he pulled up in front of a house. 'You're staying here.'

She got out of the car. He was leaving her? She walked up the path slowly, not caring enough to appreciate the pretty wooden chalet he'd just unlocked. When was she getting the 'dirt' in the weekend? Inside he'd opened the big suitcase. Carefully packed inside was all her gear—all her tools, all her unfinished work. She stared at it, then at him.

'I'm not letting you throw away this opportunity, Sophy,' he said softly, placing his hands on her shoulders. 'Not even for hot sex with me.'

'Lorenzo—'

'Give me your phone.' He held out his hand.

She pulled it from her purse and gave it to him.

He switched it off and put it in his pocket. 'You have no excuses now. You have to finish them.' His expression softened. 'I've booked you into the spa at four p.m. for a massage and whatever other treatments you feel like.'

'Really?' Her spirits lifted a fraction.

'Uh-huh.' His eyes twinkled. 'But you have to do nothing, and I mean nothing, but work until then—deal?'

'Okay.'

'And you'll have to walk down to the spa because I'm taking the car.'

'That's okay.' She nodded again. 'Thanks.'

But she was disappointed. She *ached* for him. And he'd played on that—used it to set her up. She'd cleared her weekend to be with him, but now she had nothing to do but finish her pieces for the show.

She supposed she'd thank him one day.

He kissed her, drew away way too soon. But at least he groaned as he did. He put his hands behind his back. 'Nothing but work. *Nothing.*'

She managed a laugh and watched him go. As he got to the car she couldn't stop herself calling after him through the open door. 'You'll be back later?'

'Count on it.'

She turned back inside and looked at her stuff. She had all afternoon. All day Saturday and Sunday too. With no phone, no outside contact—no one calling. Suddenly she felt it—liberation. And she did as he'd bid. It only took twenty minutes to set herself up and then she worked. In the silence, alone, she got into the zone. Her enthusiasm for it returned, as did her confidence. She studied her options, assessing the work she had completed and her pages of notes for other styles. She deliberated carefully before making a decision. She wanted her work to be thematically linked, but for each piece to stand uniquely, to showcase a broad range.

There was a harsh ringing. She literally jumped three feet in the air. Spun round, looking for the source of the noise. It was the landline of the holiday home. 'Hello?'

'You need to go now or you'll miss your appointment.'

'Oh.' She looked at her watch. 'Is it that time already?'

He chuckled. 'You've been hard at it, haven't you?'

She leaned against the bench and let the smile out. 'Yes. Thank you.' She meant it this time.

It was a ten minute walk down the hill to the thermal

pool complex, but she jogged it in five—so she had time to pick up a swimsuit from the store first. She walked straight past the leopard print but stopped at the rack of crimson costumes. There was a two piece the exact shade of part of the graffiti piece on Lorenzo's fence. She grabbed the one in her size—hoped the cut would be okay. She paid and ran—not wanting to be late.

She went for the full facial, full massage option. An hour and a half of pure bliss. At the end she couldn't have peeled herself off the table if she'd tried. The beautician left her to relax. Her private room had its own small pool of thermally heated, mineral-laden, olive-green water for her to melt into at her leisure. When she regained some kind of muscle control, that was.

She was almost asleep, lying on her tummy, when she heard him.

'Are you ready for your massage, ma'am?'

She smiled. She recognised the thread in that voice. 'I've already had my massage, thanks.'

'This one is a little special.'

She felt his hands circling over her back.

'Crimson,' he muttered. 'Good choice.'

She didn't roll over—for one thing she couldn't, for another she didn't want him to see how slight the triangles covering her breasts were. Not yet anyway—she was still getting used to them herself.

But he couldn't have been that into the bikini because in less than a minute he was pushing the briefs down. He lifted her foot, then the other to get the garment off—and when he placed each foot back he spread them a little further apart. Slid his hands hard up her calves, up the backs of her thighs...

She bit her lip, anticipation flooding her. 'Lorenzo, there are people everywhere.'

'I locked the door.' His 'massage' took an incredibly intimate turn.

'They'll hear us,' she said breathlessly.

'No, they'll hear *you*.' He laughed and bent to nip her butt while his thumbs stroked into the space between. 'Of course,' he added thoughtfully, 'you don't *have* to come. Women don't have to orgasm every time, do they? You can still enjoy sex regardless, right? It won't bother me.'

'How magnanimous of you.' She clutched the towel beneath her and tilted up to give him better access. It was one hell of a massage.

He murmured, mouth moist on her skin as he manipulated her—faster, deeper. 'Think of it as a challenge. I dare you not to come.'

She rocked, pushing harder onto him, her voice leaping three octaves. 'I can't not!'

He whipped his hands away and flipped her over. He was already naked, and in a moment was above her. He held her face hard between his hands, kissing her savagely while he surged into her. Her scream came out in another way—her fingernails raking down his back. He arched harder, his thrusts even more powerful.

It made it even better.

'Does anyone know about the show?'

They were in the water, cheeks flushed from the heat, bodies floating.

'Only Rosanna,' Sophy answered lazily. 'She got me the chance. One of her flirts sponsors the film festival.'

'And no one else?'

'No.'

'Sophy.'

'What?' She gazed at him candidly. 'It's not like you're

an open book, Lorenzo. You keep everything from everybody.'

He frowned. 'Only the bad stuff.'

What, his whole life was bad? She just didn't believe that.

'Why don't you want to tell your family?' he asked.

'I'm going to. But I want them to see the stuff first—so I can see what they really think. And not just be nice because they know it was made by me.'

'What they think matters that much to you?'

'Sure,' she said. 'They're my family.'

He went quiet.

'I want them to be proud of me.' She tried to explain.

'There's no way they're not proud of you already.'

She smiled. But he was wrong. She'd let them down. 'I'm not like them.' But she didn't explain it further. Rather she let her hands slide over him—her reward for a long day of hard work. 'You were wrong.'

'What about?'

'This just can't be legal.'

He laughed.

'I'm serious. It feels too good.'

'I've got a secret for you, honey,' he whispered into her mouth. 'Only the things that are right feel this good.'

And that was the moment her heart liquefied. She tipped her head back to look up at him—a long, searching look. But his gaze slid from her and then the rest of him did.

He splashed up the steps out of the pool. 'We need to get moving.'

'You've got to be kidding.'

'A couple of my growers are coming in to Hanmer and we're going out to dinner.'

'What, like at a restaurant?'

'Yeah.' He turned on the shower.

'And it's okay for me to turn up in my bikini?'

He laughed under the stream of water. 'Absolutely.'

'Well, what else am I going to wear? My crushed suit from today?'

She was *naked*.

He left the shower running for her and wrapped a towel round his hips. While under the hot jet she watched him open his backpack. He pulled out another pair of jeans and tossed them on the massage table for her.

She switched off the water. 'I'm not going to meet people wearing your clothes.'

'Sophy—' he sent her a look '—relax. It's not a fancy restaurant. Just nice people, nice food.'

It *was* a fancy restaurant and wearing nothing but a pair of men's jeans that hung on her and a tourist tee shirt from the spa shop wasn't her idea of fancy restaurant attire. And, worse, wearing his jeans turned her on.

'Hi, Lorenzo. You must be Sophy.' So he'd mentioned her to them? She felt an absurdly warm glow about that.

To her relief the older couple were in jeans too and were full of welcoming smiles. Lorenzo explained that Charlotte and Rob Wilson had one of the largest holdings that supplied grapes to one of his labels. They were led to a table, talk turned to food and wine and business.

'Have you known Lorenzo long?' Sophy just had to do some digging while Lorenzo and Rob talked about the bar.

'Fifteen years,' Charlotte replied.

Sophy nearly spilt her wine. Wow—if there was someone who knew him it was this woman.

Charlotte was smiling at her as if she'd just read her mind. 'He used to work as a hand in the picking season. Right from when he was a teen and had nowhere to go in the holidays.' She looked at Sophy. 'I tried to spoil him but he wouldn't have it. I'd leave baking in his cabin and hope he got it. The tin was always empty when he left so I figured he did. Later on Alex used to come and work too. It was more fun for him then, I think.'

Sophy swallowed. 'He was lucky he worked with you.'

'He worked on another vineyard when he was still at school too. The McIntosh property.' Charlotte shook her head. 'I've never known someone to be so driven to succeed. And he has.'

Yeah, but was he happy with it? Sophy was increasingly worried there was a huge depth of unhappiness in him.

'Now he's invested in this bar. Who knows what he'll turn to next? He's a natural entrepreneur. He's a genius.'

Okay, so Charlotte was his number one fan.

'What are you talking about?' Lorenzo turned to them.

'You.' Charlotte smiled at him. 'When are you going to be satisfied, Lorenzo?'

'I don't want to get bored.'

Sophy smiled as the woman laughed. But her nerves stretched. Bored—as he had been with the woman who'd no longer turned him on? He was busy—always busy—and frequently moved to newer, even more challenging projects. He did that with women too, didn't he? She had to try to remember that.

'Did you know Jayne McIntosh is trying to sell,' Rob said. 'I bet her father regrets not backing you now.'

'Would you be interested in Jayne's property, Lorenzo?' Charlotte asked quietly.

Was it Sophy or had he gone a bit stiff? Who was the Jayne? Was this the McIntosh he'd worked for? He reached for his wine and took a small sip. 'No. I don't think so. We have enough for the label and I'm diversifying elsewhere.'

'He was stupid not to come in at the time.' That was Rob again.

'He was doing what he thought best.' Lorenzo shrugged.

'He made a mistake,' Charlotte muttered.

'No.' Lorenzo's face went blank. 'He did me a favour. He made me want to fight even harder.'

'You were already fighting hard enough,' said Charlotte.

Lorenzo just laughed and put his hand on the older woman's arm.

The rental car was roomy and sleek and, even though it was only a ten-minute drive, she was asleep by the time he parked the car. He switched the engine off and just looked at her in the dim light from the moon and stars. Her hair was amazing. He'd been with her every moment—she hadn't nipped into a salon to have it styled in the two minutes he'd had his back turned. She hadn't even used a hairdryer. But it was in that old Hollywood movie star style again—a straight bob at the top ending in curls at her shoulders. She'd run a comb quickly through it, made sure the part was straight and put a clip in. That was it. Utterly effortless perfection.

That was her all over. But she didn't seem to know it. Always she strived to be more—to be and do everything for everyone. She should just chill out and believe in herself more. Because she was gorgeous—inside and out.

He went round to her side of the car, opened her door and roused her gently.

'Oh, sorry.' Her eyes were slumberous, deep blue.

He held her hand tightly and guided her into the lodge. She blinked as he put the lights on.

'You have been working hard,' he said looking at the table. It was covered. But it was the one lying on the small mirror that caught his attention. The blue was the exact colour of her eyes.

'Put it on for me,' he said, his voice woefully husky.

'It's only dress jewellery.' She played it down as she put it on. 'It's hardly diamonds or pearls.'

'It doesn't need to be. It's beautiful. You're really talented.' He'd known that. It was some of what had driven him to offer her the room, to bring her down here.

But it wasn't the only reason. There was the totally selfish reason as well—to have her for the weekend, all to himself. With no one else making demands on her, no interruptions, no brother or sister or mother calling all the time, scheduling errands for her to run. No, she was here for when *he* wanted. And he wanted her all the time.

He took her on the floor then and there. With her naked other than the beautiful necklace—the blue burning into him as he moved closer, closer still. He couldn't resist touching, couldn't stop touching.

He went back to the vineyards early the next day but finished up hours before he ought to. It didn't matter, much of what he needed could be done by phone. It was more just to see the team face to face. But his mind was elsewhere—and his body ached to catch up with it.

Not good. He rebelled against the unfettered need rising inside. Where was his restraint? His self-control was slipping. It was all wrong—he'd worked so long to gain mastery over his emotions. So why wasn't the passion waning? Why was it getting worse?

'Come for a run.'

Sophy looked up as Lorenzo stalked in. The electricity in the room surged—she wouldn't have been surprised if all the light bulbs had suddenly blown. 'Is exercise your answer to everything?'

'It is if I'm stuck on a problem or angry or something—it works for me.'

And was he stuck on a problem now, or feeling something stronger? 'You get angry a bit, Lorenzo?'

'I used to.'

Maybe he'd had a bit to be angry about. Casually she put down the pliers. 'Tell me about it.'

He looked at her, his eyes like burnt black holes. 'What is there to tell, Sophy? I was my father's punch bag. Eventually I got taken away but went from foster home to foster home. I didn't adjust well.'

She stared, shocked at the sudden revelation, at the painful viciousness underlying the plain statement of facts. Not many people would 'adjust' to that.

He looked uncomfortable, twisting away from her. 'But I'm not like him. I've never hit a woman, Sophy. And I've never hit anyone who wasn't hitting me first.'

He didn't need to tell her that. 'And you don't get angry any more?'

He relaxed a fraction. 'I prefer to get passionate.'

Yeah, he channelled his aggression elsewhere.

'Passionate about exercise,' she teased softly, wanting to lighten his mood. She knew his bio in the company literature was tellingly sparse. Now she saw his work with the Whistle Fund revealed far more. Art camps, for one thing. Sports days. All the work geared to underprivileged, at risk kids. He identified with them. He'd *been* one. 'Did you get into trouble?'

'Totally.'

'What things did you do?'

He didn't answer.

'How bad?'

'A few stupid things.' He was fudging it. 'The school was good.'

'What kind of stupid things?' Sophy leaned towards him. 'Graffiti?'

His grin flashed. 'You figured it out?'

'You have that place totally secure—there are security cameras, you live on site. And that massive piece appears overnight? No way would you have let that happen.'

He shrugged. 'You got me.'

'You're quite good.' He was better than good. 'Spray cans?'

He nodded. 'But I wipe my own slate clean now. And I only decorate my own property.'

'What else?'

He shook his head. 'Nope. If we're doing the twenty questions, then it's your turn to answer.'

She giggled, thrilled inside that he'd opened up just that touch. 'Okay, what do you want to know?'

'Past boyfriends.'

'No. Really?' That was the most pressing thing he wanted to know about her?

'Uh-huh.' His head bobbed, eyes glinting.

'Not a lot to tell. Dated a couple of boys at high school. Only one serious when I was at university.'

'How serious?'

'We got engaged.'

His eyes widened. 'What happened?'

'I changed my mind.'

'You don't strike me as the kind of person to break a promise easily.'

'It wasn't easy. I left the country.'

'Where did you go?'

'France for most of the time.'

'Why did you come back?'

'I missed my family.' She shrugged. 'Stupid huh?'

'No. Not stupid.' He went to his pack and pulled out his training gear. 'What did you do at university?'

She'd started law, of course. Had done okay, but didn't have the family brilliance. 'I didn't graduate.'

'Snap. I left to build the business. Why did you quit?'

She swallowed. 'That boyfriend. Bad news.'

'What did he do?'

Cheated, of course. He'd been a law student a few years ahead of her. But he'd only wanted to be with her because of her family's prestige. She didn't want to go there. 'It's more than past your turn for a question. Past girlfriends?'

He bent and tied his trainer laces. 'No relationships Sophy, remember?'

'What about Jayne McIntosh?'

His fingers stilled. 'What did Charlotte tell you?'

Barely anything—it was a guess. So was her next question. 'It wasn't that she didn't turn you on any more, was it?'

He stood. 'I never liked this game.'

'What happened?'

'Nothing that matters,' he said shortly. 'I'm more interested in what's happening now. Not the past, not the future, but now.'

'And what is happening now?' She drew in her lip, wondering if he'd go *there*—dissect their affair at all.

He paused too. Finally turned—away from her. 'We're going for that run.'

They got her some running shoes and shorts from a shop in the town and then he led the way up the hill, round and down through the forest, finally returning to town and the thermal pools.

Back at the chalet she dressed in his jeans and he cracked the whip.

'You get back to work.'

It was all right for him—he was sprawled on the sofa reading the paper. But she was on target so found going back to work wasn't so hard at all.

A couple of hours later he went out, brought back some Thai takeaway for dinner. After they'd eaten Sophy felt as playful as a kitten—the happiness made her feel sparkly from the inside out. She'd had a wonderful afternoon, was pleased with her progress for the show, and had loved his quiet company. She stood up from the sofa, stretched her arms out and twirled round the room.

'What are you doing?'

'Expressing myself.' She lifted her tee shirt and his smile widened. Oh, it was so easy to have fun with him. 'Come into the bedroom and watch me express myself some more,' she invited.

She danced the way through, peeling the tee shirt from her body. He followed, and she pushed him onto the bed and knelt over him, enjoying the dominant position. Well, she was wearing his trousers, so she'd be in charge. She knew he liked it slow, and she could do slow for him. She toyed with the edges of her bikini top. He reached out and teased one triangle down a little lower so her nipple was almost exposed.

She slapped his hand away from her. 'No. My job.'

His mouth made an 'oh' and his grin went wider. And thirty seconds later his fingers were back teasing—ruining her concentration.

'Stop it.' She batted his hand away again.

'Make me.'

She paused, an idea bolting in. 'Okay.'

She got off the bed and went out to the table covered in all her supplies. The ribbon was scarlet, a thin smooth satin. She picked up some scissors too.

He saw them as soon as she went back into the bedroom. Guessed her intention immediately. 'Oh, no.'

'Hands up.'

'No.'

'Why, Lorenzo—' she knelt on the bed '—you wouldn't be afraid, would you?'

He gave her a piercing look and held out his hands with a pained sigh. 'There was me thinking you were straight-laced.'

'Maybe I've discovered a ribbon of recklessness,' she joked. It was his fault. His influence. His touch. He made her feel free. He made her feel as if she could do anything, try anything, and he'd still accept her.

She bound his wrists together. Wrapped the ribbon around the headboard and tied that too, so his arms were caught above his head. She looked down at his face. He had a smirk. As soon as she finished, he flexed, the ribbon went taut.

His smirk vanished. He stiffened and pulled harder.

'I don't think you can break it.' She leaned closer to him, letting her breasts touch as she taunted. 'We girl scouts know how to tie knots.'

He pulled again. She saw it dawn in his eyes—that he really couldn't get free. 'Sophy. Untie them.'

'No.' She straddled him.

'Sophy. Joke's over.' He looked very serious, his eyes black.

'It's no joke. And it's not over.' She tickled her fingers up the underside of his arms—his biceps bulging as he tried to rip free of the ribbon again. 'Don't worry,' she whispered. 'I won't hurt you.'

The tenor had changed completely—he really wasn't comfortable with this, was he? She studied him. Raw, vulnerable, yet fiercely proud. Something pulled deep in her heart. This powerful, independent man was at her mercy—and he didn't like it.

And what had begun as an almost kinky, definitely playful tease, turned devastatingly intense. She spread her fingers wide, ran her palm slowly up the centre of his chest, feeling the warm skin, up to where she could feel the thudding of his heart. Had he ever lain back and just let someone *love* him?

No. He never had. And he didn't want to let her now.

But she wanted to love him—so much. And just this once, she would.

She moved off him, knelt at his side and started— slowly—even more slowly than when he'd tormented her that first time. She touched him, forgot time as she felt him, entranced in her exploration in seeing how she could make him respond. Making love to every inch of his skin and trying to go deeper—right into his bones, into his heart. He said nothing. Nor did she. But his breathing changed. She watched the straining in his body—knew what he wanted. She was breathless too—filled with yearning. She kissed him all over, her fingers either trailing or kneading every part of him—but the most obvious. She was saving the best bits 'til last. It was too wonderful to rush it.

But eventually she moved closer—her hands working together in sweeping circles—ever decreasing—narrowing in on her target. She heard his breath catch.

'Sophy.'

She smiled and took him in her mouth. His harsh groan was the sweetest melody to her ears. He moved beneath her—arching, seeking.

'I want to touch you,' he ground out, his hips rising— chasing her caresses.

'You already are.' It was her turn to be fiercely proud—

of the way she could make his powerful body buck, of the way she could make him cry out for her. The pleasure she could give him. She wanted to make him feel joy—as being with him filled her with joy. And the feelings surged through her, she lifted up looked down into his eyes. The beautiful eyes that she loved.

She kissed him like crazy—pouring it all into him. He met her, his kiss equally fervent. Then his body went rigid beneath her as he strained to be free of the bonds, but the knots held.

'I have to have you.' He sounded so raw. 'Please.'

Finally she couldn't take it any more herself—needed to feel him deep within her. She straddled him. Held his pulsing erection in her hand and sank onto him in one swift movement. They both cried out. He arched up, trying to lead the rhythm, but she pushed her hands down on his shoulders, using them as anchors so she could ride him hard—her way. She threw her head back as the bliss ravaged through her.

'Sophy, Sophy, Sophy.'

She looked back down into his eyes as she heard his agonised call to her. Saw him stripped bare. The vulnerability unconcealed—the bottomless depth of need in him revealed. Her fingers tightened on him as she saw the anguish there. She leaned forward to kiss him again—a kiss offering all she had. And felt the shudders racking him as he accepted it.

A long time later she still lay on him, running her hand gently over his chest as she felt his heartbeat slow. She said nothing, didn't expect him to either—and he didn't. Eventually she moved, lifting to look at him. His eyes were closed, his brow smooth. She pulled the coverings up. He'd gone to sleep. She reached down to the floor and got the scissors. She caressed his jaw, pressing a soft kiss to his cheek. And then she snipped the ribbon.

He moved faster than she'd ever have thought possible. Grasping both her hands in his, he flipped her onto her back, his eyes open and blazing as he crushed her half beneath his body. The scissors clattered to the floor. Breathless, she twisted her head to the side—could see the red marks on his wrists from where he'd fought against the knots. She bit her lip, braced as she looked back into his face—afraid of the anger she would find there.

But the flames weren't frightening. Instead the faintest smile appeared as he pushed down to emphasise each word. 'No one. But. You.'

CHAPTER NINE

LORENZO could hear Sophy playing with the necklace—picking it up, rolling the beads between her fingers, letting it drop. And then picking it up again. He kept his gaze on the dark grey bitumen that was fast sliding under the car. The airport was a rush of bodies and noise and interminable waiting—even though they arrived only five minutes before the check-in for their flight closed. Too soon they landed in Auckland. Too soon he was driving her home.

And he was not going in with her.

'Are you pleased with your designs?'

She nodded, dropping the necklace against her skin once more.

'I'll take them back to the warehouse. You can do any finishing there this week.' He couldn't bring himself to sever it completely. Not yet.

'Thanks.' She didn't look him in the eye. And he didn't look for long to see if she did.

Breathing space. He couldn't wait to be alone so he could reclaim his equilibrium. Alone was good. Alone was comfortable—this wasn't. The discomfort was bigger than the silence that ballooned between them.

He reached into his pocket and pulled out her phone.

The shock on her face sent a welcome flash of pleasure through him. Yeah, she'd forgotten he had it. She'd forgotten everything else the whole weekend except her work. And him.

That pleased him far too much, and in the wake of the warm glow the discomfort barged back.

'See you tomorrow, Sophy.' He drove away as soon as she was out of the car.

Something had changed. He knew when it had, but he wasn't sure how. She'd held him and he'd been more vulnerable than ever before in his life. But it wasn't because she'd bound his hands.

He didn't care to think about what had happened—what he might have revealed or what she thought she might have seen. But the need to have more of what she'd given had driven him. Just for today he'd taken it—holding her, playing with her, laughing like the carefree kid he'd never been. She'd done some work—not that much—they'd swum, they'd rested. A lovely, lazy Sunday for anyone normal.

But he wasn't normal—was fundamentally different from most and especially someone like Sophy with her perfect world and her perfect family. And now—back on normal ground—he was feeling more alien than ever.

Restless in his apartment, he tried to catch up on some work—went through the motions of checking his messages. He felt as if he'd stolen someone else's life for a day and he was going to get caught out any moment. His heart pounded the way it had when he was a kid and had known trouble was coming. His concentration splintered, reformed—focused on only one thing.

He went down to the room she'd taken as a workshop. Went into the cupboard at the back and pulled out the crate of paint. Twelve hours later he was still working on it in his office, hating the way he was so wired about seeing her.

'Stay late tonight—I've got something to show you.' He poked his head into her office halfway through the next day, not staying to explain, glad she had the temp with her so he couldn't go and kiss the hell out of her as he wanted. He was a touch embarrassed. She might not like what he'd done. And wasn't he just getting himself in an even stickier mess? He should be pulling away, not going in deeper.

Lorenzo was no stranger to hardship—well used to going without. So a bit of abstinence should be nothing. But she was the first thing—the only thing—that he wasn't sure he could give up.

He'd noticed she was missing something for the show and he was certain she hadn't had time to do it herself. She was up to her neck just trying to get the pieces done. She came to his office on the dot of five. He'd abandoned work hours ago—had been shooting hoops half the after noon, was now sitting waiting.

'It's upstairs.' He almost blushed. But the screen of his computer up there was bigger—that was why not because up there was private and had his huge bed waiting. She said nothing, just followed. He swung the computer screen round so she could see. 'I did some designs for you. If you want to use any I can get them printed.'

She stopped in front of the computer and stared at the images he'd pulled up. 'For business cards?'

He nodded. 'And labels for each piece—you can write on the details by hand or do them on the computer individually.'

Her eyes were wide as she bent to take a closer look. 'You're a man of many talents, aren't you?'

'Some good, some not so good.'

'Lorenzo, they're amazing.' She looked so thrilled he was even more embarrassed. 'I can't believe you did this for me.'

He shifted uncomfortably. 'It didn't take anything. It's really easy.' Okay, it hadn't been that easy. He'd stayed up half the night painting and then spent half the morning getting them into digital form. And then playing some more with them.

'I won't mind if you don't want to use them.'

'Of course I want to.' She was already fiddling with the mouse, tapping words. 'Lorenzo, this is fantastic. Thank you so much—I love them.'

'Okay.' He felt the relief whistle through him. 'Well, you want to work on them now? Then I'll get them printed. You'll be right on schedule.'

He went to the coffee machine. Hadn't slept all night, didn't need the hit now, but it was something to do. He glanced over to his workspace—she'd pulled up the seat and was busy adjusting his designs, experimenting with the text to go across the swirling design he'd created as her logo.

His heart thudded even more uncomfortably as the edge of panic sliced into him. He glanced at the door. This wasn't just his place, but his *escape*—his private lair. So why the hell had he tainted it with her scent again? It had taken days to fade after the last time she'd been here— when he'd been stupidly sick. And her scent had tormented his fever then. It was swirling round him now—tempting, choking him.

He shouldn't feel annoyed she was here—he'd invited her, after all. But now he wished he hadn't. He needed to get out before he did something stupid. All he could see was the memory of her lush mouth sucking him in, the look in her eyes as she'd arched above him.

'Um…' he walked away '…I'm going for a run.'

She looked up from the computer. 'Now?'

'Uh-huh.' He moved as fast as possible. If he didn't the

concrete would set around him and he'd be stuck completely.

As soon as he changed into shorts and trainers he got out onto the pavement and pushed it from the off. But with every pound of his feet the pull sharpened. It was like being torn in two. He pushed harder. Aimed to go further. But...he couldn't fight it. Any hope of restraint faded. He turned back.

The door slammed behind him. His breathlessness didn't ease. His erection grew harder. He'd run from her yet in less than twenty minutes was running back to her faster than before. His fingers curled tighter in his fists. She looked up as he strode across the room. He winced as her cool gaze swept over him. No way could she fail to see the state he was in. He walked across the room.

'You're going to shower?'

He nodded and strode faster. The torment infuriated him. He faced the shower head, turning the jet onto full power. Not caring that the gush of water was slightly too hot and needling his nipples. His sensitive nipples. He'd managed to go without all kinds of things before—why not now? He braced his hands on the wall and pushed his face into the rush of water, wanting to wash away the desire he felt for her. Wanting the emptiness back. It was easier—so much easier.

A hand slipped around his body. He gasped as she grasped his straining erection. He could feel her soft body against his back. And then her other arm wrapped round him too, her fingers teasing circles around one of those too sensitive nipples—tormenting him further. 'Sophy, don't.' The words hurt. Everything hurt.

'Do you really mean that?'

'You don't know what will happen.'

Her mouth moved across the skin stretching across his tense shoulders. 'Don't I?'

He pushed harder against the wall with his hands, desperate to thrust his hips. This would all be over in a second if he didn't get a grip. But it was her grip that tightened—pulling up his length with faster, harder strokes.

'Sophy.' He whirled around and pulled her close.

She shivered as he brushed his lips up the length of her neck in the gentlest ever touch—the sweeping caress a complete contrast to the rough, hard hold of his hands. He struggled to soften that hold—but couldn't, so made his kisses light instead.

'I want you so bad,' he confessed.

'That's not a bad thing.'

Oh, but it was. The water thundered in his ears. She was so soft—so heart-meltingly soft. But it was because she was so soft that he should be staying away. Instead he leaned into her, his lips trailing over her jaw, sucking her lip. He felt the insane need to touch strengthen again. His need to be with her was unstoppable now.

'Are you too sore?' He tried to slow down—they had been so physical yesterday and he was sure she must be tender.

'No.'

'Are you sure?'

She arched, lifted her legs to curl them around his thighs—opening to give him all access. And as he felt the wet heart of her sliding against him he lost it. Couldn't stop now even if he tried, the last shred of control gone. His hands moved, fingers gripping tight, holding her so she couldn't move.

He was hardly conscious of her cries as he mindlessly pumped deeper and deeper, growling as he strove for the bliss only a stroke or two away.

Instinctive, elemental, shattering—*peace*.

For a long moment he remained still, rammed into her

body, trying to stop his weak shuddering in the aftermath. The hot water cascaded over him but inside the chill was spreading fast and painfully. So out of control. He'd been so hopelessly out of control. He didn't even know if—

Oh, God, what had he done?

'Better now?' She ran her hand lightly down the side of his neck.

He screwed his eyes shut, wanting to reject her touch.

Because, no, he was *not* better. His body might be spent, but he still wasn't satisfied. He didn't know if he ever would be. The feelings scared him. He couldn't suppress them. It had never happened before. Never been like this. 'I'm sorry.' He shook his head and made himself look at her. 'You didn't have time.' Hell—had he hurt her?

'Didn't I?'

He saw a smile stretch her puffy lips, the pure satisfaction glowing from inside out. 'Really?' But it didn't ease his conscience.

She closed her eyes, tilted her head to let the water flow over her face.

Her beauty hurt him. Everything about her hurt him.

Because he could have hurt her. He wouldn't even have known—certainly wouldn't have been able to stop. In those moments just now, he'd totally lost it. The wild animal he knew was caged inside him had been freed— he'd been operating on blind, raw emotion and been utterly unable to think, to be aware of anything but his need to let that emotion have free rein. Just as he had all those years ago. Only then he'd pulverised some random person's car—had taken a bat to it in a blind rage, had smashed and destroyed, his anger thermonuclear. Unstoppable. Uncontrollable. Terrifying.

Loss of control over his emotions was unacceptable. It didn't matter what emotion—lust was as bad as anger. And if he'd lost it over one, he could lose it over another just as easily. The years of hard work, the self-discipline gained from physical training and concentration meant nothing now. He'd thought he could manage it? He didn't have a hope.

And hurting anyone—hurting *her*—was not an option. He'd always choose isolation over running that risk. And he'd enforce it now.

He looked at her—she wasn't even naked. She'd only stopped to take off her knickers before reaching to touch him as he'd showered. And now she was wet and bedraggled and beautiful.

Her eyes opened and in that moment he saw it—the vulnerability, the confusion, the *questions*. His blood ran cold. He couldn't possibly answer those questions.

He pushed away, switched the water off and got out of the intimacy of the shower room. 'Here.' He handed her a towel. 'Strip off and I'll hang your clothes to dry.'

They needed to talk. It was a talk they should have had the day before but she'd been too scared. Honestly she was still too scared. She didn't want to shatter this fragile moment—this happiness seemed so fleeting.

But it was disappearing anyway. She could see him retreating. His face had frozen, the brooding look back in his eyes. She tried not to let it hurt her. But that was like trying to stop the sun from rising.

'Don't worry,' she said, suddenly realising what might be bothering him. 'I've started the pill. I won't get pregnant.'

'What?' He spun to face her.

She blinked. 'In the shower just now, we ah…' She didn't finish.

His eyes had widened in horror. 'You've started taking the pill?'

'I thought it was for the best.' She didn't want babies yet. Judging by the look on his face he didn't want babies at all. So it was better not to run the risk of accidents. She'd known it was the wise thing to do.

'When?'

When had she started taking it? 'Last week.'

'Oh.' He still looked shocked, only now a frown had overlaid the discomfort on his features too. 'I'll, um…just find you a robe.'

He hurried from the bathroom.

An affair. She rubbed her skin hard with a towel and tried to remind herself that that was all it was. A one night fling that was having a few replays—okay, was on a continuous loop. But she couldn't make herself believe that was all there was to it despite his rapid cooling off now. If she were sensible, if she were reading the signs, she'd stop it. Walk away. But she was utterly lost in the web of desire for him. Her body held in thrall by his. And there was more than that.

She was in love with him. Head first, totally, desperately in love with this complicated, lonely, generous man. She ached to give him everything—and could only hope that maybe he'd ask for it, maybe accept it. She couldn't end it now—it would be like ripping out her own heart.

She walked back to the living area, looked at the cards he'd designed on the computer. He'd clearly studied her work—because he'd done the samples in her favourite colours, the swirling design that she saw was a key part of her style. He really did have an eye. The fact he'd done them for her blew her away—and gave her hope. Then she turned and looked at the way he was frowning into the fridge, seeming to take hours to decide what he was looking for.

Suddenly she knew what she had to do—there was even a song about it, wasn't there? About setting something you loved free. 'You know, I can get my clothes to-morrow. If you wouldn't mind me borrowing your robe and you running me home?'

He looked up quickly. 'You don't want to stay?'

Of course she did. But his relief was heartbreakingly obvious.

'No.' She pulled the robe closer around her. It was a warm day but she was growing colder by the second. He didn't want her to stay. Her heart shrank from the truth. She didn't want to be where she wasn't really wanted. He'd just had all he wanted.

Stupid girl.

She stayed away from work the next day—phoned through to Jemma the temp and explained she had family stuff to tend to. Not an untruth. She always had family stuff to tend to. Lorenzo didn't call, didn't come to her flat that night. She pretended to sleep. He'd never called her phone before—there was no need to be checking it every three minutes all night.

On Wednesday she went in—had to finish up the last details and pack everything up to take it to the theatre. She checked with Kat on the way in, hoped she hid her disap-pointment when the receptionist told her Lorenzo was scheduled to be out at meetings most of the day. It was a good thing really—she still had a few hours' work to do. She didn't need the distraction.

She worked hard—the labels and business cards were printed and in a box waiting on the table. She was thrilled with the finished product, for the first time feeling excite-ment about the show. She'd done her best work and now she was excited about showing it to the world. Late in the day she heard the heavy tread on the stairs, couldn't stop from flying to the doorway with an all over body smile that was impossible to hold back.

'Why are you looking so happy?' The brooding shadows were dark beneath his eyes.

Some instinct warned her not to admit that it was because he'd just appeared. 'I've found the most fabulous frock to wear tomorrow night.'

The smallest of smiles lifted his expression and he came into the room. 'Of course. Shopping maketh a woman smile.'

Oh, no, in truth it was just him. 'I'm actually starting to look forward to it now.' And she was. Sure, she was nervous about what her family would think of her designs, but at least she did have a stellar outfit to go in—and an even better escort. 'Are you wearing a tux? It's formal dress.'

His eyes narrowed a fraction and he turned away. 'I'm not going.'

She looked after him, stunned. 'Not going? You're not coming to the opening?'

He walked over to the window. 'No. We're not a couple, Sophy. I said from the start that this wasn't ever going to be a public thing.'

What? But he was the one who'd taken her out to dine with some of his oldest colleagues last weekend. She tried to stay cool. 'Well, you don't have to be there with your arm around me. You could just be there as a friend.'

'You don't need me there.'

'Yes, I do.' She didn't want to go without a friend. Rosanna was away on another buying trip so she wouldn't be there. But that was beside the point—she wanted Lorenzo with her, even just his presence on the far side of the room would be calming—like a secret injection of confidence. He believed in her, she knew he did. And she drew strength from it.

'No. You don't.'

She'd have to face her family's judgment alone. She swallowed. Okay, she could handle those nerves. But she was hurt by him now. 'Why don't you want to be there?'

'I don't like those foreign type movies.' He shrugged.

'Then why do you have some in your DVD collection?'

'You went through my collection?'

'You know I did.'

'Look, Sophy—' he turned to face her '—leave it. I'm not going.'

'You really don't want to be seen with me?'

'I'm not interested in complicating our arrangement.'

Their *arrangement*? What the hell did he mean by that? 'Then why have you been helping me so much if you're not interested? You want me to do well—why don't you want to be there to see if it happens?'

He turned, irritable. 'It's just sex between us, Sophy— some down and dirty release. It's what you wanted, remember? You can't go changing it now.'

'I'm not.' Her voice rose. 'You've *already* changed it. You were the one who took me away for the weekend. You're the one doing these things for me.'

'That was just so you could get your work done. You were so busy doing everything for everyone else. I thought it was a good way for you to catch up.'

'And that's not showing you care about me—not even just a little?' She held her breath.

He went utterly still. 'Nothing special, Sophy, no.'

She flinched but forced herself to take a step closer. 'And there was nothing in that weekend for you? Nothing *special*?'

He stared at the floor, answered with inhuman control. 'No.' He lifted his head sharply, like a beast sensing blood. 'Now don't get upset.'

'How can I not when you say there's nothing special?' He was denying everything—denying her, denying himself and above all denying the truth. She couldn't stop the hurt brimming in her eyes as she cried, 'You're lying to me, Lorenzo. And you're lying to yourself.'

'No. I'm being honest.'

She clutched the back of a chair. Was he? Being brutal to be kind? She stared at his rigid body, his masklike face. 'I don't believe you are.'

'It's just sex, Sophy.' His mouth moved, but his eyes were like dull stones. 'Just a tawdry affair that no one need ever know about.'

'You really think that?'

'We have nothing in common. We're good at screwing, that's all.'

She blanched at his crudeness. They didn't screw—she didn't just bang him for the momentary thrill. She'd made love to him—again and again. She had offered everything inside herself to him—wordlessly at least, on more than one occasion.

But she wasn't going to offer it again now—not in the face of such determined denial and such cold anger. No—she had very little left in her right now, but she did have that last drop of dignity. 'Then if that's all it is, Lorenzo, you won't mind that it's over.'

She walked past his stock-still figure and straight down the stairs.

CHAPTER TEN

SOPHY slowly buttoned the royal blue nineteen-forties vintage frock she'd found in an exclusive retro store earlier in the week. She pushed out the fantasy she'd had about twirling in it in front of Lorenzo. She spent ages on her face, going with forties style make-up to match—full foundation, lush red lips. She breathed slowly to try to check her nerves.

She'd spent half the afternoon in the theatre foyer setting up the display, had received gratifying comments from the staff there about her designs. But they weren't the people who mattered. She was going to those people now. It was only a ten minute walk to her parents' home in the heart of Auckland; they were going to the theatre together from there.

'I'm looking forward to the movie. It's had great reviews,' her mother chatted, oblivious to Sophy's stress.

Of course, they didn't even realise the exhibition was on in the foyer. Sophy clutched her purse, trying to hide the way her fingers were shaking as her father drove them. Her heart raced. This wasn't good. She'd even done a Lorenzo and gone for a run earlier—too bad if her cheeks were still flushed from it, she'd needed to burn off some of the adrenalin. But she might as well have not bothered.

Her body felt wired, on fire, yet she was cold to the bone. She wanted the movie to start—not have a whole hour of the pre-drinks to get through with her stupid baubles on show. But her parents were only too willing to relax, quietly chatting in the foyer to friends and generally acting like the reserved pillars of society that they were. How had she ever thought this was a good idea?

Her brother and sister were already there. And it was her sister and sister-in-law who pointed out the gleaming display cabinets of vintage inspired jewellery to her and her mother.

'What do you think of them?' That was her sister-in-law, Mina.

'I love this one—look at it, Soph, it's just gorgeous,' Victoria said.

'Are you okay, Sophy? You've gone all pale.' Her brother, Ted, stared at her. 'Now you're gone all red.'

'I'm fine,' she squeaked.

Her mother turned to look at her. 'Are you sure?'

'Mmm hmm.' She nodded, not bothering to try to talk more.

'This one would really suit you.' Mina, her sister-in-law, hadn't been paying attention. 'It would go beautifully with your eyes.' She was looking at the blue necklace she'd made in Hanmer.

Ted, her brother—the one with the IQ too high for anyone's good—had picked up one of the business cards on the table.

'"Designs by Sophy,"' he read aloud. 'Even has your mobile number listed.' He gave her a sharp look 'Got something to share, baby sis?'

'*You* made these?' Her mother whirled, her face beaming.

They all turned and looked at her.

'Umm.' Sophy was a dehydrated flower withering under the heat of her immediate family's collective stare. 'Yes.'

'But this is amazing! Edward!' Her mother raised her voice. 'Edward have you seen these?'

He had—her father put his arm around her, smiling in that quietly pleased way he had. 'Well done, Sophy.'

'You're *so* talented.'

'When did you learn to do this?'

'I could never do anything so intricate.'

Victoria and Mina got in on the act. Oh, the squeals were embarrassing.

'She got it from my side of the family,' her father said with his usual assured authority. 'Which is your favourite, darling?' He turned to her mother. 'I'm going to buy it.'

'You don't have to do that, Dad,' Sophy mumbled, beyond embarrassed by their effusiveness now.

'Oh I do. I am.' He was halfway through the crowds— off to find the manager who was in charge of the sales.

Sophy looked at them. It was weird how her heart could sink and lift at the same time. Wasn't this what she'd wanted? To have their approval? To 'wow' them like this? So why was she feeling so deflated? 'Guys, you don't have to.'

And she realised the problem. It wasn't them she'd wanted to impress. She wanted Lorenzo with her—here to witness it, here to stand beside her. She'd be so proud then.

Her anger flared within—with herself. She'd spent so long wanting this moment—for her parents to be proud of her. How could she let a guy, especially one whom she'd known for all of three weeks, ruin it all? Why was what he thought suddenly so much more important than everything else?

She made herself smile. 'I'm really glad you like them.'

'Like them?' Her mother looked stunned. 'Sophy, we had no idea.'

Sophy shrugged her shoulders. 'You've been busy. I've been busy too—I did it in my own time.'

'Why didn't you tell us you were displaying them tonight?'

'I wanted an honest reaction.'

Her sister frowned. 'You were that insecure?'

'Yes,' she admitted. 'I guess I was. Still am.'

'Oh, Sophy,' her mother scolded but folded her into a hug at the same time.

Sophy smiled. They did look good. The jewellery gleamed in the cases, the display was slick, professional and *different*—vintage inspired but thoroughly modern.

'Darling, I can't buy that necklace.' Her father came back.

Sophy looked up.

'It's already sold.' He was beaming now. It was just like the smile he'd worn when Ted and Victoria had both graduated with their first class law degrees, the smile she'd never seen him bestow on her before. 'Apparently it was the first item that went. Several of the other pieces have sold now too. It's a huge success, Sophy.'

Sophy flushed with pleasure.

'Apparently it sold within five minutes of them opening the doors tonight. Someone was obviously keen.'

Sophy's flush deepened. Her thoughts instantly flicked to Lorenzo—had he done it? Was he here for her as a surprise? Had he bought the necklace because of what they'd shared? Was this his way of apologising?

Her heart soared with hope.

'Sophy, there's someone here wanting to talk to you.' Her brother touched her shoulder.

Sophy spun, blood thundering in her ears as she looked through the crowds. He was here—he'd come. Someone tapped her other shoulder and she turned again, getting hopelessly giddy, and too full of hope.

'Surprise!'

'Oh!' Sophy gasped. 'Rosanna!' She threw her arms around her friend and hugged her close—hiding her disappointment in her friend's shoulder and her tight hug.

'You didn't think I'd really miss it did you?'

Sophy shook her head. She couldn't speak, her heart full and yet bleeding at the same time. She had such a great friend, such a great family. She had no right to be feeling so crushed. She looked into her friend's smiling face. 'Oh, thank you so much for coming.'

Lorenzo sat in his car, still too shocked to even turn the key. He was parked just down the road from the theatre—had been since ten minutes before the doors opened and that was an hour ago now. Fool that he was, he hadn't been able to resist.

He'd been going to go—say sorry, or something. He hadn't meant a word of what he'd said yesterday. He'd done it deliberately—pushed at her until she pushed him away. But she was right, he'd been lying. Of course she was special. She was so special he was terrified.

So here he was sitting in his damn monkey suit and everything because he couldn't let her down completely. But thank goodness he had. Because now he knew.

Braithwaite. It wasn't that common a surname. He should have made the connection sooner. But he hadn't bothered to ask too much. And she offered almost as little info about her family as he did his. Now he knew why.

The collar of his shirt seemed to be tightening round his neck—choking him.

He'd seen them arrive before he'd got out and got in there. For once the fates had shown him some mercy. Because the last thing he'd have wanted was to have met the man again in front of Sophy.

Edward Braithwaite—*Judge* Braithwaite—the man he'd stood before all those years ago. The one who'd condemned him and yet who had offered him that one last chance.

For half an hour tonight, while dressing, he'd deluded himself into thinking he could have fudged it—hadn't enough time passed? Jayne's father had sent him packing—he wasn't good enough for his daughter, wasn't good enough to invest in back then. And she'd agreed— had laughed at his dreams. He'd just been sex to her.

But ten years had passed since then and things had changed. Some things anyway. So maybe, if it was someone else, he could have pulled it off—skirted round his history and talked up his present successes. But Judge Braithwaite knew everything—had seen him at his worst. He knew the whole sorry story. And no way would he want him anywhere near his precious baby daughter.

Society might give second chances, fathers didn't. Fathers wanted only the best for their daughters; hell, Lorenzo understood that—*he* wanted only what was best for Sophy. And that wasn't him.

He bowed his head over the steering wheel and faced it: it was always going to be this way—as it had been before, it would be again. And it was why he should never have let her get so near to him. The past was inescapable. The perfect life he'd been imagining for just a few moments was a mirage—something that he just wasn't meant to have. He'd managed his life fine without until now anyway—forging his career, working so hard. He had his hugely successful business, the charity, he had a couple of good friends. But any other intimacy? A woman, a life partner—there could be none.

He would never be good enough for a woman as wonderful as Sophy and he wanted none but her. It didn't matter how much money he made, how successful his business became, there was always that part of him—that fundamental truth that he always tried to hide even from himself.

But her father knew that truth, and, knowing how much her parents' approval mattered to Sophy, Lorenzo knew it was over.

She deserved a perfect family, a perfect lover. But it would never be him. He had never been part of a family. Had never been wanted in a family. Damn well didn't want one of his own. Being alone was what he was used to—secure, uncomplicated. And he had been a fool to think he could ever deal with anything more—or be dealt anything more.

He had to stay away now. He'd let the end he'd engineered her to declare truly be the end. So there was only one thing left for him to do. He'd go to Vance's bar. And he'd get really, really drunk.

Sophy didn't remember a thing about the movie that screened. Afterwards she went with her family for coffee and cake—Rosanna came too. But all she could think of was the necklace that had sold so quickly. She knew it was crazy, that she'd read too many romance novels and watched too many Hollywood movies, but she couldn't help hoping that he'd bought it for her. Maybe he'd sent someone in to buy the necklace. Maybe he'd present it to her in a romantic gesture, an apology for not being there. It was going to be his way of making it up to her. Oh, how she'd love something like that—for someone to go over the top for her, someone going to lengths to do something wonderful for her.

She was such a sad unit.

'Are you okay?' Rosanna curled her legs up on the café's sofa after Sophy's parents and siblings had called it a night.

Sophy nodded and flopped back into the big armchair. 'I'm just a bit tired.'

Rosanna reached forward and put her glass on the table carefully. 'Lorenzo wasn't there.'

'No. He said he wouldn't be.'

Rosanna's eyes had narrowed. 'But—'

'My mother loved those earrings. Did you see her?' Sophy interrupted. 'I never thought she'd be into ones that are so dangly.'

'I know.' Rosanna went along with the change of topic. 'So are we going out to party now?'

Sophy laughed and shook her head. It was after one a.m. already. 'I don't think so.'

Rosanna shrugged. 'I can come home if you want.'

'And eat chocolate ice cream? No, I'm going straight to bed.'

'Okay. But if you wanted to do the ice cream, you know I'd ditch the plans.' She paused. 'I'm going to meet up with Vance.'

'What about Emmet? And Jay?'

'Oh, they're going to the bar too.'

It was the most genuine laugh to burst from Sophy in days.

Rosanna's face lit up. 'I have a surprise for you—close your eyes.'

Sophy obeyed, waited for what felt like ages. 'Are you still there?'

'Yes.' Rosanna chuckled. 'Okay, you can open them now.'

Sophy did—and stared. Rosanna was wearing the necklace—*her* necklace.

'I just loved it.' Rosanna angled her shoulders one way and then the other, showing off the sparking necklace with its looping swirl.

Sophy made herself swallow the disappointment and bring up a smile. 'It suits you.'

'Don't worry about the display.' Rosanna leaned forward. 'I promised I'd bring it back in tomorrow and leave it for the duration of the festival, but I wanted to surprise you tonight.'

And she had.

Sophy gripped her cup closer to her chest. 'You didn't have to buy it. I'd have given it to you.'

Rosanna flashed her huge smile. 'I know, but I didn't want you to. I wanted you to be a success tonight so I bought it straight away. But then so many others sold too—you're a legend!'

Sophy was so disappointed it was embarrassing. She'd really thought it had been him. That it was going to be some grand gesture, to have her unwrap it as part of an apology and declaration—of what? His *love*?

As if.

Hot tears prickled her eyes.

'Sophy!' Rosanna looked horrified. 'I've made you cry.'

'It's okay.' She tried to pull it together, but the salty water trickled down her cheeks. Yeah, she had wanted that. It had been the private fantasy that had got her through the last few hours. 'Thanks so much for doing that. It means a lot.'

It hadn't been him, of course it hadn't. She'd been an idiot to think it ever could have been. No, it was her best friend who'd done it for her. She'd been the one to turn up. Sophy knew she should stick to the sisterhood. Men were overrated. 'You know what?' She sniffed and reached for her handbag. 'I *am* going to come out with you tonight.'

She was not going to go home and wallow. She wasn't going to waste one more minute of her life mooning over Lorenzo. She had too much to celebrate tonight. She was going to go dancing.

The bar was pumping. Sophy followed Rosanna to the dance floor. Rosanna had sent a text ahead and Emmett and Jay were waiting with drinks for them.

'Thank you, darlings.' Rosanna kissed them both.

Sophy managed a smile and downed half her glass's contents in one shot.

Jay's brows lifted and he took her arm. 'Come on, you look like you need a laugh.'

Oh, she did. Jay was a great dancer—held her close, had slick moves and didn't once make her feel as if she was his second choice partner—though she knew full well she was. She felt her body relaxing into the relentless beat—it blocked all thought from her head and dulled the pain. Yeah, this had been a great idea. She'd dance 'til dawn and then maybe she'd be able to sleep. She stood on tiptoes so he had a chance of hearing her. 'Thanks, Jay. I'll put in a word for you.'

He slid his hand round her waist and chuckled. 'Every little bit helps. But it's not Emmett I'm worried about. It's the bar dude.' He nodded over to the side.

Sophy turned to look. From behind the bar Vance stood tall, positively glaring over at where the four of them were dancing. She couldn't stop the little laugh. But then it died because someone else stepped up from the back of the bar. Even taller than Vance, Lorenzo was glaring even harder—right at her.

She spun back to face Jay. 'Shall we dance some more?'

'Sure.' He pulled her closer.

But her heart was racing and she could hardly hear the music above the noise in her ears. Only one song later she pushed away. 'I'm just going to freshen up.'

She ran cold water over her hands and wrists, trying to cool down and slow her pulse. Then she got her lipstick out and took care repairing her slightly worn look. Then she simply stared at her reflection and wished she could teleport out of there. She really hadn't liked the look in Lorenzo's eyes.

Finally she left the room. He was leaning against the wall in the corridor, his eyes fixed on the door. She paused—stood back to let another woman past before taking the step clear of the doorway. But she kept her distance from him. Knew getting past him was going to be difficult. He looked like a panther about to pounce.

'You look like you're having a good time,' he drawled.

So did he—his hair was tousled, his eyes burning. He looked as if he'd been propping up the bar for hours.

'I am.' She made herself act perky.

'With one of Rosanna's cast offs,' he muttered.

'He's charming. He's good company. He doesn't take himself too seriously.'

Was that a snort?

She glared at him. 'Why are you so dressed up?' Although the tie was gone it was definitely a tux he was wearing. And even though he wore it carelessly, he wore it too well for her comfort.

He shrugged. 'How did it go?'

'I didn't think you were interested.' She couldn't stop the bitchiness.

He lifted away from the wall. 'Sophy.'

'No.' She straightened, getting ready to move. 'I've got someone waiting for me.' She moved fast to get past. But he pounced—just as she'd known he would.

Damn, his hands were fast and he was too strong. In seconds he'd pulled her into a room and locked the door. A toilet. Really classy.

But before she could even start in on the fury she felt he'd pulled her close. His hand cupped her chin, tilting her head back for him to kiss.

But he didn't go for her mouth—no, it was her jaw, her neck, that spot beneath her ear that they both knew was so sensitive. She could smell the alcohol on him, could feel how thin his control was and then she felt his lips. That damn sweet tenderness that made her feel as if he was worshipping her with his mouth. She fell back, melting into the kisses; his furious passion rose in a flash, sweeping her away.

It had been three days. Three long, lonely days in which she hadn't felt his touch—and as soon as she did she flamed for him. Despite her hurt and disappointment she still wanted him—desperately.

His kisses deepened as she softened. She panted as he kissed her with ravenous abandon, his hands cupping her butt and rhythmically pressing her against his hard erection as his mouth scalded her skin.

But as his touch grew bolder, more intimate, her brain started screaming at her. He didn't want to go out with her—be seen together by their friends or family. But he'd whisk her into the nearest, tackiest place he could so he could get his hands on her? He was the proverbial dog in the manger. Not wanting her but not wanting her to have fun with anyone else? Not fair. Not right.

She grabbed his chin and forced it up, making him look into her face. Her nails curled into the vulnerable space just below his jawbone. If she were truly part animal she could kill him this way—pierce the skin and slice his throat. But that wouldn't serve her purpose at all. She wouldn't scratch him, couldn't hurt him—not that way at least—despite the anger burning inside her, and the bottomless well of pain that was feeding it.

For a long moment she looked into his eyes—saw her anger reflected. What bothered him so much? Surely not her dancing with Jay?

No, this anger was too deep for that. And too old. It was the bitterness she'd seen in him before, only tonight it was burning out of control.

She looked away, caught sight of their reflection in the mirror—her face pale, her lips that ridiculous bright red from her forties fashion look.

She turned back to him, brushed her lips against his jaw and then looked at his skin. All praise to the modern cosmetics companies with their long-lasting lip colours—but they'd yet to make them smudge free.

She kissed his jaw again, then down his neck, pressing her lips hard all the way down to the starched white collar of his shirt—and then across that. As she made her mark she let her hands tease him, inflame him, distract him.

'Sophy.'

She swore she'd heard that old thread of laughter then—yeah, he was so confident of her surrender. She let her hands slip lower—harder.

She heard his hissing breath, felt the surge of energy and braced herself.

But nothing could prepare her for what happened. His hands twisted in her hair as he held her firm and gazed at her. His burning black eyes bored into hers—but there was no laughter in them, not even a smile. He was all serious, so intense and, if she was right, so sad.

It began as the softest kiss. Then his arms went tight around her, sealing their length, and she felt him straining against her, his touch scorching, his need overwhelming.

Finally the kiss eased. It was then that she found it—the strength to push him away. To her surprise he let her, his head snapping back as she shoved him hard in the chest.

She blinked away the tears—of bewilderment, resentment and plain old hurt.

'Gosh, Lorenzo—' her voice shook '—you have lipstick stains all over your face and all over your shirt.' Her bitter laugh turned into a sob halfway through. 'How are you going to hide your dirty little secret now?'

The fury that flashed made her run.

'Sophy!'

How she got the door open she never knew. But she ran through the crowded bar, desperate for an escape.

Jay materialised in front of her, eyes wide. 'Sophy?'

Yeah, her little paint job meant she had more than a make-up malfunction now, she probably looked like a reject from clown school with the slut red lipstick smudged all over her chin. 'Walk me to a cab, would you?' She had no idea where Rosanna was but would get Jay to pass the message on later.

'Of course.' He moved instantly.

'I'll do that.' Lorenzo was on the other side of her.

'No, you won't.' She pushed past him.

'Are you okay?' Jay muttered, putting his arm around her, glaring over her head at Lorenzo, who silently stalked next to them.

'Never better. Will you tell Rosanna I've gone home?'

'Sure.'

They got outside. Jay kept a protective arm looped

around her shoulders as he stepped to the kerb and waved his spare arm at the taxi rank not far down the road. The first one peeled off and came towards them. Jay stayed with her, holding the door—blocking it from Lorenzo while she got in.

'Sophy.' Deadly quiet but she heard him anyway.

Just before she slammed the door she answered. 'Not now, Lorenzo. I'm too angry, and you're too drunk.'

CHAPTER ELEVEN

SOPHY hadn't been home fifteen minutes when the thudding on her door started.

She opened the door and glared at him. 'I said not now.'

'I'm not drunk.'

'Oh, please.' She looked at the way he was breathing, at the flush in his cheeks. 'Did you run here?'

He shrugged.

'You shouldn't run in those shoes. It'll be bad for your feet.'

'Says the woman wearing stupidly high heels.'

She whirled away and walked down the hall. 'What is it you want, Lorenzo?'

She heard him close the door and walk after her. 'I just wanted you to know it's not you. It's me.'

She stopped and turned back to stare at him. 'You've got to be kidding me.' She laughed. 'That's the line you're giving me?'

'I was jealous as hell watching you dance with him. Even though I knew there was nothing in it, I was wild. I can't even blame the booze. I'm sorry.'

'*You* could have danced with me.'

He shook his head. 'You're too good for me.'

'Oh.' She clasped her hand to her chest. 'Another great

line. Whatever will be next? Let me guess, "I just don't do relationships, darling,"' she said, dropping her voice a ridiculous octave. '"I was born to be alone." Am I on the right path?'

He'd gone pale. Stopped halfway down the hall. 'Why did you want me to meet your family?'

'I didn't. It wasn't like I was going to introduce you to them as my boyfriend or anything, Lorenzo. Heaven forbid.' She rolled her eyes. 'I just wanted you to be there. I wanted your support.'

'No.' Lorenzo took a deep breath in and reminded himself that he was not going to lose it. Not again. Now was the time for some honesty. He owed her that, at least. 'I've met your father before.'

'You have?'

'He was the presiding judge when I was up in court.'

'What?'

'Youth court. I was thirteen.'

'What had you done?'

He shrugged. 'Graffiti, theft, destruction of property. It wasn't the first time.'

'What did he do?'

'Ordered some community service. Made the order to send me to that school.'

'Dad did that?'

'Yes. I had "potential." They thought it might bring it out.' And it had—to a degree.

She lifted her brows. 'And you think what? That your past would put him off you now?'

Of course it would.

'Doesn't all you've done in the last eighteen years count for anything? Or are you stuck in some kind of time warp? You don't think what you've done with your life since matters?'

He shook his head. She just didn't get it.

'So tell me the truth, then.' She squared up to him. 'The wine label—it's a front for money laundering, isn't it?'

'What? No.'

'Is it drugs, then? You're secretly growing pot in the vineyards?'

'Of course not.'

'Oh.' She sounded disappointed. 'No illegal activities. You're not much of a crim then are you?'

'Sophy.' He so didn't need the sarcasm right now.

She didn't stop. 'Have you ever been back in court?'

He shook his head.

'So what's the problem?' She folded her arms and eye-balled him. 'My father believes in justice, Lorenzo. You had a problem. Did some things you shouldn't have. You did your hours of community service or whatever. Put the wrong right. And he got you into a place that would actually help you. It's finished. Behind you.'

'He wouldn't see it like that.'

'How do you know?'

'I just do, all right?' She was so naïve. 'Do you really think he'd be okay with what I'm doing with you?'

'Well—' her colour deepened '—I don't think he'd want to know any intimate kind of details about anyone I'm with but—'

'No father wants a man like me to be with his daughter. No father.'

She lifted her head. 'Someone's said that before?'

'More than once,' he exaggerated. 'Not good enough.'

'You need to lose the chip, Lorenzo,' she said coolly. 'Anyway—' she lifted her head proudly '—I don't live with them. I'm grown up. I make my own choices. I can see whoever I want.'

'You say that but we both know that what your family thinks means everything to you. You've been tied up in knots for weeks over what they'd think of your work. What they think of your lover would be even worse.' He watched her swallow. Knew he'd scored a hit.

'You're making far too much of something that happened for ever ago. And even if it did bother Dad initially, it wouldn't be a problem once he got to know you now.'

'You just don't get it. I am not the kind of person who should be with you.'

'What kind of person do you think you are? Because I know you. And I know—'

'You don't know me,' he interrupted. 'You've got no idea, Sophy.'

'Tell me, then,' she shouted back.

'Tell you what, Sophy? The ugly truth? How rough it was? How rough I am?'

'Yeah.' Her anger flared. 'Why not tell me some more clichés—the abused-boy stories.'

His vision burst with red. 'What would you know about it? Having to be taken away from your own parents because of the way they treated you? Your father saying you should have been the scum in an abortionist's bucket?'

Sophy recoiled.

'Oh, that was nothing, darling,' he sneered. 'That was just words and not even the worst. Wait 'til you hear the rest.'

'Lorenzo, I'm sor—'

He shouted over her. 'I was beaten for answering him wrong, for not answering soon enough, for not answering at all. It didn't matter what I did, it happened anyway. With fists, sticks, belts—whatever he had to hand. I wasn't wanted by him, wasn't protected by her, and I wasn't wanted by anyone else after. I'd go to a new house, a new home. Meet a new family. Again and again.' He was shaking, bunched his fists to try to stop the uncontrollable jerking of his hands.

'Lorenzo, please—'

His sharp gesture shut her up.

He took a step backwards down the hall, away from her as his agony boiled over. 'You think you can possibly know about it? I sought approval, Sophy. I tried. I would have done anything to make it okay. And I tried everything. But it never worked. It was me that was wrong—every time. So I stopped trying so hard. Because every time it was the same. *Too difficult. Out of control. Angry.* I always stuffed up. Labels stick, so why bother trying? Because in the end you know they don't want you anyway. They never want you.'

'I want you,' she whispered.

It made him incensed. 'No, you don't.'

'I do.' She walked after him.

'You like the sex,' he yelled, taking more steps back. 'This is just an excursion for you. As hard core as you've ever gotten. Your ride with the bad boy. In another week you'll be over it. Go back to someone perfect, Sophy. Someone from the right background, who'll fit into your perfect family.'

'My family aren't perfect.'

He laughed then. 'Oh yeah? Your parents love you. You think they don't but of course they do. They call you all the time, you do things for them all the time. It wouldn't matter what you do, Sophy, no matter how awful, they'll still love you, they'll always love you. But no matter what I did, mine never loved me. And you know the result?' His throat hurt as he hurled the truth out. 'I'm *damaged*, Sophy. Treat someone like an animal and they *become* an animal. And there's no changing that.' That was what her father knew too. 'You have no idea of the rage I can feel. I frighten myself. And I refuse to frighten you.'

He stopped, breathing hard. He couldn't stay in control of anything around her. And it terrified him.

'You don't frighten me, Lorenzo.'

'I can't control it,' he said flatly, admitting the worst. 'I don't want to hurt you.'

'You're hurting me now.'

He shook his head. No, he was protecting her.

'I love you, Lorenzo. Let me love you.'

'No one can love me.' He denied her—he had to. 'And I can't love. I won't.' His back was right up against the door now. 'I can't be part of any kind of family. I tried. And I failed every single time. I won't try again, Sophy. Not even for you.'

'You don't have to. It can just be me, Lorenzo.'

He turned and opened the door. 'It can't,' he said heavily. 'You know it can't. You want it all—and you should have it. The nice guy who loves you, who'll stand at the barbie and talk sport with your father, who'll be a good father to your babies.' He looked over his shoulder at her. 'What the hell kind of dad would I make?' The knife dug deep in his heart and he screwed his eyes tight against the pain. 'I don't need it. Don't want it. Not happening. Not ever happening.' He stood in the open doorway, the cold pre-dawn air chilling the hall. 'I'm sorry I manhandled you tonight. You were right. It's over.'

Sophy cried. Curled into a ball in the hall and sobbed her heart out. So ironic, wasn't it, that the 'perfect' boyfriend had only wanted her for the kudos he could get from her family, while the one she loved wanted nothing to do with her *because* of them—at least in part? After an age she moved, sat staring at the dining table for hours, barely seeing the pattern in the wood as the conversation circled in her head. And her anger with him grew.

Coward. The selfish, bitter coward.

Yet she hurt so much for him—the hell he'd been through. He'd missed out on so much. As a result he didn't understand love. And she wanted to help him understand it. She had to talk to him again, had to show him. Somehow she had to get through to him—or at least try.

By the time she summoned the courage it was after nine the next morning. He was out the back of the warehouse already. He was in jeans, but had no tee on, hadn't shaved. He'd been at it for a while because his body was gleaming. But he didn't stop bouncing the ball. Didn't stop to look at her.

'You're wrong, Lorenzo. You know you're wrong.'

He said nothing.

'You can't stop me loving you.'

He took the shot but missed the hoop.

'You're using it as an excuse. You *like* playing the tortured loner type. It's safe for you. You won't let anyone close because you can't bear to be rejected again. But I wouldn't reject you.'

'You would.' His mouth barely moved.

She stepped in and snatched the ball, forcing him to look at her, to pay attention. 'You're right, my family do love me. No matter what they'll love me. And if they know how happy you make me, they'll love you—regardless of your past. But you won't give them or me a chance because it's easier not to.' She took a shot but missed too. She turned to him as the ball bounced away. 'You're lazy. And you're a coward.'

He looked at her, but there wasn't the fire she'd hoped for. Just the dull stones.

'I can't presume to understand what you went through. I wouldn't dare to. But I do know this—you can't let it ruin the rest of your life. You can't lose faith in everybody. And I don't believe you have. Why else do you try to help those kids? Why else did you give Vance a chance with the bar? You try to keep yourself shut away but you can't quite do it. And you couldn't do it with me. Only now you're scared. Now you're trying to run. But you don't have to, not from me.'

She stepped closer and took in a deep breath. 'Everyone has problems, Lorenzo. We all do. But problems are best solved with help—and with support from the people who love you.' He didn't have to face his demons alone. She'd stand by his side and help him slay them. As he helped her.

He jerked, looking away from her and going back to the fence to get the ball. She stood, helplessly watching as he started the relentless practising again. She was waiting long moments for what—to be ignored?

She gulped, the burning hurt too strong to be held down any more.

'You know, maybe I do know something of what you went through,' she choked. 'Maybe I do know something about loving someone, of wanting to be loved back but only to be rejected. Not wanted.' The tears suddenly streamed down her face. 'But at the end of the day it's your loss. You could have had everything, Lorenzo. I would have given you *everything*.'

She ran then, wanting to get as far from this hell as she could. Everything—her hope, her heart, her love—was in tatters.

She didn't hear it, didn't see it, as she blindly ran as fast as she could. The last thing she was conscious of was the piercing screech of rubber on metal, and the animal scream in her ears.

CHAPTER TWELVE

THE door opened. Lorenzo turned his head as the woman burst in.

'Where—?' She broke off, gulping as she saw the pale figure in the bed. 'Oh, Sophy.' The tears sprang just like that. 'Is she going to be okay?'

Lorenzo stood but didn't answer and didn't move away. He looked beyond her to the man who'd stopped on the threshold. After a moment that man walked to the other side of the bed and looked down at his daughter for a time, his expression rigid. Then he looked at Lorenzo for even longer, even more frozen.

'I know you.' He didn't smile.

'Yes.' Lorenzo still held her hand. His fingers tightened instinctively. 'I'm not leaving.'

'I can see that.'

'Yeah.' Lorenzo sat down again.

'Beth, this is…' He kept staring at Lorenzo.

'Lorenzo. Lorenzo Hall.'

'That's right.' He nodded slowly. Lorenzo just knew it had all come back to him now.

'Do you know each other?' Her mother looked from her father to him.

Lorenzo looked at the man who had once judged him. Who'd once before given him a chance. And waited.

'Not really.'

Lorenzo looked down at the bed.

'You're a friend of Sophy's?' her mother asked.

'Yes.'

In the silence, nothing more was said.

The guilt was swamping him. It was his fault. If he hadn't made her so upset. If she'd hadn't been at the damn warehouse. If she hadn't run so fast, so blindly from him.

Her blonde hair was spread on the pillow with its perfect curls on the ends. Her skin was unnaturally pale with the ugly bruise deepening. He still couldn't believe there were no broken bones—or worse. He'd waited, utterly distraught, while they'd done their tests. A bad bump to the head, that was all, despite being knocked to the ground, clipped by the edge of the car. It was only the driver's quick action in pulling on the wheel that had saved her from more serious injuries.

The doctors would monitor her for the night, but they didn't think there was anything they'd missed. But even now, despite their words, he feared there was damage beyond what he could see.

'Why don't you call Victoria and Ted, darling?' Sophy's father spoke. 'Go into the lounge area. I'll come and get you if there's any change.'

Lorenzo knew they were communicating behind his back. He didn't care. He wasn't leaving the damn room.

As soon as the door closed behind her he lifted his gaze and met the judge's. He had the same blue eyes as Sophy's—only his were colder. 'Things have changed for you since we last met, Lorenzo.'

'A lot.'

'I'm glad.' He looked serious. 'Does Sophy know?'

'Yes.' Lorenzo swallowed.

'And she's your…friend?'

He knew what he was asking. 'Yes.'

The judge's face tightened. 'You had a lot of potential back then. But when I saw you, you were too angry to use it. Too angry to let anyone care for you. Anyone who tried had it thrown back at them.' His voice changed, to the implacable, imperative word of law. 'Don't you do that to my daughter.'

Lorenzo didn't answer, just looked at the small fingers resting limply in his. He couldn't bring himself to admit that he'd already done exactly that.

Sophy's head really hurt. She blinked. Tried again, squeezing her eyes open just that little bit. 'Lorenzo?'

No answer. But he was here. She was sure of it. She could smell him. She could feel the warmth from the pressure of his hand—he'd been holding it, hadn't he? 'Lorenzo?'

'He's not here,' a deep voice answered. 'I told him to go.'

'What?' she wailed. 'Dad!'

A warm hand touched hers, but it wasn't the right hand.

'Sophy?' Her mother bent over her. 'Honey, are you okay?'

Had she just sobbed? Just a little bit?

'He'll be back. He'll come back, I'm sure. We just told him to go get some coffee. He hadn't moved for almost two hours.'

Okay, so she had sobbed. She closed her eyes again. Felt the wet on her cheek and turned her head away, pressing deeper into the pillow. He wouldn't be back. He didn't want to be near her family—or any family.

'Sophy?'

'Should we get the doctor?' Her mother's voice rose.

'No,' Sophy croaked. 'No. I'm okay.' And with every word she spoke her voice grew stronger. 'What happened?'

'You were hit by a car. You ran straight out onto the road.'

'Were you running away from something, Sophy? Someone?' her father asked quietly, but she heard the tone, the condemnation, the conclusion.

She shook her head, wincing as it hurt. 'Not what you think, Dad.'

'I don't know what to think, sweetheart.'

Carefully she opened her eyes, looked at her father. 'Do you remember him?'

'I remember all of them,' her father said sombrely. 'But some stick in your mind more than others.'

The tears welled again, stinging her eyeballs.

'He was very angry back then. But he had a lot to be angry about.'

Sophy's heart was breaking. She needed her father to know, to understand. 'I love him, Dad.'

The sharp intake of breath was audible—but it didn't come from either of her parents. Sophy turned her head. Lorenzo stood in the doorway.

'You're awake. Are you okay?' The edge of panic was evident both in the speed of the question and the hesitancy as he hovered.

She licked her horribly dry lips.

'Edward, let's go get some fresh coffee.' Her mother suddenly stood. 'Come on. She can't have too many people in here at once. She'll get too tired.'

Sophy watched the two men looking at each other—saw some message she couldn't interpret pass between them.

Lorenzo moved closer, where she could see him better. He was so pale.

'Sophy.' His voice broke. 'I'm so sorry.'

'It was my fault. I should have been watching where I was going.'

He shook his head. 'I shouldn't have made you so upset. I never wanted to hurt you like this.'

The brush-off. Again. It was so embarrassing. Dully she admitted the truth. 'I shouldn't have pushed for something you never wanted to give.'

'You're right,' he said. 'But not about that. I'm scared— just like you said. A coward. You scare me to death—how you make me feel scares me.' He moved quickly, sat in the seat near her head. 'I don't know that I can give you what you want from me.'

'Lorenzo.' She took in a deep breath. She'd take all there was—no matter how little. She loved him. She wanted him. She was happy when with him. She didn't need all the bells and whistles. She just needed him. 'All I want is whatever you have to give.'

He stared at her. The dark eyes tortured, the unhappiness hurting her more than the relentless pounding in her head and in her heart. 'But you deserve so much more than that. So much more than me.'

'No.' Her eyes filled. She didn't want him to push her away like that. No one else could give her what he could. 'I want you. That's all. Just you.'

'And I want you. But I don't want to make you unhappy. And I have.'

She opened her mouth but he kept talking.

'It's all new to me. You know that—the whole big family thing. But I'll try, if you want me to.'

She trembled and his hand quickly covered hers.

'What made you change your mind?'

'Nearly losing you today.' His voice wavered again.

'I got a bump on the head. I'm not about to die—'

'If you had seen yourself you wouldn't say that.'

'Lorenzo, I'm fine.'

'Well, I'm not. I don't think I'll ever recover from seeing you crumple like that.' He closed his eyes and bowed his head, both his hands firmly clasped around hers. 'Can you be patient with me?'

'Yes.' She had him. Nothing else mattered. She didn't need the grand gestures, the romantic flourishes. She just needed him.

He leaned across, kissed her tenderly on the lips. Not enough for her.

'You're staying in here tonight.'

'No.' She frowned. 'I'm not.'

'You are. Observation. You probably have concussion. You need to be monitored.'

'I can be monitored at home. Rosanna will—'

'Rosanna is away,' Lorenzo said sharply. 'I'll wait with you today. Come back to pick you up in the morning. Unless—' he breathed out '—you'd rather your parents did?'

'I want you to.'

His hand cupped her face so gently. 'I don't deserve you.'

'You do,' she said, angry tears springing again. 'You *do*.'

She would make him understand that—somehow. She loved him. But she couldn't say it again—wouldn't—because she didn't want him to feel the pressure to say it in return. She didn't know that he'd ever be able to say it. It didn't matter. Her tortured warrior spoke with actions. And he was here. That was enough.

Twenty-four hours later Lorenzo finally went to do some work for a bit—having instructed her to phone down if she needed anything. He paused halfway down the stairs. Rosanna was on her way up, a sheaf of flowers across one arm.

She waggled her finger at him. 'You don't take my best friend home to your place and think you're not getting me too.'

He laughed. 'She'll be pleased to see you. She's bored and getting restless.'

'I've got some magazines.'

His grin faded as she got closer. 'You're wearing her necklace.' His throat went tight as he saw it.

She touched it. 'Stunning, isn't it? I bought it at the exhibition the other night. Made sure I did it as soon as I got there. I wanted her to have one "sold" sign really early on.' She grinned. 'Not that I needed to worry—she sold most of them in the first hour. But she was so nervous.'

He nodded. 'I know.' He should have thought to do that. That should have been him. But he'd been thinking too selfishly. 'You're a good friend to her.'

'Only because she's wonderful to me. It's nice to be able to do something for her for once,' Rosanna said. 'She does so much for everyone else.'

'Yeah.' She did. She bent over backwards for the ones she loved. She was bending every which way for him. And he wasn't happy about it. She deserved so much more. The feeling inside his chest tightened.

She was going to take him—like this—with nothing extra. She was too generous. And he wasn't going to let her get away with it. Not any more. No matter the cost to him, she was too important. Her happiness was too important.

He could do it, sure he could—because she deserved it.

'I've got a few other things I need to do for her.' He swallowed and bit the bullet. 'Are you up to helping me?'

Rosanna looked sharply curious. 'What kind of things?'

'Top secret things.'

'Spend money kind of top-secret things?'

'Lots of money,' he acknowledged.

'Then you've got an able assistant.'

He'd grin if he weren't feeling so freaked. 'Fantastic.'

CHAPTER THIRTEEN

SOPHY let Lorenzo guide her to her seat. Honestly, she was over the cotton wool treatment. Four days since her accident and he was still handling her as if he was afraid she'd break any moment.

'You're into taking this risk a second time?'

'The first wasn't such a risk,' she teased back. 'It's not like you've asked me for my passport.'

He put his hand in his pocket and pulled out two small blue books.

'No way.' Sophy stared at them. 'You got my passport? How did you do that?'

He didn't answer. Just grinned at her in a lazy way.

'That was at my parents' house.' She frowned. 'At least, I think it was. You didn't break in there, did you?'

'I never did breaking and entering. Not my strength.'

'Don't be ridiculous. You're capable of anything you set your mind to,' she muttered. 'It's scary.'

'Are you scared?'

She met his serious gaze. 'No.' She did up her seat belt. 'Actually I'm hoping you're going to make me a member of the mile high club.'

He laughed but she wasn't kidding. He'd kissed her since the accident, but they hadn't had sex. And she needed it—badly wanted to connect with him. There was a distance between them. She sensed his tension, as if he was keeping something back from her.

'Are we going back to Hanmer?'

He just smiled.

She was sure of it when they got into the rental car in Christchurch and he took the road north again. Fine by her—she couldn't think of anything nicer than making love with him in that wonderful warm water again.

But he turned off on a side road well before he should. Then took another, a gravel road this time. The building appeared out of nowhere. One of those churches that had been built a century ago and now was stuck in the middle of a field with nothing else around—no other buildings, no cars, nothing.

'Sophy.'

He switched off the engine. He was so pale she was seriously worried.

'Lorenzo?'

He turned to face her. 'Will you marry me?' It was only once he'd asked it that he looked directly into her eyes.

She blinked, stunned at the question that had come so suddenly out of the blue. 'Yes. Of course I will.' Her heart thudded hard enough to burst from her chest.

But he didn't smile. Didn't look even a smidge more relaxed. He just jerked his head in a sharp negating gesture. 'But will you marry me right now?'

She stared from him, to the church in front of them. *'Now?'*

'Right now.' He sat still as marble.

'Of course I will.' She answered in a heartbeat.

'You're sure? You're absolutely sure?' He was the colour of marble too.

'Yes,' she said. 'But are you?'

He smiled then. It was as if the full power of the sun had burst through the storm clouds—scattering them to the furthest edge of the universe. He got out of the car, strode round to her door and opened it.

She stepped out carefully, looking cautiously at him as he took her hand and led her to the closed doors of the old church.

'We can't really get married now can we?' She climbed the stairs doubtfully. She didn't think there was a minister in there—there wasn't a car in the yard, there didn't seem to be another soul around for miles.

Unless he meant to do some little personal made-up thing for just the two of them? Well, that would be fine by her. She wanted to be with him. She was happy.

He pulled the heavy door open and was a half-step behind her as she went in. She blinked in the dim light, suddenly saw the movement. The turning of heads. The smiles.

The church was full of people. *Full.*

She looked at Lorenzo—saw the colour had leeched from his skin again. A tall streak came flying up the aisle to her.

'Rosanna, what are you doing here?' Sophy asked, utterly shocked.

'I'm your bridesmaid, silly.'

'You're serious.' Sophy stared. 'You're not serious.'

'I'm dead serious,' said Rosanna.

'So did you mean it?' Lorenzo asked quietly. 'You'll marry me right now?'

'No, I need at least ten minutes with her first.' Rosanna again.

Sophy ignored Rosanna. Took a step closer to him, reached up on tiptoe and pressed her lips to his.

'Five minutes, okay?' He whispered, cupping her jaw. 'Don't be late.'

She saw the anxiety hidden not so deep in his eyes. 'I won't be.'

Rosanna dragged her by the hand out of the church and around the back to the vestry entrance. 'Didn't you hear the man? Five minutes is all we have.'

'You're not wearing black.' Sophy stared at her stupidly.

'It's a wedding, not a funeral.'

Sophy clapped her hand over her mouth to stop the crazed giggle bursting out.

'Ta da.' Rosanna held up the hanger.

Sophy's jaw dropped and she took a few steps closer. 'Where did you find it?'

Rosanna shrugged. 'Darling, I'm a buyer. I shop for a living—you know this.'

'But, Ro—'

'I know, even for me it's outstanding. Now strip.'

Rosanna held the dress for Sophy to step into. Fixing the zip for her and smoothing the skirt, holding the new shoes that were the exact shade to match.

'It all fits.'

'Of course. I am a professional.'

'Oh, Ro—'

'No getting emotional. Not yet,' Rosanna said tartly. 'Now, we can do a better job of hiding this bruise.' Despite her astringent tone, Rosanna swept the brush gently through Sophy's hair, quickly but carefully put in some clips. 'A rub of lipstick. You don't need any other make-up—you're glowing as it is.'

Sophy needed a distraction—otherwise she was going to hyperventilate, or get hysterical, or run into the church right now, half-ready, just to make sure it really was happening. She looked at her friend's demure French navy frock. 'Is Vance here?'

'Yes.'

Sophy glanced—that was an arctic-sounding answer. 'Are you not getting on?'

'We've never got on. We just got *it* on a few times.'

Yeah, but Sophy had suspected, just for a fleeting second, that maybe Rosanna had finally met her match. 'So what happened?'

'He told me I had to give up the others. It was him and no one else. An ultimatum, no less.'

'How unreasonable of him,' Sophy remarked dryly. 'What did you say?'

'I said no, of course.'

'Oh, Rosanna—'

'Be quiet or I'll spread lipstick all over your cheeks.' Rosanna looked down. 'You know me, Soph. I'm thrilled for you, I am. But you know the whole monogamous happy-ever-after thing isn't for me. The only time I'll ever walk down an aisle is right now, as your witness.'

'I know.' Sophy put her hand on her friend. 'And you know how much I love you for doing it for me.'

Rosanna shrugged, reverting back to snappy. 'It was fun spending Lorenzo's money.' She stood back and assessed her handiwork. 'Okay, you've got something old—the dress. Something new—the shoes. Now for something borrowed and something blue.' She looked sly, undid the clasp on the necklace she wore round her neck.

'Rosanna.' Sophy's heart melted even more.

'You have to wear it. He loves it on you.'

The necklace she'd made. 'I'm giving it back to you after.'

'Of course, it's borrowed.' Rosanna smiled. 'You look like you've put that stuff in your eyes. They're all big and sparkly.'

'Deadly nightshade?'

'Dad!' Sophy whirled around.

'You look beautiful.' He walked towards her, looking super-establishment in his grey suit. But he was smiling that wonderful, proud smile. 'Would you like me to walk up the aisle with you, Sophy?'

'Oh, Dad.' She took the two paces and he folded her into his arms. 'Just the one way.'

He laughed. 'Yes, you have the exit covered already.'

'How did this happen?' She couldn't believe it.

'Lorenzo's spent the last three days organising it.'

'But is it legal?'

'I'm a judge, honey. Of course it is.'

'But how?'

'He's a good man. And he knows how to get things done.'

Sophy nodded. 'He's very strong. He's wonderful to me.'

'I can see that. It's obvious how much he cares for you. A person who loves you like that, we'll always welcome.'

Sophy bit her lip. Did Lorenzo love her? In his own way she knew he must—he'd never be doing this otherwise. And maybe one day he'd even be able to tell her.

Her mother came to the door. 'Hurry up, the poor boy is out there looking paler than a ghost.'

The poor boy? Sophy choked back the laughing sob and gave her mother a hug.

'No tears, you two,' her father said gruffly. 'You'll both ruin your make-up.'

'Hold it together, Renz. She won't be a minute.'

'I won't be happy until it's done.' Until she was his. He breathed out a long breath—trying to control the racing pulse, the nerves slowly killing him. 'Thanks for being here.'

'I wouldn't have missed this for the world. Dani is beside herself with excitement. You should have heard her on the flight—"I can't believe it, I can't believe it" over and over.'

'I'm sure you figured out a way to shut her up.' Lorenzo flicked a quick glance to where his friend's wife sat sandwiched between Kat and Cara, who had her new baby cuddled to her breast. They were out of the neo-natal unit and thriving. Her husband looked like a doting fool. Lorenzo went even more tense—could barely dare hope that he'd be like that one day. His attention swerved straight back to the door at the back of the church. Where was she? Had this all been a huge mistake? Was she working out a way of backing out of it without embarrassing him?

'Relax.'

Easy for Alex to say. But Sophy was his one hope of salvation. The link to the vulnerable humanity he knew he'd hidden away a long time ago. But with her he had the courage—and the desire—to open up and be everything. To do everything. To embrace all that life had to offer.

He cleared his throat. Okay, so maybe the courage bit was fading. He needed to see her. Had he done the right thing? Her whole family was here. All thirty thousand of them. There was music all of a sudden and an expectant hush descended. The whole congregation stood for her.

Lorenzo couldn't remember the last time he'd cried. Decades ago probably, as a kid getting a hiding. But the lump in his throat now was like a burning ball of metal—only instead of melting it was getting harder and harder and bigger.

He staved off the tears by sheer will—based in the raw desire to see her clearly at this moment. No stupid salty water blurring the vision of her walking to meet him.

Man, she was beautiful. The dress was white and slim fitting and frothed to the floor. Her blue eyes, almost painfully bright, looked nowhere but right into him.

She smiled. And his heart burst open.

He followed the minister's instructions—repeated the words, listened to her cool, clear voice say them back to him.

So he could kiss her now. But there was something he needed to do first—here and now and in front of a hundred witnesses.

He cleared his throat, took a deep breath as he turned to face her, gazing right into her beautiful blue eyes.

And finally he said it—the thing he'd never said to anyone before. Had never dreamed he'd ever be capable of saying, let alone actually feeling.

'I love you.' Suddenly he was freed from the terrible tension he'd felt for ever. 'I love you.' He said it again with a smile—louder that time as he recognised it as the beginning of a whole new meaning to his life.

She crumpled and he caught her to him, tasting her tears as he kissed her.

He did. He really did love her—the power of it was beyond anyone's control. Certainly his. But that was okay. That was better than okay.

Sophy heard him whispering it again as he held her in a bear hug so tight she couldn't breathe. But she wasn't letting him get away with just one kiss. Not after that. She put her palms on his face, blinking through the tears, feeling her soul sing as she touched her lips to his. She was tight in his arms again, literally swept off her feet as they kissed.

There was cheering and clapping and, for her, utter reluctance as they drew apart. Sophy turned, faced the sea of smiles and sparkling outfits for only a second. Then she turned back to him and was centred again. He was her anchor. And she his. Together they'd form a foundation from which they could do anything.

He kissed her again, the way she needed to be kissed—with love and heat and fierce intensity.

'I love you, Lorenzo.'

He smiled, that rare, shining, carefree smile that she hoped would now be much more common.

She'd known there were people. As she'd walked up the aisle she'd seen them in her peripheral vision. But all her attention had been on the man waiting for her at the altar. Stock-still, pale, looking at her as if she were an illusion—as if fearful she'd disappear in a wisp of smoke if he so much as blinked.

Now, as they walked back down the aisle together, her arm tightly clamped to his side, she saw them all properly—her parents, her brother and sister, aunts, a few cousins, Rosanna's boys, several other friends. And she recognised the Wilsons, Vance, Kat, Cara, some others who she guessed were vineyard workers. All were here to celebrate with them.

From somewhere—who knew where?—a couple of large buses had appeared out the front of the church. They all climbed aboard and were taken to the reception in a marquee in the middle of the Wilsons' vineyard. They dined and danced and laughed. It seemed Lorenzo really had impressed her father. The two of them bonded over fine wine and possible investments. Her mother was just floored by him. Sophy understood that all too well. Sophy gazed round at the gleaming silverware, the white and silver decorations making the room sparkle.

It was the grandest gesture anyone had ever done for her. She who'd organised this and that—the surprise parties here, the celebrations there. The biggest day of her life had been arranged by all who loved her. In an old church in the middle of nowhere the man she loved had given himself to her—unreservedly.

'I can't believe you did this for me.' She gazed up at him as they danced together on the specially constructed wooden floor.

'I wanted to do something nice for you.' He smiled faintly.

'You've done a lot of nice things already, Lorenzo—you gave me workshop space, you gave me time in Hanmer, you did those designs for me.'

'But it was all with conditions. There are no conditions on this.'

'Other than that I promise to be your wife and to love you always.'

'Just that little thing, yeah.'

'Unconditionally given.'

He pulled her closer. 'Do you mind not getting to organise your own wedding?'

'Mind?' She laughed. 'I'm so relieved I don't have to. No stress. I could just enjoy it.'

'Rosanna was fantastic.' He brushed her cheek with the backs of his fingers. 'So were your parents.'

'Thank you so much.'

'They love you.'

She nodded, unable to speak any more.

'Sophy?'

She turned into his arms, hiding her tears in his neck. 'I love you.'

She looked at him then. He was smiling, his face light, his eyes warm and free of shadows. 'If I'd known how good it felt to say it, I'd have said it back that day when you rang for the doctor in my apartment. I wanted to make love to you then—I'm going to now.'

She reached up to him, placing the palm of her hand on the slightly rough cheek. 'Thank goodness,' she sighed. 'I was worried you'd taken a vow of abstinence.'

'I did,' he said soberly. 'I wasn't going to be with you again until you were my wife.'

'And now I am.'

'Yes.'

They whispered quiet goodbyes to the others, then slipped away in the night—running together down the rows of vines, to the small cottage at the far corner of the land. It had been decked in flowers, the sweet scent filling the air.

His arms were tight about her. 'Thank you, thank you, thank you.'

'For what?'

'Everything.' He looked down, a half-smile quirking his lips. 'I talked to your father.'

'You did?' She felt some nerves twinge.

'When I asked him for his blessing. It was a pretty frank talk.' He looked rueful. 'But he reckoned it's impossible to control feelings or to stop them, but that it's better to accept them. And then to deal with them.' He laced his fingers through hers. 'I want to deal with my love for you. Now and every day to come.'

And then he did—showing her the tenderness she'd made him feel, the happiness she'd brought to life in him. She cried as he told her, showed her, loved her. And she held him, loved him, until he shook in her arms.

'Not alone,' she whispered. 'Not any more.'

He buried his hot face in her neck and she stroked him until both their tears were spent.

'Are we staying here?' She was finally back on earth and able to absorb something of her surroundings.

'For a few days.'

'Then why do you have my passport?'

He chuckled. 'So you couldn't say no and run away overseas.'

'I'd only want to run away with you.'

'And we will. Very soon. But I thought we could decide where together.' He twirled her hair round his finger. 'You're tired.'

She was. But so happy. She snuggled closer to him and discovered she wasn't *that* tired. 'Once was not enough, Lorenzo.'

'Demanding wench.' He rose onto his elbow. 'You're always asking me for more.'

She laughed. 'And isn't it just such a hardship for you?'

'No,' he said, pulling her closer, binding her in his arms. 'It's heaven.'

Pure heaven.

* * * * *

THE FAR SIDE
OF PARADISE

BY
ROBYN DONALD

Robyn Donald can't remember not being able to read, and will be eternally grateful to the local farmers who carefully avoided her on a dusty country road as she read her way to and from school, transported to places and times far away from her small village in Northland, New Zealand.

Growing up fed her habit. As well as training as a teacher, marrying and raising two children, she discovered the delights of romances and read them voraciously, especially enjoying the ones written by New Zealand writers. So much so that one day she decided to write one herself. Writing soon grew to be as much of a delight as reading—although infinitely more challenging—and when eventually her first book was accepted by Mills & Boon she felt she'd arrived home.

She still lives in a small town in Northland, with her family close by, using the landscape as a setting for much of her work. Her life is enriched by the friends she's made among writers and readers, and complicated by a determined corgi called Buster, who is convinced that blackbirds are evil entities. Her greatest hobby is still reading, with travelling a very close second.

CHAPTER ONE

STONE-FACED, Cade Peredur listened again to the tape of his foster-brother's final call—a frantic, beseeching torrent of words recorded just before Peter Cooper killed himself.

'Cade, where are you? Where the *hell* are you—oh, with Lady Louisa, I suppose. Damn it, Cade, I need you more than any woman could—why aren't you home? *Why can't you be there for me?*'

A short pause, broken only by his breathing, jagged and irregular, and then, 'Cade, I've been such a fool—such an idiot.'

Not a muscle of Cade's face moved at the sound of choked weeping.

At last Peter said in a thick, despairing voice, 'Taryn was my last—my *only*—hope. It hurts—so bloody much, Cade, so much…' Another wrenching pause and then, in a voice Cade had never heard before, Peter said, 'There's nothing left for me now. She laughed when I asked… *laughed*…'

The silence stretched for so long that when he'd first heard it Cade had been sure the call was over.

But eventually his brother whispered, 'It's no good, Cade. I'm sorry, but it's no good any more. I can't—I just can't live with this. She's gone, and she's not coming back. Tell the parents I'm sorry to be such a useless son to them, but at least they'll still have you. You're the sort of man they wanted me to be, and God knows I tried, but I've always known I didn't have what it takes. Get married, Cade, and give them some grandchildren to adore. They'll need them now...'

He stopped abruptly. Then he said unevenly, 'Try not to despise me, Cade. I love you. Goodbye.'

Cade switched off the tape and walked across the luxurious room to look unseeingly across the London cityscape, fighting to control the rush of blind rage threatening to consume him. The call had come eight hours before he'd arrived home and by the time he'd got to Peter's apartment his brother was dead.

Peter had worshipped him, emulated and envied him, then finally grown away from him, but Cade had always been intensely protective of his younger brother.

Hands clenching, he turned and walked into his office, stopping at his desk. The photograph on it had been taken at his foster-parents' fortieth wedding anniversary a few months before Peter's death—Isabel and Harold Cooper all smiles for the camera, Peter's grin revealing a hint of feverish excitement.

As always, Cade was the odd one out—taller than the other two men, his features harsher and his expression unreadable.

His brother's suicide shattered that secure, tight family unit. A fortnight after the funeral, Harold Cooper had died from a heart attack, and while Isabel was still trying to come to terms with the wreckage of her life she'd stepped out into the path of a car. Onlookers said she'd moved as though in a daze.

She'd wanted to die too, but not before she'd begged Cade to find out what had driven her son to suicide.

He'd held her hand while she'd whispered painfully, 'If...if I knew why...it wouldn't be so bad. I just want to *know*, Cade, before I die.'

'You're not going to die,' he said harshly. 'I'll find out what happened.'

Her lashes had fluttered up again, revealing a spark of animation in her gaze. 'Promise?'

To encourage that hope, that flicker of determination, he'd have promised anything. 'I will. But you have to keep going for me.'

She'd managed a pale smile. 'It's a deal.'

That had been the turning point; valiantly she'd gathered her reserves and struggled back to cope with everything life had thrown at her. It had taken months of rehabilitation, and she was now adjusting to living the rest of her life in a wheelchair.

The letter Peter had left for his parents lay in its envelope on Cade's desk. He flicked it open and read it again. Unlike the telephone call, it was free of overt grief. Peter had told his parents he loved them, that he was sorry to cause them pain, but his life was no longer worth living.

No mention of the woman who'd reduced him to this depth of despair. He'd never introduced her to his family, only spoken of her once or twice in a casual, throwaway fashion. The last time he'd gone home—to celebrate his first big commission as a sculptor, a work for a public park in a market town—he hadn't referred to her.

So why that anguished, cryptic mention in his final call?

Cade turned away, his hard, arrogantly contoured face set. What part had Taryn Angove played in Peter's death?

Had something she'd said, something she'd done,

precipitated his final, fatal decision? It seemed possible, although she'd left for her home country of New Zealand eight hours before Peter's suicide.

Cade had always known that revenge was a fool's game; he'd seen the hunger for it eat into the intellect, destroy the soul.

Justice, however, was a different matter.

Progress had been infuriatingly slow. He knew now her return to New Zealand had been organised well before Peter's death. He knew she and Peter had been good friends for almost two years, almost certainly lovers.

He knew Peter's bank account should have been flush with a large advance to buy materials for his commission. Indeed, the money had arrived—and immediately a substantial sum had been taken out and paid directly to Taryn Angove. But the rest of the money had been siphoned off in large weekly cash payments, so that when Peter had died there had only been a few hundred pounds left.

If—and it was only an *if*, Cade reminded himself— Taryn Angove had somehow got her hands on it all, that could be why Peter had killed himself. Unfortunately, so far there was nothing, apart from that initial payment, to connect her with its absence.

But now, thanks to dedicated work by his security people, he knew where she was in New Zealand.

Cade looked across at the suitcase he'd just finished packing. His arrangements were all made and his actions from now on would depend on the woman he was hunting.

All day it had been still, the horizon a hazy brush-stroke where simmering sky met burnished sea, the forest-clad hills around the bay drowsing in the fierce glare of a sub-tropical sun. Cade narrowed his eyes against the intense light to watch seabirds made dumb by the heat fight silent battles over their catch.

Even the tiny waves on the shore were noiseless; all he could hear was the thrum of thousands of cicadas vibrating through the forest-covered hills behind the bay—the prevailing summer sound in this long northern peninsula of New Zealand.

The sibilant hum was penetrated by the imperative summons of his cell phone. Only his personal assistant had that number, so somewhere in his vast holdings something had gone wrong.

From halfway around the world his PA said, 'A few matters pertaining to this meeting in Fala'isi.'

'What about it?' Because of his business interests in the Pacific Basin, Cade had been asked to attend a gathering of high-powered Pacific dignitaries to discuss the future of the region.

Dealing with that took a few minutes. His voice a little tentative, Roger, his PA, said, 'Lady Louisa called.'

Arrogant black brows almost meeting across the blade of his nose, Cade said, 'And she wanted…?'

'Your address. She was not happy when I wouldn't give it to her. She said it was urgent and important.'

'Thanks.' Cade didn't discuss his private life easily, but he did say, 'We are no longer together.'

A pause, then, 'You might need to work on convincing her of that.'

His voice hard and cold, Cade said, 'Ignore her.'

'Very well.'

Cade's mouth curved in a sardonic smile. Louisa wouldn't follow him to New Zealand—it was completely out of her orbit. His *ex*-lover craved luxury and fashion and the heady stimulation of admiration. This remote paradise couldn't satisfy her need for the envy of others.

'Ah…not to put too fine a point on it, but she sounded stressed.' Roger paused. 'Actually, desperate.'

Her father had probably refused to pay a bill. Cade shrugged broad shoulders. 'Not your problem.' Or his. 'How is your daughter?'

His PA hesitated before saying in a completely different tone, 'We hear the results of the first lot of tests tomorrow.'

What the hell did you say to a man whose child could be suffering a terminal illness? 'If you need leave or any help at all, it's yours.'

'I know. Thanks—for everything.'

'No need for thanks—just let me know what I can do.'

'Thanks. I will. Keep in touch.'

Cade closed down the cell phone, his eyes flinty. Against the fact that a three-year-old could be dying, Louisa was a very minor consideration. A sensuous, satisfying lover until she'd decided Cade—influential, moving in the 'right' circles and exceedingly rich— would make the ideal first husband, she'd been careless enough to let him overhear as she discussed her plans on the telephone.

It had needed only a few questions in the right ears for Cade to discover she'd run through most of the fortune inherited from her grandfather. With no chance of support from a father whose income had been decimated by financial crisis, marriage was the obvious solution.

Like Louisa, Cade didn't believe in the sort of love poets wrote about. However, although experience had made him cynical, he intended to marry some day, and when he did it would be to a woman who'd value him for more than the size of his assets. He'd choose carefully, and it would last.

Cade's expression hardened. If Louisa was desperate enough to follow him, he'd make sure she understood that he was not and never would be a suitable husband—first, last or intermediate—for her.

After eyeing the hammock in the dark shade of one of the huge trees bordering the beach, he succumbed to an unusual restlessness that drove him down onto the hot amber sand. He stared out to sea for a long moment before turning. Only then did a drift of movement in the cloudless sky catch his attention.

Frowning, he stared at it. At first nothing more substantial than a subtle darkening of the blue, the haze swiftly thickened into a veil, an ominous stain across the sky.

In the grip of its severest drought in living memory, the province of Northland was under a total fire ban. The manager of the farm he'd rented the holiday house from had impressed on him that any smoke anywhere had to mean danger.

Muttering a word he wouldn't have said in polite company, Cade headed towards the house, long legs covering the ground at speed. He grabbed his car keys and cell phone, punching in a number as he headed towards the bedroom.

'I can see smoke in the sky,' he said curtly when the farm manager answered. 'South, and close—in the next bay, I'd say, and building fast.'

The farm manager swore vigorously, then said, 'Bloody free campers probably, careless with a campfire. OK, I'll ring the brigade and round up a posse from here. With any luck, we'll be able to put it out before it takes hold.'

Cade eyed the growing smoke cloud. 'I'll go over and see what I can do.'

'Man, be careful. There's a tap in the bay, but the creek's probably dry. If you've got a bucket there, grab it.' Possibly recalling that the man renting the farm's beach house was an influential tycoon, he added, 'And don't try to be a hero.'

Cade's swift grin vanished as he closed the cell phone. The smoke suddenly billowed, forming a cloud. Until then there had been no movement in the air, but of course the instant some idiot lit a fire the wind picked up.

The faster he got there, the better. He hauled on a long-sleeved shirt and trousers with swift, economical movements, then wasted precious moments looking for a non-existent bucket before giving up.

Not, he thought grimly as he got into the car, that a bucket would be much help, but it would have given him an illusory feeling of control.

He drove too fast along the track to the boundary gate; unlocking it wasted a few more valuable seconds so he left it open to give the manager and his men easy access. Lean hands tense on the wheel, he swung the four-wheel drive onto a narrow public road that led to the next bay.

It took too long to manoeuvre his vehicle around the tight corners through thick coastal scrub that would go up like a torch the moment a spark got into it. When the car emerged into searing sunlight a glance revealed no tents on the grassy foreshore or beneath the huge trees—nothing, in fact, but an elderly car parked in the deep shade cast by one of those trees.

And a woman in a skimpy bikini far too close to an area of blazing grass.

What the hell did she think she was doing?

Putting his foot down, Cade got there as fast as he could. He turned the vehicle, ready for a quick get-away, and was out of the car and running towards the woman before he realised she was directing a hose at the flames.

Tall and long-legged and young, she had a body guaranteed to set a man's hormones buzzing in anticipation. Smoke-smeared and glistening with sweat, she exuded unselfconscious sensuality.

At that moment she turned, pushing back a mane of copper-coloured hair that had been fanned across her face by the hot wind from the flames.

A flame flared up only a few inches from her feet and she jumped back, water from the hose splashing gleaming legs that went on forever.

The woman was crazy! Couldn't she see she wasn't achieving anything except putting herself in danger?

Cade covered the ground between them in a few seconds, watching the woman's expression turn to undisguised relief.

She thrust the hose into his hands and commanded brusquely, 'Keep directing it anywhere the flames try to get away. If they make it to those bullrushes the whole place will go up. I'll wet my towel and have a go at it from the other side.'

'Get dressed first,' he suggested, turning the pathetic dribble of water onto the flames.

She gave him a startled look, then nodded briskly. 'Good thinking.'

Taken aback and amused by her air of command, Cade watched her race across to her car to haul on a pair of inadequate shorts and a T-shirt and jam her feet into elderly sandshoes. Only then did she sprint down to the waves to wet her towel.

A sudden flare almost at his feet switched Cade's attention, but as he sprayed water onto it he wondered why on earth he was bothering. It was a losing battle; a wet towel would be as useless as the meagre trickle from the hose. Yet clearly the woman had no intention of giving up and doing the sensible thing—getting out of there before the fire made retreat impossible.

Cade admired courage in anyone, even reckless, blind courage. She might have lit the fire, but she was determined to put it out.

When she came running up from the shoreline she thrust the heavy, sodden towel into his hands. 'I'll take the hose—you're stronger than me so you'll be more efficient with this. Just be careful.'

The next few minutes were frantic. And hopeless. Working together, they fought grimly to hold back the flames but, inch by menacing inch, the bright line crept closer to the stand of bullrushes, pushing first one way and then, when frustrated, finding another path through the long, dry grass.

'Get back,' Cade shouted when flames suddenly flared perilously close to those lithe bare legs. Two long strides got him close enough to put all his power into beating it out.

'Thanks.' Her voice sounded hoarse, but she didn't move, directing that inadequate spurt of water with a stubborn determination that impressed him all over again.

She looked down at the towel, which was beginning to scorch. 'Go down and wet the towel again.'

'You go.' Cade thrust the towel into her hands and grabbed the hose from her.

Sensibly, she didn't waste time in protest, turning immediately to run across the sand.

His foster-mother's influence was embedded so deeply he couldn't evade it, Cade thought wryly, stamping out a tuft of grass that was still smouldering. Women were to be protected—even when they made it obvious they didn't want it.

He glanced up the hill. No sign of the fire brigade yet. If they didn't appear damned soon he'd grab the woman and, if he had to, drag her away. It would be too late once the bullrushes caught; they'd be in deadly danger of dying from smoke inhalation even if they took refuge in the sea.

Panting, she ran up from the beach and almost flung the dripping towel at him. Her face was drawn and smoke had stained the creamy skin, but she looked utterly determined. Clearly, giving up was not an option.

Cade said abruptly, 'The brigade should be here soon,' and hoped he was right.

His arms rose and fell in a regular rhythm but, even as he beat out sparks along the edge of the fire, he accepted their efforts were making very little headway. No way could they stop the relentless line of fire racing through the grass towards a stand of rushes so dry their tall heads made perfect fuel.

If they caught, he and the woman would have to run, but not to the cars. The beach would be their only refuge.

Once the fire got into the coastal scrub it would take an aerial bombardment or heavy rain to put it out. The cloudless sky mocked the idea of rain, and a helicopter with a monsoon bucket would take time to organise.

And if the wind kept building, the blaze would threaten not only the beach house he'd rented, but the houses and barns around the homestead further up the coast. Cade hoped the farm manager had warned everybody there to be on the alert.

A muted roar lifted his head. Relief surged through him as the posse from the station came down the hill on one of the farm trucks, almost immediately followed by two fire engines and a trail of other vehicles.

'Oh, thank God,' his companion croaked, a statement he silently echoed.

Taryn had never been so pleased to see anyone in her life. Smoothly, efficiently the firemen raced from their vehicles, the chief shouting, 'Get out of the way —down onto the beach, both of you.'

She grabbed a bottle of water from her car and headed across the sand. Without taking off her shoes, she waded out until the water came up to her knees, and only then began to drink, letting the water trickle down a painfully dry throat.

Heat beat against her, so fierce she pulled off her T-shirt, dropped it into the sea and used it to wipe herself down. The temporary coolness was blissful. She sighed, then gulped a little more water.

The stranger who'd helped her strode out to where she stood. 'Are you all right?' he demanded.

He was so tall she had to lift her face to meet his eyes. Swallowing, she said hoarsely, 'Yes. Thank you very much for your help.'

'Go easy on that water. If you drink it too fast it could make you sick.'

Taryn knew the accent. English, clipped and authoritative, delivered in a deep, cool voice with more than a hint of censure, it reminded her so much of Peter she had to blink back tears.

Not that Peter had ever used that tone with her.

The stranger was watching her as though expecting her to faint, or do something equally stupid. Narrowed against the glare of the sun on the sea, his disconcerting eyes were a cold steel-blue and, although Taryn knew she'd never seen him before, he looked disturbingly familiar.

An actor, perhaps?

She lowered the bottle. 'I'm taking it slowly.' Stifling a cough, she kept her eyes fixed on the helmeted men as they efficiently set about containing the flames. 'Talk about arriving in the nick of time!'

'I wouldn't have thought the village was big enough to warrant a fire station.'

A note in his voice lifted tiny invisible hairs on the back of her neck. He was very good-looking, all angles and strong bones and lean distinction. Not exactly handsome; that was too neutral a description for a man whose arrogantly chiselled features were stamped with formidable self-assurance. His aura of cool containment was based on something much more intimidating than good bones. An odd sensation warmed the pit of Taryn's stomach when she met his gaze.

Unnerved by that flinty survey, she looked away, taunted by a wisp of memory that faded even as she tried to grasp it.

'They're a volunteer group.' She took refuge in the mundane and held out her bottle of water. 'Would you like some?' Adding with a wry smile, 'I've wiped the top and as far as I know I have no diseases you need worry about.'

'I'm sure you haven't,' he drawled, not taking the

bottle. 'Thanks, but I've already had a drink—I brought my own.'

Stick to social pleasantries, she told herself, rattled by a note in his voice that came very close to mockery. 'Thank you so much for helping—I didn't have a hope of stopping it on my own.'

'Didn't it occur to you that lighting a fire in the middle of a drought could be dangerous?'

No, not mockery—condemnation.

Controlling an intemperate urge to defend herself, Taryn responded evenly, 'I didn't light it. I came down for a swim but before I got that far I noticed someone had had a fire on the beach above high tide mark to cook *tuatua*—shellfish. They didn't bother to put it out properly with sea water so I hosed it down, but a spark must have lodged somewhere up in the grass.'

'I see.'

Nothing could be gained from his tone or his expression. Stiffening, she said coldly, 'As soon as I saw smoke I rang the emergency number.'

'Ah, so that's why they arrived so quickly.'

Screwing up her eyes in an effort to pierce the pall of smoke, she said, 'It looks as though they're winning, thank heavens.'

Heat curled in the pit of her stomach when her gaze met his, aloof and speculative. Something in his expression reminded her she'd been clad only in her bikini when he'd arrived. And that the shorts he'd ordered her to get into revealed altogether too much of her legs.

Shocked by the odd, primitive little shiver that tightened her skin and set her nerves humming, she looked away.

He asked, 'Are you a local?'

'Not really.' She'd lived in the small village a mile away during her adolescence.

'So you're on holiday?'

Casual talk between two strangers abruptly hurled together...

Taking too deep a breath of the smoky air, she coughed again. 'No.'

'What do you do?' He spoke idly, still watching the activity on the grass behind the beach.

'I'm a librarian,' she responded, her tone even.

The brows that lifted in faint surprise were as black as his strictly controlled hair. In an abrupt change of subject, he said, 'Should you be swimming on your own?'

Taryn parried that steel-blue survey. 'This is a very safe bay. I don't take stupid risks.'

How did this man—this *judgmental* man, Taryn decided—manage to look sceptical without moving a muscle?

In a bland voice, he said, 'Fighting the fire looked risky enough to me. All it needed was a slight change of wind and you'd have had to run like hell to get to the beach safely. And you probably wouldn't have saved your car.'

That possibility had occurred to Taryn, but she'd been more afraid the fire would set the coastline alight. 'I can run,' she said coolly.

His gaze drifted down the length of her legs. 'Yes, I imagine you can. But how fast?'

His tone invested the words with a subliminal implication that summoned a swift, embarrassing heat to her skin.

That nagging sense of familiarity tugged at her again. *Who was he?*

Well, there was one way to find out. Without allowing herself second thoughts, she said coolly, 'When it's necessary, quite fast,' and held out her hand. 'It's time I introduced myself—I'm Taryn Angove.'

CHAPTER TWO

CADE'S heart pounded a sudden tattoo, every nerve in his body springing into instant taut alertness. This young Amazon was *Taryn Angove*?

OK, so courage didn't necessarily go with attributes like compassion and empathy, but she was nothing like the women Peter usually fell for. They'd all been startlingly similar—slight and chic, with an intimate knowledge of fashion magazines and the latest gossip, they'd pouted deliciously and parroted the latest catchphrases.

Cade couldn't imagine any of them trying to put out a fire, or throwing commands at him.

Mind racing, he took in the implications.

Did she know who he was?

If she did, she'd suspect that although this meeting was a coincidence, his presence in New Zealand wasn't. So she'd be wary...

Chances were, though, that Peter wouldn't have spoken of him. An unpleasant situation some years before, when Peter's then lover had made a determined play for Cade, meant that Peter rarely introduced his girlfriends to his family. He'd once admitted that although he referred to Cade occasionally, it was only ever as his brother.

Cade knew the value of hunches; he'd learned which ones to follow and which to ignore. One was warning him right now to keep quiet about the connection.

'Cade Peredur,' he said smoothly, and shook Taryn Angove's outstretched hand. 'How do you do?'

He could see why Peter had fallen for her. In spite of the smoke stains, she was very attractive—beautiful, in fact, with fine features and creamy skin set off by coppery hair.

Not to mention a lush, sinfully kissable mouth...

Ruthlessly, Cade disciplined an unexpected kick of lust. Nowhere near as easily affected as his brother had been by a lovely face and lissom body, it exasperated him that Taryn Angove had a definite and very primal impact on him.

Which he had to suppress.

His investigation team hadn't been able to turn up a single person who wasn't shocked and astonished by his brother's death. The police had been unable to add anything beyond the fact that there had definitely been no foul play.

Peter had taken Taryn Angove to the theatre the previous night. She'd stayed with him that night and then he'd delivered her to Heathrow for the flight home. He'd cancelled an appointment with friends the following evening, but he'd spoken by telephone to them and he'd seemed perfectly normal.

Yet only a few hours later he'd killed himself.

From New Zealand, Taryn been asked to do a video interview with the police, but it revealed nothing; she hadn't mentioned anything that might have upset him, so they didn't consider her a person of interest. Although sympathetic, for them there was no doubt that Peter had committed suicide, and so there was nothing to investigate.

So she was the only person who might be able to help Cade find out why Peter had done it.

And there was the question of what had happened to the money...

Looking down into the wide green-gold eyes lifted to his, noting their subtle darkening and the faint flush visible even under a patina of smoke, Cade decided a change of tactics could be in order.

He'd come here determined to use whatever weapons might be necessary to find out what she knew. He'd try appealing to her better instincts—if she had any—and, if that failed, then intimidation might work. Or paying her off.

Now he'd met her, he wondered whether such weapons would be necessary. Taryn seemed nothing like he had expected. In order to choose the best method of persuading her to talk, he'd have to find out what made Taryn Angove tick.

Which meant he needed to get to know her.

Ignoring the electricity his touch zapped across her nerve-ends, Taryn concentrated on his grip—firm but not aggressive and completely confident.

Just her luck to be sweaty and smoky, with stringy hair clinging to her probably scarlet face. How did he manage to look so...so much in control?

Not that it mattered. Too late, she remembered who he was—periodically, she'd seen photographs of him in the press and appreciated his sexy, angular impact. He was a big player in financial circles and appeared occasionally in the gossip magazines a flatmate in London used to devour.

In them, he was usually squiring a beautiful titled woman with very expensive taste in clothes.

When he released her hand she said calmly, 'Thanks so much for coming to help when you saw the smoke.'

Broad shoulders lifted again dismissively. 'It was a matter of self-interest.' At her enquiring look he enlarged, 'I'm holidaying in the next bay.'

Had he bought Hukere Station? She dismissed the idea immediately. High-flyers like Cade Peredur didn't invest in remote agricultural areas in New Zealand's subtropical north; they went to the South Island's glorious mountains. Anyway, he didn't look the sort to want a cattle station; from what she remembered, his interests lay in the cutthroat arena of finance and world-shaking deals. And sophisticated English aristocrats.

In that cool, slightly indifferent tone he told her, 'I saw smoke in the air so I came to see what I could do.'

Taryn looked past him and said with a shiver, 'I'm so glad you did. I wish the idiots who lit that fire could see what their carelessness has led to. The thought of all these pohutukawa trees going up in flames is horrifying. Some of them are over five hundred years old. In fact, Maori legend says that the big one along at the end of the beach was used to tie up the first canoe that ever landed here.'

His gaze followed her pointing finger. 'It looks old enough, certainly.'

Taryn shrugged mentally at his lack of enthusiasm. He was English, and on holiday—why should he share her love for the ancient trees? It was enough that he'd come to help.

'It will take a lot of time before this place gets back to its previous loveliness,' she said. 'It's such a shame.

It's the only good swimming beach close to Aramuhu township, but no one will want to come here until the grass grows again.' Her nose wrinkled. 'It looks horrible and it smells beastly, and everything—and everyone— would get covered in soot.'

Cade accepted the opportunity she'd offered— whether deliberately or not, he couldn't tell. 'If you'd like to swim, why don't you try the beach I'm staying at?' He nodded towards the headland that separated the two bays.

Startled and a little wary, she looked up. Caught in an ironic blue-grey focus, she felt her pulse rate surge and automatically ignored it. 'That's very kind of you,' she said without committing herself.

'It seems only fair.'

For the first time he smiled, sending languorous heat curling through Taryn. 'Fair?' she asked, only just stopping herself from stuttering.

'You might well have saved the beach house from going up in flames—and me with it,' he replied, noting that the farm manager was on his way towards them with the fire chief.

Noted too, with something close to irritation, the swift appreciative glances both men gave Taryn Angove.

Not that he could blame them. Those shorts showed off her glorious legs, and her bikini top accentuated her more obvious assets; only a dead man would ignore them.

The thought no sooner formed in his mind than he realised how bleakly appropriate it was. A man as dead as Peter...

'Hi, Jeff.' The smile Taryn gave the farm manager was friendly and open, but the one she bestowed on the grey-haired fire chief sparkled with mischief. 'Mr Sanderson.'

The fire chief gave a brief grin. 'Why am I not surprised to find you trying to put out a fire with nothing more than a garden hose?' he asked in a not quite fatherly tone before turning to Cade.

The farm manager introduced them and, as they shook hands, Cade said, 'It didn't take you long to get things under control.'

Hugh Sanderson nodded. 'Easy enough when you've got the men and the equipment. However, I'll leave a gang here to keep an eye on it. Just as well you both kept at it—probably saved a lot of destruction. Do you know how it started?'

'Ms Angove's theory seems logical,' Cade told him. 'All I saw was smoke in the sky.'

She flashed a green-gold, glinting glance at him as she explained what she thought had happened.

'Yeah, that would be it.' The fire chief indicated the sign that announced a total fire ban. 'Some idiots think a fire on the beach doesn't count. Thanks for keeping it away from the bullrushes—although I damn near had a heart attack when I saw you two trying to put it out.' He transferred his gaze to Taryn. 'No more heroine stuff on my patch, all right? If that fire had got into the rushes you'd have been in serious trouble, both of you. You OK?'

'Fine, thanks.' Her radiant smile made light of smoke stains and sweat.

The older man grinned. 'You never were one for keeping out of mischief. Patsy was just saying the other day she hadn't seen you for a while. Come and have a cup of tea with us when you're in town next.'

Cade waited until they'd gone before asking thoughtfully, 'What sort of mischief did you indulge in?'

She flushed a little, but laughed before explaining, 'When we first came to Aramuhu I was twelve, and I'd spent the previous eleven years living with my parents on a yacht in the Pacific. Fruit grows wild in the islands and I was used to just picking something off the nearest tree whenever I was hungry. At Aramuhu we lived for a few months next door to Mr and Mrs Sanderson and one day I took a cherimoya from his orchard.'

'Cherimoya?'

'It's bigger than an apple, sort of heart-shaped with bumpy green skin. Cousin to a custard apple.' Her voice sank into a sensual purr. 'They have the most delicious taste in the world. My mother marched me over to apologise and offer to work to pay for it. Mr Sanderson decided I could weed the garden for an hour, but once I'd done that he gave me a bag of them to take home. Even when we moved to a new house he made sure we were supplied with ripe ones in season and he still likes to tease me about it.'

Cade wondered if that husky tone was reserved for fruit, or if she murmured like that when she made love. His body tightened—and then tightened again for an entirely different reason at another thought.

No doubt Peter had also found that sleepy, sexy note both erotic and beguiling...

In an ironic tone that banished the reminiscent softness from her expression he said, 'Ah, small town life.'

'Where everyone knows your business,' she agreed with a swift, challenging smile. She focused her gaze behind him and he looked over one shoulder to see a racy red car hurtling boisterously down the road.

When he turned back she was frowning, a frown that disappeared when she asked, 'Did you grow up in a big city, Mr Peredur?'

'I was born in one, yes.' When taken away from his mother, he'd been living in the stinking backstreet of a slum. 'I'm going back to the beach house now. The invitation to swim is still open.'

And waited, concealing his keen interest in her answer.

She hesitated, then said lightly, 'I'm sticky and hot and I'd love a swim, thank you. I'll follow you in my car.'

'Right.'

Taryn watched him stride towards his Range Rover, long legs carrying him across the sandy ground in lithe, easy paces.

In a word—*dominant*. He compelled interest and attention by sheer force of character.

The swift fizz of sensation in the pit of her stomach startled her, but what made her increase speed towards her own car was the arrival of the one driven by a journalist for the local newspaper, an old schoolfellow who'd made it more than obvious that he was angling for a relationship.

Although she'd tried as tactfully as she could to show him she wasn't interested, Jason didn't seem to understand.

She fought back an odd clutch of apprehension beneath her ribs when she saw the possessive gleam of his smile as he swung out of the car, camera at the ready.

'Hi, Taryn—stay like that and I'll put you on the front page.'

'I've done nothing—showcase the men who put out the fire,' she returned. From the corner of her eye she noticed that Cade Peredur had opened the door of his vehicle, but not got in; he was watching them across its roof.

'Babe, they don't look anywhere near as good as you do.' Jason gave a sly grin and lifted the camera.

'No.' She spoke more sharply than she intended.

He looked wounded. 'Oh, come on, Taryn, don't be coy —we'd sell a hell of a lot more issues with you in those shorts on the front page instead of old Sanderson in his helmet. How about coming out with me tonight? I've been invited to a soirée at the Hanovers' place and they won't mind if I bring along a gorgeous girl.'

'No, thank you,' she said, keeping her voice even and light.

'Going to wash your hair, are you? Look,' he said, his voice hardening, 'what is it with you? Think you're too good to go out with an old mate now, do you? I'm not trying to get into your pants, I—'

He stopped abruptly as a deep voice cut in. 'All right, Taryn?'

'Fine, thank you,' she said quickly, adding rather foolishly, 'Jason and I went to school together.'

'Hey,' Jason exclaimed, ever the opportunist, 'you're Cade Peredur, aren't you? Mr Peredur, I'm Jason Beckett from the *Mid-North Press*. Can I ask you a few questions about the fire?'

'The person to tell you about it is the fire chief,' Cade said evenly. He looked down at Taryn. 'You go ahead— I'll follow.'

'OK,' she said, fighting a violent mixture of emotions.

Cade watched her walk across to her car and get in, then looked down at the reporter. Yet another man smitten by Taryn Angove's beauty; he should feel a certain amount of sympathy for the good-looking kid even if he was unpleasantly brash.

Instead, he wanted to tell him to keep his grubby hands and even grubbier statements to himself, and stay away from her if he valued his hide.

Shrugging, Beckett said, 'Well, that's women for you, I guess.' He produced an ingratiating smile. 'Are you planning to buy Hukere Station, Mr Peredur? I've heard rumours of development, a farm park…'

'I'm on holiday, nothing more,' Cade said evenly, nodded, and strode back to his vehicle.

In her car, Taryn took a deep breath and switched on the engine. The hot air inside the vehicle brought a moment of giddiness, but at least it wasn't too smoky. Grimacing, she looked down at her legs, stained and sticky with a vile mixture of sea water, perspiration and smoke. The swim she'd been promising herself all week had never seemed so desirable, but she should have said, *No thanks, Mr Peredur*, and headed back to the small studio unit that was her temporary home.

So why hadn't she? She turned the key and waited patiently for the engine to fire.

Partly because she'd wanted to get away from Jason. But more because she was curious—and that forbidden tug of response excited her as much as it alarmed her.

Her mouth curled into a wry smile as she eased the car up the hill. It would take a woman made of iron to look at Cade Peredur and not feel *something*. As well as innate strength and authority, he possessed a brain that had taken him to his present position. Add more than a dash of ruthlessness to that potent mix, and the fact that he looked really, really good…

Yes, definitely a top-of-the-list male.

But not a man any sensible woman would fall in love with.

Not that *that* was going to happen.

Bitter experience had taught her that although she could feel attraction, when it came to following through on it she was a total failure.

In a word, she was frigid.

Without volition, her thoughts touched on Peter, the jumble of shock and sorrow and bewilderment assailing her as it always did when she recalled his proposal—so unexpected, so shatteringly followed by his death. Guilt lay permanently in wait, making her wonder yet again whether her response had driven him to take that final, lethal step.

If only she'd been a little less incredulous—if she hadn't laughed—would he have made a different decision?

If she'd stayed in England as he'd wanted her to, instead of coming home, would she have been able to help him get over her refusal?

All those *if*s, and no answers…

The car skidded slightly. Feeling sick, she dragged her mind back to driving. Although the station road was well maintained, it still required concentration.

At Anchor Bay she pulled up and switched off the engine. Cade Peredur's big Range Rover stopped beside hers and he got out, appraising eyes coolly intent as he surveyed her.

Tall as she was, a little more height would be a distinct asset when it came to dealing with this man. Taryn tried to dissipate another tingle of sensation by collecting her bag. As she walked towards Cade she felt embarrassingly self-conscious. She glanced away, gaze skimming a huge flame tree to one side of the bay, and caught sight of the house.

It was a relief to be able to say something impersonal. 'Oh, the bach is still here,' she exclaimed. She'd half-expected some opulent seaside mansion, suitable for very rich holidaymakers, against the bush-covered slope that backed the lawn.

'Bach?'

'The local term for a small, basic cottage, usually by a beach or a lake.'

Cade said, 'Obviously you know the place.'

'When I was at school, the previous owners allowed the school to hold its camps here—it's a very safe beach. The bach was just a ruin then. Possums used to nest in the ceiling, and I've no doubt there were rats under the floor.' She looked around reminiscently. 'Over there, under that pohutukawa, when I was thirteen I was offered a cigarette by a boy I was madly trying to impress.'

'And did you accept it?'

She gave him a mock-scandalised glance. 'Are you kidding? My parents are doctors! I stopped trying to impress him right then.'

He smiled. 'Good for you. Would you like to see what's been done to the house?'

It was difficult to match the abandoned shell she recalled to the house now. It had been almost completely reconstructed, its stone outer walls repaired and the timber ceilings stripped and oiled so that they gleamed.

'It looks great,' Taryn said, gazing around the long living room.

Although it must have cost a mint to renovate, it didn't look glossy or smartly out of place. Comfortable and beachy and cool, it had shelves containing a large collection of books and some seriously good pictures hung on the walls. Somehow it suited Cade Peredur.

He said, 'There's a changing room and a shower in the cabana over by the flame tree. You can leave your bag and your clothes there—I'll join you in a few minutes and bring you down a towel.'

She summoned a bright smile. 'Thank you. And then I can prove to you how competent I am in the water.'

Cade's answering smile didn't soften his face. In fact, Taryn thought as she walked across the coarse warm grass to the beach hut, the curve of his firmly chiselled mouth had made his striking, hard-edged face seem both cynical and forbidding.

Safely in the small building, she wondered if anything ever did soften those arrogant features. When he kissed…?

She tried to imagine being kissed by Cade Peredur. Heat sizzled through her at the thought, but she couldn't see his face softening into a look of…well, *love* was out of the question, but what about lust?

The word *soften* just didn't fit the man. In his world it took an intimidating blend of brains, courage and formidable will to reach the top of the tree. When he kissed a woman it would be as a conqueror…

Hastily, she stripped off her clothes, pulling a face as she discarded them. They smelt disgusting—a mixture of smoke and sweat. They looked horrible too, both shorts and T-shirt smeared with ashy smudges and black marks. Even her bikini stank of the fire.

So, probably, did her hair and her skin.

Blissfully, she washed it all off in the sea's warm caress. A few minutes after she waded into the water, she caught movement on the beach from the corner of her eye and inched her head around so she could watch Cade Peredur stride across the sand.

Her heart jumped, startling her. Formidably and blatantly male, he seemed like some potent, elemental figure from the dawn of time—sunlit bronze skin and a perfect male body showing off sleek muscles that proclaimed strength and energy.

Some of which she could do with right now. Deep in the pit of her stomach, that hidden part of her contracted and sent another hot wave of sensation through her.

Lust, she thought, trying to douse it with a prosaic and practical attitude.

Although she'd never experienced anything so powerful before, this keen urgency that alerted every cell, tightening her skin and making her heart race, was merely run-of-the-mill physical attraction.

And if she tried to act on it, she knew exactly and in humiliating detail what would happen next; it would vanish, leaving her cold and shaking with that familiar fear. But even those mortifying memories couldn't banish the shimmers of sensation that pulsed through her, stimulating and undisciplined.

She turned away when Cade dropped his towel and made a fluid racing dive off the rocks at the side of the bay. An unexpected wave caught her—unexpected because she was too busy drooling over the man, she thought furiously as she inhaled water. Spluttering, she spat out a mouthful of salt water and coughed a couple of times to clear her lungs, opening her eyes to see her host heading towards her, strong arms cutting through the waves.

Oh, how…how inane! She'd probably just convinced him she wasn't safe in a shower, let alone the sea.

Sure enough, he trod water when he reached her and demanded, 'Are you all right?'

The sun-dazzled sparkles of water clogging her lashes surrounded him with an aura, a dynamic charge of power that paradoxically made her feel both weak and energised at the same time.

'Fine,' she returned, only a little hoarse from the dousing. Her heart was thudding as though she'd swum several kilometres through raging surf.

Get a grip, she commanded.

The last time she'd felt anything remotely like this she'd been nineteen and amazingly naive. She'd decided it had to be love, and became engaged on the strength of it. What a disaster that had turned out to be!

But there was nothing girlishly callow about her response to this man. Her body throbbed with a dark, potent sexuality unlike anything she'd ever experienced before.

She'd deal with that later. Right now, she had to get herself back onto an even keel.

Somehow she managed to produce a smile and said the first thing that popped into her head. 'Race you to shore.'

Cade's brows shot up as though she'd surprised him, but he recovered instantly. 'You get a handicap.'

'OK,' she agreed.

However, even with the handicap, he beat her comfortably. At least swimming as fast and as hard as she'd ever done worked off some of that wildfire energy.

When she stood up he said, 'You're good.'

'I was brought up almost in the water,' she said, breathing fast. He too, she noted with satisfaction, was breathing more heavily than normal. She added, 'My parents love the sea so much they called me after it.'

'Taryn?'

'No, Taryn is apparently derived from an Irish word meaning *rocky hill*. I had an Irish grandmother. But my second name is Marisa, which is from a Latin word meaning *the sea*.'

He observed dryly, 'It's a very pretty name, but I don't think it would help if you got cramps and there was no one around to help.'

'I've never had even the slightest twinge of cramp,' she said defensively, extremely aware of the way water gleamed along the muscular breadth of his shoulders, highlighting the effortless power beneath the skin. 'Anyway, I know how to deal with it.'

'Those medical parents?'

'And a Pacific upbringing,' she said shortly. 'Want to know how it's done?'

He laughed. 'Like you, I've never had cramp, but just in case—yes, demonstrate.'

When he laughed he was really something, she thought confusedly. Trying to speak prosaically, she said, 'First you change your kick. That often works. If it doesn't, take a deep breath and float face down, then pull your leg up, grab your foot and yank it upwards.'

She demonstrated, glad to be able to hide her face in the water for a few seconds. When she'd finished, she stood up and said, 'That almost always does the trick, I'm told.'

But he wasn't going to let her off so easily. Bumblebees zoomed through her bloodstream when he scanned her face with hooded blue-grey eyes. 'And if it doesn't?'

'Assume the same position and massage the offending muscle,' she told him succinctly, taking a surreptitious step back before her brain scrambled completely, overcome by all that bronzed skin, sleeked by water and backed by muscles and hard male authority.

He laughed again, teeth very white in his tanned face. 'Fine, I'll accept that you can deal with cramp. Are you on shift work to be able to take the day off?'

The abrupt change of subject startled her. 'I'm not working right now.'

His brows met over the distinguished blade of his nose. 'Really?'

Was there a hint of disparagement in his tone? Taryn bristled. Parrying a keen, questioning look, she said with cool reserve, 'I've been overseas, and when I came back I took a job selling souvenirs to tourists. It's getting close to the end of summer and tourists are slackening off, so I'm no longer needed.'

'Is there plenty of work around here?' His voice was casual. 'The village looked to be pretty small.'

Aramuhu was small, and there were very few jobs. But her future was none of his business. 'I'm sure I'll find something,' she said dismissively.

He smiled. 'I'm sure you will.'

Something in his tone caught her attention. Their gazes met, clashed, and the glint of awareness in his eyes summoned an intense, elemental response from her.

Taryn forced herself to ignore the shiver scudding down her spine, the tingle of anticipation.

Her breath stopped in her throat and she had to fight an odd belief that those few seconds of silent combat were altering the very fabric of her life, fundamentally changing her so that she'd never be the same again.

This unexpected attraction *was* mutual. Cade felt it too and, if she were willing, he'd probably enjoy a light-hearted, temporary affair.

Taryn didn't do casual affairs—didn't do *any* sort of affair. She'd had more than enough of the stark embarrassment when men realised that, although she could shiver with desire, when it came to actually making love she froze.

Her impetuous youthful engagement had caused such fierce disillusionment she'd been left emotionally bruised, so wary she'd never allowed herself to feel anything more than friendship for the men she'd met. Over the years she'd developed effective methods of brushing off unwanted approaches, yet this time temptation whispered seductively through her.

She'd stay well away from him—not give herself any chance of weakening. Turning away, she dived back into the welcoming water.

CHAPTER THREE

CADE didn't follow her. Taryn told herself she should be pleased. She'd be prepared to bet her next year's income—always providing she had one, she thought uneasily—that on his home turf he'd be hip-deep in swooning women. He had to be in his early thirties and he wasn't married. Most men with his financial and personal assets would enjoy playing the field.

As she hauled herself up onto the rocks she decided acidly that when he did make up his mind to marry he'd probably choose a glamorous model or actress. After five years or so he'd divorce her and marry a nice girl from his own strata of society—whatever that was— who'd give him the required couple of children. And in his fifties he'd divorce the second wife and marry a trophy one thirty years younger.

And she wouldn't want to be any of those wives.

That thought made her grin ironically before she slid back into the water.

Half an hour later she'd showered and reluctantly got back into her smelly shirt and shorts, emerging from the luxurious cabana to meet Cade, his muscled elegance defined by clothes that made her feel like a ragamuffin.

Only for an instant. The appreciative gaze that skimmed her bare legs did considerable damage to her composure. How on earth could he convey leashed interest with one swift glance—a glance that set her treacherous blood fizzing?

Possibly she'd misread his attitude, because his voice was coolly impersonal when he asked, 'Would you like a drink?'

'No, thank you,' she said at once, squelching a pang of regret. 'I smell of smoke and I really want to get out of these clothes.'

And could have bitten her tongue out. Would he think she'd made an unsubtle proposition? If he said something about a Freudian slip she'd have to bite back an indignant reply in case he guessed what she'd been thinking.

But he was too sophisticated to take her up on her clumsy choice of words. Not a muscle in his face moved when he said, 'Then some other time, perhaps.'

'That would be nice.' Taryn thought in self-derision that platitudes were so useful for filling in awkward moments.

Then Cade's smile hit her like a blow to her solar plexus. It turned her thoughts into chaotic, disconnected responses—all of which indicated, *He is utterly gorgeous...*

And he knew the effect that smile had on the opposite sex too.

Calmly, he said, 'If you want to swim, come and do it here. Nobody is going to want to swim in the next bay for a while.'

'I... That's very kind of you,' she said automatically. Yet another platitude.

Of course she wouldn't accept. Yet some traitorous part of her couldn't help wondering if this surprising invitation was the first step in—what?

Nothing, she thought sturdily, but heat scorched her cheeks and she hastily bent to pick up the bag containing her togs.

'So that's agreed,' he said calmly.

Taryn had never met another man with his uncompromising aura of authority and controlled, potent sensuality. She preferred her male companions to be interesting and unthreatening.

Like Peter.

That memory drove the colour from her skin. She produced a meaningless smile and said, 'Actually, it isn't, but it's very kind of you to offer, and I'll probably take you up on it.'

She got into the car, frowned as the engine took a sluggish couple of moments to power, waved with one hand and drove off.

Cade watched the elderly vehicle, its persistent rattle deepening his frown. It certainly didn't look as though she had all Peter's money; if she did, she'd have been able to buy a brand-new car. The amount he knew for certain she'd received wasn't enough for that.

Perhaps she was canny enough to save it.

Unfortunately, he didn't know enough about her to make any reasonable judgement.

But that, he decided, could be dealt with. If she needed a job, he could provide her with one for long enough to find out whether she was a money-grubbing opportunist...

Taryn stopped at the top of the hill to look down into the next desolate bay. One fire engine remained there and a couple of the firemen were checking the perimeters of the burn but, although wisps of smoke still drifted up, the fire had clearly been controlled.

No little red car, either, she noted. Her frown

deepened. Jason was becoming rather too pressing, a nuisance.

But not dangerous.

Unlike the man she'd just left.

Dangerous? She gave a snort and muttered, 'He's a *businessman*, for heaven's sake.'

Tycoons Taryn had seen on television or in the news were sleek, well dressed and well manicured. The thought of them being dangerous anywhere but in the boardroom was laughable.

So what made her foolish mind fix on that word to describe Cade Peredur?

Instinct, she guessed,

And Cade had certainly *looked* dangerous when he was scotching those greedy tongues of flame. He'd used her wet towel like a weapon, flailing it with an economy of movement that showed great strength as well as determination.

Also, there had been something in his manner when he approached Jason that had indicated a formidable male threat—one Jason had recognised.

OK, Cade was dangerous, as any strong man could be. But he was in complete control of all that strength. And none of it was directed at her.

So she didn't have to worry or feel intimidated.

Images of his powerful body filled her mind. Water-slicked and gleaming, every long muscle lovingly delineated, he'd stolen her breath away.

Yes, her decision to see no more of him had been the right one. She glanced down, frowning at the sight of the tight fist pressed against her heart, and let her hand drop, spreading out the fingers before shaking them so they relaxed.

Plenty of women must have felt the same surging

chemistry when they set eyes on Cade Peredur. Some of them would have ended up in his bed.

'Lots, probably,' she said aloud to a fantail flirting its tail from a nearby bush as it kept its beady black eyes fixed on her.

Smiling, she confided, 'Men like Cade Peredur—men who positively *seethe* with masculine confidence—always know they've got what it takes to make a woman happy in bed.'

Unless she was inherently cold...

But not one of his lovers had managed to make their liaison permanent.

And when—*if*—she ever fell in love properly, with a man who'd understand her fear of sex and help her overcome it—she wanted permanence, a lifelong alliance like that between her parents. She wanted trust and equality and a family, laughter and commitment and security...

None of which immediately brought Cade to mind.

'So forget about this love business,' she told the fantail. 'Because I don't think the sort of man I want exists in this world.'

And she'd keep away from any more chance meetings with Cade Peredur. Next time she was struck by the urge to go to the beach she'd slake it with a shower. She wouldn't have to keep it up for long; he had to have things to do and places to go—empires to run, worlds to conquer, women to overwhelm—so he'd soon leave New Zealand.

And, once he was gone, her life would return to normal. No chills, no cheap thrills when those hard blue eyes met hers, no shivering awareness of his sheer physical impact...

For several moments more she stood looking down

at the blackened landscape, frowning at the ugly stain across the grass and the rank smell of incinerated vegetation.

Then she stiffened her spine and got into the car and drove back to the sleepout she rented in an orchard a few kilometres from the village. Basic but comfortable, it boasted a miniature kitchen and a slightly larger bathroom, and the wide terrace outside made up for the lack of space within.

Clean once more, and in fresh clothes, she picked up an apple from the bowl on the bench and dropped into the lounger to demolish the fruit, carefully not thinking of Cade Peredur.

She needed to find work. She'd quite enjoyed selling souvenirs to tourists, but the summer wave of visitors through the village had receded, leaving her behind.

Jobless and drifting…

Ever since Peter had killed himself, an aching emptiness made her question the value of her existence.

'Time to stop it,' she said out loud, and made a sudden resolution.

Drifting was for slackers, for losers.

It was more than time to find some direction to her life. Before she'd gone to the United Kingdom, she'd enjoyed her work in one of Auckland's largest libraries. In London she'd worked in a coffee shop run by a New Zealand friend until she met Peter. They'd clicked straight away and he'd introduced her to his friends—a very earnest, intense artistic circle who'd treated her as a kind of mascot.

Peter had even found her a new job; she'd been in her element cataloguing the immense library collected over fifty years by the deceased uncle of one of his acquaintances.

Although she and Peter had become close, there had been no sexual spark between them, so his proposal had come as a shock. She'd thought he was joking and burst out laughing.

Only he hadn't been. And then she'd had to refuse him as gently as she could.

His death had horrified her. She should, she thought wearily, have realised it wasn't artistic temperament that caused his bouts of depression, always followed by tearing high spirits. She had wondered if something was wrong, but it had never occurred to her that *she* might be the cause.

Assailed by questions for which she'd never know the answers, and bitter remorse at not handling the situation better, she'd come back to Aramuhu, the only place she'd ever really called home.

But there was nothing here for her, no answers. So now what? The future stretched before her, featureless and uninviting.

'I need to make a plan,' she said aloud, resisting an impulse to give up. Unlike her parents, she was not a born rover. Yes, she wanted some purpose in her life, and she'd like to settle somewhere like Aramuhu, with a steady job in a nice library.

Unfortunately, the village was too small to be able to afford a salaried librarian. Like the fire brigade, the busy little library was run by volunteers.

OK, so if she were Cade Peredur, how would she go about making a worthwhile life?

A list of all the things she had to offer would be a good start. 'So what's stopping you from doing that?' she asked the empty room, and got out of the chair.

The following morning she surveyed the list with a frown. It looked reasonably impressive—she hoped.

Much more impressive than the bank statement she'd just opened. It told her she had enough money to last for two weeks. Something perilously close to panic pooled icily beneath her ribs.

Ignoring it, she sat down and wrote at the bottom of her list: *Stay here?*

That had to be her first decision. Living was cheap in Aramuhu—but the sleepout was used for kiwi fruit pickers in season, so it was temporary. She could stay there for another couple of months, perhaps.

She could go to her parents in Vanuatu, but she had no medical skills, and they didn't need a librarian or even a secretary. Besides, it would only ever be a stopgap.

Frowning, she added a final few words: *If so, disengage from Jason.* Not that he seriously worried her, but she was beginning to feel uneasy at his refusal to take no for an answer.

An abrupt summons from the telephone startled her.

Not Jason, please.

'Yes?' she said cautiously.

And recognised the voice instantly when he said, 'Cade Peredur here.'

How did he know her number? Her stomach tightened when he went on without pausing, 'Do you have decent computer skills?'

Startled, she glanced at her ancient laptop. 'They're not bad.'

'I've just been called to a business meeting at very short notice, and I need someone to assemble and collate information for me from the Internet and possibly transcribe notes. Would you be interested?'

That crisp, deep voice showed no indication of any

interest in her but the purely businesslike. 'Well, yes,' she said cautiously.

'You are still looking for work?'

'Yes, but...' Taryn gathered her scattering wits and took a deep breath as that forbidden word *dangerous* appeared in red letters across her brain. Common sense demanded she say no, and mean it.

'What's the problem?' he enquired.

Pushed, she responded tersely, 'None, I suppose, if I discount the fact that we met for the first time yesterday, and I don't know very much about you at all.'

There was silence, as though she'd accused him of some deviant behaviour, before he said, 'I can probably come up with a reference. Who would you like to give it?'

Flippantly, she returned, 'How about the Prime Minister?'

'United Kingdom or New Zealand?'

Funny man.

Or seriously influential. 'Oh, don't bother,' she retorted. 'Where is this business meeting?'

'Fala'isi.'

An island basking in the tropical sun... Firmly, she pushed back memories of halcyon days. 'I didn't realise it involved travel.'

'Have you a current passport?'

'Yes, but—'

'It's only a short flight from Auckland.'

Fala'isi was a small island nation known for its good governance, safety and lack of corruption. However, she said, 'There are good temping agencies in Auckland—'

'It's a long weekend,' he said evenly. 'I've tried, and everyone's away on holiday.'

Of course, it was Anniversary weekend. Torn, Taryn wavered.

Into the silence, Cade said with cool, crisp detachment, 'I can assure you I have no designs, wicked or otherwise, on you, your body or your well-being. I've been called in to advise at an informal meeting of political and influential figures from around the Pacific Rim. It will last a week. My personal assistant in London is unable to help—he has family problems. I need someone who can type well, find information on a wide variety of subjects, check its accuracy and collate it in time for me to be armed for each session. Someone who's discreet. You'll be busy, but there should be enough time for you to swim and otherwise enjoy yourself. Obviously, you'll be well compensated for your time.'

The lick of irritation underlying his words angered her, but was oddly reassuring. It sounded as though she were merely the easiest solution to an unexpected difficulty. And in Fala'isi it was highly unlikely she'd come up against any situation she couldn't deal with.

However, it was the thought of her bank balance that made the decision. She needed the money. And she wasn't likely to lose either her head or her heart in a week.

'All right, I'll do it,' she said quickly, before she could change her mind. 'But I'll need an address and contact details.'

She'd give them to her landlady. Just in case…

Three hours later Taryn was sitting in a sleekly luxurious jet feeling as though she'd been tossed without ceremony onto a merry-go-round. Cade had taken over, efficiently organising their departure.

The first shock had been the helicopter ride to the

international airport at Auckland. The second arrived hot on its heels when, after swift formalities, Cade escorted her to this plane. The third came when she realised that not only was it private but they were the only passengers.

Feeling ridiculously as though she'd been kidnapped, she obeyed the pilot's instructions and strapped herself in, and they were soon streaking northwards over an ocean as serene as its name. Taryn knew how swiftly the Pacific Ocean could turn violent, but today it was rippling watered silk, agleam all the way to the horizon beneath a sky just as blue and benign.

Not that she could concentrate on it; a few moments ago Cade had finished concisely briefing her on what she'd be expected to do in Fala'isi.

She said warily, 'I assume you won't want me attending the social occasions.' He'd spoken of cruises, dinners, a cocktail party...

His brows lifted. 'I don't expect you to work for the entire time. If you don't want to attend any of the social occasions that's not a problem. You grew up in the tropics—have you ever been to Fala'isi?'

'No.' She paused, then said lightly, 'But, from what I remember, tropical islands in the Pacific have coconut palms and coconut crabs, and most of them are surrounded by lagoons of the most amazing blue on the planet. There's glorious singing, and whole families somehow manage to perch on little motor scooters.'

'Your parents were brave taking a young child so far from civilisation.'

There was no condemnation in his tone but she had to control a spurt of defensiveness. Her parents didn't need defending. 'They're experienced sailors. And they were desperately needed—still are. There are very few doctors in the outlying islands. My parents are kept busy.'

'So they settled in Aramuhu for your schooling?'

'Yes,' she said briefly.

'Where are they now?' Cade asked, his blue-grey eyes intent.

'Back in the islands,' she told him, wondering a second too late if she should have hedged, let him believe they were within reach. 'In a bigger, more easily sailed yacht that's also a mobile clinic.'

A clinic that the unexpected and very generous donation from Peter had helped to fund. When he'd received the advance for his sculpture, he'd transferred the money into her account.

Horrified, she'd wanted to return it, only to have him grin and say, 'Let me do this, darling girl—it's probably the only time I'm ever going to do anything altruistic. You bring out the best in me.'

He'd had to talk hard to persuade her, but in the end she'd accepted it. He'd been pleased when she'd shown him a photograph of the yacht...

Hastily, she glanced away to hide the tears that stung her eyes.

'Do you see them often?' Cade asked.

'No.' Something in his expression made her say crisply, 'I suppose that sounds as though I don't get on with them but I do—and I admire them tremendously for what they're doing. I think I told you I'd been overseas for two years, having a ball in London and working there to finance trips to the Continent.' She added with a smile, 'Known to all young Kiwis as the big OE—overseas experience. It's a rite of passage.'

Cade leaned back in the seat and took a swift glance at her profile. 'When did your parents go back to the

Pacific islands on their mission of mercy?' he asked, keeping his voice detached.

'Once I'd settled at university,' she said cheerfully. 'And now I've revealed some of my story, how about yours?'

Ironically amused, he met coolly challenging green-gold eyes, their size and colour emphasised by dark lashes and brows. No way was he going to tell her of his early childhood; he'd padlocked those memories and thrown away the key years ago.

Cade wondered if she realised just how much she'd revealed. *Admire* didn't mean the same as love. It sounded as though her parents had seen her through school and then more or less abandoned her.

And he was beginning to believe she didn't know that he and Peter had been brothers. If she did, she'd have been a little more wary when she'd spoken of her time in London.

He said economically, 'My life? Very standard. Good parents, good education, a university scholarship, first job in the City, then striking out on my own.'

'And then success,' she supplied with a smile.

Cade caught the hint of satire in the curve of her mouth.

Yes, she was challenging him, and not just sexually, although he was extremely aware of her in the seat beside him. His body stirred at the recollection of the silky texture of her skin and the smooth curves her bikini had displayed.

'That too,' he said non-committally. 'Does success interest you?'

She considered the question, her forehead wrinkling. To his surprise, he realised he was waiting for her answer with some expectation. Which was reasonable;

he'd hired her to remove her from her comfort zone so he could find out what sort of person she really was.

Of course, he wouldn't allow himself to be distracted—he didn't do distraction. Not even when it came as superbly packaged as Taryn Angove.

'It interests everyone, surely,' she said at last. 'But it depends on how you define it. My parents are hugely successful because they're doing exactly what they want to do, which is helping people—making a difference to their lives. Sometimes *saving* their lives.'

'So that's your definition? Success means following your passion?'

She gave him a startled look, then laughed, a sound without much humour. 'Seems to be.'

Something more than idle curiosity persuaded him to ask, 'Do you have a passion?'

He saw her withdrawal, but she answered with a rueful smile, 'Not one I've discovered yet. What's your definition of success?'

That had changed over the years, from his initial instinctive need to survive a neglectful, drug-addicted mother. He had no intention of divulging his motivations to anyone, let alone Taryn, who'd made out a list that ended in *disengage from Jason*.

The list had been on the table, as though she'd dropped it there when he'd arrived to pick her up a few hours ago. She'd gone into her bedroom to bring out her pack, and deliberately and without guilt he'd read down the items. He needed all the ammunition he could muster to remind him that her reaction to Peter's proposal had so shattered his brother he'd killed himself.

When had she added that last significant note? After they'd met yesterday?

Jason presumably had been her lover; the journalist

had certainly bristled with a territorial air when he'd been talking to her.

So she hadn't mourned Peter for long.

CHAPTER FOUR

THAT thought grated so much Cade turned his head and looked out at the sea below.

One thing the years with an erratic mother had taught him was to read people. As soon as he'd met Taryn he'd noted the subtle signs of her response to him. What he hadn't anticipated was his own reaction to her—a quick, fierce hunger he was having difficulty controlling.

But what worried him was an unexpected and alarmingly unwelcome inclination to believe every word she said. Cade was cynical rather than suspicious, but his life and career had taught him not to trust anyone until he knew them.

And that, he reminded himself, was why Taryn was sitting beside him—in order for him to gather information about her.

He said, 'I suppose my definition of my own success is to do whatever I do well. And to keep faith with the people who rely on me.'

She waited as though expecting more, then nodded, her expression thoughtful. 'Sounds good.'

And meant very little, she thought a touch sardonically. If she'd hoped to get something other than platitudes from him, she'd just learned he wasn't going to open up to her.

After all, he was now her employer. There were protocols to be observed, a suitably respectful distance to be kept. Possibly, in a subtle English way, he was indicating she'd better forget the informal, unconventional circumstances in which they'd met.

Glancing up, she met hooded steel-blue eyes, unsparing and probing. Sensation sizzled through her and she said the first thing that came to mind. 'I hope I can do the job.'

In an indifferent voice, he said, 'Having second thoughts, Taryn?'

When she shook her head he went on, 'Fala'isi is a civilised place, and all I expect from you is a week of quite straightforward work.' His voice hardened. 'Because you are beautiful there will be people who misunderstand our relationship, but I'm sure you're sophisticated enough to deal with that.'

Heat burned across her cheekbones. Cade's tone had been casually dismissive, as though in his world beauty was taken for granted.

He was far too perceptive. She'd barely recognised the caution in herself, a warning based on nothing more than her own response to him. Time to show him she could be completely professional.

'Of course I can,' she said. She added, 'And I don't suspect you of ulterior motives.'

He nodded. 'Good.' And began to talk of their destination, of the two cultures that had been so successfully integrated by the family that ruled Fala'isi, and of the vibrant economy that made the island state one of the powers in the Pacific.

Taryn listened and commented; from her parents she knew enough about island politics to appreciate the sharp intelligence of his remarks, the astute judgement and skilful manipulation of information. Not that he revealed much of his feelings; he probably felt they were none of her concern.

And he was entirely right; this inchoate desire to understand him was neither comfortable nor sensible.

But he did say, 'It's more than possible that somebody might try to pump you for information about me.'

'They'll fail,' she said promptly, 'because I don't know anything about you.'

He raised his eyebrows. 'You didn't research me on the Internet?'

'Yes, of course.' As far as she'd been able. She'd downloaded a couple of pictures of him with stunning women, and read several articles about his business tactics, but she'd found nothing personal about him. 'Just as anyone else could.'

He showed his teeth in a mirthless smile. 'I'm sure I don't need to tell you to be discreet.'

'No,' she said shortly.

'Good.' He looked up as the cabin attendant came through.

Taryn welcomed the interruption. She was probably imagining the unspoken undercurrents that swirled beneath the mundane words he'd spoken. Yes, he'd called her beautiful—but in a tone of voice that gave no indication what effect she had on him.

She wrenched her mind away from such a subversive thought. OK, so she was acutely conscious of Cade—and she now knew he liked what he saw when those hard, crystalline eyes roved her face, but she understood how little that superficial appreciation meant.

What would her parents think of the man beside her, at present intent on a sheaf of notes?

Her gaze traced the arrogant lines and angles of his

profile, the olive skin and arrogantly perfect line of mouth and chin...

Physically, he was magnificent. And after searching the Internet the previous evening she knew he was renowned for his ferociously brilliant mind and what one commentator called his *iron-bound integrity*. Another had commented on his almost *devilish good luck*.

What were his parents like? She'd found a reference to his *climb from the stifling mediocrity of middle-class England* but nothing else personal.

Unless you counted the photographs of him with exquisite women. At the thought of those women—bejewelled, superbly groomed, confident—a foolish pang of envy darkened her mood.

He looked up and for a moment their eyes locked. Her confusion turned into a flash of fire at the base of her spine, in the pit of her stomach.

It was quickly dampened by his drawled question. 'Something bothering you?'

'No,' she said swiftly and not, he suspected, entirely truthfully.

He was convinced of it when she added, 'I was wondering if you have a Mediterranean heritage.'

Cade shrugged negligently. 'Not that I'm aware of.'

He didn't know who his birth father was—it could have been anyone. His real father, the one who'd loved him and disciplined him and shown him how to be a man, was ruddy of complexion and blue-eyed, but Harold Cooper had handed on far more important things than superficial physical features.

Cade had no illusions as to what his life would have been if he hadn't been fostered by the Coopers.

He'd have grown up on the streets and probably ended up in jail, possibly dying young like his wretched mother before him. Instead, he'd been loved and cared for, given rules to live by, taught everything he needed to make a success of his life.

Even when his new parents had had their miracle— the child they'd been told would never eventuate—their love for Cade had never faltered. Peter had been a joy to them all, a beloved small brother for Cade to protect and help.

He owed the Coopers everything but the fact of being born—and he was prepared to do anything to give his mother the closure she craved.

Why had Peter chosen to end his life? It had to be something to do with Taryn.

Cade was accustomed to finding answers, and he needed this answer more than any other. His mother feared that Peter had died because he hadn't felt valued by his parents.

The Coopers had certainly been worried about Peter's choice of career, but he had real artistic talent and, once they'd realised he was determined to make his own path, they'd stopped suggesting he choose something steady and reliable.

One way or another, Cade would get to the truth. It shouldn't take him long to discover Taryn's weaknesses and use them to find out what he needed to know.

He glanced across; she'd picked up a magazine and was skimming the pages, stopping now and then to read more carefully. She was beautiful in a healthy, girl-next-door kind of way, her clear green-gold eyes seeming to hide no secrets; her attitude was candid and direct. Cade could see nothing in her to suggest she'd mock a man's offer of love.

Yet she must have cut Peter's confidence to shreds for him to choose death rather than face life without her.

Into Cade's mind came that final note on the list she'd made out: *disengage from Jason*.

Had she *disengaged* from Peter too, then gone on to view the world with that same innocent gaze?

It would be interesting, he thought grimly, to see Taryn's reaction when she found out the accommodation waiting for them on Fala'isi. She knew he was rich; she'd sensed he was attracted to her.

How would she accept sharing the same luxurious beachfront lodgings with him?

Would she see it as an opportunity? With cold self-derision, he fought the kick of desire in his groin and forced his attention back to the papers in his hand.

Taryn looked around the room, furnished in tropical style with lush green plants cooling the flower-scented air. One wall was highlighted by a magnificent *tapa* cloth in shades of tan and cream, black and cinnamon, and in a corner a serene, smoothly sculpted figure of a frigate bird in flight seemed to hover above its pedestal.

Peter would have loved it...

The knot of apprehension in her stomach loosened when Cade said, 'Choose whichever bedroom you'd like.'

Helpfully, the porter said, 'That room over there has a very beautiful view of the lagoon, madam, and the one on the other side of the *fale* has a lovely intimate view of the pool and the terrace garden.'

She looked at Cade.

Shrugging, he said in a tone that edged on curtness, 'I don't mind where I sleep.'

Taryn responded equally crisply, 'In that case, I'll take the one with the pool view.'

The porter, tall and magisterial, smiled his approval as he scooped her very downmarket pack from the trolley and headed towards the bedroom.

Shoulders held stiffly, Taryn followed him. She'd not expected to be whisked by luxury launch from the airport on the main island of Fala'isi to a fairy tale atoll twenty minutes offshore, nor to be ushered into a beachfront bungalow she was expected to share with Cade Peredur.

That was when she'd faltered, only to feel foolish when Cade said, 'There are two bedrooms.'

'Each with its own bathroom, madam,' the porter had supplied in a reassuring voice that made her even more self-conscious.

OK, so for a moment—but only a moment—she *had* wondered if she'd walked into a situation she didn't even want to think about. But there was no need for the glint of satirical amusement in Cade's hard eyes. She was not an overwrought idiot, seeing danger where there was none!

After a quick survey of the room she'd chosen, she smiled at the porter when he set her pack tenderly onto the luggage rack.

'Thank you, this is perfect,' she said.

'The lagoon is excellent to swim in, madam,' the porter told her before ushering her into the bathroom, where he demonstrated the switches that lowered the blinds and showed her how to work the multitude of jets in the shower.

The bathroom was circular, its walls built of rock topped by a glass ceiling that allowed a view of palm fronds against a sky of such intense blue it made her blink.

The porter noted the direction of her gaze. 'The rocks

are from the main island—from a lava flow of ancient times.'

His warmth and innate dignity brought back child-hood memories and lifted her heart. If it weren't for her unusual response to the man in the next room, she'd relish this return to the tropics.

But without Cade Peredur she wouldn't be here.

She did her best to repress an excitement she hadn't allowed herself to feel for years—since the debacle of her engagement to Antony. Since then, any time she'd felt an emotional rapport, she'd reminded herself that men wanted more than affection. For them—for most people—love included passion.

She'd been utterly convinced she loved Antony, and just as certain that the stirrings of sexual attraction would progress to desire.

Her mouth twisting into a painful grimace, she turned and walked back into the bedroom, thanking the porter as he left.

She'd been so wrong. Making love with Antony had been a disaster. Try as hard as she could, she'd been unable to respond. In the end, her frigidity had caused their love to wither and die in pain and bitter acrimony.

Which was why she'd been so relieved when Peter had shown no signs of wanting anything more than friendship...

And dwelling on a past she couldn't change was fruit-less and energy-sapping.

Although this exclusive, secluded retreat had prob-ably been built with extremely wealthy honeymooners in mind, this was a business situation. If she kept that in mind and stayed utterly, coolly professional, she'd enjoy her stay in Fala'isi.

She allowed herself a single wistful glance at the aquamarine pool before unpacking her meagre allowance of clothes and indulging in a quick refreshing shower. For a few seconds she dithered, trying to decide on the most suitable garment.

Which was silly. As part of the office furniture, no one would notice what she wore. Firming her mouth, she slipped on a pair of cool, floaty trousers and a soft green shirt, combed her hair into a smooth cap and tied it back, then re-applied her only lipstick and after a deep breath walked back into the big, airy living room.

Her treacherous heart bumped at the sight of Cade, tall and dark in casual clothes, standing on the terrace. He turned before she'd taken more than a couple of steps into the room and watched her come through the huge glass doors to join him.

That cool scrutiny set every nerve twanging with eager, anticipatory, thoroughly scary awareness.

'Everything all right?' he asked.

'Absolutely.' She tore her gaze away to examine the surroundings. 'Whoever set this place up certainly homed into the romantic ambience of the South Seas.'

Palms shaded the bamboo furniture, luxuriously upholstered in white. Impressive boulders—probably also relics of the fiery creation of the main island—skilfully contrasted with vast earthenware pots holding lushly foliaged shrubs and, a few steps away, thick white rope provided the hand-rail in the shimmering pool. Bold, brilliant flowers danced in the sun, their colours clashing with a sensuous bravura Taryn envied.

'The Chapmans—the family who rule Fala'isi—are famous for their acumen and their commitment to excellence,' Cade said coolly. 'They know what people expect from a place like this.'

'They're also noted for steering Fala'isi so well the islanders now have the highest standard of living in the Pacific Islands. And that,' Taryn finished, 'is much more important.'

He gave another of those piercing looks, as though she'd startled him, and then to her surprise he nodded. 'I agree.'

So he wasn't as cynical and arrogant as she'd suspected.

He resumed, 'We'll eat lunch here, and then I have some facts I'd like you to check and validate while I attend a preliminary meeting. It shouldn't take much more than an hour, so once you've finished I suggest you do some exploring, swim if you want to.'

'On my own?' she couldn't help saying.

His short laugh acknowledged the hit. 'It would be extremely bad for business to allow anyone to drown here.'

'Does that mean there's always someone keeping watch?'

'Discreetly,' he said, a sardonic note sharpening the word. He surveyed her face and said with the perception she was beginning to expect from him, 'You don't like that.'

'Not particularly.'

He didn't say *Get used to it*, but that was probably what he was thinking. Thankful she didn't live in his world, she added, 'But that won't stop me swimming.'

And wished she'd stayed silent when she recognised a note of defiance in her tone.

'Somehow I didn't expect it to. You seem to live life on your own terms.'

For some reason, his comment startled her. 'Doesn't everyone?'

'You're remarkably innocent if you believe that,' he said cynically. 'Most people meekly follow society's dictates all their life. They buy what they're told to buy, live where they're told to live, in some societies even marry whoever they're told to marry. You appear to be a free spirit.'

'I don't think there's any such thing as true freedom,' she said slowly, then stopped.

She did not want to open herself up to Cade Peredur. It would be safer to establish boundaries, a definite distance between them, because instinct told her that even this sort of fragile, getting-to-know-you exploration could be dangerous.

There's that word again...

She laughed and finished brightly, 'And I've never thought of myself as a free spirit. It sounds great fun.'

And braced herself for another sceptical Peredur scrutiny.

Instead, he picked up a sheaf of papers. 'Around five I might have notes for you to transcribe—not many, as this afternoon's meeting is a procedural one. At seven we'll head off to pre-dinner drinks, and dinner will be at eight.'

Startled, she stared at him. 'What do you mean—*we*? You told me I wouldn't be expected to go to any of the social occasions.'

'That was because I hadn't realised most of the men were bringing their wives and significant others.' He stemmed her impetuous protest with an upheld hand. 'Don't bother pointing out that you're neither. I've just been down that road with Fleur Chapman, the wife of the man who's convened this conference. She wouldn't hear of you being left out.'

Colour stung her cheekbones. Of course he would

have objected; social occasions were not in this job description. 'I'm here as your researcher, not to attend parties.'

He responded just as crisply, 'Mrs Chapman has heard of your parents' work, and can see no reason why you shouldn't attend. In fact, she was appalled to think of you staying hidden in the *fale* like a shameful secret, as she put it.'

Dismayed, Taryn stared at him. He—and Mrs Chapman—had cut the ground from under her feet, and she suspected he knew it. Possibly he resented being forced to take her with him.

No more than she did, but the Chapman family had ruled Fala'isi for a couple of centuries, not only were they extremely rich, they were a powerful force in the Pacific where their descent from the ancient chiefly family of Fala'isi gave them huge prestige.

If the Chapmans were interested in her parents' work, she thought suddenly, there was a chance they might be prepared to help. With so many worthwhile calls on charity spending, her mother and father scrabbled for enough money to keep their clinics going.

This was possibly something she could do for her parents.

But she made one further effort. 'I haven't brought any suitable clothes.'

Dispassionately, Cade said, 'Naturally I'll organise that.' Overriding her instant horrified objection, he went on, 'The manageress of the boutique here will be along about three to discuss what you'll need.'

'I can't let you pay for my clothes,' she blurted.

One straight black brow lifted. 'You can't stop me,' he observed with cool amusement. 'Whether or not you wear them is entirely up to you.'

The prospect of appearing in public with him—in clothes he had paid for—sent prickles of apprehension across her skin. There would be sideways glances and assumptions, some of them almost certainly salacious, and the sort of gossip she despised.

Apparently he could read her mind, because he startled her anew by saying in a hard voice, 'If anyone—anyone at all—says anything untoward, I'll deal with it.'

Of course he wasn't being protective, she thought, alarmed by the swift rush of warmth his words caused. She quelled it by telling herself that he wouldn't want them to be connected in any way.

Office girl and tycoon? Not with the lovely Lady Someone in his life.

Stoutly, she responded, 'I'm quite capable of looking after myself, thank you.'

Anyway, she doubted if anyone would mistake her for Cade's latest lover; no matter what she wore, she couldn't achieve that elegant, exclusive, expensive look.

'I've noticed,' he said dryly, 'but in this case you won't need to.'

When she looked up he was smiling. Her heart flipped, honing her awareness into something so keen and compelling she felt it in her bones. Tension pulled through her, strong as a steel hawser, and it took all her will not to take a step towards him.

She managed to resist, but couldn't conquer the reckless impulse to smile back at him, although her voice was uneven when she said, 'How often does someone tell you you're a very dictatorial man?'

Involuntarily, Cade responded to her smile; it was pure challenge backed by a hint of invitation, and he guessed she was trying to force a reaction from him, judge for herself why he'd brought her here.

It took an exercise of will to clear the urgent hunger that fogged his brain.

OK, he wanted her—but, much more than that, he wanted what she knew. Instead of confronting her directly about Peter's death, he'd decided on a more subtle approach—one that did *not* involve acting on this elemental attraction, as unwanted as it was powerful.

However, he couldn't stop himself from saying, 'Calling me dictatorial makes me sound like some blood-thirsty despot intent on holding on to power by any means, no matter how cruel. How often does someone tell you you're beautiful and ask you why you're still unattached?'

Her eyes widened, then were veiled by thick, dark lashes. 'Rarely,' she said curtly. 'And usually it's as a sleazy pick-up line from a man I wouldn't be seen dead with.'

'Touché.' OK, so he'd been blunt, but what the hell had caused the frozen shock he'd seen for a millisecond before her expression had closed him out?

Something shattering. Peter's suicide? Possibly.

Damn, he thought, as sounds from outside heralded the arrival of waiters with lunch. *Damn and double damn*. Their inopportune arrival might have cut off a chance to introduce the subject.

He was going to have to, sooner or later, yet he found himself intensely disinclined to raise the matter. And that was a worry.

'Ah, here's lunch,' he said, his voice as clipped and curt as he could make it.

It was impossible to tell what she was thinking, but she responded calmly, 'Good, I'm hungry. And I'm really looking forward to diving into the lagoon. It's too long since I swam in really warm water.'

Into his head flashed a tantalising image of her in her bikini, all slender limbs and silken skin, a gleaming, golden nymph from one of the raunchier legends.

Angered by the violent involuntary response from his body, Cade headed for his own room, but stopped at the door to say over his shoulder, 'When you do swim, make sure you use sunscreen.'

'Yes, sir,' she responded smartly. 'New Zealand spends summer under a huge hole in the ozone layer, and wearing hats and slapping on sunscreen at frequent intervals has become part of our national character.'

Cade had to hide a smile. Over lunch, served on the terrace, he asked her about her childhood and, although she spoke readily enough about that, she was surprisingly reticent about other aspects of her life. He already knew she'd been engaged once, but when he'd provided her with an opportunity to mention it, she hadn't.

Which proved nothing, he thought, irritated by a potent mixture of feelings—the sensual hunger somehow magnified by a growing protectiveness. Clearly she didn't feel her parents had abandoned her. In fact, she'd snapped at the bait he'd dangled in front of her by mentioning that Fleur Chapman might be able to help them in their mission of mercy.

So the fact that they'd more or less left her to her own devices once she'd left secondary school didn't seem to concern her. He felt an odd sympathy, remembering his own parents' sacrifices—the money saved for a trip to France, the gap year they'd insisted on financing...

During the afternoon meeting he found it surprisingly hard to concentrate; his mind kept slipping back to the smooth fall of Taryn's hair, turned by the sun into a flood of burnished copper, the way her crisp voice was softened by an intriguing husky undertone, her open pleasure in the food.

And that, he thought grimly as he headed back to their *fale*, was something new; no other woman had come between him and work. He'd liked his lovers, enjoyed spending time with them—even Louisa, before she'd decided to change the rules of their relationship. But his previous women had only occupied a small niche in his life.

Taryn Angove was different. How different? He searched for a word to describe her, and could only come up with fresh—*fresh* and apparently frank, intensely seductive.

Had Peter too thought she was different?

Cade welcomed the acid bite of that thought; it dragged his mind back to focus. He couldn't afford to let his hormones overpower his brain cells.

A call on his cell phone interrupted him; he stopped beneath a large spreading tree with brazen scarlet flowers and spoke to the private detective who'd been investigating Taryn.

When the call was over he pocketed the cell phone and punched one hand into the palm of his other. Beneath his breath, he said explosively, 'Why the hell did you have to do it, Peter? Why didn't you just laugh straight back in her face and find a woman who could love you? Why take the coward's way out?'

The bitter words shocked him into silence. He lifted his gaze to the sea, but saw Taryn walking across the sand towards the *fale*, the *pareu* slung across her hips emphasising their seductive sway. Water turned her hair into gleaming copper and gilded her skin so that she seemed to walk in a golden, shimmering aura. She was even more alluring than the images his brain had been conjuring all afternoon.

Heated desire gripped him so fiercely he had to turn away. It would be no hardship to seduce her, he thought grimly, no hardship at all.

Yet he could not. Dared not. Never before had hunger fogged his brain, whispering a temptation he wanted to yield to.

CHAPTER FIVE

CADE dragged his gaze away from Taryn, trying to clear his mind by fixing his attention on the hibiscus bush a few feet away. The fiercely magenta heart of each flower glowed in a silken gold ruff, hues so intense he was reminded of the time he'd visited an official mint and watched molten gold being poured.

Taryn had a quick, astute brain and plenty of character, so she was unlikely to be drifting without purpose. Yet since she'd got back from England her only job had been selling souvenirs to summer tourists, and she certainly didn't seem to be in a hurry to find more work.

He found himself strongly resisting what should have been the obvious reason. If she had most of Peter's advance in her bank account, she wouldn't need to worry about working for some years.

Everything pointed to her being the one who'd accepted—or stolen—the money from his brother. There was no proof, yet no other person had been close enough to Peter to make it seem likely he'd have given them money. If he'd showered her with it, only to have his proposal turned down with mockery and laughter, then that could have been a reason for Peter's tragic decision.

And she hadn't mentioned Peter. Or shown any signs of grief.

An innate sense of justice forced him to admit he didn't expect her to break into sobs every half hour. That wouldn't be her style.

Nor his, yet he grieved deeply for his brother.

So, was she as good as he was at hiding her feelings—or did she have none? His eyes narrowing, he watched her stop at the outdoor shower set under a big poinciana tree. She tossed the length of fabric around her hips over a shrub, turned on the tap and lifted her face to let the water flow over her.

The bikini was decorous enough but, moulded against the clean curves of her body by the veil of water, she might as well have been naked.

Was this a deliberate pose, letting him see what she had on offer?

Lust tugged urgently at him, swamping his cold calculation with a hot, angry hunger. Abruptly, he turned away, overcome with self-disgust. He couldn't let himself become too fixated on her. He'd always been in charge of his physical reactions; it was humiliating to want a woman who might be everything he despised.

He had to persuade her to open up so he could better judge whether to trust her version of what had happened. He needed to see for himself what she'd felt—if anything—for his brother.

Mouth set in a firm line, he headed down the shell path to the *fale*.

Taryn almost hummed with pleasure beneath the shower, but water was likely to be precious on a coral atoll, so she turned off the tap and wrapped her *pareu* around her again to mop up.

She was so glad to be back in the tropics. Stroking through the silken waters of the lagoon, she'd felt a surge of something very close to renewal. Oh, the warm sea against her skin, the sand shimmering white against the green bushes beneath the coconut palms—they all had something to do with it but, although the sun beat down with a languorous intensity only known in the tropics, her raised spirits were caused by something deeper than delight at being back, a feeling much stronger, much more intimate than a sensory lift, welcome though that was.

It was strangely like a rebirth, an understanding that life could be worthwhile again.

And it had *nothing*—not a thing—to do with being here with Cade, whose controlled dynamism was a force to be reckoned with. Perhaps she'd finally accepted that she'd never know why Peter had changed so abruptly from a best friend to a would-be husband...

Or whether her shocked refusal had led to his suicide.

Her bitter remorse at her stunned response would always be with her. But from somewhere she'd found a renewed sensation of confidence, of control of her own destiny.

Once she got back to New Zealand she'd find a job—move to Auckland if it was necessary—and start this next stage of her life.

There was no sign of Cade when she reached their accommodation. Squelching a stupid disappointment she walked through the glass doors into her bedroom, bare feet warm against the cool smooth tiles on the floor.

Perhaps she could put her skills as a librarian to use in some tropical area?

She smiled ironically. If she managed to find such a position she wouldn't be living in a place like this, subtly groomed and organised to give rich, demanding clients the illusion of paradise.

Strange that here, in a spot dedicated to a romantic idea of leisure and sensuous relaxation, she should feel a resurgence of the energy she'd lost when Peter died.

She was dressed and combing her wet hair back from her face when movement caught her eye. Swivelling, she realised that Cade had walked to the edge of the terrace and was bending to pick a hibiscus flower.

For some peculiar reason, her heart lurched at the sight of his long fingers stroking the ruffled, satiny petals—only to freeze a moment later when a casual, dismissive flick of his fingers sent the exquisite bloom onto the ground.

It shouldn't have affected her so strongly. Yet she almost gasped with shock, and took an instinctive step sideways to hide from sight.

After a few seconds she told herself she was being ridiculous. She forced herself to breathe again and glanced sideways into an empty garden. Her heartbeat settling into its usual steady rhythm, she scolded herself for being so foolishly sensitive. Nothing had happened. He'd merely picked a flower and tossed it away.

Later, when she emerged from her room, Cade was standing just outside the glass doors with his back to her. He had to have excellent hearing because, although she moved quietly, he turned the moment she came into the big, cool living room.

Their eyes met, and another little chill ran the length of her spine until he smiled. 'Enjoy your swim?' he asked.

'It was lovely,' she said, oddly disconcerted. Had he seen her walk up from the beach? She repressed a sensuous little shiver. She'd been perfectly decent with her *pareu* draped around her—and he was probably bored by the sight of women parading around in bikinis.

'How did you find the computer set-up?'

She blinked, then hastily reassembled her wits. 'Oh, excellent. No problems.'

He nodded. Now, he thought stringently—give her that opportunity now. Yet it took all his notorious drive to say casually, 'Your computer skills would have come in handy when you were in London.'

Taryn smiled. 'Not at first. I worked in a coffee shop, until a friend found me a job cataloguing a library, which was perfect. I could dash over the Channel or around the country whenever I wanted, providing I got the work done.'

'A very good friend,' Cade observed. 'One who knew you well.'

'Yes, a good friend indeed,' she said tonelessly.

Cade sent a keen glance, but could read nothing from her smooth face. He let the silence drag on but all she did was nod.

Cade held out a sheaf of notes. 'I'd like you to get these down now.'

Heart thudding, Taryn took the notes and escaped into her room. It was a relief to sit down at the desk and concentrate on the swift, bold handwriting, and an even greater relief when he left to meet someone.

When she'd finished getting his clear, concise notes into the computer and backed them up, she closed things down and stood up. Cade had just returned and the sun was heading towards the horizon. It would seem to fall more quickly as it got closer to the clear, straight line where sea met sky, and there might be a mysterious green flash the instant it slipped over the horizon. She'd seen it a couple of times, and looked forward to seeing it again.

She picked up the printed copy and walked into the

sitting room. Cade got up from the sofa where he'd been reading the work she'd collated after lunch.

After a quick perusal of the copy, he said, 'This is exactly what I need, thank you.' He glanced at his watch. 'You have half an hour to get into whatever you're wearing to cocktails and dinner.'

When she frowned, he said smoothly, 'I assume you've chosen something suitable to wear.'

Under the boutique manager's interested survey she'd chosen something, but whether it was suitable or not time would tell. Impulsively, she said, 'It still seems too much like gatecrashing for me to feel comfortable about going.'

'We've already had this conversation. You've been personally invited.' His mouth curled up at the corners. 'Of course, if you met someone on the beach you'd like to further your acquaintance with—'

'No,' she interrupted, startled.

'Then what's your problem?'

Taryn hesitated. Impossible to tell him that for some reason she hated the thought of being tagged as just another of his women, a holiday convenience.

But his cool, speculative gaze demanded an answer. Gathering her wits, she snapped, 'I'm your researcher, not arm candy.'

His smile stopped any further words, a smile that, allied to such a powerful presence, made him a walking, breathing, potently dangerous adrenalin rush.

'Candy is sweet. Your tongue is far too sharp for you to be considered anything like that.' He took her hand. 'If you don't get going we'll be late.'

It was like brushing against an electric fence, she thought wildly. Breathing was impossible. Dumbfounded by the wildfire intensity of her reaction to his touch, she let him turn her towards her room.

'Off you go,' he said calmly, and started her off with a movement so gentle it could hardly be called a push.

Taryn's body responded automatically and she got halfway to her room before her dazzled brain came to life. How dared he? Frowning, she swung around and, in her most forthright voice, said, 'I'm not a child to be told to go to my room. And please don't ever push me like that again.'

His brows climbed. 'I'm sorry,' he said unexpectedly, adding abruptly, 'And you don't need to be afraid of me. I don't hurt women.'

The words burst out before she could stop them. 'I'm not afraid of you!'

Cool it! She was overreacting, giving too much away, allowing him to see how strongly he affected her. After a jagged breath, she said crossly, 'I just hate it when people stop a perfectly good rant by apologising.'

That spellbinding smile made a brief reappearance. 'I take your point, but you haven't time for a really good rant right now. Later, you can let go all you like.'

An equivocal note in his voice dried her throat. She could read nothing in the starkly handsome face, and surely he wasn't hinting...

He resumed, 'You flinched when I touched you.'

Wishing she'd ignored it, she said, 'Not because I was afraid. I just wasn't expecting it. And, although I'm delighted you don't hurt women, how are you with children and animals?'

He subjected her to a look she could barely parry. Silkily, he said, 'Superb.' She was choking back laughter when he added, 'And, to reassure you, from now on I'll only touch you after asking permission.'

His smile, and the glinting look that accompanied it, stopped her breath again. He *was* flirting with her!

Common sense warned her she was way out of her league—but there was no reason to let him know that.

Rallying, she said, 'So you'll say, "Taryn, I want to push you out of the way of that shark. Is that all right?" And then wait for my answer?'

'If that happens, I might force myself to ignore this conversation,' he said smoothly.

A note in his voice produced a swift wave of heat across her cheekbones. This was dangerous stuff. Put an end to it right now, she commanded herself.

But how?

OK, she'd pretend to take him seriously, as though his eyes weren't gleaming with amusement and her blood wasn't pumping a suspicious and inconvenient excitement through her veins.

In her most prosaic tone, she said, 'Well, that's all right then.' She glanced at her watch as if checking the time. 'And if I'm to be ready on time I'd better get going.'

And managed to force her suddenly heavy legs to move away from him. *Cold shower* was her first thought once she reached the sanctuary of her room.

Icy water would have been good, but she had to content herself with a brisk splash in the lukewarm water available. However, by the time she'd knotted a sleek *pareu* that fell from her bare shoulders to her ankles in a smooth column of gold, her pulse had calmed down—almost.

After a careful examination in the mirror, she gave a short nod of satisfaction. The inexpensive *pareu* looked almost as good as the designer clothes the shop manageress had brought to show her. Her own slim gold sandals made no concession to her height; she could wear ten-centimetre heels and still be shorter then Cade.

Exactly twenty-five minutes after she'd left, she walked back into the sitting room, to meet a narrow-eyed glance from Cade that sent her pulse rate soaring again. In tropical evening clothes, he was *stunning*, she decided faintly, trying to control the overheated reactions ricocheting through her.

His quizzical expression made her realise she was staring a little too openly. Without censoring the thought, she said, 'I hope this is suitable.'

'I'm not an expert on women's clothes,' he said, his level voice mocking her turmoil, 'but no man in the place is going to think it other than perfect.'

She pulled a face. 'It's not the men I'm worried about.'

Hard mouth easing into an oblique smile, he said, 'The women will be envious. You look fine.' A little impatiently, he finished, 'Let's go.'

Nerves tightened in the pit of her stomach as they walked down a shell path beneath the coconut palms to the venue for the cocktail party, a wide terrace open to the sea and the sunset.

Taryn's swift glance told her that every other woman there was clad in designer resort wear, the sort of clothes featured in very upmarket magazines as ideal for the captain's cocktail party.

And, judging by the massed array of jewels sparkling in the light of the westering sun, she was the only employee. Worse, a man who turned to watch them walk in smiled sardonically and said something in a low voice to his companion, an elegant blonde who moved so she could see them both clearly.

Taryn gave them a coolly dismissive glance, tensing when Cade slid a firm hand beneath her elbow.

'Ignore them,' he said in a low, inflexible voice, looking over her at the couple.

Taryn didn't see his expression, but the glance he sent towards them must have been truly intimidating. Their rapid about-face almost amused her, and helped to ease her chagrin.

He commanded, 'Relax.'

Ignoring the rush of heat to her cheeks, she blurted the first thing that came to mind. 'You were going to ask before you touched me again.'

'I did make an exception for sharks,' he said soberly.

She spluttered, then laughed, and he released her. Feeling an abrupt chill, almost as though she'd been abandoned, she took a quick look around, turning as a handsome couple came up to them, their hosts Luke and Fleur Chapman.

After introducing them, Cade said, 'Luke's family are rather like feudal overlords here.' Then he added, 'But you know this, of course. As well as their strong New Zealand connection, your parents keep you up-to-date with Pacific affairs.'

Taryn said cheerfully, 'Ever since a Kiwi married Luke's father we've considered the Chapmans of Fala'isi to be honorary New Zealanders.' She gave a comradely grin to Fleur Chapman. 'And of course our newspapers and every women's magazine had a field day when another Kiwi married Luke.'

Both their hosts laughed, but Fleur said thankfully, 'They seem to have lost interest in us now we've settled into being a boringly married couple.'

The glance she exchanged with her husband made

Taryn catch her breath and feel a sudden pang of something too close to envy. Nothing *boring* in that marriage, she thought.

What would it be like to have such complete trust in the person you loved?

Fleur turned back to Taryn. 'And we've heard of the wonderful work your parents do. Later, when we have time, we must talk more about it.'

Their warmth and friendliness set the tone of the evening. Her tension evaporated, and with Cade at her side she felt oddly protected—and that, she realised, was both ridiculous and more than a little ominous.

About the last thing she needed was a man's protection; she'd been looking after herself quite adequately since she left secondary school.

As she smiled and chatted with people she'd previously seen only on the news, she observed their reactions to Cade. Intrigued, she saw that respect for his formidable achievements was very much to the fore, mixed with a certain wariness.

If anyone else was speculating on the relationship between Cade and her, it didn't show. Most of the women noted her clothes, and an observant few even recognised her *pareu* to be a cheap beach wrap from the boutique.

Only one mentioned it, a charming middle-aged Frenchwoman who said, 'My dear, how clever of you! You put us all to shame with sheer powerful simplicity!'

The unexpected compliment brought a flush to Taryn's skin, making Madame Murat laugh as she turned to Cade. 'I hope you appreciate her.'

Cade's eyes narrowed slightly, but he favoured her with a smile. 'I do indeed,' he said blandly.

Which left Taryn wondering why she felt as though she'd been observing to some covert skirmish.

'I think our hostess is indicating it's time for dinner,' Cade observed.

Obediently, she turned, only to stop in mid-step. 'Oh,' she breathed. 'Oh, *look*.'

With the suddenness of the tropics, the sun vanished below the horizon in a glory of gold and crimson, allowing the darkness that swept across the sea to make landing in a breath of warm air. Torches around the terrace flared into life, their flames wavering gently in the gardenia-scented breeze, and from the distant reef came the muted thunder of eternal waves meeting the solid coral bulwark that protected the lagoon.

'Sometimes there's a green flash,' she said quietly, eyes still fixed on the horizon.

For the first time since Peter's death, Taryn felt a pang of joy, a moment of such pure piercing delight she shivered.

'Are you cold?' Cade murmured. 'Do you need a wrap?'

Taryn couldn't tell him what had happened. Not only was the exaltation too intimate, but in a subversive way Cade's presence had contributed to it, making him important to her in a way beyond the solely physical.

And that was scary. Magnetic and disturbing, yet underpinned by a solidity she found enormously sustaining, Cade was getting too close.

'I'm not cold,' she told him with a return to her usual crispness, 'but somehow I got the idea that the cocktail party and the dinner were two separate events. I'd planned to collect a wrap from the *fale* to wear to dinner.'

'My mistake,' he said blandly. He nodded at a waiter,

who came across immediately. Cade said, 'Describe the wrap.'

'It's draped over the end of my bed,' she said, touched by his thoughtfulness. 'A darker gold than this—bronze, really—with a little bit of beadwork around the sleeves.' And when the man had moved off she said, 'Thank you.'

He nodded, but didn't answer as they walked through a door onto another terrace. A long table was arranged exquisitely, candle flames gleaming against silver and crystal and lingering on pale frangipani flowers and greenery.

Foolish resentment gripped Taryn at the sideways glances Cade was receiving from a very beautiful woman in a slinky black sheath that played up her fragile blonde beauty.

Grow up, she told herself. This was ridiculous; she had absolutely no claim on him. OK, so she felt good. That showed she was getting over the shock of Peter's death. Beyond standing beside her at a sensitive moment, Cade had nothing to do with it.

Nothing at all.

CHAPTER SIX

WHEN Cade took her arm again, Taryn was rather proud of the way she managed to restrain her wildfire response to that casual touch. Too proud, because he sensed it. Fortunately, he put it down to nervousness.

'Relax,' he advised crisply. 'These are just people—good, bad or dull. Often all three at different times.' Without pausing, he went on, 'I asked Fleur to seat us side by side so that you wouldn't have two total strangers to talk to.'

In other words, he thought she was a total social novice. Well, when it came to occasions of this rarefied nature, she *was*, she thought ruefully.

He guessed her reaction. 'Normally, I'm sure you're able to hold your own,' he told her.

'How do you do that?' she asked impulsively.

He knew what she meant. *How do you read my mind?*

After a long considering look that curled her toes, he smiled. 'You have a very expressive face.'

Whereas he'd elevated a poker face to an art form.

Before she could answer, he went on, 'I thought you might be jet-lagged.'

'I don't think so, thank you.' Then she tensed again as his lashes drooped. Her breath locked in her throat.

She swallowed and added a little too late, 'But it was kind of you.'

His hooded gaze matched his sardonic tone. 'I try.'

The odd little exchange left her with stretched nerves. Fortunately, the waiter arrived with her wrap and handed it to Cade, who held it out for her. She slid her arms into it and wondered if the brush of his fingers against her bare skin was deliberate or an accident.

Whatever, it sent sensuous little thrills through her as she sat down.

She turned to greet her neighbour, a pleasant middle-aged man from Indonesia. Cade's other dinner partner was the blonde woman with the come-hither gaze and, to Taryn's secret—and embarrassing—irritation, she made an immediate play for the attention he seemed quite happy to give her.

Cattily, Taryn decided that if the woman had anything on beneath the clinging black sheath it would have to be made of gossamer. Her moment of delight evaporated and the evening stretched before her like a punishment.

Several hours later, she heaved a silent sigh of relief when the evening came to an end. Goodbyes and thanks were said and, perhaps emboldened by excellent champagne, the woman in the clinging sheath flung her arms around Cade's neck and kissed him. Although he didn't reject her, he turned his cheek so that her lips barely skimmed it and then, in a gesture that seemed to be steadying, held her away from him.

Not a bit embarrassed, she gazed into his eyes and said huskily, 'I'll look forward to talking to you about that proposition tomorrow.'

Taryn struggled to control her shock and the concentrated venom that cut through her. Jealousy was a despicable emotion—one she had no right to feel.

Nevertheless, she had to tighten her lips to keep back an acid comment when she and Cade were walking away.

Coconuts lined the white shell path, their fronds whispering softly above them in the slow, warm breeze. Taryn struggled to ignore the drowsy, scented ambience that had so seduced the original European explorers they'd thought the Pacific islands the next best place to paradise.

Desperate to break a silence that seemed too charged, she said, 'I once read that human life in the islands would have been impossible without coconuts.'

'When you say *the islands*, you mean the Pacific Islands?' Cade queried.

'Well, yes.' Good, a nice safe subject to settle the seething turmoil inside her.

Somehow, seeing another woman kiss Cade had let loose something primitive and urgent in her—a female possessiveness that sliced through the restraint she'd deliberately imposed on herself after the violent end of her engagement.

It needed to be controlled—and fast. After swallowing to ease her dry throat, she said sedately, 'It's convenient shorthand for New Zealanders when we refer to the Polynesian islands.'

'So are coconut palms native to this region?'

Judging by his cool, dry tone, Cade wasn't aware of her feelings. Thank heavens.

'Possibly.' Yes, her voice sounded good—level, a little schoolmistressy. 'No one seems to know where they originated because they populated the tropics on this side of the world well before any humans arrived here. The nuts can germinate and grow after floating for years and thousands of miles.'

When he didn't reply, she looked up in time to see something dark and fast hurtling down towards her. She gave a choked cry and ducked, stumbling as a vigorous push on her shoulder sent her lurching sideways into the slender trunk of the nearest palm.

She grabbed it and clung. Cade too had avoided whatever it was and as she sagged he pulled her upright, supporting her in a hard, close embrace.

Heart thumping, stunned by the speed of his response, she asked in a muted, raw voice, 'I think...was it a fruit bat?'

He was silent for a few tense seconds. 'It certainly didn't hit the ground, so it was flying.'

'That's what it would be, then.' Her tone wobbled—affected by a wild onrush of adrenalin, she thought feverishly.

And by Cade's warmth, the disturbing masculine power that locked her in his arms...

No!

Yet she didn't move. 'I'd forgotten about them,' she babbled. 'They don't attack, of course—they just scare the wits out of people who aren't used to them.'

She had to fight the flagrant temptation to bury her face in his shoulder and soak up some of the formidable strength and composure from his lean, powerfully muscled body.

Lean, powerfully muscled—and *aroused* body...

As if reacting to the heat that burned through her, he relaxed his grip a little and looked down.

Taryn's mouth dried and her pulse echoed in her head, drowning out any coherent thought. Sensation ran riot along insistent, pleading nerves.

Mutely, she met the probing lance of his scrutiny, her lashes drooping as the shifting glamour of moonlight played across the angles and planes of his face, so rigid it resembled a mask.

Except for that glittering gaze fixed on her lips.

As though the words were torn from him, Cade said roughly, 'Damn. This is too soon.'

Taryn froze, every instinct shrieking that this was a bad, foolish, hair-raisingly terrifying statement.

Every instinct save one—the primal, irresistible conviction that if Cade didn't kiss her she'd regret it for ever.

Her lips parted. 'Yes,' she said in a husky, faraway voice. 'Too soon.'

'And you're afraid of me.'

She dragged in a deep breath. Oh, no, not afraid of Cade.

Afraid—*terrified*—of being shown once more that she was cold, too cold to satisfy a man...

But she didn't feel cold. This had never happened before—this wild excitement that shimmered through her like a green flash at sunset, rare and exquisite, offering some hidden glory she might perhaps reach...

She stared up into narrowed eyes, saw the hard line of his mouth and knew he was going to step back, let her return to her chilly, isolated world. Somehow, without intending to, Cade had breached her defences, challenged that self-imposed loneliness, making her want—no, *long*—to rejoin the real world, where people touched and desired and kissed and made love without barriers.

'No,' she blurted, desperate to convince him. 'Not of you—of myself.'

Frowning, Cade demanded, 'Why?'

She had to tell him, but her voice was low and shamed and bitter when she admitted, 'I'm frigid.'

His brows shot up in an astonishment that strangely warmed her. 'Frigid? I don't believe it. Tonight, I saw you literally stopped in your tracks by a sunset. No one who responds so ardently to sensory experiences could possibly be frigid.'

When he bent his head she stiffened, but he said in a quiet voice, 'Relax. I would never hurt you, and I'm not going to leap on you and drag you into the bushes.'

The image of controlled, disciplined Cade losing his cool so completely summoned a spontaneous gurgle of laughter.

He smiled, and traced the outline of her lips with a hand that shook a little. The shame and fear holding her rigid dissipated a fraction, soothed by the sensuous shiver of delight that almost tentative touch aroused.

His voice deep and quiet, he said, 'There are very few frigid women, didn't you know? It's usually a term imposed by clumsy, carelessly inconsiderate men. Who slapped you with that label?'

When she hesitated, he said swiftly, 'If it's too painful—'

'No,' she said wonderingly, because for the first time ever she thought she might be able to talk about it. In his arms, his heart beating solidly against her, she felt a strong sense of security, almost—incredible though that seemed to her bewildered mind—of peace.

Nevertheless, she had to swallow before she could go on. 'It's just that I was engaged but I wasn't able to respond. It upset my fiancé and in the end it mattered too much.'

She stopped. She didn't tell him—had never been

able to tell anyone—of the shattering scene that had ended the engagement.

'So, if you truly are frigid, why are you snuggling against me so comfortably?'

Taryn said huskily, 'I don't know.'

'Do you feel completely safe?'

'Yes,' she said instantly.

'So if I kiss you, you're not going to be scared, because it's only going to be a kiss?'

Her whole body clenched as a wave of yearning swept through her—poignant, powerfully erotic and so intense she shivered with it. 'I'm not afraid,' she said, adding a little bitterly, 'Well, I suppose I am, but it's only of freezing you off.'

He lifted her chin. Eyes holding hers, he said above the wild fluttering of her heart, 'Well, let's see if that happens.'

And his mouth came down on hers.

Somehow, she had expected an unsubtle, dominant passion, so she was startled at first by his gentle exploration. Yet another part of her welcomed it and her mouth softened under his, her body responding with a languorous lack of resistance, a melting that was bone-deep, cell-deep—*heart*-deep.

As if he'd been waiting for that, he lifted his head. 'All right?'

The taut words told her he was holding himself under intense restraint, every powerful muscle in his big body controlled by a ruthless will.

Taryn could have been scared. Instead, a wave of relief and delight overwhelmed her and she turned her head and said against the hard line of his jaw, 'It's— saying that is getting to be a habit with you. I'm absolutely all right.'

He laughed, deep and quiet, and this time the kiss was everything she'd hoped, a carnal expression of hunger, dangerously stimulating, that sent unexpected shivers rocketing through her in a firestorm of reckless excitement.

He raised his head and slid his hands down to her hips, easing her closer. When he resumed the kiss, her breasts yielded to the solid wall of his chest. He was all muscle, all uncompromising strength, summoning from an unknown source in her an intense, aching anticipation that promised so much.

This time when he lifted his head Taryn's knees buckled and she couldn't hold back a low, sighing purr. Cade held her a little away and surveyed her with such a penetrating stare that she closed her eyes to shield herself.

Instantly, his arms loosened, leaving her chilled and bereft, her breasts aching with unfulfilled desire, her body throbbing with frustration.

He asked, 'Did I hurt—?'

'No,' she broke in, and her tender lips sketched a weak smile. 'Of course you didn't—I'd have punched you in the solar plexus if you had.'

An odd half smile curled his mouth. 'You could have tried,' he said, dropping his arms. 'But I suspect that's enough experimentation for now.'

Disappointment clouded her thoughts. For a moment her mind flashed back to the fragile blonde in her clinging black sheath. 'I'm not a frail little flower, easily bruised,' she said tersely.

Why were they talking when they could be repeating those moments of shattering pleasure?

She parried his unreadable survey with a lift of her

brows, only to suffer an odd hitch to her heartbeat when his mouth curled into a smile.

'Far from it,' he said and stepped back, away from her. 'And I think we've proved pretty conclusively that you're not frigid, don't you?'

Taryn banished a forlorn shiver. What had she expected? That he'd sweep her off her feet and prove in the best—the *only* way—that Antony had been completely wrong, and she was more than capable of feeling and responding to passion?

Seduce her, in other words. A hot wave of embarrassment made her turn away. There would have been precious little seduction to it—she'd gone up like a bushfire in his arms.

Cade was a sophisticated man. He'd been far more thoughtful than she'd guessed he could be, but a few *experimental* kisses from her weren't going to mean anything to him. And he was making sure she understood it too.

So it was up to her to seem just as worldly, just as relaxed about her newly discovered sexuality as he clearly was with his. 'I...yes,' she muttered. 'Thank you.'

He'd stayed totally in control, whereas the second he touched her she wouldn't have cared if they'd been in the centre of some huge sports stadium as the sole show for tens of thousands of spectators.

With whole banks of spotlights and television cameras focused on them, she enlarged, hot with humiliation.

Kissing Cade had been mind-blowing—and stupid. Out of the frying pan into the fire...

Her grandmother's domestic saying seemed the perfect way to describe her situation. Desperate to get away, she started to walk off.

Without moving, he asked, 'Did you leave something behind?'

Taryn stopped, cheeks burning, when she realised she'd set off in the wrong direction. If he was smiling she'd...

Well, she didn't know what she'd do, but it would be drastic. Pride stiffened her shoulders and straightened her spine as she turned to face him.

He wasn't smiling.

No emotion showed on the arrogant face—no warmth, nothing but a mild curiosity that chilled her through to her bones.

Just keep it light, casual, everyday. After all, she'd kissed quite a few men in her time.

It took most of her courage and all her will to set off in the right direction and say cheerfully, 'No, and I'm blaming you entirely for scrambling my brains. If you want any respectable work from me, I don't think we should allow that to happen again.'

His expression didn't change as he fell into step with her, but his tone was cynical. 'For some reason, I don't think of respectability when I look at you.'

Taryn had to bite her lip to stop herself from asking what he did think of. He might be the sexiest man she'd ever met, and he certainly kissed like any woman's erotic dream, but he was her employer, for heaven's sake.

Worse than that, she admitted with stringent—and strangely reluctant—honesty, she was far too intrigued by him. Letting Cade's addictive kisses get to her could only lead to heartbreak.

If his lovely blonde neighbour at dinner had shown her anything, it was that there would always be women around him, only too eager to fall into his arms and his bed.

'Well, I am respectable. And we have a professional relationship,' she said stiffly.

'We did.' He paused, and when she remained silent he added, 'I suspect it might just have been converted into something entirely different.'

His cool amusement grated. 'No,' she said firmly.

She'd had little experience when it came to emotional adventures, and she'd never known anything like the response that still seethed through her like the effect of some erotic spell.

Well, she'd just shown she could be as foolish as any eighteen-year-old, but she didn't do sensual escapades.

So, if he still wanted to play games, she'd—what?

The sensible reaction would be to run as if hellhounds were after her.

'No?' he asked almost negligently.

'You've been very kind and understanding, and I am grateful.' She paused, unable to summon any sensible, calm, sophisticated words. In the end, she decided on a partial truth. 'But, although you helped me discover something about myself I didn't know, I don't expect anything more from you than a resumption of our working relationship.'

Cade glanced down. She wasn't looking at him; against the silver shimmer of the lagoon through the palm trunks her profile was elegant, sensuous—and as determined as the chin that supported it.

Oddly enough, he believed she'd been convinced she was frigid. He'd deduced something of it even before she'd told him; her reactions to his touch had warned him of some emotional trauma. Suppressing an uncivilised desire to track down and punish the man who'd done such a number on her, he wondered if this was why she'd refused Peter.

No, she'd *laughed*… That implied a certain crudity—or cruelty.

She'd rejected Peter in a manner that had left him so completely disillusioned he'd been unable to live with the humiliation.

So was now the time to tell her who he was?

Not yet, Cade decided. There was more to Taryn than he'd thought, and he'd only got just below the surface.

Why was she back-pedalling? She must realise she had no need to whet his appetite; he was still fighting to control a ferocious surge of hunger. In his arms she'd been eager and passionate, her willingness summoning sensations more extreme than anything he'd felt since his untamed adolescence.

But she had every right to remind him of their professional relationship. And he had every right to tempt her into revealing herself more. He stamped down on the stray thought that his desire might be gaining the upper hand.

'Fair enough,' he said, finishing, 'Although I should warn you that I'm particularly fond of exceeding expectations.'

And waited for her reaction.

CHAPTER SEVEN

TARYN gave him a swift, startled glance, faltered on a half step, recovered lithely and looked away but, beneath the shimmering gold *pareu*, her breasts lifted as though she'd taken a deep breath. The languorous perfume of some tropical flower floated with voluptuous impact through the warm air as they turned off the main path towards their accommodation.

Was she resisting an impulse to take the bait? Cade waited, but when she stayed silent continued with a touch of humour, 'However, as we're back to being professional, here's what's happening tomorrow.'

He gave her the programme, finishing with, 'And the day ends with a dinner cruise on the harbour.'

At her nod, he said blandly, 'To which you are, of course, invited.'

'I've given up protesting,' she said, irony colouring the words.

Cade permitted himself a narrow smile as he opened the door. 'And of course you'll be perfectly safe with all those people around.'

'I'm perfectly safe anyway,' she returned a little sharply, and said a rapid, 'Goodnight,' before striding gracefully towards the door of her room.

The fine material of her *pareu* stroked sinuously

across the elegant contours of the body beneath it, and he found himself wondering how she would look when it came off...

He waited until she reached for the handle before saying, 'I've always believed that the best strategy was standing and fighting, but retreat is probably the right tactic for you now. Sleep well.'

She turned her head and sent him a long, unwavering look before saying, 'I shall,' and walking through the door, closing it quietly but with a definite click behind her.

Safe behind it, Taryn dragged air into famished lungs and headed for the bathroom, churning with such a complex mixture of emotions she felt as though someone had pushed her head first into a washing machine.

A shower refreshed her marginally, but sleep proved elusive.

Every time she closed her eyes she relived those searing kisses, so midnight found her wide awake, staring at the drifts of netting that festooned the bed.

Was Cade looking for an affair? Just thinking about that made her heart jump nervously and stirred her senses into humming awareness.

If so, she'd refuse him. He'd accept that—and, even if he didn't, she didn't need to worry about her safety, because he wasn't the sort of man to force her.

Repressing a shudder at old memories, she wondered why she was so sure.

For one thing, the blonde woman in her skimpy black shift would be only too eager to indulge him if all he wanted was a quick fling. And, judging by various covert glances Taryn had intercepted, several other women at dinner wouldn't mind being seduced by his muscled elegance and magnetic impact.

But what convinced her was his restraint, his complete self-discipline when he'd kissed her. She'd dissolved into a puddle of sensation, and he'd known it, but he'd not tried to persuade her into bed.

Her physical safety was not an issue.

So how about her emotions? Was she falling in love?

Restlessness forced her out from the tumbled sheets. She pushed back a swathe of filmy mosquito netting and walked across to the window, staring out at a tropical fantasy in silver and black, the moon's path across the lagoon as bright as the stars in the Milky Way.

No, this passionate madness had very little to do with love. Love needed time; it had taken her several months to realise she loved Antony.

She let the curtain drop and went back to bed. That love, however sincere, hadn't been enough, and she'd been sufficiently scarred to believe she lacked passion. She'd accepted Antony's disillusioned statements as truths.

Possibly that was why she hadn't seen anything more than cheerful camaraderie in Peter's attitude to her.

Bitterly, uselessly, she rued her mistaken impression that he'd been joking when he'd asked her to marry him. She was still haunted by her last sight of him—smiling as she'd waved goodbye and turned into the Departures area of the airport.

A few hours later he was dead. Why? The often-asked question hammered pitilessly at her.

Why hadn't he confided in her? They'd been friends—*good* friends—and she might have been able to help.

Oh, who was she kidding? Peter hadn't wanted friendship; he'd wanted love. If she'd given in to his pleading she'd have been replaying the wretchedness of her engagement, because she hadn't desired him—not as she desired Cade...

Cade's presence had pushed memories of Peter to the back of her mind. He was vital, compelling in a way that completely overshadowed Peter. Guilt lay like a heavy weight on her mind, in her heart—an emotion she'd never appease.

She sighed, turning to push the sheet back from her sticky body. The netting swayed in the flower-scented breeze. She felt heavy and hungry, aching with a need so potent she felt it in every cell.

Cade—tall and dark, and almost forbidding in his uncompromising masculinity, yet capable of consideration. Cade, who possibly wanted an affair.

Cade, who made her body sing like nothing she'd ever experienced before...

A stray thought drifted by, silken with forbidden temptation. What if she embarked on an affair with him?

She didn't dare risk it.

And why, when she'd loved Antony, had his passion never stirred her as Cade's kisses did? Dreamily, she recalled how it felt to be locked in Cade's arms, shivering with eager delight.

When sleep finally claimed her it was long after midnight. The next thing she knew was a voice saying incisively, 'Taryn, wake up!'

She opened her eyes, blinked at a steel-blue gaze and bolted upright. 'Wha—?'

'You've overslept,' Cade said curtly, and turned and left the room.

Stunned, still lost in the dream she'd been enjoying, Taryn stared around her.

Why hadn't her alarm gone off?

Leaning over, she pushed back the hair from her face so she could check, only to bite back a shocked word and twist off the bed.

She hadn't heard the alarm because last night she'd forgotten to set it.

And she'd forgotten to set it because she'd been too dazzled by Cade's kisses to think straight.

So much for professionalism!

Not only that, she'd kicked off her bedclothes. She was sprawled on top of the sheet in a pair of boxer shorts and a skimpy singlet top that had ridden sideways, revealing almost every inch of skin from her waist to her shoulders.

All of which Cade would have been able to see through the fine drift of mosquito netting.

Hot with delayed embarrassment, she dived across the room, performed her ablutions, changed into a business-like shirt and skirt and walked out into the living room with her chin at an angle and every nerve taut.

Cade was standing at the table checking out a sheaf of papers.

'Sorry,' she said rapidly.

He lifted his head and gave her a long, cool look. Last night's kisses—and whether he'd just seen more of her than was *respectable*—clearly meant nothing to him.

All thought was blotted out by a stark, fierce surge of hunger when he crossed the room towards her. Desperately clinging to her splintering composure, she tried to ignore the powerful, masculine grace of his movements and the erratic beat of her heart.

'Jet lag reveals itself in different ways,' he said laconically. 'Here's what I want you to do after you've had breakfast.'

She forced herself to concentrate, only to be startled

when he finished by saying, 'Drink plenty of water today and try a nap after lunch. It might help.' He looked at his watch. 'I have to go. I'll be back around midday.'

Taryn took a deep breath, letting it out on an explosive sigh once she was safely alone.

'Breakfast,' she said to the silent room, then started at a knock on the door. Fortunately, it heralded a delicious concoction of tropical fruit with good toast to back it up.

And excellent coffee... Mentally thanking that long-ago Arabian—or had he been Ethiopian?—goatherd who'd noticed how frisky his goats became after grazing on coffee berries, she ate breakfast before setting to work.

Although she still felt a little slack and listless, by the time the sun was at its highest she'd finished nearly everything Cade had set out for her.

When he arrived back in the *fale* he glanced at her work. 'Thank you. This is just what I need. I'm having a working lunch but you can eat here or in the restaurant, whichever you prefer.'

'Here,' she said.

Cade's nod was short, almost dismissive. 'And take that nap.'

Clearly he regretted those feverish kisses as much as she did.

Perhaps for him they hadn't been feverish. Had he been taken aback—even dismayed—by the intensity of her response?

Even if he hadn't, his aloofness was understandable; basically, he was indicating that although he'd forgotten himself enough to kiss her, he regretted it and she wasn't to presume on it.

Kiss in haste, repent at leisure—a classic case of the

morning after the night before, she thought, smarting with something close to shame.

Ignoring the tight knot in her stomach, she worked through lunch, and afterwards followed instructions to take a short nap, only to wake with heavy limbs and a threatening headache.

A swim in the lagoon revived her considerably. On her way back to the *fale*, she met the Frenchwoman with impeccable style who'd admired her *pareu* the previous evening.

Beside her was a much younger woman, a stunning opera singer. After giving Taryn an indifferent nod, she began to complain of boredom.

Madame Murat listened to her complaints with a smile, before saying, 'It would be my dream to spend the rest of my life in this lovely place.' She looked at Taryn. 'You, my dear, are here to work, are you not?'

'Yes.' Taryn added brightly, 'But working in paradise is no effort.'

The younger woman gave a significant smile. 'No effort at all when you're sharing…' she paused, before adding on a husky laugh '…*accommodation* with a hunk like Cade Peredur. Lucky you.' Another pause, before she asked, 'What's he like—as an employer, I mean, of course.'

'Very professional,' Taryn said woodenly.

'How maddening for you,' the other woman said, odiously sympathetic. She gazed around the shimmering lagoon and pulled a petulant face. 'I didn't realise we were going to be stuck on this tiny little dot of land all the time we were here.'

After a nod to each of them, she walked away. The Frenchwoman said tolerantly, 'Poor girl—she had hopes of a resort holiday, I think, with handsome men to admire her and a chance to display her jewels. Instead, there are only other wives while our men are working.' She glanced past Taryn. 'Ah, here comes your employer. They must have finished talking for the afternoon.'

Startled, Taryn looked up. Sunlight shafted down between the palms in swords of gold, tiger-striping Cade's lean, powerful form as he strode towards them. Her heart fluttered and her body sang into forbidden warmth as the memory of his kisses sparked a rush of tantalising adrenalin. She blinked against suddenly intense colours, so bright that even behind her sunglasses they dazzled.

Unexpectedly, the woman beside her said, 'Wise of you not to move, my dear. Unless you love him and know it is returned, never run towards a man. This one is coming to you as fast as he can.'

Flushing, Taryn said swiftly, 'He's my employer, that's all.'

'So far, and you are wise not to surrender too soon.' Her companion smiled wryly. 'My children say I am very old-fashioned, but I do not approve of modern attitudes. There should be some mystery in a love affair, some greater excitement than finding out how good in bed a man—or woman—is. A meeting of minds as well as of bodies.' Just before Cade came within earshot, she finished, 'And this man—both mind and body—would be a very interesting one to explore.'

She bestowed a frankly appreciative glance on him as he came to a stop before them and in a voice coloured by amusement she said, 'I hope you do not intend to scold your charming secretary for spending time with an old woman.'

The smile he gave her held cynicism, but was warmed by male appreciation for her soignée chic and elegant femininity. 'I don't see any old women around,' he said, 'and the days of wage slavery are long gone. Taryn would soon put me in my place if I tried to keep her immured in work.'

Madame Murat chuckled and steered the conversation into a discussion of the Pacific economy but, when Taryn admitted ruefully to knowing very little about that, adding that she'd been in London for the past couple of years, the older woman changed the subject to her favourite sights there.

None of them, Taryn thought when she was walking back to their suite with Cade, were sophisticated 'in' places; the older woman had concentrated on museums, galleries and parks—the sort of spots a tourist would be likely to visit.

'Do you like Madame Murat?' Cade surprised her by asking.

'Yes.' It came out too abruptly. She was too aware of him, of his intimidating assurance—and gripped by memories of the compelling sensuality of his kisses.

After clearing her throat, she said, 'Very much.'

His smile was narrow. 'She was fishing.'

Startled, she glanced at him. 'You mean—'

She stopped when she met his cool, cynical gaze. Yes, he did mean it. It hurt to think that the charming Frenchwoman might have targeted her.

He shrugged. 'She was laying ground bait. Her husband is very enthusiastic about a scheme I'm positive will fail, and he's almost certainly suggested she find out what you know of my plans.'

'I don't know anything of your plans,' she said shortly, angry with him for some obscure reason. 'And, even if I did, I do know how to hold my tongue.'

'I'm sure you do,' he returned smoothly, 'but it's always best to be forewarned. What's the matter?'

'Nothing.' When he sent her an ironically disbelieving glance, she enlarged reluctantly, 'Just that I liked her. It sounds ridiculous and overdramatic, but…it feels like a betrayal.'

Cade's eyes were keen. 'Of course you like her—she's a charming woman and a very intelligent one. She and her husband make a formidable team. She won't hold your discretion against you, and might well be useful to you in the future. As for betrayal—' His shoulders lifted and fell. 'It happens.'

Thoughtfully, Taryn said, 'I don't think I like your world much.'

A black brow lifted. 'My world, your world—what's the difference? Every world has its share of innocents and those who prey on them, of honest people and scoundrels. Unless you understand that, you run risks wherever you are.'

Shocked, she asked directly, 'Don't you trust anyone?'

Cade didn't answer straightaway. When the silence stretched too long, she looked up into an austere, unyielding mask.

He gave another barely noticeable shrug. 'A few. And only when they've proved trustworthy. Do you trust everyone you meet?'

After a moment's pause, she said, 'Of course not. Only a fool would do that.'

'And you're not a fool.'

A note in his voice made her uneasy. 'I try not to be,' she returned, irritated by her defensive tone.

The conversation was too personal—almost as personal as his kisses—and, strangely, she felt he was attacking her, trying to find some hidden weak spot he could use.

Don't be silly, she scoffed. *He's just making sure you can be trusted not to give away secrets...*

He asked, 'Did you manage to get some sleep after lunch?'

Hugely relieved at the change of subject, she said, 'Yes, for a short time.'

'I found your notes. You did a good job.'

She tried to suppress a warm pleasure. 'Thank you. I assume there's more.'

'Yes, although I don't need it until tomorrow afternoon. Have you ever been to the main island?'

'Only yesterday when we arrived,' she said dryly.

'In a couple of days I plan to check out the local fishing industry and I'd like you to come with me.'

Taryn said, 'All right. Do you want me to take notes? I can't do shorthand, but I could take notes by hand, or talk into a recorder—or even use the laptop.'

'I've got a recording device you can use. And I won't force you to trek around fishing factories or dirty, smelly boats,' he told her. 'We'll be meeting with the people who run the show, not the fishermen.'

She gave him a swift, amused look. 'I bet I've been in more dirty, smelly boats than you have.'

Cade liked her frankness—a little too much, he conceded sardonically. It could have been an indication of inner honesty—except that she'd shown a chilling lack of empathy for Peter.

Could that have been because of her crass fiancé? He must have been a total fool, because she certainly wasn't frigid by nature.

Quelling a sharp shock of desire, Cade banished the memory of her incandescent response to his kisses. It could have been faked, of course. Unpleasantly aware of a desire to find excuses for her behaviour to Peter, he had to remember to keep an open mind.

'You've spent a lot of time on such vessels?' he enquired as they approached the gardens that shielded their *fale* from the others on the island.

She grinned. 'My parents and I used to spend the holidays travelling for a charity that sent medical aid to the islands. We sailed mostly on traders—and trust me, although they did their best, those vessels smelt and they were quite often dirty. The tropics can make things difficult for anyone with a cleanliness fetish.'

'You didn't think of following your parents into medicine?' he asked casually.

'Yes, but it didn't work out.'

'Why?'

She shrugged, her breasts beneath the *pareu* moving freely. Cade's groin tightened. Seeing her almost naked in her bed that morning meant he knew exactly what the brightly coloured fabric covered. He had to dismiss an image of his hands removing the thin cotton that covered her, then lingering across the satin-skinned curves he'd revealed.

Without looking at him, Taryn said, 'About halfway through my first year of pre-med study I realised that I simply didn't have the desire or the passion. It was my parents' dream for me, not mine.'

'How did they feel about that?'

Her narrow brows met for a second. 'They weren't happy,' she admitted, her tone cool and matter-of-fact. 'I felt really bad about it, but I couldn't see myself being a good doctor. For me, medicine would have been just a job.'

'Whereas for them it's a vocation?'

Her surprised glance sparked irritation in Cade, an emotion that fought with the swift leap of his blood when she turned her head away and the sun transformed her wet red locks into a coppery-gold aureole.

Clearly she hadn't thought him capable of recognising altruism. For some reason he wasn't prepared to examine, that stung.

'Yes,' she said simply. 'They made big sacrifices for me. Because they wanted to give me a good secondary education, they came back to New Zealand and bought the practice at Aramuhu. As soon as they'd organised me into university, they went back to the islands.'

Cade felt an odd, almost unwilling sympathy. Although philanthropic, her parents seemed to have been as casual about her as his mother had been. Had traipsing around after them on their missions of mercy given her a distaste for a lifetime of service?

It bothered him that he didn't blame her.

Her chin lifted and her green-gold eyes met his with a direct challenge. She said firmly, 'So I studied for librarian qualifications—much more my thing.'

'And you've not regretted it?'

'Not a bit.' In the dark shelter of one of the big rain-trees, Taryn sneaked an upward glance. Nothing showed in his expression but casual interest, yet her voice tightened so she had to hurry over her final remark. 'My parents are perfectly happy with the way I've organised my life, and so am I.'

In any other man, she'd have accepted his words as idle chit-chat, the small coin of communication, but she was pretty certain Cade didn't do casual. When he asked a question, he really wanted the answer.

A hot little thrill shivered through her as they walked out into the sun again. His kisses had indicated one sort of awareness, but did this conversation mean he felt more for her than uncomplicated lust?

Startled by a swift, passionate yearning that went deeper than desire, far deeper than anything she'd experienced before, she blinked and pretended to examine the shrubs beside the path.

Those hard eyes saw too much and, although she didn't understand him in any real way, somehow he stirred a secret, unsuspected part of her. She longed to warm herself in the intense primal heat she sensed behind the uncompromising exterior he presented to the world.

Abruptly, she stopped walking. Keeping her face turned away from Cade, she touched a hibiscus flower, letting her fingertips linger on the brilliant satin petals. It took all her self-possession to say in a level voice, 'Only a flower could get away with this combination— vivid orange petals with a heart as bright and dark as a ruby. The colours should clash hideously, but somehow they don't.'

Control restored, she lifted her hand and turned back to him, insides curling when she realised he wasn't looking at the bloom. Instead, his gaze was fixed on her mouth. Sensation ricocheted through her, tantalising and tempting.

Without haste, he said, 'It's all part of the forbidden, fated lure of the tropics, I believe.'

'Forbidden? Fated?' She let the flower go and resumed walking. In her most prosaic tone, she said, 'The European sailors who first explored these islands thought they'd found paradise.'

'Ask Luke Chapman to tell you about the first Chapman who arrived in Fala'isi. His story might change your mind about that.'

'Oh, the Polynesians were warlike, of course,' she admitted, keeping her voice practical. 'But they were hugely hospitable too, and although there were episodes when the two cultures clashed badly—like Captain Cook's death in Hawaii—they weren't common.'

Wanting Cade Peredur was asking for trouble. Better to keep her distance, stay safe behind the barricades, not waste her time and emotional energy on a man who—at the most—would suggest an affair.

Probably one as brief as tropical twilight, and with as little impact on him.

And there was always the possibility that her body was playing tricks on her, luring her on with a promise it couldn't fulfil. In spite of Cade's kisses, if they made love her desire might evaporate as swiftly as it had with Antony. She could do without a repeat of that humiliation.

Mouth firming, she bade her erratic heartbeat to settle down as they reached the *fale*.

'Those first explorers called them the Isles of Aphrodite,' he said, surprising her again. 'Love has to be the most dangerous emotion in the world.'

Her brows shot up. 'Dangerous? I can see that sometimes it might be,' she conceded. 'But fated and forbidden? That's a bit extreme. Plenty of people fall in love and live more or less happily ever after.'

'Plenty don't. And love has caused huge amounts of angst and misery.'

'Like any extreme emotion,' she agreed, heart twisting as she thought of Peter. Trying to ignore the sad memories and guilt, she said quietly, 'But there are different kinds of love. The love of parents for their children, for instance. Without that, the world would be a terrible place.'

Cade's face froze. 'Indeed,' he said evenly.

What had she said that had hit a nerve?

CHAPTER EIGHT

FOR a highly uncomfortable few seconds Cade looked at Taryn from narrowed eyes before asking abruptly, 'So what do you plan to do once you're back in New Zealand?'

'Find a proper job.' She grabbed at her composure and, once they were in the cool sitting room of the *fale*, said daringly, 'I'm thinking of asking you for a reference about my research abilities.'

'I expected as much.' His voice was level and lacking in emotion. And then he drawled, 'However, I'll need a little more experience of your skills before I can give you a reference that would mean anything.'

The words were innocuous enough—quite reasonable, in fact—but a note in his voice set her teeth on edge.

Meeting eyes that were narrowed and intent, she said crisply, 'I don't like the sound of that.'

His brows lifted. 'Why?'

Wishing too late she hadn't opened her mouth, Taryn knew she had to go on. 'Because that almost sounded like the sort of thing a sleazy employer might say to a defenceless employee.'

The half beat of silence tightened her nerves to

screaming point, until he laughed with what seemed like genuine amusement.

'You're far from defenceless,' he said coolly, 'and I rather resent you suggesting I'm sleazy. If you need the reassurance, any reference I write for you will be based entirely on your work, which so far I've found to be excellent.'

'Thank you,' she contented herself with saying.

He asked in that objective voice she was beginning to distrust, 'You're a beautiful woman. Do you have to set boundaries whenever you take a new position?'

'No.' Too brusque, but she wasn't going to elaborate.

However, he said, 'But you have had to before.'

'Do I act as though I expect every employer to try to jump me?'

His look of distaste made her stiffen and brace herself.

He said, 'No, but it's clear that you've developed ways to defend yourself. Unsurprising, really, since your parents deserted you once you left school.'

His tone hadn't altered, which somehow made his statement even more startling. Taryn said indignantly, 'I wasn't deserted! We kept in touch all the time—if I'd needed them, they'd have been there for me. They still are.'

One black brow lifted, something she realised happened whenever he didn't believe her. 'How long is it since you've seen them?'

She paused before admitting, 'A couple of years.'

'It sounds pretty close to being abandoned.'

'No, you don't understand—'

'I understand abandonment.' His voice was coldly deliberate. 'My birth father I never knew. My mother abandoned me at birth to be brought up by my grand-mother. When she died, I lived with my mother, but I was eventually taken into care. I lived—happily—with foster parents after that, but recently I've lost my foster-brother.'

Shocked and horrified at what her innocent words had summoned, Taryn said quietly, 'Yes, you obviously do understand abandonment, and I'm very sorry for that, but my parents haven't abandoned me. I'm a big girl now, Cade—Mr Peredur—and quite capable of looking after myself without needing them to shepherd me through life.'

'Oh, call me Cade,' he said negligently. 'We might not have been introduced formally but last night in my arms you called me Cade without hesitation.'

Colour burning through her skin, she said, 'I haven't thanked you for making sure that fruit bat didn't blunder into me.'

He shrugged. 'At the time I thought it was a fallen coconut I was rescuing you from. You've been digging trenches and laying barbed wire along your defences since you woke up this morning. Why? Because we kissed?'

'Of course not.' Immediately she'd spoken, she wondered if she should have told him the exact opposite.

Then he wouldn't have smiled—the cool, easy smile of a conqueror—and lifted his hand. Her eyes widened endlessly in fascinated apprehension, but all he did was push back a lock of sea-damp hair that clung to her cheek. His fingers barely grazed her skin, yet she felt their impact like a caress, silkily sliding through her body to melt every inhibition.

Dropping his hand, he said, 'It's quite simple, Taryn.

If you don't want me to touch you, all you need to do is say so.'

Neither his face nor his tone revealed any emotion beyond a wry amusement.

She resisted the need to lick suddenly dry lips. Cade's touch had paralysed her, banishing everything but a swift, aching pleasure from his nearness. He filled her gaze, blotting out the seductive lure of the tropical afternoon with a potent male magnetism that sapped both her energy and her will.

Again Cade held out his hand but this time, instead of touching her, he waited, his expression cool and challenging. Desire—hot and irresistible—pulsed through her, overwhelming her fears in a honeyed flow she felt in every cell in her body. He was watching her with an intensity that was more seductive than any caress or polished words, as though she were the most important thing in his life.

Slowly, eyes locked with the steel-sheen-blue of his, she fought a losing battle against the impulse to take what he was offering and ignore the common sense that urged her to say no.

Yet she didn't say it. Couldn't say it.

'What is this?' The words stumbled huskily from her, almost meaningless, yet he seemed to know what she wanted from him.

He said, 'You must know—since last night, if not before—that I find you very attractive. And you seem to reciprocate. But, if you're not interested, all you have to do is refuse. However, if I'm right and this—' his mouth twisted '—*attraction* is mutual, then we should decide what to do about it.'

Plain words. Too plain. And he knew damned well that the attraction was mutual! For a moment she suffered a pang of angry rebellion. Why didn't he woo her with passion, with heady kisses?

She knew the reason. Because he wanted her to know that whatever he felt was not love, not even a romance. He'd made it quite clear—he trusted no one. If she succumbed, it would be a business affair with no promises made and no hearts broken, just a clean cut when it was over.

Her only sensible response must be that simple syllable of refusal.

Yet still it wouldn't come.

Would succumbing to his offer be so dangerous...?

Or would it finally free her from fear, from the poisonous aftermath of Antony's violence?

Fighting a honeyed, treacherous temptation, Taryn searched for something sensible to say, words to get her out of the situation before she got too tangled in her rioting emotions.

None came.

She glanced upwards. As usual, she couldn't read anything in the arrogant features. Indignantly, she thought that his enigmatic look would be etched into her memory for ever.

In the end, she said as steadily as she could, 'In other words, why don't we both scratch an itch?'

Cade inspected her from the top of her head to her toes, his cryptic gaze fanning that treacherous desire deep inside her.

But when he spoke his voice held nothing but detachment. 'If that's how you see it, then yes.'

She bristled, made angry by a foolish, obscure pain.

Still in that judicial tone, he continued, 'But for me there's more to it than that. I've met a lot of beautiful women. I don't believe many—if any—would have held that hose and, in spite of knowing she hadn't a hope of doing it, still tried to stop the forest going up in flames.'

And, while she silently digested that, he went on, 'I want you. Not just because you make my pulse leap whenever you come into the room, but because I find you intriguing and I enjoy your company.' His broad shoulders sketched a shrug. 'If you want a declaration of undying love I can't give it to you. I know it exists—I just don't seem to be able to feel it myself. Why are you shaking your head?'

'I'm not asking for that.' Yet she hated the thought of being just another in the parade of women through his life.

He frowned. 'Then what do you want?'

'I don't know.' She hesitated, before adding in a troubled voice, 'To be reassured, I suppose—and I don't even know what I mean by that, but it makes me sound horribly needy and clinging, which I am not.'

'You most emphatically are not,' he agreed dryly. 'Well, what is it to be?'

When she didn't answer, he said in an entirely different voice, 'I could kiss you into agreement.'

Taryn opened her mouth to deny it, then closed her lips over the lying words.

Quietly, he said, 'So which will it be?'

Her thoughts tumbled in delirious free fall. Making love to Cade would be a step into a wildly stimulating unknown. Yet, in spite of being convinced she'd respond to Cade's lovemaking as eagerly as she had to his kisses, at the back of her mind lurked the dark cloud of apprehension that had been her constant companion since her engagement.

Now was a chance—perhaps her only chance—to find out whether she could be what Antony had called *a real woman*—one who enjoyed passion and could give herself in that most fundamental way.

And what harm could possibly come from a short affair when both she and Cade knew the rules?

None at all, that reckless inner part of her urged. Love had no part in this, so she'd be unscathed when the time came for them to part. And if—*if* she could surrender to desire fully and without shame, she'd be free at last of humiliation and able to consider an equal relationship some time in the future.

Slowly, reluctantly, she lifted her eyes and met Cade's gaze, which was narrowed with desire—for *her*—and, as she thrilled with a potent, spontaneous surge of sensuous hunger, she knew her answer.

If she didn't take this opportunity, she'd always regret her cowardice. Whatever happened, even if it ended in tears and heartache, she was desperately in thrall to a need she didn't want to resist.

But her voice wobbled when she said, 'I… Then it's yes.'

Cade fought back a fierce satisfaction—so fierce it startled him. With it came a driving, insistent hunger and something he'd never expected to feel—an intense need he immediately tried to block.

Because it was still too soon. Those enormous green-gold eyes and her soft trembling mouth certainly betrayed desire, but he sensed fear too.

For the first time in his life a headstrong passion had almost overridden his mind and his will. If he took her now he could wreck everything. She needed to be sure of his ability to rouse her, confidence that he wouldn't hurt her before she could come to him without restrictions, without fear or shame.

She needed gentling. Wooing...

He needed to know her better.

He shied away from that thought. And he, he thought grimly, needed to find a way to control this almost desperate sexual drive.

Watching her so he could gauge her reaction, he said with as much resolution as he could muster, 'It's all right, I'm not going to drag you off into a bedroom right now.'

'I didn't think you would,' she returned smartly. 'I'm sure your motto is always business first.'

He permitted himself a narrow, humourless smile—probably looking more like a tiger ready to pounce, he thought with grim humour. 'So why are you still holding yourself as stiffly as a martyr facing the stake?'

'I'm not!' But she was; already she could feel her shoulders start to ache.

And Cade's response didn't relax her at all. 'You need time to get to know me better,' he said.

Taryn paused, her mind racing against the thud of her heartbeats. In the end she nodded. 'Yes, I do,' she admitted, chagrin colouring her voice. 'Everything's happened so fast I feel as though I've been whisked off by a tornado. And you obviously need time too.'

'I know what I want.' He gave another of those twisted smiles, as though he understood the riot of emotions clouding her thoughts. 'It's all right, Taryn. There will come a time when we both know it's right. Until then, we'll carry on as we have been.'

Abruptly, that shaming relief fled, to be replaced by a disappointment so acute she almost changed her mind there and then. But he was right, she thought, clinging to a shred of common sense. She needed time.

He glanced at his watch, then out into the western sky, already lit with the pageantry of a tropical sunset. 'If we're going to be in time for the dinner cruise on the lagoon we'd better get going.'

Business first, of course, she thought as she nodded and hurried into her room, frustrated yet relieved. Her insides quivered. If only she didn't freeze...

Then she thought of what she'd learned about him, and her heart shuddered. She wanted to know so much more than the few spare statements he'd delivered in that chillingly impersonal tone, but the thought of him as a child, at the mercy of a neglectful mother, hurt her in an almost physical way.

No time for that now, she told herself after a harried glance at her watch. What to wear? The gold *pareu* again? Not entirely suitable for sailing—although the vessel that had anchored in the lagoon that morning looked more like a mini-liner than a yacht.

A swift search through her wardrobe made her decide on a gift from her mother. Pacific in style, the loose top of fine, silky cotton echoed the colours of handmade *tapa* cloth. Its soft cream-white fabric, patterned in chocolate-brown, tan and bronze, made her skin glow. With it, she wore sleek tan trousers and a cuff bracelet of tiny golden mother-of-pearl beads.

When she reappeared Cade gave her a swift smouldering look. Her stomach swooped and colour surged along her cheekbones. She had to steady her voice before she could say, 'I hope this is OK.'

He said, 'Infinitely more than merely OK. You look radiant. We'd better get going or I'll succumb to temptation and try to persuade you to skip the damned evening.'

A stripped, corrosive note in his words lit fires deep inside her.

Some hours later, Taryn leaned against the rail of the opulent vessel, which was owned by one of the most powerful businessmen in Australia.

She'd had an interesting evening. She'd been admired, patronised and ignored; she'd been entertained by Madame Murat, who'd revealed a charmingly indiscreet side that made Taryn chuckle; she'd fended off attempts at flirtation by various men and she'd eaten a delicious Pacific buffet meal beside Cade. He'd shown no overt possessiveness, but he'd clearly been keeping an eye on her.

She turned as someone came towards her, stabbed by sharp, unexpected disappointment when she saw not Cade but the son of the yacht owner. Tall and cheerfully laconic, he'd made no secret of his interest.

'Alone?' he said against the babble of talk and laughter from the big entertaining deck. 'Are we boring you?'

'No. I'm admiring the skies.'

He stopped just a little too close beside her. 'They're stunning, but if you want fabulous you should come to the Outback. Nothing beats the stars over the Australian desert. Check them out one day—we've got a cattle station so remote you'd think there was nowhere else on earth. I'd like to take you star-watching there.'

'It sounds amazing,' she told him, keeping her voice non-committal. A flurry of white in the water caught her attention. 'Oh—what was that?'

'What?'

When he turned to see where she was pointing out

she took the opportunity to move along the rail away from him. 'A splash—perhaps dolphins jumping? I presume there must be dolphins here.'

'Might be a whale,' he said, examining the water. He gestured towards a waiter, who came rapidly towards them. 'Binoculars, please,' he said, and turned back to her. 'Sounds as though you're used to dolphins jumping around you when you swim.'

'Not exactly,' she said, 'although pods often turn up off the coast of my part of Northland.'

He smiled down at her. 'What part of Northland? The Bay of Islands?'

'A bit farther north than that,' she said vaguely. He was good-looking and charming in an open, friendly way. Normally, she'd have flirted happily enough with him. But this wasn't normality; nothing had been normal since last night when Cade had kissed her and tilted her world off its axis.

The arrival of the waiter with binoculars eased things. 'Try these,' her companion said, offering them to her.

She squinted into them and suddenly caught a pod of dolphins arching up from the water in a free-wheeling display of gymnastics, graceful and joyous and gleaming in the starshine.

'Oh, lovely,' she breathed, turning to hand over the binoculars, only to discover her companion was now standing behind her, so close she actually turned into him.

'I'll get out of your way,' she said crisply and thrust the binoculars into his hands, ducking sideways.

Cade came striding towards them. Something about him made her stiffen; behind him, a group of people watched, clearly intrigued. Without thinking, she lifted her hand and beckoned, then pointed out to sea where the dolphins played.

'Dolphins,' she said, hoping her smile conveyed nothing more than simple pleasure.

The man beside her took the binoculars away from his eyes. 'They look as though they're moving away.' He looked beyond her, his demeanour subtly altering when he saw Cade approach.

'Hi, mate, take a look at this,' he said, handing him the binoculars. 'We'll go across to them so everyone can see them close up.'

'No, don't do that,' Taryn said swiftly.

Both men looked at her. 'Why?' Cade asked.

'At home we're told not to interfere with them—it disturbs them, especially if they have young with them. If they come across to us of their own accord, that's fine, but deliberately seeking them out isn't.'

Both men looked at each other, then the Australian grinned. 'OK, anything for a pretty lady. I'll get them to break out all the binoculars on board.'

Cade waited until he'd gone before checking out the dolphins.

Eyes narrowing as she watched the sea creatures, Taryn said, 'They look as though they've turned—they are heading this way, aren't they?'

'It seems so.' He lowered the binoculars and looked at her. 'Enjoying yourself?'

'Yes, thank you. It's a fantastic night and the food is delicious, and the people are very pleasant.'

As well as Fleur and Luke Chapman, she'd recognised a couple of business tycoons from New Zealand, one with his wife, a Mediterranean princess. A media baron and his fourth wife were in a huddle with several politicians from countries around the Pacific Rim, and an exquisite rill of laughter came from the opera star as she flirted with her husband.

Which made a change from flirting with Cade, Taryn thought waspishly. She said, 'Everywhere I look, I see faces from the television screen.'

And they all seemed to know each other well; she was the only outsider.

Just then someone else saw the dolphins, now close to the yacht, and called out, and there was a concerted move to the rails.

Taryn said, 'We'll get the best view up in the bows.'

Cade examined her face for a brief second, then nodded. 'Let's go.'

Several people followed them. Taryn tried hard not to wish she could stand alone with Cade in the moonlight watching the glorious creatures ride the bow wave with consummate grace, their curving mouths giving them the appearance of high delight. Silver veils of water garlanded their rounded, muscular backs while they dipped and pirouetted and leapt from the water, gleeful and wild in their unforced joy.

And then, as quickly as they'd come, an unheard command sent them speeding away to an unknown destination. And people who'd been lost in silent wonder broke out into a babble of noise that broke the spell.

Cade said, 'What was that sigh for?'

'Anything beautiful makes me feel sad—in an odd, delighted way,' she said, then laughed. 'They're such magnificent creatures, so wild and free, and they seem to get a huge kick out of wave-riding. You could just *feel* their pleasure, couldn't you?'

He nodded, his eyes searching as he looked down at her. 'I'm glad you saw them.'

Taryn would have enjoyed the rest of the evening

much more if anticipation hadn't been tightening inside her, straining her nerves and clamouring for the evening to end so that she could go back to the *fale* with Cade.

However, once they were alone, he closed the door and turned to her, eyes narrowed and gleaming, his face a mask of intent. She felt a sudden clutch of panic.

'You seemed to have a good time,' he said.

She nodded. 'Did you?'

'No.' His smile was brief and mirthless. 'I kept having to stop myself from striding over and establishing territorial rights every time I saw some man head in your direction.'

Taryn's hiccup of laughter was cut short when he slipped his tie free and dropped it, then shrugged out of his jacket. 'Surely you couldn't have thought that—'

She stopped, watching the way the powerful muscles flexed and coiled beneath his white shirt. Her breath came short between her lips. In a voice she didn't recognise she admitted, 'I understand the feeling.'

He looked at her and said in a completely different tone, 'All night I've been wondering whether that elegant and very suitable garment is as easy to remove as it seems to be. One night I'll find out. And if you want me to keep to our agreement, you'd better get into your room right now.'

Taryn dragged her gaze from his, blinked several times and said in a muted voice, 'Goodnight.'

She heard him laugh as she closed the bedroom door behind her, the low laugh of a man who had his life in order.

The three days that followed were a lesson in sorely tried patience and silent escalating tension. In public Cade treated her with an understated awareness. In private he touched her—her hand, her shoulder, an arm slipped around her waist occasionally.

Taryn knew what he was doing—getting her accustomed to his touch, his nearness, like a nervous filly being broken to the saddle. And the subtle courtship worked; each touch eased her fears, set up a yearning that grew with the hours until she found herself dreaming of him, an erotic dream that woke her into a shivering hunger unlike anything she'd ever known.

Twisting onto her side, she stared past the misty swag of the netting into the warm night, and knew that for her the time of waiting was over.

Her breath eased, but restlessness drove her to switch on the bedside lamp and pick up her watch. Almost midnight—not called the witching hour for nothing, she thought and switched off the light, settling back against the pillows.

Only to toss sleeplessly. Eventually, she got out of bed and opened the screens onto the terrace. The air outside was marginally cooler against her skin.

A blur of movement froze her into stillness.

CHAPTER NINE

IT WAS Cade, gazing out at the night. He turned to watch her as she stood in the doorway. A silver bar of moonlight revealed the strong male contours of his face and the fact that he was still fully clothed.

He didn't speak. Very much aware of her skimpy singlet top and shorts, Taryn swallowed to ease a suddenly dry throat and said abruptly, 'I've had enough time.'

Almost expressionless, a muscle in his jaw twitched as he held out his hand. 'So come to me.'

Taryn looked at him, toughly formidable, his handsome face almost unyielding in its bold angularity. He radiated power and an uncompromising male authority that should have warned her not to push.

Instead, it evoked something close to defiance. He was so clearly accustomed to being in charge, to taking women on his terms, not theirs.

'You come to me,' she returned and, although each word was soft and slightly hesitant, there could be no mistaking the challenge in both words and tone, in her level gaze and the tilt of her chin.

She expected some resistance and was startled when his beautiful mouth curled into an appreciative smile. Noiselessly, he walked across the terrace and, without any further comment, drew her to him, enfolding her as though she was precious to him.

Held against his lean, muscled length, she sighed and relaxed. It was too much like coming home. Lashes fluttering down, she hid her face in his shoulder, every sense languorously accepting and eager.

A finger under her chin lifted her face, gentle but inexorable.

'Look at me,' Cade said, his voice rough and deep.

But she couldn't—didn't dare. Panicking, she thought, *Don't be such an idiot. If looking at him seems too intimate, how are you going to make love with him?*

Shivers raced across her skin when she felt the warmth of his breath on her eyelids, and then the soft brush of his mouth across hers.

His voice was deep and low, pitched so only a lover would hear. 'Open your eyes, Taryn.'

When he repeated the command she slowly lifted her lashes to meet a hooded, glittering gaze that melted her spine.

Instantly, his arms locked around her, crushing her breasts against his broad chest, and the intimate contact of his thighs made her vividly, desperately aware of his arousal.

And her own. Need consumed her, tearing at her with insistent velvet claws. When his mouth came down on hers, she opened her lips to his bold claim and gave him what they both wanted—her surrender, joyous and open and exultant.

Eventually, when she was clinging and helpless with longing, he raised his head. Eyes glittering, he asked, 'Was that so difficult?'

'No,' she said on an outgoing breath and, before she

could change her mind, 'But three days ago I should have told you I don't believe in one-night stands.'

Releasing her, he said calmly, 'Neither do I.'

He trusted very few people and presumably that applied to her too, but there was genuine understanding in his tone. He'd recognised the fears that swayed her—fears and caution that now seemed flimsy and foolish—and didn't think any the less of her for them.

Yet when he took her hand, she hesitated.

'Second thoughts, Taryn?' His voice was aloof.

She reached up and touched his jaw, fingertips thrilling at the slight tactile roughness there. Cade held her hand against his mouth and kissed the fingers that had stroked his skin.

'No,' she whispered. 'No second thoughts. I just need to know you'll respect me in the morning.' A tremulous smile belied the steadiness of her gaze.

Cade's eyes hardened. Tension thrummed between them, fierce and significant.

Until he bent his head and kissed the corner of her mouth. 'Not a whit less than I respect you now,' he said deliberately.

Renewed confidence surged through her. She let him turn her and went with him into her room. Excitement beat through her, quickening as she turned to face him.

'Do you want the light on?' he asked, barely moving his lips.

'No.' She didn't want any other light than that of the moon, a silvery, shadowy glow full of mystery and magic.

Cade's eyes kindled into diamond-bright intensity, burning blue as the heart of a flame. 'You take my breath away,' he said gutturally and pulled off his shirt, dropping it onto the floor.

Taryn's breath stopped in her throat. He was utterly overwhelming, all fluid muscle and bronzed skin and heady male charisma. Acting on instinct, she reached out a tentative hand and skimmed his broad chest, fingertips tingling at the contrast of supple skin and the silken overlay of hair. Her heart pumped loudly in her ears and she sucked in a sharp breath at the raw, leashed strength that emanated from him, balanced by masculine grace and an aura of power.

She muttered, 'And you are…magnificent,' and pulled her little singlet top over her head.

Cade's mouth hardened. For a second she froze, her eyes fixed on his face, but when he kissed her, deeply and sensuously, taking his fill of her, she forgot everything but his mouth on hers and the hands that slid across her back to hold her upright when her knees would no longer carry her weight.

When the kiss was over he scrutinised her face, his glinting eyes narrowing in the taut silence while his hands moved again, one down to her hips, the other lingering to trace the curves of her breasts before finally, just when she thought the tension inside her would have to be released in a groan, he cupped them.

Stunned and charmed, she shivered as he bent his head and kissed an expectant tip.

Desire uncoiled through her so swiftly it shocked her. Nothing, she thought helplessly when he eased her across his arm so that he could take the pink crest of a breast into his mouth—*nothing* in her previous life had prepared her for this charged, voluptuous delight.

At the sensuous tug of his lips, erotic little shudders tightened her skin and she closed her eyes, swamped by the sheer immensity of the sensations sweeping through her.

Dimly, she realised that all her fears had been wasted—whatever had kept her from enjoying sex previously no longer applied. Shivering with a passionate intensity, she was transformed, taken over by a desperate craving for something she didn't recognise, didn't understand. Her back arched in unconscious demand, and Cade lifted his head and subjected her to a darkly probing survey.

Shaken by the hunger surging through her veins, she gasped as he eased her onto the bed. Colour burned through her skin and her lashes fluttered down when he stripped completely.

But once he came down beside her, she turned into him, seeking his strength to appease the hunger burning inside her. His arms tightened around her and he kissed the wildly beating pulse in her throat.

'Open your eyes.' It was a command, not a request.

She tried to steady her voice, force it into something like its normal sensible tone, but the words came out in a husky, languorous whisper. 'It's too much...'

'What is?' And when she didn't answer he bent his head again and his lips closed over the other tightly budding peak.

'Everything,' she croaked, her pulse racing so fast she thought she might faint with the delicious thrill of his caress.

By the time he'd eased her remaining garment from her she no longer remembered that once she'd lain frozen and repelled by just such a caress. His hand moved between her legs and he began to press rhythmically and without haste, setting up a powerful sensuous counterpoint to the exquisite tug of his mouth. Insistent, demanding pleasure built in the pit of her stomach, a driving, powerful ache totally beyond her experience.

'Look at me,' Cade breathed, lifting his head so that Taryn felt his lips brush against her breast with each word.

Molten rills of sensation raced through her—beautiful, devouring, possibly destructive fire, but it was too late to call a halt now.

Not that she would, even if she could. Heat from his body fanned her passionate reaction to the subtle masculine scent that was his alone, and the intoxicating seduction of his skilled caresses had gone straight to her head.

'I think I'm shy,' she muttered, not surprised when he laughed deep in his throat.

Except that a shy woman wouldn't have yielded so quickly, so easily.

She'd wanted Cade from the moment their eyes met, her body surrendering to an elemental hunger her mind had refused to recognise. That hidden, barely registered excitement had tangled logic and caution into knots, sneakily undermining them and persuading her she'd be perfectly safe going to Fala'isi with him.

'Shy?' he murmured, his voice thick. 'A little, perhaps, and tantalisingly elusive, but so intriguingly responsive.'

His fingers slid deeper, towards her acutely sensitive core, and suddenly desire fractured into light that filled every cell in her body with shimmering transcendent sensation, a rapture that took her totally by surprise.

Her lashes flew up. Hugely dilated shocked eyes locking with his, she came apart in his arms, so abandoned to the magic of Cade's lovemaking she had no defence against her wild surrender.

He silenced the gasp that escaped her with a kiss so fierce and sensual she didn't register the flare of satisfaction in his eyes. Her lashes drifted down and she lay cradled against him for several minutes while her heartbeat slowed into normality and the vivid consummation faded into the sweet laziness of sated desire.

Until Cade moved, positioning himself over her. Then, in a reaction she couldn't stop, her body tensed. Bleak despair roiled through her. Willing her muscles to relax, she had to force herself to meet the keen, polished steel of his gaze.

'It's all right,' he said abruptly. 'I won't hurt you.'

'I know.' Hardly breathing, she tried to unlock her muscles.

He bent and took her breast into his mouth again. And somehow, miraculously, passion conquered fear, floating through her in pleasurable ripples that almost immediately coalesced into a mill race of urgent, clamorous anticipation.

Cade lifted his head, narrowly examining her face, then said, 'Yes?'

'Oh, yes,' she breathed.

Blue eyes held her gaze as he eased into her by slow, sensuous increments and began to move almost sinuously, his male strength and power controlled by a will she dimly recognised.

Hunger poured through her in a violent rush, easing his passage with a flood that summoned voluptuous tremors through her. Instantly gauging her response, he thrust more fiercely and she gasped again, hips arching off the bed to meet him, the carnal rhythm projecting her into a world where all she had to cling to was this heady, dazzling sensation and the driving measure of their hearts against each other.

Lost in rapture, almost immediately she crested again in an infinitely more complex, intense culmination that hurtled her through some unmarked boundary on a soaring wave of ecstasy. Just when she was certain she couldn't bear any more pleasure, his breathing became harsh and he flung back his head. Through barely open eyes she saw him reach his fulfilment, his arrogant face a drawn mask of sexual pleasure, every muscle in his body cording in hard tension.

Eventually, while the erotic satiation faded into a dreamy daze, Taryn tried to sort her scattered thoughts. Stupidly, strangely, she longed for some tenderness from him, some acceptance of their mutual ecstasy, but without speaking, he twisted away and settled beside her on his back.

Close, so close, yet not touching. And she needed his touch now, so much she felt the need aching through her.

'All right?' he asked, his voice rough.

Hold me, she almost begged, but a remnant of common sense barred the abject plea. Terrified she might betray herself by letting the words free, she whispered, 'I didn't know it could be like that.'

His mouth crooked in a humourless smile and, without speaking, he turned onto his side and scooped her against him. His chest lifted as he said, 'He must have been a crass fool, that fiancé of yours.'

'Oh, no,' she said quietly. 'He loved me. But we were both so young...and I didn't...couldn't...'

His arms tightened when she stumbled, giving silent support. Oddly enough, it was as though the rapture she'd found with Cade had opened a door she'd slammed shut years ago.

When he asked, 'How young?' she told him.

'Nineteen, and he was twenty-one. Far too young, my parents said, and they were so right, but...at first everything was like a romantic fairy tale. Only once we were engaged he wanted to make love, and he was bewildered—and hurt—when I couldn't...'

She stopped and took a deep breath. Possibly without realising it, Cade was stroking her back and the slight, slow caress was soothing something more than her laboured heartbeat.

In a soft, dragging voice she said, 'I still don't know why I froze every time. He was experienced—I wasn't his first lover. He said I was frigid. And I thought it was true because I was so certain I loved him. But I just couldn't relax...'

Cade said quietly, 'So he found someone new?'

'Oh, no.' She swallowed. 'He tried everything... I think he saw my coldness as a challenge to his masculinity.'

She couldn't go on. Antony had been utterly determined to overcome her frigidity. Sex with him had become an ordeal of new techniques, new attempts at seduction—from watching pornography with her to licking chocolate from her body—in his efforts to discover the magic caress that would miraculously turn her into the willing, eagerly passionate partner he wanted.

His dogged efforts had only made her more tense, eventually creating a rift, one that had rapidly spiralled out of control.

Cade said quietly, 'That doesn't sound like love.'

In a low, shaken voice, she said, 'He got so angry—as though I was doing it deliberately. I didn't know how to handle it—' She stifled a laugh that sounded too much like a sob. 'I wanted to run home to my mummy and daddy like a little girl and have them make things all better for me.'

'But they weren't there for you.'

'They were dealing with an outbreak of dengue fever that was killing people.' Her voice strengthened. 'So of course I didn't tell them.'

'What happened?'

When she shivered his arms tightened around her again. Keeping her face hidden in his shoulder, she mumbled, 'We were fighting a lot…and he…in the end I told him I didn't want him and never would, and he… and he…' She stopped, unable to go on.

'It's all right.' In a tone so devoid of emotion it was more threatening than anger, Cade said, 'Let me guess. He raped you.'

Taryn shuddered. 'Yes,' she whispered, adding swiftly, 'Afterwards he was shattered. He said he still loved me, even though I'd turned him into a monster.'

Every muscle in Cade's big body tightened. 'And you believed that—that self-serving, righteous—' he paused before clearly substituting another word for the one that must have sprung to mind '—*rubbish*?'

'At first I did,' Taryn admitted quietly. 'And even when I realised he had no right—that he was responsible for what he did, I still believed…'

'That you were frigid,' he supplied when she couldn't go on, his voice hard with anger. 'Well, now you know you aren't. Far from being frigid, you're delightfully responsive, all any man could ask for. If he wasn't able to make you respond, it was probably because you sensed the propensity for violence in him. No man has the right to take out his frustration in rape. It's every bit as criminal and brutal as beating a woman.'

Something that had been wound tightly inside her for

years eased, dissipated, left her for ever. She felt oddly empty, yet light and free.

More shaken than she'd ever been, she said, 'I don't know why I told you all this.'

'Feel better?'

She sighed. 'Yes. Thank you.'

Thank you for everything. Thank you for making a woman of me...

'You don't need to thank me,' he said abruptly. 'I've done nothing—you always had the capacity for passion. It was your bad luck you thought you loved someone who didn't know how to arouse it.'

'Stupidity, more like,' she murmured.

He laughed quietly. 'Who isn't stupid at nineteen?'

Comforted, she luxuriated in the heat of his body, the smooth lift and fall of his chest, the sensuous, languid delight of being there with Cade. The world righted, reassembled itself, and she yawned.

'Do you want me to stay?' he asked.

Taryn's acrobatic heart jumped in her breast. It was utterly stupid to feel that this was more important than making love with him; that his question even implied some tenuous commitment...

In a voice she hoped sounded lazily contented, she murmured, 'If you want to.'

His smile sizzled through her. 'At the moment I don't think I can move,' he said and stretched, his big, lithe body flexing before he settled himself back beside her. There was a note of humour in his tone when he finished, 'But if you'd rather sleep alone I'll make the effort. A little later.'

'Mmm.' Another yawn took her by surprise.

'Sleep now,' he said, tucking her against him again.

Taryn had never actually slept with anyone. She and

Antony had always made love in his flat and afterwards she'd gone back to hers, but having Cade beside her felt so natural—so right—she drifted almost immediately into slumber.

Cade waited until her breathing became deep and regular before easing her free of his embrace and turning onto his back, folding his arms behind his head as he stared out into the soft silver-hazed darkness.

Only when she moved away from him did he look at her. Even through the netting, the light of the moon shone strongly enough to pick out the long, elegant line of her sleek body and burnish her skin to a pale ivory quite different from its daylight colour of warm honeyed cream.

His hooded gaze traced the curves of her breasts and waist, the pure line of her profile, the lips his kisses had made tender. Astonishingly, his senses stirred again, startling him.

She'd been a willing and lusty lover, her response deliciously sensual. Yet there had been that intriguing element of…not exactly shyness, more like delighted bewilderment when she'd unravelled in his arms.

Although he was still furious with the man who'd abused her, the realisation that no one else had been able to elicit that shuddering primal response produced a visceral, addictive kick of satisfaction.

Of course, the whole story could be a lie…

His instinctive vehement resistance to this possibility warned him he was on the brink of making a huge mistake—of forgetting the reason Taryn was with him. All he'd intended was to get closer to her, find out what made her tick, why she'd laughed at Peter's proposal— what had made Peter decide his life was no longer worth living if she wasn't in it.

But he'd let himself get sidetracked. Seducing her had not been part of the plan.

Unfortunately, he'd wanted her from the moment he'd seen her. Worse than that, he'd let his hunger eat away at his self-control.

Had that happened to Peter? Was that why he'd killed himself—because she'd bled him dry and then left him?

Cade fought back a cold anger, realising with icy self-derision that he didn't want to picture Taryn in his brother's bed. Shocked to realise his hands had clenched into serviceable fists, he deliberately relaxed every muscle.

He wouldn't let such a stupid adolescent emotion as jealousy crumble his hard-won self-control.

Life had taught him that ignoring inconvenient or unpleasant facts and possibilities invariably led to foolish decisions and bitter consequences.

Why did the thought of Taryn responding to Peter with the same passion and heady desire she'd shown a few short minutes ago make him feel like committing some act of violence?

His mouth tightened. Because he'd allowed her to get to him. Somehow, in spite of everything he knew and suspected about her, he'd let down his guard.

A seabird called from above the palms, a sorrowing screech that lifted the hairs on the back of his neck.

Ignore the damn bird, he thought grimly. Face facts.

Lust meant nothing—any normal man would look at Taryn's beautiful face and lithe body and wonder what she was like in bed. But he'd made love to her knowing—and ignoring—the fact she was the only person who knew what had driven Peter to take his life.

He needed to know the reason, and not just because he'd promised his mother he'd find out. For his own peace of mind.

He suspected Peter had always felt slightly inferior. It hadn't helped that he'd never been able to match Cade physically, or that after their father's frightening bout of cancer when Peter was at school both parents had tended to rely more and more on their elder son.

Certainly his brother's behaviour at university hadn't convinced them he was someone they could rely on. Revelling in the freedom, Peter had wallowed in everything college offered except the opportunity to study.

Cade frowned, remembering how worried their parents had been. Fortunately, his brother's discovery of talent as a sculptor had ended that period of dissipation. To everyone's surprise—possibly even Peter's—his interest had become his passion.

He'd been *good*. He might eventually have been great. To die without ever fulfilling his potential would have been bad enough, but to kill himself because a pretty thief laughed at his offer of love and marriage was a bitter travesty.

Cade took a harsh breath, freezing when Taryn moved beside him. He waited until she settled her long legs and tried not to think of them around his hips, to banish from his mind the way she'd given herself utterly to desire.

To him…

His inglorious satisfaction at that thought both shamed him and brought his body to full alert again.

Staying in her bed had been a stupid, passion-addled decision. As soon as she was sleeping soundly enough he'd leave. Until then, he'd concentrate on the fact that she'd almost certainly spent the money Peter had given her. If she still had any of it, she wouldn't have had to resort to a job in a dead-end village.

Perhaps she'd given it to her parents to finance a clinic or a hospital somewhere?

Angered by this futile attempt to provide an excuse, he stared unseeingly across the room.

Think logically, he commanded. It had to be a possibility; although he might think her parents had a very cavalier attitude towards her, she clearly didn't. She'd been very quick to defend them.

Possibly he could find out if an unexpected amount of money had arrived in her parents' coffers. He'd get someone onto it tomorrow morning.

A slight breeze shimmered through the white mosquito netting. Again Cade glanced across at the woman beside him. As though his gaze penetrated the veils of sleep, she murmured something and turned back to him. A lovely, sensuous enigma, she lay like a child, one hand under her cheek, her face calm except for a tiny half smile that curled her lips. Long coppery hair tangled across her shoulder, half covering her breasts.

Once again, Cade's body stirred into urgent hunger. He swung his legs over the side of the bed and stood up. Lashes fluttering, Taryn gave a little sigh, but her eyes remained closed and almost immediately she sank back into deeper sleep.

Moving with a noiseless tread, Cade scooped up his clothes and headed for the door before he could yield to the temptation to get back into the bed and stroke her into wakefulness, to make love to her again…

No, not to make love.

To have sex with her again, he reminded himself savagely, silently closing her bedroom door behind him.

Back in his own room, he threw his clothes onto a

chair and strode across to the windows, pushing back the shutters to drag warm sea-tangy air into his lungs. It had seemed so simple, so logical to bring her to Fala'isi so he could study her more closely. Instead, he'd got himself into an emotional tangle.

No, not emotional. He was *not* in love with her. He didn't know what love was about, so whatever he was feeling right now was—irrelevant.

CHAPTER TEN

DAZED by memories and dreams, Taryn woke from the best sleep she'd experienced for months and smiled sleepily at the crooning of the doves outside. When she'd first heard them she'd been astonished at such a European sound here, but after only a few days they'd become an intrinsic part of Fala'isi for her.

She'd always remember them—along with last night.

Colour burned up through her skin. She was glad Cade had left before she'd woken, yet some weak part of her mourned his absence.

She flung the sheet back, stretching and wincing a little at the protest from rarely used muscles. Making love with Cade had been a considerably more athletic exercise than she was accustomed to.

He'd known exactly what to do to make her body sing with desire, to waken that urgent, exquisite hunger, then send her soaring into an alternate universe where the only thing that mattered was sensual rapture.

She glanced at her watch, muttering as she leapt off the bed. A quick shower left her no time for memories, she pulled on a cool shift that seemed almost formal in this relaxed atmosphere, but had to summon her boldest face when she finally walked out of her room.

Only to find he wasn't there.

He'd written a note, about as personal as a legal document, telling her he'd be back some time in the afternoon. However, he left her with work to do.

It took her all morning to track down and collate the information he asked for, and when she'd finished she looked along the white coral path for any sign of him.

Nothing. The island drowsed in the bright glow of tropical heat. For once the feathery palm fronds were silent and still against a sky so blue and bold it hurt her eyes. Even the lagoon was too warm when she swam, its silky waters enervating rather than refreshing.

She met him on the shell path just after she'd rinsed off the salt water from her body. Although a *pareu* hid her wet bikini, his gaze kindled and he reached out to touch her shoulder but, to her disappointment, immediately let his hand drop.

'Enjoy your swim?' he asked.

'Very much, thank you.'

Sensation churned through her, exciting yet making her apprehensive. She'd never felt like this before—as though the world was fresh and new and infinitely alluring—and she didn't know how to deal with it. Would he expect her to be blasé and sophisticated?

He broke into her thoughts by saying abruptly, 'I've cancelled the trip to check out the fishing industry.'

After a startled upwards look, she nodded. 'OK.'

His black brows lifted. 'No protests? No insistence that you've been looking forward so much to it?'

She grinned. 'I'm not a liar, unless it's polite white lies. And even then I try to avoid them if I can. I'd find the trip interesting, I'm sure, but business is business. And you're the boss so you get to make the decisions.'

They'd set off walking towards the *fale*, but he

stopped in the brief shade of the palms and demanded, 'Is that how you think of me?'

When Taryn hesitated he said, 'The truth, Taryn.'

'Until yesterday,' she said, hoping he couldn't see that she was hedging.

'Just that?'

She sent him a level glance. 'Do you really want to know, or are you pushing me to prove that I always tell the truth?'

Emotion flashed for a moment in his gaze before his lashes came down. When they lifted again his gaze was steely and relentless. 'Both.'

'I don't like being tested,' Taryn said steadily and set off again, her emotions in turmoil. She didn't know what he wanted from her, but she certainly wasn't going to tell him that last night had changed her in some fundamental way.

If she did, he'd probably send her home.

Making love with him had been like setting off into dangerous, unknown territory with no map, no provisions and no equipment, furnished only with hope. Last night it had seemed simple and right. Today she was more wary. If she wanted to keep her heart free and unscathed, she suspected she should be making plans to get back to New Zealand.

And knew she wouldn't.

Abruptly, she said, 'You already know that I found you very attractive right from the start. But until we changed the rules yesterday I did my best to regard you as my employer.'

'And now?'

He was ruthlessly pushing for something from her, an answer to a question she didn't understand.

Half exasperated, half distressed, she said, 'I have

no claim on you, just as you have none on me. We both know this is a temporary arrangement between us. If you want to forget about it, tell me and we'll call it quits.'

And held her breath, feeling as though her whole future depended on his answer.

Cade said in a voice that brooked no argument, 'I shouldn't have started this out here. We'll talk once we're back in the *fale*.'

In the cool dimness of the living room he glanced at the pile of papers on the table and then, blue eyes hooded, examined her face. 'I want to make sure that the fact that I'm your employer had no bearing on your charming surrender last night.'

'I haven't been to bed with any other of my employers,' she said stiffly, obscurely hurt.

'I didn't intend to insult you,' he said, his voice hard. 'I certainly didn't mean to imply that you slept with all—or any of—your employers. I just wanted to make absolutely sure that you didn't feel pressured into making love.'

Taryn shook her head vigorously. 'No.'

And stopped, because anything more might reveal too much. But couldn't he tell that she'd surrendered wholeheartedly, with everything she had, everything she was?

Once again that flinty gaze probed hers for long heart-stopping seconds, until he seemed to relax and drew her towards him. Almost abstractedly, he murmured, 'You're the only employee I've ever made love to.'

His head came down and he kissed her throat, saying against her skin, 'You taste like the sea, sun-warmed and salty, scented with flowers and the wind.'

Unable to hold back, she turned her face into his and

they kissed, and he found the knot of her *pareu* and it dropped in a wet heap on the floor, leaving her only in her bikini. Cade made a deep noise in his throat and his arms locked around her. Without further resistance, she lifted her face for his kiss, body pressed to body as desire—torrid and compelling—flashed between them.

'And you taste of you,' she said on a sigh when he finally lifted his head.

Taryn expected him to loosen his arms, but he didn't. Resting his cheek on her wet hair, he said, 'Not regretting anything?'

Regret? How could she regret the most wonderful experience of her life so far? Last night had been utterly magical, a revelation to her.

Was being a good lover a talent, something instinctive? How many women had Cade practised with to gain that mastery? Not only had he divined which parts of her were acutely sensitive to his touch, but he'd been slow and subtle and erotically compelling, seducing her until she'd had no thought for anything beyond the enchantment he worked on her willing body and mind.

'Not a thing,' she said huskily.

He smiled dangerously and let her go, but his grip slid down to fasten around her wrists so he could lift her hands to his mouth.

Tiny shivers chased the length of her spine as he kissed each palm. Be careful, some part of her warned. Be very careful. You don't want to lose your heart to him. Remember, he might want you but it's not going to last.

His tone amused, he said, 'Then we're suited in every way,' and kissed her properly again.

Joy fountained through Taryn. Once again, she felt

the swift, piercing surge of desire, brazen as the tropical sun, and this time she had no forebodings, no fear about whether or not she was going to be able to respond. This time she could make love to Cade with complete confidence that the same rapture that had taken her to paradise the night before was waiting for her again.

'You'll get all wet,' she said against his throat.

'Mmm,' he murmured. 'Somehow, keeping dry is not a priority right now.'

'What is?'

He looked into her face with half closed eyes and the fierce smile of a hunter. 'Making it to a bed.'

They got there, but only just, and later, in a dreamy daze as she listened to him breathe beside her, Taryn decided she'd never been so happy before, never felt so completely at one with the world.

She drifted into sleep, but stirred when he got up. Opening her eyes, she smiled mistily at him, that flame of awareness beating high within her again at the sight of him, lean and bronzed and beautifully made, as powerfully built as he was desirable.

He dropped a kiss on her mouth but, before she could reach out and pull him down, he straightened. 'Dinner,' he said succinctly.

'Help, yes!' She swung her legs over the side of the bed and sat up. Tonight they were having dinner with the Chapmans.

Gaze darkening, Cade said, 'Don't move—try not to even breathe—until I get out of the room.'

Thrilled by her effect on him, she obediently froze.

Laughing softly, he left, scooping up his clothes as he went.

I'm in love with him, she thought, suddenly assailed

by a wild mixture of apprehension and delight. *I'm in love with Cade Peredur.*

No, that was just foolish post-coital bliss scrambling her brain. She straightened her shoulders; she was perfectly content with the rules they'd made. Love had nothing to do with this. Eventually, they'd go their separate ways and she'd grieve for a while and miss him like crazy.

She'd gone into their affair with her eyes open and when it ended she'd get on with real life, grateful to Cade for showing her that she was a normal woman who could make love with abandon and joy.

So she'd accept this fantasy interlude for what it was—an enchantment that would end once they left the seductively sensuous lure of the tropics. And, if all went well, she might one day find a man she could both desire and truly love, one who'd love her.

Dinner with the Chapmans was fun; Fleur was an excellent hostess, Luke an interesting man with the same inbuilt authority that marked Cade. Afterwards, they drank coffee and watched the moon rise over the ocean, and Cade mentioned her parents.

'They do magnificent work,' Luke Chapman said. 'I believe they've just acquired a new yacht.'

Taryn nodded. 'A much bigger one. They've had it converted into a sort of mini-hospital and it's working well, but Dad's next project is to find the finance for a shore-based hospital on one of the outlying islands. And, after that, they want to set up a trust that will help local people study as nurses and doctors. He wants to make sure that when he and Mum retire—if they ever do—they leave a working system behind.'

'Big ambitions,' Luke observed.

'And expensive ones,' Cade supplied. 'Where do they find the money to keep going?'

Taryn laughed, then sighed. 'So far it's been mainly donations. Dad's quite shameless when it comes to asking for it.'

'That's a chancy, hand-to-mouth way for a charity—especially a private one—to exist. Setting up the new yacht must have cost them a packet,' Cade said.

'They were lucky—they got a big donation at just the right time.' Sadness struck her at the thought of Peter, who'd been so insistent on donating it.

And, emboldened by the Chapmans' obvious interest, she looked directly at their host. 'They want something along the lines of the health service you have here.'

Which led to further discussion. The Chapmans made no promises but, as she and Cade left, Luke said, 'I'll give you the name of the man who runs our health service. Your father could do worse than get in touch with him.'

Out of earshot, Cade said thoughtfully, 'You're a good daughter.'

Flushing, Taryn replied, 'My parents deserve all the help they can get.'

He said nothing more and she wondered whether he too was thinking of helping her parents. If so, perhaps they might keep in touch...

Don't, she told herself in sudden anguish. Don't hope for anything more. It wasn't going to happen, and wishing for it would only make it harder to recover.

Because now her heart was involved. Oh, she'd tried so hard to ignore it but, as they'd talked over the coffee table, she'd looked across at Cade and *known* she loved him. The knowledge had pierced her like a sword—

transcendent yet shattering. Life without Cade stretched before her, bleak as a desert.

She looked up into a sky so brightly lit by the moon the stars were tiny pinpricks against black velvet. No sign of fruit bats, she thought wistfully.

If it hadn't been for that low-flying one, would Cade have ever kissed her?

Another question she couldn't answer.

Back in the *fale*, Cade glanced at his watch. 'I'm expecting a call from London in a few minutes, so I'll say goodnight now.'

It was like a blow to the heart. She felt her expression freeze and said hastily, 'Oh! Goodnight then.'

He surprised her by kissing her lightly, an arm round her shoulder holding her without passion.

'Sleep well,' he said and left her, walking into his room.

But, once there, he stood indecisively for a few moments, looking around as though he'd never seen the room before.

Every instinct was telling him to get out. He was in too deep and tonight he'd slipped over some invisible boundary, one he hadn't known existed. The whole evening had been—he struggled to find the right word and could only come up with *satisfying*. Satisfying in some deep, unplumbed way that scared the hell out of him.

He was falling and, if he didn't stop the process, he had no idea where he'd land. Damn it, it had been a quiet dinner with a couple he called friends, yet for some reason he'd accessed a level of—again, he searched for a word, finally settling on *contentment*—that still clung to him.

Contentment! He got to his feet and paced the room, angular face dark with frustration. Contentment was for the old, those with no further ambitions to pursue. He had plenty.

Yet, sitting under that voluptuous moon, watching the way its aura cooled Taryn's red hair and turned her skin to satin, listening to the low music of her laughter, he'd found himself thinking that life could hold nothing more for him.

Making love to her had been the most stupid thing he'd ever done.

No, bringing her to Fala'isi was that; their lovemaking had only compounded a problem he'd refused to face. Still didn't want to face.

There was only one thing to do. Before he lost his head and did something irretrievable, he had to tell her who he was, and what he wanted from her.

Surprisingly, Taryn slept well, waking next morning to sunlight and the muted coo of the doves against the slow thunder of the distant waves against the reef. And an aching emptiness because last night Cade had left her alone.

When she emerged, Cade was standing beside the pool, talking into his phone. He glanced up when he heard her, nodded and strode to the other end of the pool, the tension in his powerful back and lean, strong body warning her that something had gone wrong.

The terrace table had been set for breakfast for two, so she poured herself some coffee and spooned passionfruit pulp over golden slices of papaya.

She couldn't hear what Cade was saying, but his tone echoed his body language. He was angry.

When he strode over she asked a little warily, 'Trouble?'

'Problems.' Dismissing them, he sat down opposite

her and examined her face, his expression flinty. 'All right?'

'Of course,' she said automatically. Much more than all right, in fact. Her heart was singing and every cell in her body responded with pleasure to the sight of him. 'Is there anything I can do?'

'No—just a business rival thinking that being on the other side of the world means I'm not keeping my eye on the kitchen. However, there is something I must tell you,' he said shortly. 'Did Peter Cooper ever tell you he had a brother?'

Taryn's spoon clattered into her plate. Searching his face, she swallowed. Nothing showed in the grey-blue eyes but an icy determination. 'Yes,' she answered automatically.

'Did you know I am—was—his brother?'

Taryn had never fainted in her life but, as she felt the colour drain from her skin, she thought dizzily that this was going to be the first time.

He said abruptly, 'Put your head down.' And, when she didn't move, he got to his feet and swivelled her chair around so he could push her head below her heart. The heavy, sick feeling beneath her ribs dissipated but she couldn't think—couldn't even make sense of the words jumbling through her mind.

After a few seconds the dizziness faded and she croaked, 'Let me up—I'm all right.'

'Sure?' He released her, watching her as she straightened.

After one look at his controlled face, she asked inanely, 'How can you be his brother? You don't have the same name.'

He shrugged. 'I went to the Coopers when I was five. Peter was born four years later.'

Taryn blinked, her mind seizing on this because she didn't dare—not yet—ask why he hadn't told her right at the start who he was.

'I see.' Heart twisting at the thought of what he must have endured as a child, she concentrated with fierce determination on the cluster of hibiscus flowers in the centre of the table.

She'd never be able to enjoy their showy vividness again without remembering this moment. *Peter's brother.* Cade was Peter's foster-brother.

Taryn believed in coincidences, but not where Cade was concerned.

Cade made things happen. He must have known that she and Peter had been friends.

Had he deliberately tracked her down? Was his love-making a sham? *Why?*

Pain sliced through her, so intense she hugged herself, trying to force the mindless agony away. When she trusted herself to speak again, she asked quietly, 'Why didn't you tell me this when we first met?'

His eyes narrowed into flinty shards. In a tone that almost brought her to her feet, ready to run, he said, 'Because I wanted to find out what sort of woman you were.'

'Why?' Every breath hurt, but she had to know.

He said evenly, 'I wanted to know what the woman who laughed at his proposal was like.'

Taryn almost ducked as though avoiding a blow. White-faced and shaking, she had to force herself to speak. 'How...how did you know that?'

His beautiful mouth tightened—the mouth that had brought her such ecstasy.

'How I know doesn't matter. Are you surprised that I should want to know why he killed himself?'

Dragging in a sharply painful breath, she reached deep into her reserves to find strength—enough strength to force herself up so she faced him, head held high.

'No,' she said quietly. 'Do you think I don't regret laughing? That I don't wish I could go back in time and change how I reacted? I thought he was joking.'

'Men do not *joke* about proposing,' he said between his teeth, making the word sound obscene. 'Why the hell would you think that?'

'Because we didn't have that sort of relationship,' she cried. 'We were friends—good friends—but we'd never even kissed.'

Stone-faced, he asked, 'Never?'

Firming her jaw, she admitted, 'The occasional peck on the check, that's all. Nothing beyond that. In fact, I thought—' She stopped.

'Go on,' he said silkily.

She swallowed. 'I thought he had a lover... There was a woman...' She stopped and forced her brain to leash the tornado of emotions rioting through her. 'Or that he might be gay.'

Cade looked at her, his expression kept under such rigid discipline she had no idea what he was thinking.

'He wasn't. Far from it.' He made a sudden, abrupt gesture, his control splintering. 'So if he never made a move on you, never showed that he wanted you, never indicated he might be in love with you, why the *hell* did he propose?'

'I don't know,' she said wretchedly. 'I really did think he was joking. And I was so taken aback—so startled—I laughed. Until I realised he was serious. I never thought... I *still* find it hard to believe he was in love with me.'

'I'm finding everything you've said hard to believe,'

he said in a level judicial voice. 'I know—knew—my brother better than anyone, and he wouldn't have rashly proposed to a woman he wasn't sure of. Peter wasn't one for wild impulses.'

Taryn opened her mouth, then closed it again.

Harshly, Cade said, 'Tell me what you were going to say.'

When she hesitated, he commanded in a tone that sent a cold shiver scudding down her spine, *'Tell me.'*

'Just that as a brother you might have known him well, but as a man…how much time did you spend with him? He could be impulsive. And before he—'

'Killed himself,' Cade inserted when she couldn't go on.

'Before he died,' she went on bleakly, 'he was ecstatic at scoring that wonderful commission. It meant so much to him. He told me it validated everything he'd done before, and that he'd finally make his family proud of him. He was so happy planning the sculpture, so eager to get on with the work—almost crazy with delight.'

Shocked, she realised she was wringing her hands. She stopped, reasserted control and said without thinking, 'I swear, killing himself was the last thing on his mind.'

'Because he believed you loved him,' Cade said ruthlessly. 'When he proposed, what did you say to him?'

CHAPTER ELEVEN

TARYN flinched when she met Cade's—*Peter's brother's*—hooded, pitiless eyes. 'After I laughed, do you mean?' she asked on a half sob. 'I told him that although I liked him very much and valued him enormously as friend, I wasn't in love with him.'

'And what did he say to those noble sentiments?'

Colour flamed the length of her cheekbones, then faded into an icy chill. 'He said he hoped I'd always remember him as a good friend.'

'And it didn't occur to you he was saying goodbye?' he demanded incredulously.

'Of course not.' Then she said swiftly, 'Well…yes. Yes, of course I realised that our *friendship* was over. His proposal changed everything—and I was going back to New Zealand in a few hours. But…if he loved me, why did he leave it so late to propose?'

Cade said nothing and she went on in a low, subdued voice, 'I did…I did love him, but not the way he wanted me to, and I still can't…'

Cade remained emphatically silent while she gulped back her emotions, eventually regaining enough self possession to say in a voice drained of all colour, 'I d-don't know what I could have done to help him.'

'Nothing.' He was watching her so closely she took

a step backwards. In a level voice, he said, 'Although offering to return his money might have made some difference to his decision to kill himself.'

'Money?' She flushed when she realised what he was talking about. 'It had already gone to my parents. It was used to fit out the new yacht—and he wanted to give it to Mum and Dad, Cade. If you believe nothing else, believe that. He insisted on sending it to them.'

He shook his head. 'Not that—I know he donated it to your parents. As I said last night—you're a good daughter.'

Now she understood what he'd meant—and why he'd left her alone last night.

Numbly, she listened to him continue, shrivelling inside when he went on, 'Peter had every right to give his money to whoever he wanted to. No, the money I'm talking about is the rest of his advance for the sculpture he was commissioned to produce.'

His words rang senselessly in her ears, jangling around her head in meaningless syllables. She stared at him, met penetrating eyes that judged and assessed every tiny muscle flickering in her face.

'What are you talking about?' she asked numbly.

He lifted one eyebrow to devastating effect. 'Don't be coy, Taryn. As well as the donation for the clinic, Peter gave you a large chunk of that advance. Where is it?'

Deep inside her, some fragile, persistent hope shattered into shards, dissolved into nothingness, leaving behind a black bitterness and misery.

Cade had deliberately targeted her, tracked her down and made love to her—because he thought she'd taken money from Peter. A large amount of money. Peter had gleefully told her how much it was, and that it was to be used to buy the materials for his sculpture.

Everything Cade had done, he'd done because he was convinced she was a thief. He'd brought her here, made love to her, given her such joy—and it was all false, all lies...

Trying to speak, she discovered that her throat had closed. Her stomach turned and she clapped a hand over her mouth.

He said, 'Stay there.'

Taryn closed her eyes, shielding her misery from him. She heard a clink and felt a glass of water being put into her hand.

'Drink it up,' he advised.

Their fingers touched and, in spite of everything, a jolt sparked through her. Dear God, she thought wearily, how could her body betray her like that when she now knew exactly what he thought of her—a liar and a common thief?

She wished she could summon righteous anger at being so badly misjudged, but her only emotion was a deep, aching grief for a fantasy that had turned into a dark nightmare.

Although she was sure she'd choke if she tried to drink the water, her throat was so dry and painful she forced several gulps down.

'Thank you,' she said hoarsely, wishing he'd step back. He was too close, and she...she was as broken as though the very foundations of her world had been cut from under her.

Clutching the glass in front of her like a pathetically useless shield, she said, 'I don't have anything of Peter's—certainly not his money.'

'Taryn, if you don't have it, who does?'

He spoke quite calmly and for a brief, bewildered

second she wondered if indeed—somehow—she did have the money.

Then sanity returned, and with it some courage. 'I don't know,' she said. Her voice wobbled, so she swallowed and tried again. 'All I know is that he didn't give me any money. I'll furnish you with the records of my bank account so you can see for yourself.'

His lashes drooped. 'I want to see them, although if you took it you've had plenty of time to stash it away and cover your tracks.' He waited for a second and when she remained silent went on, 'It will be much easier if you just tell me where it's gone. Once it's returned, we'll forget about it.'

Fighting back against shock and fear and disillusionment, she drained the glass and set it down. She looked up, measuring him like a duellist of old, sensing that once again he was testing her, assessing her reactions to discern whether she'd stolen the money.

In other words, he wasn't sure.

The thought acted like a stimulant, but she forced herself to repress the wild hope that burst into life. Although her thoughts were still far from coherent, she said as calmly as she could, 'I swear to you, Peter didn't give me a cent all the time we knew each other.'

'Taryn, every financial transaction leaves a paper trail.'

When she shrugged, he finished softly, 'I can find those trails.'

It was a threat, but now she'd found a few shreds of composure she recognised it for an empty one. 'You'll discover that there's nothing to find. Cade, you'll never know how sorry I am that Peter's dead, and how sorry I am that I laughed when he proposed. I have that on my conscience, but not the loss of his money. And now I want to go home.'

Home? She didn't have a home, but if she didn't get away from Cade soon she'd crack. Now that she knew the depths of his betrayal, she couldn't bear to stay anywhere near him—let alone pretend they were lovers.

'We'll be leaving tomorrow,' he said inflexibly. 'Until then, I'll expect you to behave as you have been.'

'You must be joking!' she burst out, incredulous at his arrogant command.

'Far from it.' And when she started to speak again he said, 'You won't get off the island without my permission so don't try it.'

She stared at him, met an implacable gaze. He had to be lying—yet, perhaps not. Fleur Chapman might be a warm, compassionate woman, but her husband had the same air of effortless, uncompromising authority that marked Cade. They were also good friends.

And there were her parents—if the Chapmans were thinking of helping their mission, she didn't dare put that in question. Quietly, she said, 'Very well, I'll work for you, but that's all.'

'That's all I want,' he returned.

He turned away, stopping when she said, 'Why did you wait until now to tell me this?'

Without looking at her, he said, 'It had gone far enough.'

And he strode out of the room.

Taryn made sure she was in bed when he came back in the warm tropical night. Working had given her mind something to do—something other than returning endlessly to that moment when Cade had accused her of stealing money from Peter and stripped away her foolish, self-serving illusions.

Except that in bed, faced with the truth, her mind refused to allow sleep. Endless, scattered, anguished thoughts tumbled through her mind until she forced herself to accept that she couldn't love Cade. He'd deceived her and seduced her.

Actually, he hadn't seduced her. Besotted idiot that she was, she'd met him more than halfway there.

But she had too much pride to love a man who could deliberately lie to her—even though she accepted he had good reason to find out what had killed his brother.

Most nights a sighing breeze kept the mosquito nets breathing in and out, but tonight the sultry heat—and what felt perilously like a broken heart—kept her wide-eyed and sleepless.

On a half sob, she thought Cade had caused her more wakeful hours than anyone else in her life.

A pang of exquisite pain made her catch her breath. More than anything, she wanted to be able to blank him out, forget she'd ever met him, ever seen him. The memories hurt too much.

So she set her mind to the mystery of Peter's missing advance. He'd splashed money around a bit once he'd gained the commission, but he hadn't been extravagant. Certainly not enough to have spent it all...

She was still mulling this over when she heard Cade come into the *fale*. Her breath locked in her throat and her lashes flew up. For a few ridiculous seconds she hardly dared breathe, but of course he didn't knock on her door.

Once she left Fala'isi and Cade, surely she'd get over this aching emptiness, this sense of loss and loneliness, of being betrayed by hopes she hadn't even recognised?

Driven by a searing restlessness and a heart so sore it

felt like an actual physical pain, she got up and walked across to the window. It took her some time to realise that Cade was out there in the tropical night, a tall, dark form standing beside the pool.

Still, so still, as though he couldn't move...

Moonlight shimmered across the arrogant planes of his face, picking out in silver the sweeping strength of bone structure, the straight line of his mouth. Tears burned behind Taryn's eyes, clogged her throat. She blinked them back, focusing on the object Cade held in his hand.

A flower, she realised when he turned it and light glimmered across its silken petals. A hibiscus bloom. What intrigued him so much about the blossoms?

Wincing, she saw him throw it down as he had done before. Then she froze when he suddenly stooped and picked up the flower. Hardly daring to breathe, she watched him walk towards the *fale*.

Her breath sighed out slowly and she turned and made her way back to her bed, too heartsore to do more than wonder why he'd bothered to pick up the flower...

Eventually exhaustion claimed her, but only to dream, and wake with a start to wonder why her unconscious mind had brought her images of a friend of Peter's, famous for her artistic installations.

Peter had respected Andrée Brown as an artist and enjoyed her acid wit, but they'd had an odd, edgy relationship. Sometimes Taryn had suspected he and Andrée were lovers, and wished she could like the woman more. She'd found her heavy-going, a nervy, almost neurotic woman who lived for her art and made no secret of her disdain for people without talent.

Grimacing into the humid air, Taryn used every technique she could remember to calm her mind and woo the oblivion of sleep. But when it arrived it was disturbed by chaotic, frightening dreams so that she woke in the morning unrefreshed and heavy-eyed.

Work was penance; treating Cade with cool dispassion was hell. Doggedly, she plugged through the day, even went to the beach in the late afternoon when she judged everyone would be inside preparing for drinks before dinner.

Soon she'd be back in New Zealand; she'd never have to see Cade again, and this heavy grief that had lodged in her heart would fade. People recovered from the most appalling things; she'd recover too.

She had to...

Shaded by palms, Cade watched her swim towards shore, long arms stroking effortlessly through the water. When she stood, the westering sun kindled an aura of gold from the glittering sheets of water that poured from her. She looked like Venus rising from the Mediterranean, slender and lithe and radiant, no sign of stress in her lovely face, her hair a sleek wet cloak of red so dark it was almost crimson.

Hot frustration roiled through him. Had he just made the biggest mistake in his life?

His jaw tightened as she stooped to pick up her towel. In spite of everything, heat flared through him. Damn the woman; he'd spent most of last night lying awake, remembering how sweetly, how ardently she'd flamed in his arms.

In spite of everything, he couldn't reconcile the laughing, valiant woman he'd come to know with the woman he knew her to be.

His cell phone stopped him just as he was about to step out onto the hot sand. He said something fast and low, but the call was from his PA in London. Today was the day they were to get the results of a further series of tests his PA's three-year-old had endured.

'Yes,' he barked into the phone.

He knew the instant his PA spoke. Instead of the heavy weight of fears of the past month or so, his tone was almost buoyant. 'It's not—what we feared.'

'Thank God,' Cade said fervently. 'What's the problem?'

He listened for a minute or so as Roger told him what lay ahead for little Melinda. When the voice on the other side of the world faded, he said, 'So it's going to be tough, but nowhere near as bad as it could have been.'

'No.'

'OK, take your wife and Melinda to my house in Provence and stay there for a week. Get some sun into all of you.' He cut short his PA's startled objection. 'I refuse to believe you can't organise someone to take your place. I won't be back for another week, so things can ride until then. And buy Melinda a gift from me— something she's been wanting.'

He overrode Roger's thanks, but fell silent when his PA asked urgently, 'Have you heard from Sampson?'

'No.' Not since the investigator he'd set to track down the money from Peter's account had come to a dead end.

Cade stiffened as the tinny voice on the other end of the phone said, 'He rang on Thursday to say he might have something for you in a couple of days.'

An odd dread gripping him, Cade glanced at his watch, made a swift calculation and said, 'OK, thanks. And enjoy Provence.'

He stood looking down at the face of his phone, then set his jaw and hit the button that would get him

Sampson. As the investigator began to speak, his intent expression turned from hard discipline to shock, and then to anger. Swinging around as he listened, he strode back to the *fale*, the cell phone pressed to his ear.

An hour or so later, Taryn walked reluctantly into the *fale*, a *pareu* draped around her from armpit to ankle, only hesitating a moment when she realised Cade was already there.

He said harshly, 'I have something to tell you. Something about Peter.'

'I don't want—' She stopped, her eyes widening. He looked—exhausted. A fugitive hope died into darkness. It took her a moment to summon enough strength to say quietly, 'What is it?'

He closed his eyes a second, then subjected her to an unreadable examination. 'Did you know he was a drug addict?'

Shock silenced her, leaving her shivering. She put out a shaking hand and clutched the top of a chair, bracing herself while Cade waited, his face held under such rigid restraint she couldn't discern any emotion at all.

She whispered, 'No. Oh, no. Are you sure?'

'Yes. I've just been talking to the man I got to investigate the whereabouts of Peter's advance.' He paused, then said in a voice she'd never heard before, one thick with self-disgust, 'You'd better sit down.'

'I'm all right,' she said automatically. 'Go on.'

But he shook his head. 'Sit.'

And because her head was whirling and she felt nauseated, she obeyed, but said immediately, 'You can sit too.'

He said, 'I feel better standing.'

Taryn swallowed. 'All right.'

But he sat down anyway.

Slowly, painfully feeling her way, she whispered, 'I hate to say it, but it makes sense. Peter was mercurial—in tearing good spirits one day, then in the depths the next. I thought it was artistic temperament—made even more so when he got that commission. And asking me to marry him was so out of the blue! He was a great, good friend, but there had been nothing...nothing like...'

Nothing like the instant, unmistakeable reaction between you and me. A glance at Cade's stern face made her remember that only she had felt that wild erotic response.

Stumbling a little, she went on, 'Just nothing. Which was why I thought he had to be joking.'

Would Cade believe her now? She held her breath, her heart thumping so heavily in her ears she had to strain to hear his reply.

'He wasn't joking,' he said roughly. 'He loved you.'

But Taryn shook her head. 'He never made the slightest approach—never touched me except for the odd kiss on the cheek—the sort of kiss you'd give a child.'

'I imagine he was afraid to let you get too close in case you found out about his addiction.' Cade spoke with a control that almost scared her. 'And, although I can't be sure, I suspect he began to hope that if you married him he'd be able to beat the addiction.'

Taryn drew in a ragged breath, grateful he'd made her sit. 'It would never have got that far,' she said numbly. 'I loved him too, but not—' She stopped again, because she'd been so lost in Peter's private tragedy she'd almost blurted out *not like I love you.*

'Not in a sexual way,' she finished, acutely aware of his probing gaze. 'But, oh, I *wish* I'd known. I might have been able to help him. At the very least, I'd have known not to laugh when he proposed...'

'He would have been ashamed of his weakness,' Cade said.

'If I'd understood, I wouldn't have let him down so badly.' The words were wrenched from a depth of pain she could hardly bear.

Cade said, 'He didn't tell anyone.' He paused before saying without inflection, 'Our parents knew what addiction could do, and not only to the one with the problem. My birth mother was an addict—they'd seen what living with her had done to me. When I arrived at their house I was feral—wild and filthy and barely able to function on any level but rage. They worked wonders with nothing more than uncomplicated love and fortitude and their conviction that there was some good in me.'

She made a slight sound of protest and he went on harshly, 'It's the truth. They fostered me because they were told they'd never be able to have children. Peter was their miracle, but it appears he always felt they loved me more than him.'

He'd withheld so much about himself, so much she'd longed to know. The telling of it was clearly painful and now she wished he didn't feel obliged to. 'I'm so sorry,' she whispered.

'Damn it, I don't know why,' he said with a hard anguish that wrung her heart. 'I just don't know.'

But Taryn thought she understood. When he compared himself to Cade's compelling character and the success he'd achieved, Peter must have felt inferior.

As though driven, Cade got to his feet, moving awkwardly for so lithe a man. For once he seemed unable to find the right words. 'I thought we had a good relationship, but it appears it was not. He didn't come to me for help because he resented me.'

'No,' she said swiftly. This was something she could give him—possibly the only thing he'd take from her.

She steadied her voice. 'Whenever he spoke of you there was no mistaking his affection. He never said your name—it was always *my brother*—but he told me little incidents of his childhood, and he always spoke of you with love. He might have felt he couldn't measure up to you, Cade, but he did love you.'

He got to his feet and strode across the room as though driven by inner demons. 'Life would be a hell of a lot easier without love. It complicates things so damned much,' he said angrily. Then, as though he'd revealed far too much, he continued, 'I owe you an apology.'

Taryn's breath locked in her throat. If only he'd tell her he'd really wanted her, that it hadn't all been a fantasy...

One glance at his face told her it wasn't going to happen.

He went on in a cool, deliberate tone, 'I should have made sure of my facts before I taxed you with stealing the money. It's no excuse that I didn't want to believe it, but no one else seemed close enough to him to be a suspect. And he'd given you the money for your parents.'

He hesitated, and she waited with her breath locked in her throat.

But he finished, 'From what the investigator has discovered, it probably all went to pay off drug debts.'

Yet another thing to blame himself for, she thought bleakly, once more faced with a situation she was unable to help, unable to do anything but watch him with an anguish she didn't dare reveal.

In a softly savage voice that sent shudders down her

spine, he said, 'That supplier will be out of business very soon—just as soon as I find out who he is.'

'I might be able to help there,' Taryn said impulsively, immediately regretting her statement when he swung around, eyes narrowing. Choosing her words carefully, she said, 'Peter had a friend—an artist he respected— but it was a difficult relationship. Intense and vaguely antagonistic...'

As she spoke, she suddenly realised why she'd dreamed of the other woman. Torn, she hesitated.

'What was his name?' Cade demanded.

Taryn made up her mind and gave him Andrée Brown's name. 'I saw him handing her a wad of notes once. At the time I didn't think anything of it. It might have been perfectly innocent. Probably was.'

'But?' Cade said curtly.

She frowned, trying to put into words something that hadn't been suspicious but which she'd remembered. 'When he realised I'd seen he told me why—he had a perfectly logical reason, but his reaction was odd. Not for long, and not so much that I was at all suspicious, but just a bit *off.*'

Keen-eyed, he asked her to write the woman's name down, and when she hesitated once more, gave a hard, mirthless smile. 'Are you worried I might hound her too? I never make the same mistake twice,' he said brusquely. 'Taryn, I've treated you abominably. Whatever I can do for you I'll do.'

'Nothing,' she returned automatically, chilled to the bone but holding herself together with an effort that came near to exhausting her.

He said harshly, 'Don't be a fool.'

Taryn's heart contracted, but she steadied her voice enough to be able to say, 'I accept your apology. You had

what you thought were good reasons for your mistake—
and I understand why you wanted to punish someone
who took away your brother's hope.'

'He could have asked for help, booked himself into
rehab.'

'Poor Peter,' she said, her voice uneven. 'Would you
have helped him?'

'Of course.'

She believed him. 'And surely your parents wouldn't
have turned against him?'

He wasn't nearly so quick to answer this time. 'At first
they'd have been shocked and intensely disappointed,
but they loved him. They'd have tried to help him. I had
no idea he thought he'd failed them, and I'm sure they
didn't suspect either. If they had, they'd have reassured
him.'

Something about his words made Taryn say, 'You
speak of them in the past tense.'

He shrugged. 'My father died of a heart attack two
weeks after Peter's funeral, and my mother walked out
in front of a car a few weeks later.' After a glance at
her horrified face, he said immediately, 'No, she didn't
intend to. She'll be in a wheelchair for the rest of her
life.'

More than anything, Taryn longed to put her arms
around him, give him what comfort she could. She
didn't. His tone was a keep-off sign, a message rein-
forced by the jutting lift of his chin, taut stance and
steely eyes.

She said quietly, 'I'm so sorry.'

'You have nothing to be sorry about.' As though he
couldn't wait to be rid of her, he went on, 'I'll get you
back to New Zealand straightaway.'

Within twelve hours she was in Aramuhu, listening to

her landlord while he told her that the sleepout needed urgent repairs and she'd have to find somewhere else to live.

She nodded and must have appeared quite normal because he said, 'I'm sorry, Taryn. The roof's started to leak and I have to get it all repaired before the kiwi fruit pickers come in. You'll stay with us until you find somewhere else to live, of course.'

When he'd gone she sat down and let the slow, unbidden tears well into her eyes, farewelling the past, looking ahead at a future that loomed grey and joyless.

CHAPTER TWELVE

'TARYN, why won't you come with us?' Hands on her slender hips, her flatmate eyed her with exasperation. 'You're never going to get over The Mystery Lover by staying obstinately at home.'

Taryn's lazy smile hid the flash of pain that any mention of Cade always brought. 'I'm too tired to go halfway across Auckland for a concert—I walked up to the top of One Tree Hill this afternoon,' she said cheerfully. 'I'd be nodding off halfway through the first song.'

Isla grinned. 'You couldn't—the band's too loud. And you're not going to get over a broken heart by turning into a hermit.'

'I'm not a hermit,' Taryn told her. 'I'm an introvert. We enjoy being alone.'

Her flatmate wasn't going to be diverted. 'Piffle. It's just not *natural* for you to never go out with *anyone*.'

Taryn said with indignation, 'Stop exaggerating. I have gone out.'

'Friends don't count!' Isla flung her arms out in one of the dramatic gestures she did so well. 'Auckland has over a million people living here, half of them men, and quite a few of them looking for a gorgeous woman like you. But no, you ignore them all because you're still fixated on some man who did you wrong. You know how you're going to end up, don't you? You'll be an old maid, buying baby clothes for your friends' kids but never for your own. And it's such a waste because you're not only gorgeous, you're clever and nice as well, and you can cook and change a car tyre—the world *needs* your genes.'

'What's this about babies?' Taryn eyed her suspiciously. 'You're not trying to tell me you're pregnant, I hope?'

Isla snorted. 'You know better than that. Look, it's a fabulous night, just right for a concert in the Domain. I've got enough food and champagne to feed an army, and I happen to know that in our group there'll be one unattached, stunning man. You'll love the whole thing. And it will do you good.'

'Thanks for suggesting it, but no.'

Isla cast her eyes upwards. 'OK, OK, but I'm not giving up—I'll get you out sooner or later, just see if I don't. And that's both a threat and a promise.'

She turned away to gather up the picnic basket and a wrap, adding over her shoulder, 'Still, at least you're no longer looking quite so much like a ghost. You had me really worried for a while.'

'I'm fine,' Taryn said automatically. 'Go on, off you go. Have fun.'

'That's a given. See you.' Isla disappeared down the passage of the elderly villa she shared with her two flatmates. The other one, a man, was away for the weekend. Taryn liked them both and got on well with them, grateful for their uncomplicated friendship, just as she was grateful for the job she'd found in one of Auckland's smaller libraries.

She heard the front door open and Isla's voice, startled and then welcoming. 'Yes, she's here. In the living room—second door on the right. See you.'

Hastily, Taryn scrambled to her feet. She wasn't expecting a visitor.

The door opened and Cade walked in, somehow seeming taller than she remembered, she thought confusedly above the urgent clamour of her heart. Her stomach dropped and then a great surge of joy burst through her.

He stopped just inside the door, gaze hardening as he examined her. When her tension reached near-screaming point, he said, 'You've lost weight.'

Her head came up. Reining in the urgent need to feast her eyes on him, she said astringently, 'Thank you for that. *You* don't appear to have changed at all. How did you know where I live?'

'I've known since you got here,' he said, adding, 'and any changes in me are internal, but they're there. Are you going to ask me to sit down?'

Taryn cast a desperate glance around the room, furnished in cast offs from Isla's parents, who were short. 'Yes, of course. The sofa, I think.'

Afraid to ask why he'd come, what he wanted, she sank into a chair, only to scramble up again. 'I'm afraid I haven't got anything to drink—not alcohol, I mean. Would you like some coffee? Or tea?' She was babbling and he knew it.

'No, thank you,' he said curtly. 'How are you?'

She managed to rake up enough composure to say, 'I'm fine. Thank you. Very well, in fact.' Struggling to control the wild jumble of emotions churning through her, she sat down again. 'How are things with you?'

Shrugging, he said in his driest tone, 'Fine. I thought you'd like to know that Peter's supplier is in custody now. And yes, the go-between was Andrée Brown—who cheated Peter by telling him the dealer was demanding more and more money. In effect, she drove him to his death. She's being investigated for fraud and drug trafficking.'

Taryn grimaced, relieved to have something concrete to fix on. 'I'm glad. It's been worrying me that Peter might never be avenged. It was kind of you to come and tell me.'

Cade said harshly, 'You deserved to know. And I don't consider bringing them to account to be revenge—it's a simple matter of justice.'

Taryn realised every muscle was painfully tight, and that she was holding her breath. Forcing herself to exhale, she said, 'You said you always knew where I was—how?'

'I had someone keep an eye on you.' His mouth curved as he met her seething glance.

'Why?'

He shrugged. 'To make sure you were all right.'

Taryn didn't dare look at him in case the hope that bloomed so swiftly—so foolishly—was baseless. She said steadily, 'I'm all right, so you can go. Nothing can take away the fact that if I hadn't laughed at Peter and refused his proposal he'd probably be alive today.'

'It's no use going over what can't be changed.' He shrugged. 'You weren't to know—he must have gone to incredible lengths to hide his addiction from you—from everyone—as well as his dependence on that woman for them.'

Something shifted in Taryn's heart, and the grief that had weighed her down since she'd left Fala'isi eased a little.

Uncompromisingly, he continued, 'We didn't understand how fragile he was because he took pains to prevent anyone from seeing it. Nobody could help him because he wouldn't let us see he needed it. We can wallow in guilt until we die, but it's not going to help Peter.'

Taryn swallowed. 'You sound so hard.'

He said harshly, 'I am hard, Taryn. I suspect the three years I spent with an addict mother toughened me. And the fact that she was an addict probably explains why Peter would have moved heaven and earth to keep me from finding out about his addiction.'

Taryn dragged in a deep breath. 'What happened to your mother?'

'She died soon after I went to the Coopers.'

'Your grandmother must have loved you,' Taryn said swiftly. 'Babies need love to be able to survive, and you not only survived, but you learned to love your foster-parents, and Peter when he arrived in the family. You're not that hard.'

He shrugged. 'That sort of love, yes, but until I met you I wondered if I'd ever be able to love a woman in the way Harold Cooper loved Isabel.'

Inside Taryn wild hope mingled with bitter regret. Heat staining her cheeks, she met his unwavering regard with slightly raised brows. 'And after you met me?'

'I decided to use the attraction between us to get the information I wanted from you.' He stopped, then went on as though the words were dragged from him, 'But I made love to you because I couldn't stop myself.'

Her heart leapt and the pulse in her throat beat heavily, but she didn't dare let hope persuade her into more illusions. Mutely, she waited for whatever was to come next.

'When we were together I didn't think of Peter.' He

spoke carefully, his face bleak yet determined. 'I was too concerned about hiding my response to you. Just by being yourself, you wrecked my logical plan to win your trust so you'd confide in me.'

'Logical?' she demanded, suddenly furious. 'Cold-blooded, more like.'

He frowned. 'Yes.' He paused, then said, 'I *am* cold-blooded. Cold-blooded and arrogant.'

In a shaken voice, she said, 'That's not true—you loved the Coopers. You set out on this…this charade… because you loved Peter. The time with your birth mother must have been horrific, but I'm so glad you had those early years with your grandmother and that the Coopers took you in. They must have been wonderful people.'

He said evenly, 'They were—my mother still is. And I don't want sympathy. But a background like that probably explains why—until I met you—I found it easier to talk of wanting rather than loving. It's no excuse. I had no right to do to you what I did. I should have told you who I was when we met.'

'Why didn't you?' she asked, almost against her will, and braced herself for his answer.

He said quietly, 'I expected someone like Peter's other girlfriends—like the lovers I've had, someone charming and beautiful and chic and basically shallow, I suppose. Instead, I saw a girl with a hose trying to put out a fire she had every reason to know would ultimately get away from her, possibly put her in danger. A woman who was beautiful under a layer of smoke and sweat, a woman who ordered me around.' He stopped, then said with an odd catch in his voice, 'A woman I could love. And every sensible thought went flying out of my head. Oh, I thought I was in control, but all I wanted was to get to know you, to find out what sort of person you were. I wouldn't—couldn't—accept that I'd fallen in love at first sight.'

Taryn went white. She stared at his controlled face, the only sign of emotion a tiny pulse flicking in his angular jaw. He *couldn't* have said what she thought she'd heard.

'I'm making a total botch of this,' he said curtly. 'I didn't believe I could love. But I did, even when I was telling myself that all I was doing was finding out why Peter had killed himself. And every day that passed I fell deeper and deeper in love with you without recognising it or accepting it. Although I told myself I needed to give you chances to talk about Peter, I really didn't want to know.'

He got to his feet. Unable to stay where she was, she too stood, but couldn't move away from her chair. He paced across to the window and looked out at the rapidly darkening garden.

In a level voice that somehow showed strain, he said, 'I love you, Taryn. Even when I was accusing you—I loved you. I sent you back to New Zealand because I needed time to accept what I'd learned about my brother. And I needed to see my mother. But I came here because I couldn't stay away.'

For long moments she stared at him, his face drawn and stark, a charged tension leaping between them. He didn't move and she couldn't take a step towards him, held prisoner by caution that ached painfully through every cell in her body.

But she believed him, although it was too soon to feel anything other than relief, and a fierce desire to see everything out in the open after all the lies and secrets.

She said, 'That connection between us—I felt it

too. I'd never have made love with you so quickly—so easily—if I hadn't somehow known that beneath the hunger and the excitement there was more. I didn't know what the *more* was, but it was always there, from the moment I saw you.'

He said her name on a long, outgoing breath, and covered the distance between them in two long strides.

But, half a pace away, he stopped and examined her face with a gaze so keen she had to fight the urge to close her eyes against it. His voice was deep and hard when he demanded, 'You're sure?'

'Yes,' she said with all her heart. 'Living without you has been a lesson in endurance, but it's made me utterly sure.' She gave a half smile and searched his beloved face. 'Are you?'

'Sure you deserve more than I can give you,' he said quietly. 'These past interminable weeks have shown me that without you my life is empty and useless, bleak and joyless. Taryn, I need you to make it complete.'

As though the admission opened some sort of channel he took that final step. Her eyes brimmed when his arms tightened around her to bring her against his lean, strong body.

'Don't,' he said in an anguished voice. 'Don't cry, my love, my dearest heart. I don't deserve you, but I'll spend the rest of my life making you happy. I feel like an alien, dumped onto a strange, unknown planet with no support. It's like nothing I've ever experienced before. Once I'd realised I was falling in love, I was scared witless.'

She gave a little broken laugh. 'I understand the feeling. It's beyond comprehension. These past weeks have been…bleak. Hollow—just going through the motions.'

'Exactly. And, as I'm being honest about my feelings,

I must admit I hoped I'd get over it.' His smile twisted. 'I tried to convince myself that loving you was an aberration, something that would die once you left. In fact, I felt like that feral five-year-old—at the mercy of something so much bigger than myself I had to protect myself in any way I could.'

'Oh, no,' she whispered, understanding for the first time why he'd fought so hard against this miraculous love.

'It's all right,' he soothed swiftly. 'And that's a stupid way of describing how I feel. How on earth do people deal with such an overwhelming, uncivilised need? I had to come and ask you if there was any hope for me.'

Every cell in her body cried out for the relief and joy of his arms around her.

But she said, 'I love you with all my heart, everything I am.' And pressed her fingers over his mouth when he went to speak. 'Cade— there's still the fact that, although I didn't intend it, I caused your brother's death.'

'You didn't,' he said simply. 'Possibly, he hoped you'd rescue him but, in the end, the decision to take his life was his, no one else's.'

'Your mother—'

'She knows I'm here, and why. She's not happy about this, and yes,' he said quietly, still holding her, 'I won't say that didn't affect me but, although I love her, this is none of her business. If you come to me, Taryn, I will do my best to make you happy, to make sure that you never regret it.'

His oddly formal phrases were enough to banish the final cowardly fear.

'Is it going to be so simple?' she asked softly. 'Because I will do my best to make you happy too. Is that all it takes?'

She felt his body stir against her and a leap of excitement pulsed through her.

'I hope so. It hasn't been easy for either of us,' he said quietly. 'I had to struggle with the knowledge that I'd done you a grave wrong, one I regret bitterly. Except that out of it has come this utter commitment to you—one without any reservations.'

Taryn's heart swelled and, lifting her face so she could kiss him, she said against his mouth, 'I love you so much.'

A year later, with small Teresa Rose Peredur sleeping in her arms, Taryn watched her husband come across the room.

Love misted her eyes. She'd never been so happy as in these past months. He'd supported her through her pregnancy and been with her during their daughter's birth, and he'd been wonderful in his dealings with her parents. Not only had he charmed them and won their respect, but he'd financed the trust they'd been trying to set up, so that by the time they gave up their practice there would be local doctors and nurses to take over.

Relations with his mother were still strained. She'd made her wheelchair the reason for not attending their wedding, and she wouldn't stay with them or visit them in the house they'd bought in Buckinghamshire, but Taryn hoped that time would ease Isabel Cooper's reservations.

'Our darling daughter is going to have your nose,' Taryn said happily, turning so Cade could look at the baby's face. 'It's stopped being snub and is turning into a definite aquiline.'

He laughed, scooping the baby from her arms. 'My poor little treasure,' he said in the voice he reserved for his daughter. 'Not that it isn't a perfectly efficient nose, but it's going to look a trifle odd in that beautiful face you've inherited from your mother.'

'It will give it character,' Taryn said firmly.

He laid the baby in her crib and came across and kissed his wife. 'My mother is coming up to London next week and asked if she could stay here a couple of nights,' he said, watching her keenly.

Elation filled her. 'I'm glad,' she said, hugging him. 'It's the first step, isn't it?'

'Yes, I think so,' he said without hesitation. 'She knows you a little better now, and she's accepted that whatever happened between you and Peter was not your fault.'

'I'm so glad.' It seemed inadequate to describe the relief she felt, but a glance at his face told her he understood.

He said, 'She'd been worried about him for some time, but he wouldn't confide in her. And she suspected drugs—that you might have introduced him to them. But when it came out at the trial that he'd been sleeping with that Brown woman, she accepted that your reaction to Peter's proposal wasn't as cruel as it seemed.'

Andrée Brown and the man who'd supplied her with drugs were both in prison.

Taryn glanced across at the sleeping baby. 'Even if we take Teresa to see my parents often, a child needs at least one grandparent close by. And your mother made such a brilliant job with you, I'm sure she can teach me a lot.'

He laughed and kissed her again, and they left the nursery for their own room. As he started to change out of his business clothes, Cade said, 'Ready for next week?'

'Just about,' she said cheerfully.

Next week they were visiting her parents in Vanuatu. It would be the first time they'd seen their granddaughter, and she was excited.

'I thought you might like to drop in on the Chapmans,' he said. 'They've offered us the *fale* in Fala'isi.'

Where they'd first made love, where they'd married and spent their honeymoon...

'Lovely,' Taryn said, and hugged him exuberantly. Happiness expanded inside her, filling her with delight, but she said a little wistfully, 'It's a pity everyone can't have an ending like ours, isn't it.'

'Happy ever after?' he teased. 'My romantic love...'

'Only it's not an ending, is it,' she said soberly. 'It's a series of beginnings too, and they won't all be happy ones.'

'We'll deal with anything.' They exchanged a long look, one of perfect trust.

Heart swelling, Taryn nodded. 'Yes,' she said, smiling at his beloved arrogant face with perfect confidence. 'Whatever happens, we'll cope because we love each other. It really *is* that simple.'

RUB IT IN

BY
KIRA SINCLAIR

When not working as an office manager for a project management firm or juggling plot lines, **Kira Sinclair** spends her time on a small farm in north Alabama with her wonderful husband, two amazing daughters and a menagerie of animals. It's amazing to see how this self-proclaimed city girl has (or has not, depending on who you ask) adapted to country life. Kira enjoys hearing from her readers at her website, www.kirasinclair.com. Or stop by writingplayground.blogspot.com and join in the fight to stop the acquisition of an alpaca.

I'd like to dedicate this book to a group of women who have become sisters of my heart—Kimberly Lang, Andrea Laurence, Marilyn Puett and Danniele Worsham. Without you guys this journey wouldn't have happened—and it sure wouldn't have been as enjoyable even if it had. It seems like you've been a part of my life for as long as I can remember instead of only a few years. Y'all mean the world to me and I hope you guys know that. Love you!

1

"No, I CAN'T WAIT until next week for the delivery. You promised it would arrive today," Marcy McKinney snarled into the phone. Taking a deep breath, she pasted a smile on her lips—because you really could hear it and her dad had always taught her you catch more flies with honey than vinegar—and said, "If you can't have the building supplies here by tomorrow then I want you to cancel my order and I'll get what I need somewhere else."

Slamming the phone back into its cradle would have felt good, but Marcy resisted. Barely. She had no idea where she'd find a store that could fill her rather large order, but she'd figure that out if the dissolute man on the other end of the phone actually called her bluff.

It wasn't as if hardware stores were thick on the ground in the middle of a secluded island in the Caribbean. Escape—the resort that she worked at as general manager—was actually the only thing on Île du Coeur. St. Lucia was the closest major hub, and it was forty-five minutes by ferry.

Getting the supplies from another island would

probably double the cost…but that wasn't her problem. It was Simon's.

She should probably feel bad about making Simon's
life difficult. She didn't. It was his turn, damn it.

The resort would be closed for the next two weeks—
their off-season hiatus. In two days she had a job interview for the general manager position at a boutique
hotel in New York City. This could be her ticket off the
island and back to civilization.

And nothing, not Simon or lost building supplies,
defecting security personnel, not even—

"Marcy!"

—whatever was the latest disaster to hit her desk
could keep her here.

Tina, the front desk clerk, bellowed down the back
office hallway again.

"Coming," Marcy hollered back, modulating her
voice to a pleasantly official tone. Scrambling out from
behind her desk, she tried not to panic at the piles of
paper, messages she still had to return and color-coded
folders that needed her attention. She had so much to
handle before she could walk out the door.

And by the time she could mark one thing off her
list, three more tasks seemed to crop up to take its
place.

The minute Marcy rounded the corner she knew
there was trouble. Tina's normally brilliant smile was
tight and as fake as her long red fingernails.

A couple, sunburned and cranky, stood on the opposite side of the counter.

"Mr. and Mrs. Smith." Tina rolled her eyes. While
it wasn't their main focus, they had their share of
Smiths, Joneses, Johnsons and any number of generi-
cally named guests who were most likely cheating on

their spouses. Marcy didn't like it, but there was little she could do.

"Thank goodness. I've explained to—" the woman leaned forward and squinted at Tina's name tag "—Tina that we need to extend our stay." She held out her lobster-red arm, "As you can imagine, explaining how I received a second-degree sunburn while on a business trip to London might be slightly difficult." The woman sneered, including her companion in her raking gaze.

"And as I've told Mrs. Smith..." This time Tina couldn't help but emphasize the misnomer. Marcy probably should scold her, but she wouldn't. "We have no available rooms, as the resort is closing for two weeks tomorrow."

"We'll pay whatever."

Marcy's own smile was tight as she said, "It isn't a matter of money, ma'am." She refused to let the false name pass her lips. "The resort is undergoing construction and our insurance company won't allow any guests on the premises for liability reasons."

The woman's scowl deepened. Marcy could see the snit she was about to unleash as it built in the back of her beautiful green eyes. Cutting it off at the pass, Marcy continued, "However, I'd be happy to contact a resort on St. Lucia and see if something is available while you recover."

Instead of a tirade, a sigh of relief exited through the woman's pink and pouty lips. "Oh, yes, that would be wonderful. If you wouldn't mind." Marcy fought the urge to smack the smile off *Mrs. Smith's* face.

"Give us a minute." She ground out the words through clenched teeth as she pulled Tina into the back office behind her. "Run down the list of resorts on the island and see what you can find. Start with the family-oriented resorts. The more obnoxious the kids, the better."

Tina giggled. "Happy to."

Marcy left her to it, heading back to her desk and the pile of work waiting for her there. Despite it being afternoon, the other offices were already dark. Most of the staff were busy packing their own bags for a change. Everyone except a skeleton crew left the island for these two weeks each year. When a tropical paradise was your home, vacations usually meant visiting family you hadn't seen in forever.

Marcy had no family to see. Her mother had died when she was a little girl. Her father, a hotel manager himself, had died five years ago. She had no brothers or sisters, and only one aunt on her father's side, but the last time she'd heard from Suellen had been at her father's funeral.

She had several close friends from college, but they were all scattered around the country. And while she talked to them as often as possible, most of them were busy starting families and building careers. Several years ago they'd given up trying to plan a girls' week away. It was just too hard to work around all their schedules.

Some of the staff would stay. She'd spent last year here herself. In theory having the entire resort to yourself—including all the amenities the guests used but she never had time for—wasn't a bad thing. If she'd actually taken time to use those amenities. Instead, she'd spent the entire two weeks—weeks that were supposed to be her vacation—working.

Not this year. Tomorrow afternoon she was leaving. Marcy sighed. Two blissful weeks with no Simon—the bane of her existence.

In her opinion, no laid-back surf god should ever own a resort. It had gotten to the point where just the sight of Simon's low-riding shorts and tight T-shirts had begun to grate on her nerves. They were running a business!

Besides, no man should look that sexy while somehow still managing to appear as if donning clothing had been an afterthought. The problem with that kind of…demeanor was that most of the time she feared Simon was two steps away from shedding his clothes again just because they were annoying him. And she didn't want that. Really, she didn't. It would set a bad example for the employees.

She preferred men with more structured wardrobes. The kind who wore business suits every day…and liked it. If she discovered Simon owned a single pair of tailored pants or a silk tie—let alone a suit—she'd die of shock.

Before moving to the island she'd lived in cities. Lots of them. London, Prague, Chicago, San Francisco. And she'd loved them all. But her heart belonged to New York, where the men definitely knew how to wear their suits. And run their businesses.

Simon might have had the money to purchase the resort, but he didn't seem to care much about keeping it going. Even the disheveled blond hair that notoriously hung in his dark blue eyes bothered her. She constantly wanted to sweep it out of the way, but the one time she'd given in to the impulse her hand had tingled for twenty minutes. And that was the last thing she needed.

But it was difficult, as a woman, not to recognize that Simon was an attractive man. He was tall, his athletic body moving with a grace that seemed coun-

terintuitive considering his height. Charm and devilment mixed with his inherent sex appeal—a potentially
lethal combination.

But she refused to feel attracted. Not to her boss.
She'd learned her lesson the first time around that
block.

"Marcy." The two-way radio on her hip squawked.
"We have a problem."

Tom, their only remaining security person, thought
everything was a problem. Since the head of security,
Zane Edwards, had left to follow the woman he loved
to Atlanta and his replacement had lasted all of six
weeks, Tom was all she had right now. Marcy couldn't
really blame the guy for his "the sky is falling" attitude—he was so far out of his element. Tom was great
at watching the monitors and keeping drunken guests
in line. But at twenty-two, he was hardly ready to take
on the task of head of security for a resort as large as
Escape.

Marcy was hoping to fix that problem before she
left, as well. On her desk sat three résumés from three
very capable candidates. All were to arrive on the afternoon ferry. They'd stay the night, be interviewed
tomorrow, tour the facility and then leave on the morning ferry. Simon had balked at the expense, but after
Zane's replacement hadn't been able to handle island
life, she wasn't making that mistake again.

The last stragglers would join them. Marcy was half
packed and come hell or high water would be on the
last ferry.

Snatching the radio off her belt, Marcy huffed,
"What is it, Tom?"

"Several men—" she could hear the hesitation in his

voice "—just got off the ferry. You said not to allow anyone off."

What she'd said was not to allow any guests off. She had no doubt, based on the falter in his voice, that the group he was referring to were her construction workers.

"Do the men have toolboxes, ladders or anything else resembling construction equipment, by any chance?"

"Yes." He sounded surprised, and Marcy fought hard not to roll her eyes.

"Could they be the crew coming to handle the maintenance and renovations while we're closed?" she asked patiently.

"Maybe." He drew out the single word, telling her that he was quickly reevaluating the situation in front of him. Really, he was a good boy who could do with just a little more common sense and practical life experience. Marcy could hear a rustle as he placed his hand over the phone. Unfortunately it didn't dampen the sound enough for her to miss as he asked the men, "Are you construction guys?"

Their yes was muffled but audible nonetheless.

"Uh, yeah, they are."

"Great. Maybe next time you'll ask them why they're here first before calling me up with a non-crisis. Put them in the old bunkhouse."

The bunkhouse was left over from the days when the island had been a cocoa plantation, though it had been updated and renovated since then. The building was rarely used, but it would serve perfectly for the next two weeks. Most of the permanent employees had either bungalows at the back of the property, like hers, or living quarters close to the job, like their chef, who had a rather large apartment above the kitchens.

Great, now she had workers but no supplies for them to actually do anything.

Blowing at a wisp of hair that had fallen into her eyes, Marcy flopped back into the executive chair behind her desk, not sure whether she wanted to scream, cry or start smashing things. Probably a little of all three.

Her to-do list was a mile long. Nothing was going right.

And she had no doubt that the minute Simon realized she was leaving tomorrow he would blow a gasket. Not that her departure should surprise him, since she'd told him in person, sent him an email and reminded him a dozen times over the past few weeks.

However, if there was one thing she'd learned about Simon Reeves, it was that his brain was like Swiss cheese and his hearing was more than selective…as in nonexistent.

But that was another thing that was his problem, not hers.

Pulling up the document she'd been working on, Marcy looked at the detailed instructions she'd written in an effort to help Simon through the next two weeks—and if the interview went well, to help her replacement. Part of her had wanted to leave him with nothing, but that just wasn't her style. She'd put too much time and effort into the resort to see Simon ruin it the minute she walked out the door.

The document was currently sitting at twenty-two pages. Marcy was a little worried the sheer size of the thing would prevent Simon from reading it.

She stared at it for several seconds. *Cut it down, or*

leave it as is? It was an argument she'd had multiple times over the past few days. Ultimately she came to the same conclusion she'd come to numerous times. Once again, what Simon chose to do or not do was not her problem.

And hopefully, if things went according to plan, wouldn't ever be again.

SIMON FOUGHT THE URGE to grab the first thing and throw it at the door when a loud knock blasted through his office. The scene he was writing wasn't working and he couldn't figure out why. Frustration rode him hard and probably wasn't helping the situation. Neither was the bustling noise that even here, behind the closed door of his private office, couldn't be disguised.

The staff was happy at the prospect of having two weeks off. Frankly, he was happy to see them leave, at least for a little while. Having the place virtually to himself was going to be a godsend.

He was months behind on the deadline for his current manuscript. It was so bad that he'd actually unplugged his phone and uninstalled the mail program from his computer to avoid email from his editor and agent. If he didn't finish this thing in the next two weeks he could probably kiss his career goodbye. Again.

Thanks to Courtney's betrayal three years ago, the resulting plagiarism scandal and his fruitless attempts to prove the work was really his, his career had already dangled by a thread once. He really didn't want to go through that again.

Île du Coeur and Escape were supposed to have provided him the space and seclusion to rebuild his career. Instead, they'd both become a huge time-suck.

Buying the place had seemed like a brilliant idea. He had the capital to purchase the island, and the resort would provide the necessary revenue stream for upkeep. A manager should have taken the responsibilities off his shoulders, leaving him free to lock himself inside his office to write.

Should have. Somehow things hadn't exactly gone the way he'd hoped.

The problem was that not a soul on the island—not even Marcy—knew who he was. And he liked it that way. It protected his work. He wrote under a pseudonym and always had.

He'd wanted a clean break from the life he'd left behind. Wanted to start again and pretend the entire affair had never happened. Unfortunately, it was difficult to forget being betrayed by someone you loved.

That sort of deception tended to color your opinion of people. Always making you wonder who was going to stab you in the back next.

"Simon!" Marcy's voice exploded through the wood of the door along with the rattling of the knob that he'd locked for just such an occasion.

Knowing from experience that she wouldn't leave until he listened to her, Simon minimized his documents, brought up a gaming program he used to make everyone think he was just wasting time in here, and walked across the room. Yanking open the door, he lounged inside the jamb, one arm stretched across the gaping area so that she'd either have to stay on her side of the door or duck underneath his arm. She wouldn't do that. One good thing about Marcy—she avoided coming into contact with him at all costs.

In the beginning he'd been happy. The last thing he had time for was a romantic complication with his manager. She was there to work and make his life easier, and from his experience, mixing business with pleasure rarely made anything easier. But the more she avoided him, the more he became aware of her deliberate distance. A distance that made him want to ruffle her feathers by pushing against the boundaries she'd erected. It was pointless, but he couldn't help it.

Even now he inched his body closer to hers, crowding into her personal space just to see her spine stiffen. The infinitesimal shuffle backward was rewarding, especially when she stopped it midway, consciously determined not to let him fluster her.

A grin tugged at the corners of his lips but he wouldn't let it grab hold. Instead, he asked, "What do you need?"

She raised her hand, a sheaf of papers fluttering with the force of the motion. "*We* need to go over everything before I leave tomorrow. I sent you an appointment by email."

"I uninstalled the program."

Her eyes widened before narrowing to glittering slits. He loved it when Marcy got mad. Her blue eyes sparkled with a passion that made the muscles in his stomach tighten. She reminded him of a pixie; in fact, he almost hadn't hired her because she looked as if a good stiff breeze could knock her on her ass. But beneath that tiny frame was a spine of steel and the heart of a drill sergeant. She was good at what she did, if a little too organized and into unimportant details for his liking.

"Why would you do something stupid like that?"

Simon shrugged, not caring that she'd just called him stupid. It was by far the least offensive term she'd used for him in the past two years.

"Because I'm avoiding someone."

"Well, you can't avoid me."

If that wasn't the most obvious statement of the year he didn't know what was. He chose to let the softball setup she'd just given him slide by.

"What do you mean before you leave? Did I know you were going to be gone tomorrow? Isn't the construction crew supposed to be starting? You can't leave until you're sure they know what they're doing. I don't have time to deal with them, even for a day."

Marcy shook her head slowly, the slick blond strands of her ever-present ponytail whipping behind her. He watched the rise and fall of her chest as she took a deep breath, held it and finally let it go. As chests went, hers was…fine. He tended to prefer big-breasted women with a huge handful he could grab hold of. Although it was hard to tell where Marcy was concerned. Despite the fact that they worked in a tropical location and the dress code was fairly relaxed, she insisted on wearing business suits when she was working—which was always.

He'd decided that the slacks, skirts, blouses and tailored jackets that still somehow seemed a little too roomy over her body were her personal armor. He just hadn't been able to discover what she was hiding from. At first he'd wondered if it was men in general. He worried maybe she'd been attacked. But as he'd watched her dealing, smiling and, hell, almost flirting with their male guests over the years he'd decided that couldn't possibly be it.

And while she hadn't taken a lover in the past two years—at least not one that he was aware of, and he knew everything that happened on his island— it wasn't for lack of offers. If she hadn't said yes to anyone, it was because she hadn't wanted to. Marcy McKinney was definitely the captain of her destiny and knew exactly what she wanted at all times.

It exhausted him just to think about that kind of structured existence.

"I'm not leaving for the day."

"But you just said you were."

"No, I said I needed to go over this—" she waved the papers again; now that he looked at them, the stack appeared rather large…and the type on them awfully small "—before I leave tomorrow. I'm taking two weeks' vacation."

"The hell you say."

"We talked about this, Simon." He heard her warning tone, but chose to ignore it.

"I don't remember you mentioning you were leaving *these* two weeks." Although it was possible he hadn't been paying attention to her. He did have a habit of tuning Marcy out when she spoke. But it was usually because whatever she was saying wasn't important to him   at least not more important than the other thoughts flowing through his mind.

He'd learned early that pretending to listen and nodding appropriately were usually enough to keep her satisfied. That way, they both walked away with a smile. Win, win.

"I most certainly did. We talked. I sent you reminders. Hell, I even went on your computer and blocked the days out on your calendar."

"You went on my computer?" A nasty mix of anger, disappointment and betrayal burst through him. It was a knee-jerk reaction, the result of what Courtney had done. Not only had she stolen his work, she'd destroyed every speck of evidence that it had ever existed on his computer. She'd ruined his backup hard drive. She'd left him nothing to fight with.

He didn't like people messing with his computer.

Clenching his hands into fists, Simon invaded Marcy's space, bringing them nose-to-nose. She sucked a hard breath through her teeth, but didn't back away. Her bright blue eyes searched his, puzzled and off-kilter. It should have been enough for him, but it wasn't.

"Why did you do that?"

"Jesus, Simon, what is wrong with you?" She finally pushed against him, trying to get him out of her personal space. He didn't move. "I knew you'd ignore my emails and forget our conversation. I was trying to help."

"I didn't ask for your help," he growled at her.

Her eyes flared, the surprise quickly being overwhelmed by irritation. "Actually, you did when you hired me," she snapped.

For the first time Simon realized he was towering above her, his tall body curled over hers. Anyone else probably would have bowed backward under the intimidation tactic. Not Marcy. Sometimes it was easy to forget how tiny she was. Her confidence and competence more than made up for her size.

"Move back," she said and then waited patiently for him to do exactly what she'd ordered. Everyone always seemed to fall in line for Marcy. It was irritating.

Just once he wished she'd do him a favor and fall in line for *him*.

Instead, he slowly stepped away. She glared at him, her eyes sharp and hurt. He refused to apologize or explain his reaction.

And yet somehow the words fell from his lips anyway. "Look, I'm sorry, Marcy. I need you here during the break. I have something important that requires all my attention. I don't have time to handle the resort, too."

"Bullshit."

His molars clanked together. "Excuse me?"

"Only a few of the staff will be left. I'm interviewing the candidates for head of security tomorrow before I leave. The construction crew is here, their materials will be tomorrow. Before I leave, I'll make sure they have a clear agenda for the two weeks. These—" she waved the damn papers again "—contain every possible scenario that could come up and how to handle it. It's the perfect time for me to take a vacation. You can't afford for me to be gone while the resort is full."

She had a point there. Although in a couple weeks he should be done with this book and could probably handle things for a little while.

"I promise I'll make it up to you," he said, flashing her one of his patented grins in the hope that it might soften her up a little. It had always worked on women in the past, although somehow Marcy seemed immune. "Next month you can take as much time off as you want." Within reason, but they'd cross that bridge only when she forced him to the edge of it.

"No, Simon. You can't charm your way into getting what you want with me. I have plans."

"Change them."

"Nonrefundable travel plans."

"I'll pay the difference."

"And people waiting on me to show up. Simon, I'm leaving tomorrow afternoon. Short of you kidnapping me—and not even you are that stupid—you're going to have to find a way to deal without me for the next two weeks."

His hands clenched again and a headache began to pound behind his eyes. She didn't understand and he couldn't explain it to her, not without revealing his secret. Or telling her why his privacy was so important to him that he would hide his identity in the first place. And he just wasn't willing to make himself that vulnerable, not even with Marcy.

She was leaving, huh? Well, they'd just have to see about that.

2

THE RESORT WAS QUIET. Disturbingly silent without guests. There was no one splashing or yelling at the pool as she dragged her three matching pieces of luggage behind her. No couples strolling hand-in-hand across the warm sand. No painted-up thirtysomethings in string bikinis sipping drinks beneath cabanas and waiting to pick up whatever hot guy strolled past.

She was used to the hustle and bustle, and the place seemed almost eerie without it. As if the island itself were sad that no one was there to play and frolic.

The locals had a legend about Île du Coeur, something about finding your heart's desire—whether it was what you'd come looking for or not. She'd never really paid that much attention to it because she didn't believe in that sort of stuff, but at this moment the island felt almost alive.

As if maybe anything was possible.

The caws and whistles of the birds deep in the jungle and the ringing of hammers as the work crew repaired the restaurant roof broke through the moment. Their supplies had arrived on the morning ferry, and the last of the staff and the two candidates she hadn't hired for head of security had left. She'd been surprised when Xavier, the man she'd hired, said he was prepared to stay and start immediately. She wondered briefly what kind of person could pack their entire life into a single suitcase, but decided she didn't have time to find out. He was more than qualified for the position.

The repair of the roof was the first in a long list of upgrades and maintenance the crew would be handling over the next two weeks. Hurricane season was upon them and the last thing they needed was leaky roofs or unstable buildings. Marcy seriously hoped for their sake that everything went smoothly. She'd never actually seen Simon lose his temper, but something told her that between the distraction, the length of the list she'd left and her departure, he was precariously close to the deep end.

Too bad.

Served him right for not appreciating the long hours, detailed work and effort she'd put into this place for him. Instead of praise, she got snarky remarks and needling innuendos. Instead of understanding, she got exasperation and a locked door in her face.

Hopefully, no more. She was going to charm the socks off whomever she had to in order to get the hell off this island and back to the big city. Cramped apartments, twenty-four-hour Chinese food, men in suits, museums, shows, culture…that was her idea of paradise.

Her suitcases bumped across the raised boards of the dock. Normally she was a light traveler, preferring to fit as much as possible into one carry-on bag. The thought of losing all her luggage made her chest ache. But during her time at Escape, she'd collected more stuff than she'd realized. And hoping that she'd be able to tender her resignation from New York, she'd packed everything she owned. Well, at least anything she'd wanted to take with her. Her father had taught her that some things just weren't worth the trouble.

Arranging her luggage in descending order, Marcy lined them up perpendicular to the boards, stared out across the vacant water and then looked at her watch. She was a little early. With a shrug, she plopped her butt onto the top of her largest suitcase and prepared to wait. She thought about pulling out the novel she'd packed into her carry-on but decided it wasn't worth the effort. She had ten, fifteen minutes at the most.

But, oh, it called to her. She couldn't remember the last time she'd been able to crack open the spine of a good thriller. She loved them, a holdover from the days when her father would pass along his finished books to her. They'd shared that excitement, spending hours discussing the finer points of their favorite books over dinner.

Her love of thrillers wasn't the only thing she'd inherited from her dad. His workaholic, detail-oriented, high-expectation requirements had also come with the genes. A familiar sadness crept up on her. He'd been gone for almost five years, but it still hadn't gotten any easier.

Although she supposed there was a silver lining. He'd have been so disappointed in her over the New York debacle. Tears stung her eyes, but Marcy refused to let them fall. It had been two and a half years, and still it upset her.

She'd been so lonely. Looking for companionship and support and someone to share her life with. Marcy thought she'd found that in Christoph Fischer. Yes, she knew better than to sleep with someone she worked with—her boss, no less. But he'd swept her off her feet and she'd been helpless to resist. It didn't help that they'd spent so much time together at work.

Even before she'd started at his hotel, she'd heard rumors that he and his wife were divorcing. A year later, when he began asking her out, she assumed the divorce was final. Shame on her for not checking!

The humiliation of discovering—in the middle of a crowded ballroom filled with industry professionals—that his wife was very much still a part of his life was something she'd never forget. Neither was having champagne thrown in her face and obscenities rained down over her head. Marcy had never thought of herself as a home wrecker, had never wanted or planned to be one.

Being lied to by someone she'd trusted was terrible enough, but then he'd had the audacity to fire her. And blackball her with every other reputable hotel in the city...

She'd taken the first job that she could—Simon's offer—as far away from the city as she could get. She'd needed the time away. She'd desperately needed the job. And she'd needed the line on her résumé—a buffer between the debacle and whatever would come next.

But that was all behind her now. And this interview was the opportunity to make a fresh start. Surely, over two years later, everyone would have moved on to juicier gossip. She'd gotten the interview after all.

This job was her ticket back home. Back to civilization and structure.

A frown on her face, Marcy looked at her watch again. The tropical sun was baking her scalp and exposed legs. If she'd known she was going to sit here for a half hour she would have put on sunscreen. The ferry was definitely late. Standing, she walked to the edge of the dock and craned her neck to see if the squat vessel was visible across the water. It wasn't.

This was exactly the kind of thing that drove her crazy! The entire place ran on island time and she was so sick and tired of it. Didn't anyone respect punctuality anymore? The ferry was routinely late. People waited five, ten, even fifteen minutes on occasion, but never this long.

Maybe the ferry crew figured that with a skeleton staff and no guests to deliver, there was no hurry. With a scowl, Marcy returned to perch on top of her bag. They were going to get an earful from her whenever they did finally arrive. She had a plane to catch. Thank God she'd built some "disaster" time into her schedule.

SIMON STARED out the window at Marcy. He'd left his apartments and walked around to the far side of the building so he could watch her. Part of him couldn't help but chuckle at the agitated way she kept jumping up from her seat on that coral-colored suitcase to pace along the length of the dock, only to sit back down again.

The suitcase was unexpected—he would have thought she was more of a traditional black or brown kinda girl—but her reaction wasn't. The only reason Simon was standing there watching her was that he was a coward.

He'd meant to go down there at three, to cut her off as she reached the dock and explain that she wasn't going anywhere because he'd called and canceled the ferry service for the next two weeks. But he'd gotten involved in a scene. The words had flowed, and considering that hadn't happened in the past few days, he'd been reluctant to walk away.

And now he was going to pay the price. No doubt a tongue-lashing was in his future. Was it wrong that he sort of enjoyed riling Marcy up?

When she was angry her blue eyes flashed, reminding him of sapphires turned to catch the light. Her skin tinted a pale pink color and her jaw tightened so hard that he wanted to kiss her senseless just to startle her into letting go.

But he wouldn't allow himself to go there. She was too valuable as his manager. He had a policy of never seducing employees. And he had no desire for a relationship. He'd never been great at them before Courtney. And after, the idea of trusting someone that much again didn't sit well with him.

Marcy spun on her heel, knocking the smallest of her suitcases over and starting a domino effect that ended with all her luggage hitting the dock. He couldn't hear the bang from behind the protection of the glass, but he could imagine that it—and her growl of frustration—had been loud.

Logically, he realized the longer he waited the worse the explosion was going to be.

Taking a deep breath, he schooled his features into a mask of indifference and headed out into the afternoon heat.

Tucking his hands into the pockets of his khaki shorts, Simon ambled toward the dock. He broke through the line of rich tropical foliage to find Marcy had righted her bags and was staring in his direction, no doubt having heard his feet on the path.

"Simon," she said, her face twisted into a frown already. Not great. "What are you doing?"

Propping his hip against the wooden railing that surrounded the dock, he said, "I came to tell you that the ferry isn't coming."

"What?" she exclaimed. The already high color on her cheeks flamed even brighter. She looked behind her over the water, as if the ferry might turn a corner and prove him a liar at any moment. "The ferry comes every day. Twice."

"Not today."

"What happened? Was there an accident? Is anyone injured?"

Simon felt the pinch of guilt as he realized that her first assumption was only an accident could stop the one form of transportation on and off the island. And she was worried about other people more than her own inconvenience.

He had to come clean.

"No, no accident. I called and canceled the service."

Marcy swung her eyes back to him. They were wide with confusion. The cloud of her long blond hair, usually pulled tight into a smooth ponytail during work hours, floated around her face. He liked it down and couldn't remember a single time in the past two years that he'd seen it this way. Free. Not exactly a word he would have normally used to describe Marcy. His gaze traveled down her body and he realized she wasn't wearing her trademark suit, either. Instead she wore a pale green polo—every button done up to her throat— and a pair of crisp khaki shorts. Had he ever seen her legs bare?

Shaking his head, he jerked his mind back to where it should be. "Why the hell would you do that?"

He shrugged, knowing the inevitable shitstorm he was about to release. "Because I couldn't let you leave. I need you here, Marcy, and I'll do whatever it takes to keep you here for the next two weeks."

"You...you..." she sputtered, her eyes turning hard and sharp. "You canceled the ferry?"

"Yep." While he tried to maintain the relaxed air he'd adopted the minute he set foot on the tropical island, his eyes stayed clear and focused on Marcy. He honestly had no idea what she might do. "You gave me the idea."

"What are you talking about?"

"You're the one who suggested I kidnap you. I always try to take your advice."

She growled low in the back of her throat. It was the same sort of sound the pit bull he'd had as a child used to make when a stranger entered their yard. A warning. Only this time he couldn't shake the feeling that he was the one about to have his hand bitten.

"You do no such thing. Ignoring me has become a sort of hobby for you and we both know it."

Well, he had, but until this moment he hadn't realized she'd been aware.

"Fine," she said, her jaw hard and tight. "I'll call Rusty for a private launch."

He debated whether or not to let her make the call. He knew what Rusty's answer would be—his and that of every other private boating service on this side of St. Lucia. He'd called them all and promised to pull the resort's business from them if they accepted Marcy's request.

And where that kind of threat hadn't worked, he'd used bribery instead, offering to pay for their refusal to provide service to the island for the next two weeks.

Details were his thing, and he wasn't about to bend over backward to keep Marcy on the island only to let her get away through other means. He'd closed off every possible avenue of escape.

Marcy's phone was halfway to her ear when he decided it might be better for him if he cut her off at the pass. Perhaps hearing it from him instead of Rusty would lessen the impact...and her anger.

"I wouldn't bother. I think you'll find everyone is booked."

Her phone dangled from her loose fingers as she stared at him. "What do you mean?"

"Just that I've paid them more not to come than you could pay them to come."

And it had been worth every frickin' penny.

She raked him with prickly blue eyes, making him feel as if ice was melting down his spine. She really did know how to use that gaze to intimidate. But he was a master himself, so it just wouldn't work.

"You have no respect for anyone but yourself, do you?" she asked in a low voice that scared him even more than if she'd started yelling.

Time for the platitudes.

"Look, I'll make it up to you. Name your price. A raise? An all-expenses-paid vacation? Diamonds? What will it cost me to keep you here for the next two weeks?"

"Not everything is for sale, Simon. Do I look like I care about diamonds?"

He couldn't help it—his eyes traveled down Marcy's body, from the tip of her blond head to the pale pink toenails that peeked out from her sandals. Really, she'd almost begged him to. And he had to admit that she didn't look like the kind of woman who cared about jewels.

Oh, Marcy was stylish in a put-together business-woman sort of way. But she didn't drape herself in jewelry like some of the women he'd been known to associate with. In fact, the only jewelry she wore was a pair of small diamond studs and a single gold ring that looked suspiciously like a wedding band, only it was on her right hand.

"I had plans. Important plans. You can't manipulate everyone and everything to get your way, Simon. You are not God and no one gave you the right to meddle in my life."

His own anger was starting to kindle deep in his belly. He needed her here, damn it.

"I'm your boss, Marcy. I said I need you here. That should have been the end of the discussion. You're valuable to me. Any other boss would have given you an ultimatum."

"Right. Instead, you canceled the ferry and didn't give me any choice in the matter."

"Everyone has a choice."

Her eyes sharpened before narrowing to tiny slits that reminded him of the arrow slots he'd seen in medieval castles—deadly depending on what lay behind.

"You know what—you're right. I do have a choice. You can keep me prisoner here, Simon, but you can't make me work. You can't force me to lift a finger."

"I'll fire you."

She threw her arms up in the air, letting them fall back down, the motion disturbing the cloud of hair around her face. The laugh that accompanied the motion was far from humorous. "Go ahead. I'm tired of busting my ass for you. I'm tired of going above and beyond to make this place run smoothly, be successful and high quality. I'm tired of having to fight you every step of the way when I try to do the job you hired me for."

"Sounds like you just need a nap."

"No, what I need is a vacation, part of the reason I was leaving for two weeks."

"Only part?"

Marcy tipped her head sideways and studied him for several seconds before answering. "Yep, part. I also had a job interview in New York in two days."

Simon didn't understand. Sure, he needled her on a regular basis—it was fun to watch the steam pour out of her ears. And he often questioned her tactics and thought she bothered him with details that he didn't give a damn about.

But she worked in paradise.

"Why the hell would you want to leave here—" he threw his arms wide to indicate the beach, jungle and gleaming water that surrounded them "—for the rat race of New York? Here you have a perpetual vacation outside your door."

"One I don't ever get to take because I'm too damned busy taking care of everyone else. Just once I'd like to sit in one of those lounge chairs on the beach and sip a fruity drink and think frothy thoughts. Or get a massage."

Her eyes turned wistful for the barest moment, but he caught it before it disappeared. He'd never realized she hadn't used Tiffany's services. God, she had the most amazing hands.

Shaking his head, Simon realized he needed to keep focused on the little spitfire in front of him or risk getting singed.

"Please," he scoffed. They both knew Marcy wouldn't last fifteen minutes in that lounge chair before her body would start twitching with the need to do something. "You could have done that any time you wanted. You make me sound like a slave driver. I didn't ask you to come into the office at five o'clock every morning. Or work until seven at night. You did that all on your own."

"Because someone had to do it."

Had he really been that blind? He didn't think so. He might have his nose stuck in the Word program on his computer, but he did pay attention to what was happening around him. It was just that his idea of what was important and Marcy's seemed to be diametrically opposed. Had she needed help at some point and he hadn't realized it?

"Do you need an assistant? Is that it?"

"No, that's not it," she exclaimed, frustration pulling down the corners of her mouth. "You don't get it, Simon, and I don't think you ever will. All I wanted was for you to give a damn about this place."

"I do!" he shouted.

"Not from where I'm sitting. New York is home and I want to go back. It's where I came from and where I belong. Working here is frustrating and I can't take it anymore."

"Bullshit. You belong here. You're wonderful at your job." Hadn't he said that over and over again? Hell, he'd basically kidnapped her because he couldn't survive two weeks without her. Wasn't that demonstration enough?

"Nice to know you realize it."

"Of course I do."

Shaking her head, Marcy gathered her bags and pushed past him up the path.

"Where are you going?"

"To see if there's another way off this island."

A churning sensation started deep in his belly and quickly swirled out to overwhelm him. He knew there wasn't—he'd made sure of that—but that didn't seem to stop the nerves. Marcy couldn't leave, not today, not ever. As if he didn't already have enough reasons for keeping her here, knowing she wanted to interview for a position that would take her away permanently only made him more determined.

Over his dead body.

"There isn't. I even called the tourist helicopter services. I've covered all the bases."

Marcy whirled to face him again, framed by the thick foliage that surrounded the path. The vibrant green only seemed to emphasize the blue of her eyes, the pale blond of her hair and the deep tan of her long legs. Her fist gripped the handles of her luggage, the knuckles turning white with the force of her hold and the exertion of her control over her own temper.

Was he perverse to want to see what she'd do if she really let that temper fly? Oh, he knew she had it, but he also realized he'd never once seen the full brunt of it. He'd often thought passionate women made the best lovers because they rarely held back in life or in bed.

Marcy was the exception to that rule. He had no doubt there was passion beneath the controlled, tight, competent facade that she showed the world, despite the fact that he'd never seen it.

"Don't think you've won, Simon."

A smile twitched at the corners of his lips. From where he stood that was exactly what had happened.

Marcy couldn't leave the island and they both knew it. He also knew that despite what she might say, she was enough of a workaholic that she couldn't sit idly by and do nothing while there were things to be handled.

He was counting on her innate tendencies to override any residual anger that might still linger by tomorrow. He figured she'd stew today for sure. Tomorrow morning, bright and early, she'd be back in her office.

She just couldn't help it.

3

WHIRRING, BANGING and the loud *pa-pow* of a nail gun reverberated through Simon's skull. The construction crew had begun their noise at seven o'clock this morning. Three hours later it was getting worse, not better.

Normally, waking up that early wouldn't have bothered him—he rarely slept past five anyway—but last night he'd stayed up until 2:00 a.m. reading through a stubborn scene.

He was bleary-eyed, tired and cranky. Not to mention that the mother of all headaches pounded relentlessly behind his eyes.

After a rather loud clamor that he could only assume meant someone had dropped an entire load of metal onto a hard surface, Simon jumped out of his chair and yelled, "Enough!" Not that they could hear him.

Surely they could work somewhere else on the island for a while and give him a break. A nap, that was all he needed to get back into the groove he'd found the other day. The fact that his mind kept returning to his conversation with Marcy when it should have been concentrating on the story in front of him had nothing to do with his foul mood.

Rubbing his hands over his face, trying to clear his cloudy vision, Simon headed for Marcy's office.

Halfway down the hallway, Xavier, the new head of security Marcy had hired yesterday, walked out of the elevator.

"Oh, good," he said, stepping back onto the car and holding open the door so Simon could join him. "I was just coming to see you. I'd like to sit down and discuss the existing security measures and evaluate any improvements I'd like to make."

With a sigh, Simon closed his eyes for a moment before answering, "Our previous head of security was former CIA. Trust me when I say I can't think of a single change you'd want or need to make. Zane was meticulous."

"As am I," Xavier answered with a smile on his lips but a hard glint in his dark brown eyes. "I'd still like to meet with you. Start out on the right foot, so to speak."

"I'm pretty busy for the next few weeks. Can this wait until later?"

"Marcy mentioned the resort was closed and that a construction crew had been hired. I assume it would be more cost-effective to handle any adjustments while the crew is already here instead of having to bring them back."

The throb that had set up residence behind Simon's eyes increased in intensity. He realized Xavier had a valid point, but he really, really didn't have the time or energy to deal with this right now. Saving money wasn't always the most important objective. Something Marcy had a difficult time understanding.

It appeared that Xavier might reside in that camp, as well. Maybe putting them together was a good idea.

The elevator dinged their arrival on the lowest floor. The doors slid open silently and Simon reached to hold them back.

"I'm heading to Marcy's office right now. Why don't you follow me and discuss this with her?"

Xavier entered the long hallway, glancing back over his shoulder. "I would, but she said she no longer works here and that I'd need to deal directly with you."

Simon stopped in his tracks. "What did you say?"

"Marcy said I should deal directly with you."

"No, before that."

"Marcy said she quit or you fired her. Or maybe it was both? I didn't quite understand why she was still on the island, but I didn't figure it was my business to ask."

Simon knew exactly why she was still here. Because he wouldn't let her leave. But he hadn't thought she was serious about quitting. His threat of firing her had been a bluff. She'd known it, right? Why would he fire her and then continue to keep her prisoner here? It sort of defeated the purpose.

"Crap!" The single word exploded from Simon's mouth.

Pushing past Xavier, he headed for the offices at a sprint.

"She isn't there."

Even before Simon skidded around the corner he knew Xavier was right and the office would be vacant. First, no light shone from the small space. Second, there was no noise. Every other time he'd ventured into Marcy's territory—and he admitted exhausting all other options before giving in to that last resort—there was a flurry of activity. Phones ringing, keys being rhythmically tapped, printers whirring. Today there was nothing. The only sounds were from the construction crew outside.

A huge knot of dread tightened in the pit of his stomach. What had he done?

Backing out of her empty office, he almost barreled into Xavier, who was waiting in the hallway, his rather large arms crossed over his chest.

"Where is she?" he asked.

Xavier shrugged. "The last time I saw her she was by the pool."

With a few strides Simon crossed the lobby and headed out the front door, Xavier a few steps behind him.

"Look, we'll talk later. After I've straightened this out. In the meantime, why don't you go unpack or something?" The man had just moved his entire life to their tiny island. Didn't he have something better to do?

Raising his hands, Xavier backed away slowly. "I've already unpacked, but I suppose I can find something else to pass the time."

Bright sunlight blinded Simon, spearing straight into his already gritty eyes and making him wish he'd stopped long enough to pick up his sunglasses. And some aspirin.

The construction noise was even louder without the barrier of walls to muffle it. It almost made him want to look at the six-foot-long list Marcy had plopped onto his desk, to figure out what the hell the crew could be working on. But that was the first step down a slippery slope. Looking at the list would lead to having an opinion about what they were doing, which would lead to getting involved and the entire project would become a distraction he didn't need.

It wasn't that he didn't care what went on around the resort, but he couldn't afford to take time away from his writing. Not if he wanted to keep his career from completely tanking.

By the time he rounded the corner into the pool complex he'd built up a healthy head of steam. Unfortunately, it didn't stand a chance when faced with the vision of Marcy in one of the smallest bikinis he'd ever seen, stretched out on a lounge chair beside the pool.

He almost swallowed his tongue.

Where the hell had that body come from?

He had seen the woman every single day for the better part of two years. Simon knew that he would have remembered the firm swell of those breasts and the delicate flare of those hips if he'd ever seen them before.

He had the sudden urge to take every single power suit out of her closet and burn them all. They were doing her a grave disservice and he thought it might be his duty to men everywhere to rectify the situation.

Marcy was tiny. But she'd definitely taught him not to judge a book by its cover. That little body packed a punch…he just hadn't realized the punch was aimed straight for his gut.

Simon couldn't help himself; he had to look at her. As his eyes traveled up the length of her body the heavy weight of arousal settled at the base of his spine. With nothing more than a view of her gleaming skin, his cock turned semi-hard. It had been a long time since he'd been embarrassed by an erection—he did not like revisiting the sensation.

But this was Marcy.

And he was supposed to be upset with her.

"You're blocking my light. Could you move?" The soft, lazy tone of her voice was so out of place that it honestly took him several seconds to realize Marcy was the one who'd spoken. Although it wasn't as if there was anyone else around.

Clearing his throat, Simon managed to surreptitiously adjust his fly and desperately tried to dredge up the irritation he'd stomped out here with.

It was damn hard. Along with the rest of him. Especially when she turned to look at him, pulling down her dark tinted sunglasses just far enough to glare at him over the rims. She looked like a pissed-off pixie and he suddenly had the urge to kiss her until she forgot why she was angry.

He bit down onto the inside of his cheek, asking, "What are you doing?" instead.

"I'd think that would be obvious. Sunbathing."

"Sunbathing," he parroted like an idiot. As if the condescending tone of her voice hadn't been bad enough. Shaking his head, and hopefully reawakening his brain, he said, "I mean, why are you out here and not in your office?"

"You fired me, remember?"

"I most certainly did not. I threatened to fire you. Big difference."

"Great, well then, I quit."

"You can't."

"Oh, I can." With a wicked smile on her lips that he'd never seen before, Marcy pushed her glasses back up, pillowed her arms behind her head and leaned back against the lounge chair. The pose stretched her body, pushing the round swell of her breasts against the tiny squares of material covering them. Her stomach muscles pulled tight, drawing his gaze to the tempting little dimple of her belly button.

She was entirely too pleased with herself.

"What's it going to take to get you back to work?"

"Nothing, but an apology never goes out of style. And now that I think about it, I don't believe I've ever heard you say those two little words before."

That was because he really didn't like them.

"I'm sorry," he offered, the words tasting bitter in his mouth. But they were worth it. He'd tell her whatever she wanted to hear, just so long as it meant she'd start handling all the crap in his life so he could focus on his writing.

With a single finger she slid the glasses back down her nose and glared at him again. "That was pathetic, Simon."

He was frustrated, exhausted and slightly sick to his stomach. "What do you want, Marcy?" he bellowed. "I'll give you whatever you want. You have me by the balls—just name your price."

"I don't want your balls, Simon, and I never have."

He reached down and pulled her up out of the chair. He had no idea what he intended to do—maybe march her back inside the building and handcuff her to her desk. Hell, it had worked for his friend and former head of security, Zane. The one and only time Zane had handcuffed someone on the island he'd ended up falling in love with her.

Only, Simon had no intention of falling in love with anyone, least of all Marcy. What he did want was his damn manager back.

"Let go of me," she growled at him, deep in her throat.

"Not on your life."

Somewhere along her upward journey, her glasses had been knocked off. Her eyes blazed. Her face was flushed, not with the warmth of the tropical sun but the passion of her anger.

He found himself letting her go anyway, unwrapping his hands from around her arms slowly. The inside edge of his fingers felt scalded where they'd touched her skin. He wondered if she'd been out in the sun too long, but didn't want to risk touching her again to find out. She didn't look burned....

Once she was free, instead of pulling away as he'd expected, she pushed forward, crowding her body into his space. His chest tightened.

Her pert little nose reached just to the hollow at the base of his throat, but that didn't stop her from spearing him with her gaze. The tips of her breasts, barely covered by the pale yellow excuse for a bathing suit, pressed into the upward curve of his belly. Some sweet, floral scent mixed with sunscreen enveloped her.

The sudden vision of him rubbing the stuff into her soft skin filled his mind. He sucked a breath deep into his lungs, then regretted it when that scent swelled inside him, consuming him from the inside out.

The erection he'd somehow managed to get under control stirred again. Simon took a step backward in order to hide it from her.

"It's about damn time you had to learn how to handle this stuff on your own. I'm tired of watching you gallivant around this place like it's nothing more than a beach oasis that somehow manages to run itself. Maybe if you get a taste of what a single day of my life is like, you'll appreciate whoever comes in to take my place when I am finally gone." She returned to the lounge chair, stretching out.

"I appreciate you."

"Empty words. And since you've given me no choice but to sit here for the next two weeks, I've made it my mission to change that. I consider it my civic duty."

All Simon could think was *Oh, shit.*

MARCY STARED UP AT SIMON. She had to admit the be-mused expression on his face was somewhat reward-ing.

She wasn't nearly as upset this morning as she'd been yesterday when Simon had announced he had her trapped on the island.

She'd made a phone call to Mr. Bledsoe, the owner of the hotel in New York, and when she'd explained that she was stuck, he'd agreed to arrange a video interview with the selection committee. Tomorrow at 8:30 a.m. with any luck she'd be well on her way to a new position.

In the meantime, she'd decided to take advantage of the resort amenities that she'd never had the oppor-tunity to use before. It had been a long time—a very long time—since she'd sat on her rear and done noth-ing all day. She had to admit, at first, she'd been a little restless. Sitting idle wasn't in her nature.

She'd gotten the hang of it pretty darn quickly, though. She'd made a huge dent in the Cooper Sim-mens thriller she'd hoped to read on the plane and had managed to take a little catnap in the sun. As long as she didn't burn, those two activities seemed perfect enough to keep her busy for the next two weeks.

If she could survive Simon.

First, he honestly didn't think he'd done anything wrong by forcing her to stay on the island and screwing up all her plans. He figured he wrote her paycheck, so that made her his slave. Yeah, right.

Second, his frustrating lack of interest in the resort drove her up the wall. He kept saying he had things to do, but in two years she'd never actually *seen* him do anything but mess with his computer, snorkel and surf. It wasn't as if the man had another job. He just wanted this place to make money so he could fool around.

He was constantly locking himself inside the office or taking mysterious trips to the mainland for heaven only knew what—probably to visit his latest lover.

Marcy's right eyelid began to twitch. The thought of him with a lover made her want to snarl, although she realized she had no right to care.

"I do not need a life lesson from you, Marcy What I need is for you to do your damn job."

"I don't have a job anymore," she responded patiently. How many times would she have to say it before he got it through his thick skull? Just because she was still physically on the island didn't mean he could make her do a darn thing.

He opened his mouth to argue—she could see the stormy cast to his eyes—but a loud explosion rocked the ground beneath their feet, cutting him off before he could say anything else. It was followed by a towering spout of water.

Simon's eyes widened. A series of loud curses and raised voices came from behind the main building.

"What the hell…" he said, moving quickly toward the chaos.

Marcy tried to stay in her chair. She really did. But she just couldn't. Someone might be hurt, and while the appeal of teaching Simon a lesson was great, it couldn't trump her basic human nature.

Grabbing her towel and wrapping it around her body sarong-style, Marcy sprinted after him.

Skidding to a halt, she came inches away from barreling into the solid wall of his back. Considering he was close to a foot taller than she was, he blocked her entire view. However, the pandemonium and the loud hiss of escaping water was enough for her to realize whatever was in front of him wasn't good.

Bracing her hands on Simon's hips for balance, she leaned around him. The scene before her was something out of a comedy—a bad one.

Five big, burly, tattooed men stood around a gushing geyser of water. One of those famous tropical breezes sprayed a fine mist directly into her face.

And beneath her hands she could feel the steady rumble of anger rolling through Simon's body. For the first time she realized that her palms had heated through from the warmth of him. But there was something else, a sizzle of electricity that spiked up her arm and into her body to give her heart a little jolt. Startled by the sensation, Marcy jerked her hands away and scooted out from behind him.

"Don't worry, Mr. Reeves. We'll have this fixed in no time."

"Define no time," he said. From the corner of her eye she could see the glare Simon leveled at the single man who'd been daring enough to step forward from the pack. Although Marcy noticed the other four men had taken a rather large step backward, so it was entirely possible that his newfound status as spokesperson hadn't been intentional.

The worker glanced down at the bubbling water. At least the geyser had eased off. No doubt the pressure of the explosion had bled off the force pushing at the water.

"Um…" He scratched his head and glanced up again without actually looking Simon in the eye. "I think we hit the main waterline, so…" His voice trailed off without him actually committing to a time frame.

"You think? Really? What gave it away? I'm guessing this means you're going to have to shut off the water?"

In some perverse corner in the back of Marcy's mind she had to admit that it was refreshing to see Simon's signature sarcasm leveled at someone else for a change.

The other man nodded slowly. "Yes, sir, so we can work on the line. Anything fed by this line will be without water while we repair it."

An expletive burst from Simon. "That's everything but a few bungalows fed by the old water tanks."

Soon after coming to the island, Simon had upgraded all the outdated plumbing and as much of the electrical as possible. The few bungalows the staff used had been too far back to tie into the new system, so he'd left them on the reservoir.

"How long?"

"One, maybe two days," the other man said, but his tone didn't exactly encourage confidence in the estimate.

"Two days isn't acceptable. We have a business to run."

Marcy decided not to mention that the only person inhabiting that building right now was Simon.

"I expect this fixed no later than five o'clock this afternoon. And if it isn't, you'll work through the night until it is."

"But Mr. Reeves, how do you expect us to work in the dark?"

"I really don't care."

Simon spun on his heel. He stopped midstride, his gaze grabbing Marcy's. His dark blue eyes flashed. For just a second, beneath that laid-back surf-god exterior, Marcy saw the outline of a driven, take-no-prisoners man.

"Don't say a word."

She opened her mouth.

"Not one word."

And closed it again.

Her lips twitched. She tried desperately to keep them straight, but it was a battle she was quickly losing.

With another growl of frustration, he walked away.

Marcy tried to stop the words before they left her lips. Really, she did. But she couldn't seem to help herself.

"See, that wasn't so hard," she called out to his retreating back.

4

SIMON STUMBLED from his desk to the large windows behind him. When had it gotten dark? Stars twinkled overhead, brighter than anything he'd seen when he lived in the city. Palm trees swayed at the edge of the beach and he could almost hear the slush of water as it washed against the sand.

This was a view he'd never get tired of.

A sense of peace stole over him even as he rubbed at his tired eyes. The island had become his sanctuary. Tonight it was quieter than normal. Unlike most only children, he'd never had a problem with sharing what was his, as long as it suited his purposes. And although he'd become pretty adept at tuning out the background noise of the resort guests, it was nice to have the place practically to himself for a change.

Until a loud bang shattered the peace. Five men scrambled around the side of the building, one holding the waistband of his pants tight in a fist so they wouldn't fall as his legs worked overtime. Simon couldn't hear their words, but could definitely see the animated motion of their mouths that suggested they were all yelling.

He closed his eyes. He really didn't want to know.

The sight might have been comical if their scurrying hadn't meant his deadline was no doubt screwed.

He fought back a groan, knowing it wouldn't do any good. Crossing to the small sink at his wet bar, he flipped up the faucet handle and wasn't surprised when a gurgle of air came out.

He needed a shower, some food and a few hours away from his computer so that his brain could recover from the marathon session of writing he'd just finished. Not to mention the words on the screen had started to blur, something that didn't exactly help the creative process.

He had few options. All the guest rooms and cottages operated off the same water system as the main building, so they were out. Along with the apartments above the restaurant, where most of the other staff lived.

The bunkhouse was sourced by the old reservoir system, but he knew if he came in contact with the crew right now they were liable to get an earful…and possibly quit. He didn't need any more of that going around. However, there were several employee bungalows that the highest level of staff used.

Tony and Sara, their dance instructors, used one. The couple had elected to stay on the island during the break and Simon was loath to impose on them, since they were newly married. Xavier had been given Zane's old place, but he was just settling in and, considering the man had already tried to corner him about talking business, Simon had no desire to just drop by and give him an opening for the discussion.

That left Marcy's cottage. Simon stared out the window for several minutes, considering. On one hand, she definitely wouldn't be excited to see him. However, despite the tough outer shell she liked to present to the world, he knew she had a soft-candy center, and he thought she might find it hard to turn him away in his hour of need. Although he'd be the first to admit that he wasn't Marcy's favorite person—at least not at the moment.

Maybe if he buttered her up...

Simon stopped long enough to shut down his computer and lock his office before heading out across the island. He thought about checking on the work crew, but decided ignorant bliss was probably a better option at the moment.

A quick side trip to the wine cellar beneath the restaurant yielded a bottle of wine, a crisp chardonnay he knew was Marcy's favorite. Not that she drank on a regular basis, but the island was small and he tended to pick up on details. He'd seen her leaving the restaurant, the same bottle tucked under her arm, several times over the past two years.

Today that knowledge would come in handy.

The island was dark as he walked along the pebbled path toward the employee cottages at the back of the property. The bar was closed, without the lights, music and laughing guests that usually spilled out of the rustic structure. The soles of his shoes crunched along the path and the tiny hairs at the nape of his neck stood on end.

Oh, what he could do with a scene like this. Someone walking alone at night along the edge of the jungle...

One of the hazards of his job was an overactive

imagination. It was something he'd always had—especially as a child. His mother had explained over and over that there were no monsters under the bed, in the closet, behind the bathroom door or lurking outside his window just waiting for the moment he closed his eyes.

He no longer believed in monsters—at least of the make-believe kind. But he'd done enough research on serial killers, rapists, child molesters and the general dregs of society for him to believe wholeheartedly in the twisted, psychopathic possibilities of the human mind. There were monsters in the world, all right, but they didn't live under the bed. They walked among the rest of humanity, going largely ignored and unnoticed.

Shaking off the eerie sensation, Simon rounded the corner to Marcy's bungalow. Warm lights burned into the night, welcoming. Stepping up onto the small porch that lined the front of her cottage, he couldn't stop himself from peeking inside the large picture window... just to get an idea of what he might be up against.

But what he saw was far from what he expected.

Marcy, in a pair of small gray shorts and a bright blue tank top, was dancing around her small space. The furniture was fairly standard for the island. A large four-poster bed made of rich, warm wood. A small dining table with two chairs set against the far wall of the tiny open kitchen. And a plush sofa in a bright red color that surprised him.

The cord connecting her earbuds to the iPod clipped at her waist jerked in time to her movements as she twisted and turned around the entire place. Simon sucked in a breath when she closed her eyes and nearly slammed into the side of the coffee table. But she somehow managed to miss it.

Her hair was down, her skin flushed from exertion. The tight muscles in her calves and thighs flexed as she bounced around the cottage. Her back arched. The round swell of her breasts swayed beneath the worn cotton of her shirt. She didn't have a bra on.

And suddenly Simon couldn't swallow.

He'd never seen her like this…unfettered, alive, glowing. He should move. Knock on the door. Logically, he realized that. But his feet wouldn't budge. He just stayed there, glued to the worn boards of her front porch, and stared.

Until she spun in front of him. Her eyes popped open and connected with his through the clear glass between them.

He was caught. But right now he didn't care.

OH, GOD. Marcy was mortified.

Her feet slid against the hardwood floor as she tried to stop her movement midmotion. Her hips were thrust out, her feet pigeon-toed, and her knees collided together in mid gyration.

And Simon just kept staring.

She wasn't a great dancer. In fact, she'd skipped her senior prom because she was afraid of making a fool of herself. You always heard about the awkward girls with long limbs and gangly arms who grew into their bodies and became tall, beautiful supermodels. Well, she hadn't grown into hers. Instead, she'd gotten hit twice—awkward and short.

But she loved music, and whenever she turned it on her body just wanted to move. Her muscles twitched. Her feet flexed. Her shoulders swayed, urging her on. But she always made damn sure that she was alone before she ever gave in.

What the heck was Simon doing here? Interrupting her private time. Spying on her.

Scowling, Marcy shot across the room and snatched open the front door. Apparently he'd recovered enough from the shock of seeing her spastic movements, because he was propped against her doorjamb, a bottle of wine in his outstretched hand.

"I brought you a present."

"What are you doing outside my house in the middle of the night, Simon?"

He frowned, pulling the bottle back against his chest. Pushing away from the frame, his tall, powerful body straightened, towering over her. Marcy felt the urge to take a step back, overwhelmed by more than just the shadow that fell across her. He was too close. And the room was suddenly too warm.

"Come inside," she grumbled, "before you let all the cool air out."

Stepping away, Marcy hoped Simon would close the door behind him…because she really didn't want to reach around him. She didn't like this man, she reminded herself, even as a familiar and unwanted tingle started at the nape of her neck.

Pushing it away, Marcy went on the defensive, stabbing him with the powerful glare she'd learned to use to compensate for her lack of height. People often dismissed her because of her size, but she'd learned to use their underestimation to her advantage.

Unfortunately, that no longer worked with Simon.

"Why were you spying on me?"

"*Spying* is such a harsh word."

"If it looks like a duck and quacks like a duck…"

"I do not waddle," Simon said with mock sarcasm.

Verbal sparring with Simon was like arguing with

a silver-tongued snake. He always managed to talk in circles, never really answering a question unless he wanted to. She'd often wondered if he'd been on the debate team growing up. If he hadn't, it was a shame because he most certainly would have dominated any competition.

Taking a deep breath, Marcy asked, "What do you want?"

The smile he flashed at her was lethal for so many reasons. It was charming, no question. Bright. His eyes lowered just a little whenever he did it, connecting with hers and somehow making the whole thing more personal. As if for that moment she was the most important person in the world.

Unfortunately, she'd seen him use the same tactic many times. He was an equal-opportunity exploiter. The problem was that even though she knew his charm was hollow, it always seemed to knock her sideways a bit. Her heart stuttered. Her brain went a little fuzzy, and she found it difficult to concentrate on whatever they were talking about.

She shook her head, trying to dispel the reaction.

"To borrow your shower. And maybe your kitchen."

"No way." No way in hell. The last thing she needed right now was Simon invading her space. Her sanctuary. The one spot on the entire island she was guaranteed to find some peace because it was solely hers and no one bothered her here.

"Come on. The crew still doesn't have the water back on." He took a step toward her, and then another, crowding into her personal space. Years of refusing to be intimidated by anyone was the only thing that kept her from retreating. "You know you can't refuse someone in distress."

The scent of him overwhelmed her, filling her lungs and invading every molecule of her body as she unintentionally breathed him in. Dark, spicy and all male with a hint of something light and…salty. There was nothing artificial about it—about him. Nothing from a bottle for Simon. Nope, he was all natural.

"I really need a shower." His husky words tripped down Marcy's spine and she found herself swallowing. Hard. Trying to get control of her senses.

He certainly didn't smell in desperate need of a shower, but she wasn't about to point that out right now.

Instead, she licked her lips. She had to. They were bone-dry. And said, "If you're in distress, I'm the tooth fairy."

He didn't hesitate a moment, but popped off a comeback with the straightest face she'd ever seen. "When I'm done with my shower, will you show me your pile of teeth?"

Her lips twitched. Damn it all to hell.

How long could a shower take? Five, ten minutes at the most and then he'd be out of her hair. "Fine," she groaned

He was halfway across her bungalow before the word had even left her mouth, flashing another one of those damn smiles at her over his retreating back.

"But be quick about it. I have things to do," she added in an assertive growl just to remind them both where they stood.

He disappeared into the bathroom, his voice floating back out at her. "Like more dancing? I wouldn't mind sticking around to watch that show."

"No. No sticking, no show." Her face flushed hot with renewed embarrassment and she was grateful he couldn't see it from the other room.

"That's a shame. I could use some entertainment. It's rather boring in that big building all by myself." He stuck his head back around the frame of the door.

He was naked. At least what she could see of him. All wide shoulders and taut, tanned skin. The swell of well-defined pecs and just the hint of sculpted abs. A sprinkling of golden hair narrowed to a line down the center of his chest to disappear behind the dark wood of the door frame.

Marcy swallowed. Again. It seemed like the only thing she was capable of doing.

"I'm cooking dinner," she blurted to keep from staring, or licking her lips or asking him to walk out of that room so she could see what was hidden behind the door.

What was wrong with her tonight?

Sure, she'd…reacted to Simon before—more than she would have liked, considering he was her boss and she'd been down that road before with disastrous results. But nothing she couldn't handle. Hormones were easily controlled. He was a hot, virile male and it would have been foolish of her to expect *not* to react to him on occasion.

Maybe she was reacting so strongly because he was inside her home. She realized that in all the time she'd worked at Escape, Simon had never once come to her bungalow. That was it. It had to be.

"Dinner? Any hope of sharing? I'm starving and it's a little hard to cook without water."

Jeez, he wanted a lot from her tonight. But he wasn't going to get it.

"Not a snowball's chance in hell."

The loud sound of a zipper going down ripped through her tiny bungalow. Marcy's eyes seemed to bulge for a minute before finding their place back inside her head. He hadn't even bothered to close the door. The man was either mental or incredibly self-confident. Or possibly both.

"Need I remind you that since you quit this morning this bungalow technically no longer belongs to you?"

"Need I remind you that I tried to leave and you wouldn't let me?"

He stuck his head back around the doorway one more time. The problem was now Marcy didn't have to wonder if he was completely naked. She knew. Her mind started doing somersaults and playing tricks. It conjured up images of what he might look like fully exposed.

Unable to take it anymore, Marcy turned her back on the doorway, heading for the kitchen to cover her retreat.

"How about we consider dinner tonight payment for however long you stay?"

"Exactly how long will that be?"

"Until you come to your senses and realize you don't want to quit."

"Not going to happen."

"I brought you wine. The least you can do is feed me."

And, oh, she was going to need that wine because even as her brain said no, her mouth opened and said, "Oh, all right."

The damn man laughed as he ducked back inside the bathroom. This time he closed the door behind him. Thank God.

Although the sound of water rushing through the pipes didn't exactly help her control her wayward thoughts. Instead, it made them worse. The vision of him naked, surrounded by steam, with rivulets of water dripping down his body made her throat feel dry, scratchy and irritated.

Screwing her eyes shut, Marcy concentrated on something else. She pulled some strips of chicken from the freezer, then grabbed bell peppers, onions and squash. Chopping the veggies gave her something else to focus on—and luckily she managed not to nick a finger.

The meat sizzled in the hot skillet. She threw in a splash of soy sauce, Worcestershire and teriyaki marinade along with the veggies. The spicy scent that filled her little kitchen was pleasant and warm and Marcy found a smile curling her lips despite the fact that Simon was only a few feet away.

Cooking was a luxury she didn't often indulge in, but enjoyed. She usually thought it silly to spend the time herself when a five-star restaurant was only a few steps away from her front door. The chef was excellent, and who wouldn't appreciate gourmet meals every night?

But there was something reassuring and relaxing about making her own meal, simple as it was.

While everything cooked, she popped the cork on the bottle Simon had brought and poured a glass of wine. As an afterthought, she pulled down another glass and poured him one, as well. Maybe it would mellow them both out enough that they'd end the night without wanting to kill each other.

She threw together a simple salad of greens, tomatoes and cucumbers.

And then waited.

And waited.

And wondered what the heck was taking him so

long. His hair might be longer than some guys, but it wasn't as if it was down to his waist and needed extra conditioning. So it was a little shaggy against his collar....

He didn't have a razor or toothbrush. Hell, she realized, he hadn't even brought a change of clothes.

She stirred the chicken for lack of anything better to do. And found herself staring at the closed door... imagining.

5

SIMON WOULD NEVER TAKE warm water for granted again. The muscles running from the back of his neck down to the base of his spine ached from too much hunching over the keyboard. He hadn't realized how tense he'd become until the pounding warmth had released the knots.

He probably spent a good five minutes just standing idle beneath the spray, his mind going in pleasant, unproductive circles that he couldn't ignore.

Reaching down for the shampoo bottle sitting on a small ledge, he squirted a purple glob of the stuff into the palm of his hand. Without thought, he dumped it over the crown of his head and started rubbing.

Only to be knocked sideways when Marcy's scent overwhelmed him. It was lavender and vanilla, somehow feminine, sweet and powerful all at the same time. Not because of the actual scents but because for the past two years they'd always reminded him of her.

His body responded, his cock leaping to attention with a speed that shocked him. Need, deep and pulsing, whipped through his body and he closed his eyes tight trying to ignore it.

This had been a bad idea.

But there was nothing he could do about it now. He was here, held hostage in Marcy's bathroom by a raging erection and a desire to possess her that had blindsided him. Well, okay, maybe not blindsided, but surprised him at the very least.

Gritting his teeth, Simon looked around for a bar of soap and realized there wasn't one. Squinting at the row of bottles, he picked out one that promised silky-smooth skin and popped the lid, bringing it experimentally to his nose. Lavender. Again.

He hadn't thought to grab a washcloth. What kind of person didn't have a bar of soap in the shower? The only thing that remotely resembled something useful was a big puffy thing hanging from a hook over the showerhead. He'd seen them before, in other women's bathrooms, but never stopped long enough to care what they were for. Nine times out of ten, he'd been otherwise occupied and neither party involved had been worried about getting clean. They'd been concentrating on being very, very dirty.

Simon slammed his jaws together as a vision of Marcy, her tight little body wrapped around his waist and her back pressed against the wall of the shower, burst through his mind.

Okay, no puffy thing. Instead, he squeezed the soap out into his hand and began lathering it across his skin. He was going to smell like a pansy when this was over. But maybe that would keep him from acting on the throbbing hard-on jutting out from his hips.

He studiously ignored that entire area on the idea that pretending it wasn't there was the best course of action. Although that seemed pointless since the lather slipped down his body anyway to part around his erection and slide over his tight balls.

With a hiss through his teeth, Simon gave up. Rinsing the soap from his body, he slammed the faucet off and jumped from the confining walls of the shower. Unfortunately, even the towel he grabbed from beneath the sink smelled like lavender.

Did the woman own stock in the stuff?

Simon reached for the clothes he'd thrown haphazardly into a pile on the stool sitting in the corner of the room. The fly on his shorts pressed painfully against the ridge of his uncooperative cock. He reached down and tried to adjust for a more comfortable fit, but there wasn't one. The ache was endless.

With a snarl, he pulled his shirt back over his shoulders, leaving the tail untucked and dangling to hide the bulge. And started thinking unpleasant thoughts.

Starving children in Africa.

Stinging bees.

The workmen outside who hadn't managed to fix the water.

He waited for the erection to go away.

And waited some more.

Finally he realized it wasn't going anywhere and that if he didn't get out of this bathroom Marcy was going to think he'd drowned. And come in after him. His eyes strayed over to the shower and the drops of water that peeled slowly down the pane of glass. Despite all his efforts, the vision of her in there with him returned with a vengeance.

Which would not be good.

Snatching the knob, Simon ripped open the door and walked back out into Marcy's living area. He was greeted by a tantalizing smell. Thank god it wasn't lavender.

"Jeez, how much primping can one man do?"

Simon stared at her for several seconds, his brain spinning uselessly on her words. Until he realized what she was talking about. Perhaps her low opinion of him—and apparently his vanity—could work in his favor here.

"It takes a lot of effort to maintain this level of perfection."

"Please." Marcy's lips twitched down on one corner. "Half the time you look like you dragged the first thing out of the closet that you came to. You've needed a haircut for months. Pretty soon no one will be able to see those beautiful blue eyes behind the shaggy blond hair."

"You think my eyes are beautiful," he teased, flashing her a wide grin.

She groaned and looked at the ceiling as if hoping for help. Her eyes sparkled, just like the water outside their little island when the sun hit it just right. Her jaw tightened, flexing in a way that made him ache to give her another workout for that mouth.

"Your ego is a constant amazement to me, do you know that?"

"My ego? That isn't usually what women compliment me on."

"That wasn't a compliment."

"Sure sounded like one to me. Didn't you just say I amazed you?"

With a huff, Marcy turned and grabbed a glass of wine from the counter. The contents sloshed over the side. She reached out, snatched one of his hands, pulled it close to her body and slapped the glass against his palm.

"Drink," she ordered. "At least that'll keep your mouth occupied for a while."

His eyes unerringly strayed to her mouth. Those full lips, more often than not pulled into a tight line of frustration or concentration, were now parted. He could see the delicate pink inside her mouth and wanted to dive in and taste it for himself. He leaned closer, although he couldn't remember consciously deciding to do it.

Marcy's eyes widened. The pulse at the base of her throat began to throb and he could feel the answering echo as it shot straight to his groin. That tantalizing tongue darted out to scrape across her open lips. Simon's eyes narrowed, focusing totally on the prize that he wanted—her mouth.

With an almost inaudible gasp, Marcy turned away, breaking the connection that had caught them both.

Simon studied her as she quickly dished food from the pan on the stove onto two beautiful plates. They were thick, heavy and, on closer inspection, Simon realized probably handmade. Indigo and burgundy swirled across the surface in an abstract pattern. They were definitely not island issue, but something she'd brought with her to Île du Coeur.

And he realized it was the first touch of something personal he'd seen. Her office had no photographs, no knickknacks, no little baskets or cartoony staplers. Everything was silver, stark and professional.

Her hands were steady now, but he was almost certain they hadn't been when she'd first turned around. He'd been seducing women since puberty, so he knew the signs of interest well enough. Hell, he had the perfect tutorial outside his front door. Every night at the resort some man—or woman—was making the moves hoping to end up in someone else's bed.

Although he really didn't need the lessons.

Marcy wanted him. Physically at least. Of that he was damn sure. She might not like it, but that didn't change the facts.

She brushed past him and a blast of lavender hit him square in the face.

His body responded.

Marcy studiously ignored him as she ate her dinner. Simon, on the other hand, studiously watched her. And the more he watched the more agitated she became.

A tiny smile tugged at the edge of his lips as he slipped a piece of chicken into his mouth. She really was a good cook. He had no idea why that surprised him, but it did.

"This is excellent," He said finally, breaking the tense silence that had settled between them.

"It's nothing."

"No, it's simple and good. I didn't realize you could cook."

"There's a lot about me you don't know, Simon," she said, looking up into his eyes for the first time since she'd sat down across from him.

He quirked a single eyebrow. "Like what? Enlighten me."

"Maybe I don't want to."

Simon set his fork on his plate and leaned across the table. He stared into her azure eyes—they were so bright and clear. Such an unusual shade that he was sure she'd learned long ago to use to her advantage. She wanted to look away. He could see it in the way the corners of her eyes compressed. But she wouldn't.

Instead, she lowered her chin and silently challenged him in that frustrating way of hers.

But he was no coward and actually enjoyed the provocation. "Why not? What are you afraid of? It isn't like I'm asking you to strip naked in front of me. Just tell me where you learned to cook."

Her skin flushed a soft pink the minute the word *strip* left his mouth. But her eyes flashed and her lips thinned and he knew she'd rise to the bait.

"I taught myself. I lived most of my life in premier hotels with just my father. And while he was a wonderful man and a great father, he was a terrible cook. He'd always say that not taking advantage of the gourmet meals available to us was tantamount to committing a sin."

"Not very religious, your father, then, hmm?" he asked.

Marcy reached up and ran her hands through her hair, ruffling her bangs. The soft blond strands settled back around her face in a disheveled mess that did nothing to dampen the buzz of attraction fighting through his blood. His fingers curled against his palm, the only way to keep him from reaching out to brush the wisps away from her cheeks.

She was uncomfortable. Simon wondered if it was sharing part of her background and life that made her so, or if it was specifically sharing those details with him that flustered her.

"So why did you learn to cook? I thought you'd spent most of your adult life living in a hotel, as well."

"I did." Marcy's lips twisted into a self-deprecating semblance of a smile. "This place—" she looked around, but her gaze returned to him and Simon felt a tiny thrill blossom in the center of his chest when she did "—was the first time I'd ever had access to a kitchen, actually."

"Wait," he said. "Are you saying you taught yourself to cook while you've been living here?"

When had she done that? And for heaven's sake, why? "What's wrong with our restaurant? And why haven't you fixed it?"

"Nothing," she asserted. "There's nothing wrong with the restaurant. We get rave reviews and our chef has an excellent reputation."

Simon's eyebrows beetled. He didn't understand. "Then what in the world made you take up cooking?"

She looked away again. "I don't know. I was bored, I guess. There really isn't a lot to do after I leave the office. I'm not much for TV or movies. I guess I was used to a big city with lots of museums and theaters and social events." Her eyes wandered back and she shrugged. "It filled the time. And I discovered I was good at it. Sort of surprised me."

A smile, gentle and unlike anything he'd ever seen on her face before, curved her lips. "Dad always said my mom was an excellent cook."

There was a vulnerability there that made the center of his stomach twist uncomfortably. While he liked this softer side to Marcy, he wasn't used to it and didn't know what to do with it. *Vulnerable* was the last word he'd ever use to describe the tiny bulldog that normally ran his resort. *Capable, fearless, dominating, frustrating, enticing…*these were all words he would have used.

Searching for familiar ground, Simon grabbed on to something she'd said. "What do you mean there isn't any entertainment on the island? We have plenty!"

"Sure, if I was interested in a weekend fling with some stranger. And that's assuming said stranger wasn't just looking for T and A." Marcy looked down at her own body and frowned. "It isn't like I fit the stereotypical mold for that sort of thing."

"Putting aside your derogatory view of our guests, any man who doesn't jump at the chance to sleep with you is an idiot. You're beautiful."

Marcy blinked, appearing nonplussed. It was a new look for her, one he liked for some reason. Maybe it made her more human than he was used to her being. She was Marcy. Efficient, unflappable Marcy. But he'd made her stumble.

"I...you..." She sputtered before finding her footing. "Thank you. I think."

They stared at each other for several seconds. Simon realized that at some point in their conversation they'd moved closer to each other, both leaning over the table that separated them. Whether from the heat of their argument or the awareness pulsing relentlessly beneath his skin, it really didn't matter. The result was the same.

He wanted her.

And for the first time since she'd stepped foot on his island, he couldn't remember why that was a bad idea.

Oh yeah, she worked for him.

Or, rather, she had.

Past tense. Not anymore. Which meant there was no reason to deny what he wanted.

The fantasy that had been haunting him since he'd opened that damn bottle of shampoo burst through his brain again.

He wanted Marcy. And he was a man who usually got what he wanted.

MARCY HAD NO IDEA what was going on behind those devilish blue eyes, but whatever it was made her…uncomfortable. In fact, she'd been uncomfortable since the moment Simon walked through her door.

She reached up and fiddled with the straps of her tank top. Why was she suddenly so hot? The stove. That's what it was.

In a flurry of activity, Marcy began clearing the dishes off the table. The mundane chore allowed her to not only turn her back on Simon and the effervescent feeling he stirred in the pit of her stomach, but also to hopefully speed up his departure.

Dinner was over. He'd had a shower. And now he could leave.

Marcy's lips were suddenly dry and tight. She ran her tongue across them to try to find some relief. It didn't help.

Frowning, she turned back to grab another handful of dishes and nearly collided with Simon. His hands were full of her favorite dishes, so he couldn't reach out and steady her. Instead, he jerked the plates above their heads and pressed the line of his body against hers, giving her a solid surface to rest against.

That rolling, bubbling sensation in her stomach erupted, spilling through her entire body. Her skin tingled from the inside out, the tiny hairs running down her arms standing at attention.

She'd never in her life responded that way to a man touching her. It was overwhelming and she didn't like it at all.

Taking a step back, she put much-needed space between them. Simon simply followed, towering above her. She was sensitive to her small stature, sometimes overly sensitive. But she was used to people—especially men—looming over her. She didn't let it bother her. She couldn't afford that kind of weakness, not in the hotel business, where she had to handle not only prickly executives but also pushy guests.

Simon bothered her. Standing in front of her, his body curved slightly as if he could completely engulf her at any moment... She wanted to fidget, to slip out from under him and stand on her tiptoes. But that would show her vulnerability and she refused to do that.

Instead, she dropped her head back and stared up, up, up into his eyes. She would not let him intimidate her.

He set the plates onto the counter on either side of her. His arms stretched around her as he leaned closer. Her lungs filled with that damn scent—crisp and clean and somehow wild.... Although tonight there was something new beneath it, floral and sweet. The combination made her picture the two of them together. Naked. She tried to hold her breath so she wouldn't pull any more in. Surely now that his hands were empty, he'd move away.

But he didn't.

Instead, he gripped the counter. The heat of his body melted into her. It should have been irritating, but instead, her muscles responded. They went lax and she was suddenly glad for the edge of the counter that pressed into the small of her back and kept her from hitting the floor.

Marcy swallowed and looked up into Simon's eyes again. Her throat went dry at what she saw there. They were dark, the smoldering blue almost completely obscured by his expanding pupils. Gone was the jovial, irreverent expression that seemed to be his constant companion, replaced by a calculating intensity that scared her senseless.

She wanted to say something. To make him stop looking at her that way because it made her body do unfamiliar and uncontrollable things. A throbbing ache settled at the apex of her thighs.

This was not good.

She wanted to move, but she couldn't. Her feet were frozen to the floor.

His eyes searched her face, for what she wasn't sure, but whatever it was he found it. Leaning closer, he nuzzled the curve where her neck and shoulder met. No, *nuzzle* was the wrong word. He didn't actually touch her, but she could feel him there.

The drag of air across her skin as he pulled it deep into his lungs was almost more devastating than if he'd actually touched her. That she could have fought against. At least, that's what she told herself.

"Lavender," he whispered, the word stirring strands of her hair as they tickled her cheek.

Her lips fell open. She couldn't help herself. Her mouth tingled and pulsed with a need she didn't want.

His lips pressed against hers. He didn't overwhelm her as she might have expected he would. He didn't even press inside the open invitation of her mouth. Instead, he simply savored the connection, brushing his mouth lightly across hers.

Her fingers tightened around the counter. She wanted to reach for him, but still had enough brainpower to realize that was a bad idea. One step a little too far.

As kisses went…it was disappointing. Not because it wasn't devastating, but because it was. It was so perfect and sweet, so unexpected, that Marcy found her-

self wishing it would go on forever. And it didn't. That
was the disappointing part.

He sighed as he pulled away from her. His eyes were
heavy lidded, sexy. They glittered at her with a heat
that belied the softness of what he'd just done.

Simon wanted her.

It was obvious.

And her body agreed. It wanted to do whatever he
wanted. Lightning sensations licked across her skin,
crackling and zinging and making it hard to catch her
breath.

"Thank you for dinner," he said, taking a small step
away.

This time when her hands clenched it was because
she wanted to reach out and pull him back to her. To
plaster him full-length along her naked skin and rub
against him in an effort to find some relief for the fire
he'd built deep in her belly.

But she didn't. Instead, she nodded her head and
watched as he walked away.

The quiet click of the door was like a gunshot, finally galvanizing her into action. She crossed her home
in three strides, snatched the door open and rushed out
onto the tiny covered porch.

He was already several feet down the path leading
back to the main buildings of the resort. But he must
have heard the sound of her door, because he stopped
and turned to look at her.

The island was dark, the moon only a sliver that did
little to dispel the night. His entire face was in shadow,
but somehow his eyes still managed to flash.

His body, usually loose and languid, was straight
and tight. She could see the tension in his muscles as he

took one step toward her. She knew what he thought—that she'd rushed outside to stop him from leaving.

Instead, she shook her head, one quick motion that had him pulling up short.

There were a lot of questions swimming around inside her head. She didn't know which ones to ask. Which ones she really wanted an answer to. She settled for the most obvious—and hopefully the least dangerous.

"Why did you do that?" Her voice was low and rough, almost unrecognizable to her own ears.

His white teeth flashed in the darkness, their quick appearance her only indication of his smile. It was the first thing that felt familiar. She'd seen it often, that irreverent, self-deprecating, unapologetic twist of his lips that usually drove her crazy because she knew it wasn't real.

Taking several steps backward, he finally answered, "Because I wanted to."

6

"BECAUSE I WANTED TO," Marcy grumbled to herself. Of course he did. The man didn't care what anyone else wanted or thought. Did he ask her first if he could kiss her? No. He just went ahead and took what he wanted.

Marcy, after a restless night of tossing and turning, was building up a healthy head of steam. She was also trying to convince herself that if he had asked first she would have said no.

But the little voice inside her head called her a liar.

She ignored it.

The problem was that he didn't really want her. He didn't find her sexy. If he had, he would have shown some sign of it before now.

She ignored the *hypocrite* that reverberated through her brain. She'd been fighting her own awareness of the man for the past two years and hadn't given any indication of it. At least until last night.

He just wanted to fluster her. To set her off center. He probably hoped to use her reaction in some harebrained attempt to convince her to come back to work.

It wasn't going to happen.

Her interview had gone very well this morning. It had been difficult considering her laptop screen was small and four people—Mr Bledsoe, and three of his executives—had been present. But they'd asked tough questions and she was happy with her answers.

And to make sure Simon couldn't convince her to do something stupid—like stay—she intended to get as far away from the resort as physically possible.

Grabbing a tattered backpack from her closet, Marcy filled it with several things—a soft blanket, some paperbacks, a couple sandwiches, snacks and several bottles of water. Beneath the cutoff jean shorts and stretch-necked T-shirt, she wore her bathing suit. Including yesterday, she could count on one hand the number of times she'd worn the thing since coming to the island.

Over the next few days she planned to remedy that.

Starting with a hike out to the waterfall tucked into the heart of the jungle on the uninhabited side of the island. How many times had she heard the guests gushing about the beauty of the secluded spot? How many times had she pointed a couple to the head of the path and promised them a wonderful time?

The problem was she had to take everyone else's assurances of that because she'd never made the time to go there herself. As if she ever had an afternoon free for hiking. Or a massage or a ballroom lesson or a few quiet hours on the beach.

She flung the pack over one shoulder. Habit had her reaching for the two-way radio that sat on the charger on the small table next to the door. Her fingers brushed across the plastic before she caught herself. Pulling her hand back and cradling it against her body as if it had been burned, she stared at the thing.

Taking it would be smart. It was unusual for anyone to get lost out in the jungle, but it did happen. Just a few months ago, Colt and Lena, guests who were being photographed for an Escape ad campaign, had been stuck out there overnight. And she was hiking alone. Being able to contact Xavier if there was an emergency wouldn't be a bad idea.

And if anything else came across the radio, she'd simply turn the volume down. She didn't have to respond or pay attention.

Reaching out with a lightning motion, Marcy palmed the thing and stuffed it into the front pocket before she could change her mind.

A few minutes later the soft trill of birds and the muted chatter of unseen animals welcomed her. It was decidedly cooler beneath the cover of the trees—not that the days were sweltering or anything. While fall didn't bring the change of seasons she'd grown used to in New York, there was a difference, however small.

The biggest problem they had at this time of year was hurricanes, which was one of the reasons they always closed the resort during the fall. While they offered lots of discounts to appeal to frugal travelers, quite a few of them resisted the Caribbean and the potential for their dream vacation to turn into a nightmare with torrential rains and damaging winds. So it wasn't difficult for the resort to carve out two weeks for routine maintenance and repairs, as well as staff vacations.

They'd been lucky lately and hadn't dealt with any major storms in several years. But she knew the island had taken some pretty major hits in the past. The resort had even been closed at one time because of damage the previous owner couldn't afford to fix.

But Marcy wasn't worried about storms, not surrounded by the thickness of the jungle. The tension that had stretched across her shoulders began to ease. She took a deep breath and held it in her lungs. Everything smelled moist, green and vibrant.

The sudden urge to hurry overtook her and she began to run. The balls of her feet barely touched the ground before springing up again. The exercise felt great, something she'd definitely been neglecting in her work-focused fog. Her muscles protested after a little while—there was no question she was slightly out of shape.

She was going to fix that, though, as soon as she got back to New York. She was going to make a few changes in her priorities, starting with taking better care of herself. Although she had to admit staring at the nondescript walls of a gym would have little appeal after the natural beauty of the jungle.

Marcy heard the waterfall long before she saw it. The path became lighter and lighter, making her realize just how dark and dense the jungle had been around her. Breaking through the opening at the end of the path, she stopped to take it all in.

Despite the force of the water breaking against the rocks below, the entire place had a sense of…quiet. It was old, powerful. Marcy let her eyes wander for a few moments, taking everything in. The water looked inviting, but she wasn't ready for a swim.

Her eyes were drawn to the top of the falls. That's where she wanted to go. From up there she'd be able to see everything.

It took her almost twenty minutes to walk around the collecting pool to the far side of the falls and the only way up she could find. The rocks were a little slippery from the wayward spray of the water, but she managed to climb up safely.

There was a small patch of grass, more lush than anything below, spongy and soft. She slipped off her shoes and socks and wiggled her toes. The thick blades tickled the bottom of her feet. Sunlight, unfettered by the trees surrounding the area, fell directly over the patch.

Dropping her pack, Marcy took out the blanket and spread it in the sunshine. Her original plan was to read her book, but she barely got a few pages in before exhaustion stole through her body, weighting her limbs and eyelids.

She closed her eyes and tipped her head back. The underside of the leaves above her looked down. The loud roar of the water faded to background noise. A smile touched the corners of her lips and just as she drifted off to sleep an image of Simon popped into her head.

Towering over her—when didn't he?—he watched her with that same intense, smoldering gaze he'd used on her last night. And this time when he kissed her, he didn't pull away. And she didn't tell him to stop.

Instead, he slowly, deliberately drove her mad.

So much for escaping him in the jungle.

SIMON CROUCHED next to Marcy, running a single finger down the scrunched bridge of her nose. Even in sleep she looked frustrated. Wasn't a nap in the sunshine supposed to ease that kind of stress?

Her skin was soft. It smoothed out beneath his fingers, her entire face easing. The corners of her lips twitched and she rolled her head closer against his hand. His palm cupped her cheek, the warmth of her sun-warmed skin seeping into him. She mumbled something that he couldn't catch and then sighed his name.

Need, hard and sharp, twisted deep inside. He wanted to startle her awake, to strip her bare and take her here on the soft patch of grass. Resisting, he dropped to his knees beside her and went slowly, letting his fingers tickle across the exposed curve of her shoulder. The neck of her T-shirt was stretched out, pulled tight on one side and hanging halfway down her shoulder on the other.

Tiny freckles dotted her skin. They were cute and unexpected. He wanted to reach down and kiss every single one, but refrained. He trailed his fingers up her throat. Even in sleep, she moved toward him, revealing more skin for him to play with.

Her eyes fluttered beneath closed lids and her soft pink lips parted. Reaching with the other hand, he let it trail softly down the outside curve of her thigh. Circling her knee, he moved back up. Her legs were toned and tanned, although he had no idea when she took the time to sit in the sun. At least, not before the past two days.

She rolled beneath his caress, parting her legs and opening herself to him as he moved higher. A brief spurt of guilt shot through him, but he pushed it away. He had no intention of taking advantage of her. Although her unconscious response to him was gratifying. And probably more real than anything she'd shown him before now.

At least now he knew for sure that he hadn't been mistaken last night, or so overrun by his own lust that he'd imagined something that wasn't really there.

His fingers bumped along a small, jagged scar that

ran diagonally up the inside of her thigh. Feeling by touch, he realized it was almost two inches long. He wondered what had happened.

Without thought, he leaned over and placed his lips to the spot. It was a bad idea. She gasped, her body quivering beneath his mouth. Her skin was warm against his lips, soft and inviting. The strings from the hem of her cutoffs tickled his face, reminding him just how close his mouth was to what was hidden beneath.

Her feet scissored and tension tightened her muscles. It was his first clue that she was awake.

Turning his head, he kept his mouth close to the temptation of her body and looked up into her face. She stared down at him, her eyes now bright and vivid, definitely awake.

"What are you doing?" she whispered, her voice thick with sleep.

"Kissing it and making it better?" he asked, arching one eyebrow.

She moved again beneath him, not in an attempt to push him away, but in a restless motion that he understood. The same need crawled through his body, making his skin feel tight.

"That healed a long time ago."

"What happened?" The heat of her body seeped into his open lips, making them ache to touch her again.

"I dropped a knife. It cut me on the way down."

Had she done that here? A vision of her first clumsy attempts at cooking made his chest tighten. "When?"

"I was twelve."

He hated the idea of her in pain. His fingers brushed softly over the puckered skin. But at least she hadn't injured herself on his watch without him even knowing about it.

Rising on her elbows, Marcy twisted and pulled herself out from under him. He let her go, knowing it wouldn't be for long. Not if he had his way and he could convince her to give in to what her body obviously wanted. From where he'd been, he could smell the heady scent of her arousal.

"What are you doing here, Simon?"

"Looking for you."

"Why?"

He decided not to answer her question. He didn't want to. He wasn't entirely sure what the answer was anyway. From the window in his office he'd watched her walk into the jungle this morning. He knew where she was going. And for the rest of the morning, while he should have been concentrating, he'd been thinking about her.

Fantasies shared space with concern, knowing she was out in the jungle alone. There were snakes and jaguars and high cliffs. And while Marcy was one of the most capable people he'd ever met, she wasn't invincible.

Finally, after finishing a chapter, printing it out and adding it to the pile of work he'd already done, he gave in to the urge to follow her. The day was nice and warm. He wasn't accomplishing much anyway. Maybe if he burned up some of this need and energy he'd be able to concentrate again.

But he wasn't about to tell her that.

"You said my name."

"What?" she asked, confusion clouding her eyes.

"In your sleep. You said my name."

Her eyes widened with shock for just a moment before she hid her reaction. "I did not."

"You did. I promise."

She scoffed. "Please, a promise from you isn't worth the breath it's uttered with."

"That hurts."

She shrugged. "The truth usually does."

"I think I liked you better when you were asleep."

He expected her to make some snappy comeback. It was what they did—verbally spar. He was beginning to think all that aggression had just been an outlet for the sexual frustration that ran between them like a live wire.

Instead, she looked at him and said, "Liar. Right now you're trying to figure out the fastest way into my pants."

He rocked back on his heels. She'd surprised him. The wheels in his brain spun as he tried to figure out the best response to her candor. He wasn't sure there was one, so he decided to match her honesty.

"You wanna save me the trouble and just tell me?"

She laughed. Sunshine washed across her face and her eyes sparkled. He wasn't sure if it was from the direct light or from something more…something internal. He hoped it was more.

Her laughter eased, but even as her gaze connected with his again her body continued to quiver with fettered mirth. "No, I don't think I do."

Pushing herself up from the ground, she grasped the blanket that he still knelt on and yanked against it. It barely budged, but that didn't stop her from trying again.

Simon rose and watched as she folded it, making sure each corner matched and the final product was perfectly square. Stuffing the blanket in, she zipped her pack and moved to fling it over her shoulder. Reaching out, he snagged it from the air. Her body jerked against the unexpected weight as the pack fell suspended between them.

Using it to reel her closer, Simon stepped into her space. His eyes snagged on her mouth and he did nothing to hide his fascination. He watched as her lips jerked, almost parting, before she clamped them into a tight line.

Slowly he let his gaze travel up to her eyes. He stared at her, watching as emotions flitted through the bright blue centers. She was fighting a war that she couldn't win. But he knew she was damn well going to try.

And that was going to be part of the fun.

While he'd never been one to look a gift horse—or willing woman—in the mouth, there was something about Marcy that stirred more than just his libido. This push-and-pull thing that they had going excited him in a way nothing else had in a very long time.

Not even his work. And that cost him a lot to admit.

"You want me, Marcy. Why don't you save us both a lot of misery and just admit it?"

He didn't touch her. He didn't try to influence her. He wanted this to be her decision, her capitulation.

Licking her lips, she said, "What woman wouldn't? You're sexy as hell and you know it. You use your charm and those laid-back bedroom eyes like weapons. But you've never used them on me. Why now?"

She would ask that. She would want to understand all the angles, to analyze and inspect and pick apart the options and reasons before making a decision.

"We're here. You don't work for me anymore…."

Her decision flashed through her eyes long before it left her lips, but that was all the encouragement Simon needed. He reached for her, jerking her full-length against his body.

In his arms she felt small and delicate. There was a disconnect between his perception of her and the reality. She wasn't fragile, but it was easy to forget just how tiny she really was.

He dived in and devoured her. Their mouths met and melted together. He'd expected their first real kiss would have an edge of aggression, as their words usually did. He was wrong.

There was heat and urgency. Need. His tongue scraped against hers, shooting sparks through his entire body. Her gasp of surprise blasted against his open mouth. She tasted like oranges, chocolate and lavender all mixed together.

His hand fisted at the nape of her neck, dragging her head back so he could get more. With the other, he grasped her waist and pulled her up his body. She wrapped her legs firmly around his waist, anchoring them together and, more important, telling him she wanted this just as much as he did.

Her palms pressed against his chest, curling in and urging him closer. She ripped her head out of his hold, squeezing her thighs to push herself higher up his body. She was looming over him, and for the first time since he'd met her, he had to tip his head back to keep up with her.

She pushed in and took what she wanted. Her fingers grasped the side of his head and held him as she matched him thrust for thrust, the heat of her mouth over his as devastating as anything he'd ever experienced before.

He should have expected her to be as much of an

aggressor with sex as she was with everything else. Although it actually surprised him. He was used to women taking a backseat and letting him lead. It was sort of exhilarating and liberating to have her fight him for control.

But he wasn't about to give in. Taking several steps, he set her back against the closest tree. Shade, a cool breeze and anticipation had a shudder quaking through him.

She made a tiny sound in the back of her throat that he swallowed, the first piece of her he planned to claim. With the weight of her body resting against the trunk, his hands were free to explore. Pushing against the hem of her shirt, they scraped up the soft skin of her belly.

Her muscles jumped beneath his touch.

She writhed against him, the apex of her open thighs pressing tight to his aching erection. Denim had never seemed so thick and annoying in his life. He leaned into her, pinning her hips hard against the tree, looking for relief.

"Simon."

The radio he'd been forced to bring with him, since he was apparently in charge, squawked at his hip. He ignored it. Or tried to.

Dragging his hands higher, he wanted to cup her breasts, to fill his palms with her soft round curves. He never made it. She stopped him, slamming her own hands over his with the thin layer of her shirt between them.

Pulling back, she looked at him. "Are you going to get that?" Her words were breathy. Her lungs worked hard beneath his palms, her ribs expanding and contracting in a tantalizing way that made his hand slip against her skin.

"No." Was she crazy? Whatever catastrophe Xavier wanted to tell him about could wait. For an hour. Or maybe until tomorrow if he had his way.

"Simon!"

The screech was louder, and somewhere behind them it echoed.

With her legs still wrapped tight around his waist, the tempting center of her sex pressed against his throbbing cock, she raised a single eyebrow. Her blond hair, in complete disarray thanks to his desperate fingers, clouded around her disapproving face.

With a sigh he extricated a hand—but only one—and reached for the radio at his hip. Pressing the button, he growled, "This better be important."

Marcy's eyes flashed. He rocked his hips against her and relished her soft gasp and the way the azure depths clouded with passion once again.

But they didn't stay that way. Not when Xavier's voice floated between them.

"We've got a problem."

"I hope so, or you're about to get fired."

Marcy's lips twisted.

"Apparently the construction crew managed to get water on the main electrical panel."

"Holy crap," he muttered. "Are they completely incompetent?"

He realized it was the wrong thing to say, because Marcy began to squirm against him—and not in a good way. She was no longer overcome by passion. She wanted down. Now.

She pushed against his shoulders and dropped her legs from around his waist. Her body hung suspended between him and the tree, her toes dangling at least half a foot off the ground.

Damn it. With a frown of his own, he wrapped an arm around her waist and lowered her gently to the ground. So much for picking up where they'd left off. Although he wasn't about to just let her walk away.

Keeping her tight against his body, he asked, "What's the damage?"

"One of the crew was shocked, but he seems to be okay. Dazed."

That didn't seem so bad. Not that he wanted anyone injured, but if the man was conscious, it couldn't be life-threatening. Unfortunately, their on-staff doctor had left with most of the employees.

Xavier's voice crackled again through the connection. "And somehow a small electrical fire started. I've implemented fire protocol, but most of the staff is gone."

Before Xavier could even finish, Marcy was jerking out of Simon's hold. Grabbing her abandoned pack, she flung it over her shoulder and started down the path at a fast clip. Simon was right on her heels.

From out of nowhere another radio appeared in her hand. It was a nice trick, although Simon assumed it had been in her pack and was probably the source of the echo he'd heard. Not the cavern of the falls as he'd assumed.

"Xavier, how big is the fire? What buildings are in danger? Is someone getting the pumper truck?"

"Not big. Luckily, the panel is at the back of the main building and so far the only thing on fire is a small shed. I've called for the truck...but it won't do us much good. The water's out, remember."

Simon let out a long line of expletives. Could this get any worse?

"Oh, and the power's out all over the resort."

Why had he asked?

7

SHE'D NEVER SEEN SIMON move so quickly. His long legs ate up ground and he quickly passed her on the trail back to the resort. A hike that had taken her almost thirty minutes took ten at the fastest sprint she'd ever done. And still she arrived in the middle of the chaos minutes after Simon had.

Along the way, she'd heard him instruct Xavier to hook up the truck to the reservoir system that was still functioning. Unfortunately, that meant the truck was limited in how far the hose could reach. And by the time they'd gotten everything hooked up, the shed was completely engulfed.

It held discarded furniture, decorations and pieces that weren't used but were still in decent shape and worth keeping. No one would be devastated by the loss. The biggest concern was the proximity of the flames to the main hotel building. If that caught fire…it would be bad. Their normal emergency response team was severely limited.

The few employees left on the island crowded around, trying to pitch in and help as best they could.

Xavier stood at the end of the powerful hose, his legs spread wide and his weight grounded as he fought to keep the water trained where they needed it most.

Soot and sparks shot into the air, forming a dangerous dark cloud above them. Red-orange flames licked relentlessly up all four sides of the shed, devouring the worn wood with a crackle and hiss.

And Simon was in the thick of it.

Marcy watched as he issued instructions to the people standing around. With a few terse words he had order evolving out of the chaos. Another team hooked up a second hose to the truck and began spraying the side of the main building.

Two more men jumped in line behind Xavier, making it easier to control the powerful stream of water blasting the building.

Her heart thumped erratically against her chest when Simon rushed toward the fire. "What are you doing?" she shouted just as he slipped around the far side of the shed, way too close to the fingers of the fire for her comfort.

Idiot! She wanted to scream at the top of her lungs, but she didn't. He wouldn't hear her anyway above the noise of the truck and the sizzle of the flames. What the hell was he doing? There was nothing important enough in that shed to risk his life for.

Her feet followed him anyway. She wasn't even conscious of deciding to do it—she just moved steadily closer to the shed. Heat blasted her body as a breeze gusted through the narrow passageway between the two buildings. It was functioning as a wind tunnel, funneling oxygen to the greedy fire.

Shouting to Xavier, she told him to concentrate the water on the wall closest to the main building. The shed was a complete loss, but hopefully they could contain the damage.

Ashes and tiny pieces of charred wood rained over her head and shoulders. Squinting her eyes against the heat and blazing light, Marcy tried to find Simon.

"Simon!"

He yelled at her. She thought he told her to get back, but she ignored him. Walking farther into the passageway between the buildings, she finally saw him through the haze of smoke. He was crouched close to the ground. She couldn't see what he was next to, but it was definitely a dark shape.

She almost yelled at him then. Until she saw the shape move and realized it was someone, not just something. Two someones. From the construction crew. One was stretched out on the ground, the other crouching behind Simon next to him.

The electrical box was only a few feet away. The man on the ground must have been the one shocked.

How had Simon known they were back here? By the time she'd arrived, the smoke had been too thick to see them.

Simon threw her a dark glance when she fell down beside him. She ignored it. He could be angry with her later when the fire was out and they knew the man would be fine.

She was relieved to see that his eyes were open and his chest was rising and falling steadily. Turning to her, Simon ordered her, "Go. We're right behind you." Scooping the man up into his arms, Simon waited until she and the other man were dashing ahead of him before following.

Marcy glanced back over her shoulder several times, just to make sure he was there. Even in a crouch, staying low to the ground where the smoke wasn't as thick and carrying a two-hundred-pound man, Simon could haul ass. Their little knot burst through the end of the passageway and the small group of people around them cheered.

The panic that had been almost palpable when they'd arrived eased. The flames licking at the shed had diminished. Three sides were now only smoldering, thick curls of smoke rolling up from the jagged edges of the damp wood. The fourth side would be joining them shortly if Xavier had anything to say about it.

Marcy was impressed with how he'd handled the crisis, and if she'd still been in charge would have offered him a raise on the spot. But she wasn't.

From his position on the hose, he hollered over to Simon, "MedFlight should be here shortly. How's he doing?"

Simon grunted and laid the man gently on the soft grass away from the smoke and flames. "Okay, but I'm not taking any chances."

Frowning, Simon looked up into the sky. As if he'd conjured them, the steady *thwap, thwap, thwap* of rotor blades joined the noise around them. Leaning over to one of the restaurant staff, he shouted something in her ear. With a nod, she burst out across the resort, directing the helicopter to the closest patch of open ground big enough for it to land.

Xavier kept the stream of water directed at the still-smoking building as the force of the downdraft pushed another burst of oxygen-rich air across the fire zone. Whether because of that or the daring glare that Xavier directed at the structure, the flames stayed down.

One man stooped low beneath the spinning blades

and dashed across the resort toward the cluster of people. A couple of bags were slung over his shoulders. The equipment looked as if it weighed a ton, but his body barely reacted to the stress of it.

Two more men followed behind, a stretcher between them. They crouched and worked, assessing and preparing the man for transport to the hospital. As they were getting ready to leave, one of them came over to Simon.

"We didn't get the call that there was a fire here, just the electrical shock. Do you need me to radio in for reinforcements from St. Lucia?"

Looking across at Xavier, Simon waited for a shake of his head before declining the offer. "I think we have it handled, but thanks."

With a nod, the man rushed after the rest of the crew. Once the stretcher was strapped in, the chopper lifted off. Marcy turned her face away from the tiny pieces of debris that lashed her.

Simon wrapped his arms around her and turned her so that her face was buried against his chest. Ducking his own head, he rested his cheek on her hair.

He smelled of soot and man. His shirt was damp, but she burrowed closer to him anyway. Her body started to shake. She knew it was just a delayed reaction to everything that had happened, her muscles revolting against the stress and the flood of adrenaline that was quickly receding.

But she couldn't stop it.

She wasn't cold. Not really. But her teeth began to chatter anyway.

Simon must have felt it, because he pulled away, holding her at arm's length as he looked at her. His eyes, intent and focused, studied her face. Without looking away he shouted, "Xavier, you got everything under control?"

"Yep, we're all good. Fire's out. I'll keep someone on watch through the night for hot spots, but I don't expect any."

"Great" was Simon's only response. With a sweep of his arms, he picked her up and cradled her against his body.

Marcy sputtered, but the protest she wanted to make died on her lips.

This was a side of Simon she'd never seen. One that intrigued and—if she was honest with herself—aroused her. Where was the laid-back surf god she'd been butting heads with for the past two years? Had he been kidnapped by tree sprites and held hostage in the jungle?

The man holding her in his arms was commanding, no-nonsense and completely capable. Not that that last one really surprised her. She'd always known a capable businessman lurked beneath that jovial, joking facade. That's what had frustrated her so much.

He could give a damn—he just chose not to. As far as she was concerned, that was a complete waste of his potential. And nothing bothered her more than to watch something useful go unused.

"Where are you taking me?" she asked, finally breaking the charged silence that had settled between them.

"Where do you think?" He bit out the words through stiff jaws.

He was upset. She thought she knew why but decided, in light of this new side to Simon, she wasn't going to act on the assumption. Probably better to wait for solid ground.

Turning sharply, he headed for the main entrance to the hotel. "To get cleaned up?" she said hopefully.

A humorless chuckle rumbled through his body. She could feel the vibrations of it roll through her like the reverberations from a plucked guitar string. They rekindled the burning need that the crisis had dampened.

Better than the teeth chattering.

Pushing through the front door, he let it slam behind them. The cool interior of the building was dark and a few steps inside only the weakest light remained. Outside, she realized, it was late afternoon, but inside it felt closer to dusk.

"No water, remember. And by the time we can stop pouring water over that building, chances are the reservoir will be dry."

Marcy cursed, but there wasn't any heat behind her words. Sure, a shower would be nice, but that would mean he'd have to put her down. She didn't want to examine too closely why that idea didn't appeal to her right now.

He strode through the building, heading for the stairs. Taking them two at a time, he began the climb up four flights. She could feel the powerful surge of his muscles as they bunched and moved beneath her.

Looking down at her arms tangled tightly around Simon's neck, she realized they were dirty. Dark patches of soot covered her upper arms. Trails of naked skin peeked through where stray drops of water had fallen and rolled down.

She was nasty.

Looking up into his face, she realized she wasn't the only one covered in soot. Streaks of it ran down over his forehead and cheeks. The sharp tang of burning wood clung to their skin.

He was filthy.

She didn't care.

The vision of him running beside that burning building burst through her mind. Another surge of adrenaline accompanied it.

Letting go with one hand, she used it to smack his shoulder.

Stopping midstride, his eyebrows crashing together, he said, "Ow! What was that for?"

They were halfway up, perched on the landing for the third floor. His voice echoed through the confined space, bouncing all around them.

"That was for being stupid and heading into the fire."

His expression cleared and a knowing grin twitched at the corners of his lips.

Continuing their climb, he argued, "I didn't head into the fire."

"Semantics. You were close enough to be burned. Or overcome by smoke inhalation. How did you know they were back there, anyway?"

"One of the crew told me when I arrived. At first they thought it was safer to leave him there until the helicopter came. But then the fire spread and the smoke shifted, cutting off the passageway. They were about to go in after them and I told them to wait."

"So that you could play hero yourself."

"Because I already had one man down, possibly two, that I was responsible for. I wasn't about to let two more follow."

Damn. She had seriously underestimated this man.

Something in the center of her chest swelled, but before she could analyze it, Simon was kicking open the stairway door to the top floor.

Anticipation, desire and apprehension swirled through her, a dangerous combination that was uncomfortable and energizing at the same time. She had no illusions as to why Simon was carrying her into his apartments. They'd started something in the jungle, and despite the interruption, he had every intention of following through and finishing it.

And if she wasn't sure about that she needed to decide now. Before he overwhelmed her senses again and logical thought became impossible.

She opened her mouth to say something, although she honestly wasn't sure what, but he cut her off.

"And while we're on the subject, what kind of incompetent work crew did you hire? First they break the main waterline. Then they get one of their men injured and start an electrical fire. Really, Marcy, is that what you call doing a good job?"

He stared down at her. Despite the fact that his eyes were hard and direct, she could still see the glimmer of passion lurking in the back.

"Excuse me? I'm damn good at my job."

Simon opened his door, then pushed it closed with the heel of his shoe behind them. Instead of moving straight to the bedroom as she'd expected, he stopped in the middle of his living room. Still holding her in his arms, he stood there.

Undercurrents flew between them, even as they continued their conversation. "Were. Were damn good at your job. You quit, remember?"

"Right." And that was an important thing to remember because the minute she gave in to whatever this was between them, the possibility of working for him again would be gone forever. After what had happened in New York, she refused to sleep with anyone she worked with—especially someone she worked *for*.

"The crew I usually use was unavailable until Friday. We had a long list and a short time to complete it. We needed a full crew for the entire two weeks. I couldn't wait for them. These guys came highly recommended."

"By who? The three stooges?"

"One of the men I usually use."

"I'm guessing these guys are blackmailing him for referrals, because I doubt they could figure out which end of a hammer to use."

Dropping her arms from around his neck, she crossed them over her chest. She didn't want to be impressed by the way he compensated for the loss of her help in keeping her rear end off the floor. But she couldn't help it.

His arm muscles bunched and his chest flexed. She could see the clearly defined bulge beneath the thin, wet material of his shirt. He was built. Why had she never noticed that before? Maybe she should take up surfing instead of running if the result was that kind of muscle tone.

"Give them some credit. They fixed the roof of the restaurant with no problems. Hammers aren't their issue. I will admit that perhaps plumbing and electrical jobs are out of their jurisdiction."

"I don't have to give them credit for anything. They've cost me enough money. I'm firing them."

"And how do you propose to finish the list of repairs and renovations before we reopen?"

He leaned over her, bringing their mouths centimeters apart. His eyes flared as they toured slowly across her face to settle on her mouth. They glittered with a

promise and heat that sent awareness zinging through
her body.

He hummed, deep in his throat. The sound was wild
and sexy, a last warning of his intent.

"I guess that's my problem now. Last chance. If you
want to walk out that door you better do it now, because in sixty seconds I won't be able to let you go."

It was the sexiest thing any man had ever said to
her. What woman could resist that kind of naked admission?

Not her. Giving in was inevitable, but that didn't
mean she had to throw all caution to the wind. Caution
was part of her DNA.

"I'm not staying."

"I don't remember suggesting you would."

"I just want to make sure you know this won't
change anything."

His mouth dropped to her throat and trailed across
her skin. The sharp edge of his teeth followed the
tendon that curved from her neck down her shoulder.
He didn't hurt her, but it was hard to miss the implication that he could have…if he'd wanted to. That kind
of leashed power was intoxicating.

His words brushed softly against her skin, but that
did nothing to lessen their impact. "You're wrong. It's
going to change a lot of things."

"But not me leaving," she breathed out, trying desperately to keep hold of her thoughts.

He lifted his head and speared her with his gaze.
She felt hunted, vulnerable, desired.

"No, whatever this is won't keep you from leaving."

She dampened her dry lips, rolling them into her

mouth and swiping her tongue across them. "As long as we're clear."

"Oh, we're clear."

8

Simon stalked into the bedroom, her body tucked safely against his own.

He did not like the dirt that covered her skin. Not because it bothered him that she was dirty—it didn't—but because it meant she'd gotten close enough to the fire to be hurt.

When she'd materialized out of the smoke beside him in that tiny alley he'd wanted to growl and yell and carry her as far away from the danger as possible. Logically, he'd realized that wasn't possible. He'd needed to take care of the injured man. But at that moment logic had only barely come into play.

He moved to set her onto the dark navy bedspread covering the king-size mattress in the middle of the room. Marcy protested, a high-pitched squeak erupting from her. "Don't you dare. You'll ruin it. We're filthy."

"I don't care," he answered, dropping her onto the soft surface. He'd buy a new bed if he had to, but nothing was going to stop him from having her. Right now.

Marcy tried to keep her body off the comforter as she scrambled for the other side of the bed. She glared at him over her shoulder, but he didn't let that deter him. Grasping her by the ankle, he stopped her retreat and pulled her back to the center of the bed.

"Give it up. It's already dirty," he rumbled.

Marcy collapsed onto her stomach diagonally across his bed, her tangled hair running down her back. Without thought, he brushed the mass away, revealing the tender flesh at her nape. It was soft and fragrant as he buried his face against her. That tempting scent of hers clouded around him, overpowering the bitter smell of smoke. This was what he wanted. Something easy and beautiful to crowd out everything else.

His lips caressed her skin.

She made a small sound deep in her throat, something between a protest and anticipation. "Don't do that. I'm covered in soot."

"Not here," he whispered against her neck. He watched with fascination as goose bumps erupted across her skin. How could the rough texture of them against his mouth be this arousing?

He sucked a tiny taste of her into his mouth. Her back arched, pushing her closer against him. Breath caught in her lungs, the tiny hitch rocketing through him.

He wanted more.

Needed to see all of her, now. Pulling back, he grasped the neckline of her shirt and ripped.

"Don't—" she protested, but the threads were already coming apart in his hands. He wanted to see her that way, wild and ravaged as he pumped relentlessly inside her.

"I liked this shirt," she said with a resigned sigh. Ever practical, she wouldn't waste time fighting about something that couldn't be undone. Good for him, since the last thing he wanted to do was fight with her.

"It needed to be put out of its misery anyway. What? High school?"

"College."

His fingers slid down the exposed arch of her spine, a gentle caress that she bowed against. His fingers played beneath the string of the bikini top that circled her chest. Taking the ends, he tickled them over her skin, pulling a small moan of protest from her parted lips. Slowly he tugged at the tie until it finally let go.

His lips and fingers roamed. Her body was hot against his mouth. Her skin was soft and smooth, tempting him to take more. Even there, she had a tiny sprinkling of freckles and he paused long enough to pay homage to the few close by.

Darting his tongue out, he let it slide languidly over the tiny bumps of her spine. Her hips bucked when he reached the waistband of her shorts.

"For god's sake, take them off."

"If you insist," he said, a grin tugging at his lips.

She was as enflamed by this as he was. Knowing that only made the ache inside worse. He wanted to see the fire in her eyes as she finally broke apart beneath him. For two years he'd tried not to think about this moment, but had failed miserably.

Now he had the reality and it was so much better than anything even his imagination could have conjured up.

Marcy lifted her hips, sliding her hands beneath her to work the snap and zipper. She struggled, wiggling back and forth, and he just watched, enjoying the way her body undulated and the desperation that made her clumsy.

The waistband relaxed, slipping down and revealing the dent at the top of her ass. Without waiting for her to finish, he leaned over and ran his mouth along the newly exposed skin.

"Damn," she breathed out. Her body twisted beneath him, but with him pressed against her, she just couldn't get enough leverage to rid herself of the shorts and bathing-suit bottom.

Taking pity on them both, he curled his fingers in at her hips and pulled them off. She was beautiful.

Propped on her elbows, Marcy watched him over the curve of her shoulder. Her blue eyes smoldered, as hot as the fire they'd both just fought.

Without breaking their connection, Simon reached between her legs and pressed gently, asking her to spread wider for him. She did. The soft rasp of her thighs against the comforter as they opened for him rippled down his body.

His erection pressed painfully against his own zipper, but he wasn't about to let it free. Not yet. If he did, this would end way too soon. He wanted his fill of her first.

He ran his fingers softly up the insides of her thighs, just as he'd done when she was asleep. Only this time there was nothing to stop him from following all the way up to the soft pink center of her sex. Oh, and this time she watched him with half-lidded eyes, sharp arousal stamped on her face.

She rolled her hips, trying to hurry his journey upward, but he refused to rush. He tortured her, running his hands up and down her legs, over the curve of her ass, brushing as close to the center of her sex as possible without actually touching.

Every time he got close, Marcy's body jerked. The

response was involuntary. He knew without a doubt because he watched the warring emotions deep in her eyes—desperate need fought against a refusal to open her mouth and ask for what she wanted. It was silly, but it became a game of who would break first.

It wasn't the first time they'd played this particular game, although it was the first time they'd done it in bed. Simon had to admit this version was a hell of a lot more interesting and enjoyable.

And even if she couldn't reach him to effect a little physical torture of her own, Marcy was far from helpless. She had plenty of weapons at her disposal and had no problem using them.

Widening her legs even more, she exposed the swollen center of her sex. Simon growled, deep in his throat. She was slick, covered with the evidence of her arousal. For him. The scent of that arousal filled the air around him, making his heart pound restlessly in his chest and his fingers clamp hard around the tops of her thighs.

She rolled her hips, this time deliberately, hiding and then revealing what he really wanted. And he lost it. Without even touching him, she'd won.

He had to feel her, taste her, have her before he went mad.

Spreading the folds of her sex, he dived in and latched his mouth hard against her. She whimpered and bucked beneath him, just as devastated as he was. And that took some of the sting of his defeat away.

That and the taste of her on his tongue.

He lapped at her, enjoying her instant reaction when he brushed across the nub of her clit. He played there, relishing the way she panted, squirmed and ground harder against his mouth. His tongue speared inside her and the enveloping heat of her had a red-hot haze clouding everything, everything but her.

Somewhere in the back of his mind he realized he should probably stop, probably slow down and take a minute. But he didn't want to. Couldn't seem to find the will to do it. He'd never been this overwhelmed and out of control with a woman before in his life. He was a calculating lover. He knew exactly what to do, exactly where to touch, when to push and when to back off to give his partner the most explosive orgasm possible.

But he couldn't back off. Not this time. He wanted to feel her fall apart against his mouth. He wanted the pulse of her against his lips. He wanted the taste of her orgasm on his tongue.

Marcy arched her back, straining hard against him. She buried her head against the bed, muffling the sounds of her pleasure. But he even wanted that. He wanted everything she had and all she could give him.

Her body bowed tight beneath him, every single muscle straining for the release that he knew was so close. And when she finally gave in, her body convulsing and quivering with the force of it, he wasn't disappointed. She screamed, his name hot on her lips.

And he wanted more.

Marcy collapsed onto the bed, her body trembling with the aftermath of spent desire.

Holy shit. But despite the satisfaction rolling through her body, she wasn't fulfilled. Just getting off wasn't enough. If that was all she'd wanted, she could have handled that herself. Although it definitely wouldn't have been anywhere close to as good as what Simon had just done to her. But still…she wasn't finished, and considering his fingers continued to roam across her skin, she didn't think he was, either.

He'd better not be.

Gathering her shaking legs beneath her, Marcy pushed up and rolled over. Luckily Simon was quick on the draw, because the electrical pulses running through her body had apparently impaired her control over her own muscles. Her leg flailed, her knee coming millimeters from colliding with his chin.

His palm cupped her leg, guiding it back down to the bed. He settled his mouth at the juncture where her thigh met her hip and sucked. She nearly came off the bed again, the sensation somehow tickling and driving her crazy at the same time.

But she wasn't about to let him drag her back under. Pushing against his head, Marcy sent him rocking back onto his heels between her spread thighs. Confusion pulled his eyebrows down over smoldering eyes.

A shiver took her, a combination of aftershock and the intensity of the unspent desire she saw in his eyes.

"Take 'em off," she ordered, pointing her finger from the tip of his head down to his toes so he knew she meant every last stitch.

She was sprawled out before him, completely naked. Had acted like a wanton hussy from the moment his hands touched her body. And she was tired of being vulnerable all alone.

Scooting away, he stood at the end of the bed. Marcy propped herself up on her elbows and settled in to enjoy the show. He crossed his arms over his body, grasped the edge of his shirt and lifted it up slowly. This wasn't the mundane task of taking off one piece of clothing so it could be replaced by another. It was so much more—the first time she would see all of him, everything he hid from the world beneath those careless clothes.

And right now she wanted that more than her next breath.

Hard abs appeared and her mouth began to water. She licked her lips. It was the closest she was getting to running her tongue across those valleys and planes— at least for now.

His skin was bronzed by the sun. A light dusting of blond hair curled over the swell of his pecs, narrowing and disappearing beneath the band of his shorts.

He pulled his head through the opening of his shirt. His blond hair clouded out around his head in sexy disarray. The shirt was ruined, dirt, soot and water ground into the fibers. For the first time, Marcy noticed the singed edges and a renewed blast of fear settled heavily in her chest.

Simon could have been seriously hurt.

But he hadn't been. Studiously pushing the unwelcome and unproductive thought from her mind, she focused all her attention on the amazing body he was revealing.

Strong fingers popped the button at the top of his fly and then deliberately tugged at the tab of his zipper. The sound of metal grinding against metal filled the room and her legs scissored restlessly against the bed.

He rolled his hips and the khaki shorts hit the floor. Beneath them the tantalizing length of his erection strained against confining briefs. Red. She should have known there was nothing plain about this man. Everything about him was bold and unapologetic.

And while that bugged the crap out of her in their business dealings, she had to admit that in bed it was sexy as hell.

He knew what he wanted and he took it. Today, right now, he wanted her, and she had no problems with that.

Pushing up onto her knees, Marcy crawled to the end of the bed and knelt in front of him. Her palms bracketed his hips. The heat of him exploded through her, stealing what little breath she had left. She half expected him to take over again, to kiss her and bend her backward beneath him. But he didn't.

Moving her hands up his chest, she enjoyed the way the soft hair tickled her palms. The sharp intake of breath through his teeth as she grazed the sensitive peak of a nipple reverberated through her body. Her breasts tingled, feeling neglected.

He reached for her then, taking the sharp peaks between thumb and finger and rolling gently. She elongated the curve of her spine, pressing the aching tips harder into his hold.

Leaning into his body, she brought their mouths together and whispered, "I thought I said to take it all off."

His sharp eyes flashed, deep and fierce. "I'm a little busy. Why don't you do it?"

He continued to play with her breasts, pinching, tugging and driving her crazy before taking the soft center of his palm and rubbing in gentle circles, easing some of the ache. He did it over and over again, sending spikes of need shooting through her body straight to her sex. Arouse, relieve, arouse, relieve. The cycle was maddening.

She did what he asked, but only because it was what she wanted, too. Marcy cupped her palm around the hard length straining against the red-hot fabric. Simon groaned deep in his throat. Slipping her hand beneath the imprisoning waistband, she found him hot and hard, and squeezed.

Closing her eyes, she relished the feel of him. All silky-smooth skin, burning heat and pulsing veins, filling her palm and spilling over. She couldn't even spread her fingers and touch all of him.

"Damn, you've been hiding a lot more than killer abs beneath those rumpled clothes you like so much."

He laughed, a low rumble. And thrust his hips, pushing his length harder against her palm. A thrill raced down her spine at the thought of him buried deep inside her, filling her up and stretching her as far as she could go.

"If I'd known you were going to be this impressed I'd have shown you mine a long time ago."

"Egomaniac," she answered, even as she slid up and down, trying to memorize every inch of him.

He let her play. Somewhere along the way she managed to remove his briefs so that she could see everything she had in her hand. She devoured him with her eyes. Her tongue licked across her lips and he bucked in the tight confines of her hold.

Her fingers slipped through the evidence of his arousal, taking the clear liquid and spreading it around the sensitive head. His hips rocked with her caresses, soft at first but quickly moving faster and faster. An answering frenzy built inside her.

With hard purpose, he claimed her mouth. She tasted that same frenzy on his lips and thrilled to it. His hands were all over her, everywhere at once. And she couldn't get enough.

As he pushed her backward with the force of his kiss, she could do nothing but let him follow her down and hope that she came out the other side of this experience unscathed.

Her fingers curled into his hard hips, holding on. His body rubbed against her, all of her skin tingling beneath the caress. A whimper of anticipation slipped through her lips.

He reached above her, yanked open the bedside table, pulled out a condom and didn't bother closing the drawer again as he ripped into the foil with his teeth. Before she could process what he was doing the condom was over his erection.

Her mouth was dry. Her sex wet. Her body on fire with an aching need. It had been so long since she'd felt this way. Alive. Sensual. Wanted.

Grasping her hips, Simon pulled her back to him. Wrapping an arm beneath her knee, he crushed her leg up and opened her wide for whatever he wanted. Cold air mixed with the heat of desire and she whimpered. She was empty and she wanted him to fill her.

"Simon. Now. Please," she begged.

He speared her with a dark gaze and then with slow, sure strokes, invaded her in the best possible way. Her internal muscles protested for the space of a heartbeat before stretching around him, taking everything he'd given her.

She wanted more. He was holding back. She could see it in the concentrated strain of his face and feel it in the quiver of his muscles. Looking down at where their bodies joined, she realized he had inches left to give her. She was greedy and wanted it all.

Pulling her hips wider, she opened for him. And burying her heels into his flanks, Marcy urged him on. He resisted, pushing against her.

"I don't want to hurt you," he gritted out through straining jaws.

She clenched her internal muscles. He hissed.

"You won't," she promised, even as she surged beneath him, lifting her hips and taking all of him. He slid home, burying himself inside her to the hilt.

He hissed again. His eyes glazed over with mindless passion. Breath panted through his still-clenched teeth and his ribs contracted and expanded beneath her hands, like the flanks of a horse that had just run hell-for-leather. He was trying desperately to cling to sanity and control. Only, she didn't want him to.

She tried every trick she knew to get him to let go—undulating against him, reaching between their joined bodies to caress his tight balls, contracting her sex around him—but he wasn't giving in. He stayed there, not moving, driving her crazy.

And while she'd gotten exactly what she wanted—all of him—it left her with little space to maneuver. But, God, the hot, hard feel of him deep inside her was worth the price.

After several seconds the haze lifted and he looked deep into her, blue eyes clear and blistering. She trembled under the intensity of that gaze.

"Minx," he breathed, the soft caress against her skin jolting deep inside her. She was so close to the edge of losing it.

He pumped slowly against her, pulling out and thrusting back in. This time he didn't hold anything back. Each time he left her empty she thought she would scream, only to have him fill her so completely she wasn't sure she could ever live without the sensation again.

Her hips gyrated beneath him, meeting him thrust

for thrust, urging him higher, harder, faster. The bed trembled, and somewhere in the back of her mind she worried they'd ruin it right along with the linens.

But it would be so worth it.

She wanted this moment to last forever, to teeter on the amazing edge he'd driven them both to. But it couldn't. The consolation was that Simon broke at the same time, both of them coming together. His hips surged against her, hard. Every muscle in her body responded, contracting and pulsing and quivering.

Her cries mingled with his shouts and Marcy was grateful they were entirely alone in the large hotel. Because if anyone else had been in the place they would have heard, floors and walls be damned.

Simon collapsed beside her, half on and half off, their bodies still joined. It wasn't something that Marcy usually liked. Aside from the idea of being crushed beneath some big male body that most likely was a foot taller and fifty pounds heavier than she was, she just didn't like feeling trapped.

But she didn't mind it at all with Simon. In fact, if he'd tried to move, she probably would have protested. The weight of him against her felt like the only thing keeping her together. And the solid feel of him still inside her was reassuring as aftershock after aftershock rolled through her.

Eventually Simon pulled away. Rolling onto his back, he tucked her against him. His skin was warm under her cheek. The steady thrum of his heart was hypnotic, and exhaustion filled her. Her eyelids fluttered closed. She'd just rest for a few minutes.

Her next conscious thought was that something was tickling her hip. She swatted at it…and her fingers got tangled with Simon's. Her eyes flew open.

Moonlight filled the room.

"How long have I been asleep?" she asked, her voice still rough with sleep.

"Awhile," Simon answered. He had levered himself onto one elbow and was looking down at her, a tempting light in his eyes. She knew she probably looked awful. Her skin was no doubt flushed red, her hair a mess and soot most likely still coated her arms and legs.

He reached over to place a kiss on the curve of her shoulder and she shied away.

She didn't like his frown as he asked, "Why'd you pull away?"

"I'm still dirty," she said, lips curling up in distaste.

His frown cleared and a soft chuckle escaped. The urge to reach up and kiss him rolled through her, but she didn't give in to it. She was on shaky ground here, and didn't know what he'd consider acceptable lover behavior.

"Is that all? Most of it rubbed off on the comforter."

Marcy looked down at her arms and realized he was right. "Oh, and that makes it so much better."

The soot was mostly gone, only a few minuscule streaks left here and there. But she could still feel it on her skin. "I really wish the water was working. I'd kill for a shower."

Simon trailed a single finger down the center of her body, going through the valley between her breasts and circling lazily around her belly button.

"I don't think killing is the answer, Ms. McKinney. But I might have a solution?"

"Oh yeah, what's that?" she asked, trying desperately to keep hold of the thread of the conversation.

How could his simple, playful touch—after she'd just come twice—arouse her again so quickly?

He clicked his tongue in an admonishing sound. "What's it worth to you?"

"What do you mean?"

"Well, you were willing to kill for a shower a few minutes ago. What's my solution worth to you?"

Marcy's eyes narrowed, even as a smile touched her lips. Her fingers found their way to the nape of his neck and began playing there, twisting the strands lazily through them.

"Well, the inherent value is less because I'm purchasing an unknown."

"I promise it will accomplish the same goal as a shower."

She shrugged, the muscles of her stomach leaping beneath his touch. "I'm not in the habit of taking charming men at their word."

"Been burned a time or two?"

"Maybe."

Leaning over her, he claimed her mouth in a kiss that held every bit as much passion as the kiss in the jungle—the one that had sent them here. The only difference was this time there was a familiarity that set her a little on edge. It was nice. But it also scared her. It would be so easy to fall under the spell of this charming, gallant man. At least when he was treating her as if she were precious and unique.

"Grab a shirt out of the closet," he said, pulling back. "We'll settle on payment later."

9

DIGGING IN THE BOTTOM of a drawer, Simon pulled out some gray pajama bottoms that had never been worn. He couldn't even remember why they were there since he always slept nude, but it didn't matter.

Turning around, he was just in time to watch as Marcy pulled an old college T-shirt over her head. The sight of her covering her body shouldn't have been sexy, but it was. The hem of the faded navy fabric brushed over her skin, falling to settle halfway down her thighs. Considering he was so tall and she was so short, it more than covered the important bits. But he knew what waited underneath.

And he had every intention of seeing it again. Tonight.

Grabbing her hand, he pulled her out of his apartments and through the hotel. Their bare feet pattered softly against the stairs.

Every few feet they passed beneath the red circle of an emergency light, but in between they were surrounded by darkness. He could barely see her in the blackness. There were windows in the stairwell, but it was the middle of the night.

They burst onto the first floor of the hotel. Here soft moonlight fell through the wide windows fronting the lobby, gilding everything in silver. A shadowy figure moved silently through the space ahead of them. Simon stopped, and with the connection of their joined hands, pulled Marcy in close behind him.

There might be more light here, but it wasn't enough to tell who was in front of them. The figure was tall and lean and, Simon decided, male. Although his shoulders were slightly slumped. The initial burst of surprise and concern eased—definitely not a defensive or antagonistic posture.

And when the figure said, "Simon," he felt all the tension leave his body.

"Xavier."

"I was just coming to find you."

He wanted to say, *What now?* But one look at the exhaustion on Xavier's face as he walked through a brighter patch of light had the words dying on his lips. "You look awful, man."

His lips twisted. "Thanks."

Marcy stepped from behind Simon, pulling her hand out of his in the process. He let her go, although something deep inside gave a silent growl and urged him to grab her back. He ignored it.

Tugging self-consciously at the hem of the shirt, Marcy asked, "What's wrong?"

"Nothing. Nothing." Xavier ran his hand through his hair, ruffling the dark brown mess, which was still wet. All he managed to do was stand it on end, making him resemble a porcupine.

"I wanted to give you an update before I grab some

sleep. Paul and Christine are patrolling the site of the fire, although I wouldn't expect any flare-ups. There's enough water on the sucker that you could advertise you now have a mud bath available."

They all chuckled softly.

"Any news on the guy they took out by MedFlight?" Frowning, Simon asked, "Anyone even know his name?"

Marcy bit her lip, drawing Simon's attention. He pulled his gaze away — now wasn't the time.

"I didn't get all of their names, but the leader's name is Jake," she said.

Xavier nodded. "I spoke to Jake. The injured worker's wife met the chopper at the hospital. He appears fine. They're keeping him overnight for observation, but so far no adverse effects."

"Wonderful." Simon sighed with relief.

The guy might have been trying to take on a project he didn't have the experience to tackle, but that didn't mean Simon wanted him to pay permanently for that bad decision. He didn't want anyone hurt on his watch.

He reached out and clamped a hand on Xavier's shoulder. "Excellent work. That was a real baptism by fire, and it could have been much worse without your quick thinking and strong leadership. I don't believe I've ever given anyone a raise in their first week, but I'm all for breaking the rules. See me tomorrow and we'll talk."

Xavier nodded, not even really responding to the praise Simon had just heaped on his head. Not that Simon blamed him. It was obvious he was running on empty.

"Get some sleep," he said, squeezing Xavier's shoulder before letting go.

Simon and Marcy stood silently, watching him as he turned and walked back out of the building.

"He deserves every penny that you're going to give him," Marcy said.

Looking down at her, he realized they stood shoulder to…well, her head. He grasped her hand in his again. Turning, she looked up into his face.

"Now, you promised me something equivalent to a shower." She raised a single eyebrow—question, dare, invitation.

Raising one of his own, he paused long enough to claim her lips before leading her through the lobby and out into the night. It was so quiet, even the ever-present sound of crashing waves seemed muted.

It didn't take them long to reach the pool complex. Usually surrounded by laughing people, it was now empty. Well-placed vegetation gave the area a sense of privacy that Simon knew was an illusion—one he'd conjured on purpose. Even the concrete shell for the showers and changing rooms at the far end of the pool was camouflaged with brightly colored flowers and lush green bushes.

The water was calm and clear, inviting.

"No way," Marcy said, tugging softly against his hold on her hand. She tried to walk backward, pulling him with her. She didn't get far, only the length of their fully outstretched arms.

"What do you mean, no way?"

"I am not swimming naked in a public pool." Spearing him with her gaze, she said, "That is what you had in mind right, considering neither of us has a bathing suit?"

"Well, I suppose you could swim in my shirt, if you really want." His eyes toured slowly down Marcy's body.

This time he knew exactly what waited for him under the material of her clothing—lush curves and soft skin. Immeasurable pleasure. Maybe it was a good thing she'd always worn those nondescript, boxy business suits around him, because if he'd known earlier what was hidden beneath... Yeah, it wouldn't have taken him two years to get a taste, that was for sure.

Her skin flushed, but her eyes sharpened. "Please."

He'd seen that expression more times than he cared to count. It was her stubborn, taking-a-stance-and-not-gonna-budge expression. They'd just have to see about that.

"Do you think I'm stupid? You've already ripped one shirt. The minute I get in that water this one's toast."

His lips twitched. "I ripped *your* shirt. I happen to like that one." He gestured at it with their joined hands. "I have no intention of ruining it."

"So if I get in that pool, you promise not to try and get this shirt off me?"

"I didn't say that."

"That's what I thought."

She tugged again at their joined hands. Instead of letting her go, he jerked on the hold and used the momentum of her surprise. She stumbled against him and, lightning quick, he had his arms wrapped tightly around her, crushing their bodies together.

That scent, the one that was now entirely hers, enveloped him. He could feel the speeding thrum of her heart against his chest. Probably could've kissed her and convinced her to do whatever he wanted, but that would backfire on him later when it was all over and her temper flared.

Instead, he cajoled with words. "Everyone's asleep."

"Except for Paul and Christine."

"They're on the opposite side of the hotel. They can't see us from here. Hell, they can't even hear us. You know you want to, Marcy. For once in your life walk on the wild side."

"I walk on the wild side plenty," she countered, her nose wrinkling cutely as she frowned.

"Please. You don't know the meaning of the word *wild*. I've never met anyone as structured and uptight in my life."

She sputtered. He enjoyed seeing her at a complete loss for words. It didn't happen often.

"I am not uptight."

"Look, I don't have a problem with you being uptight. Actually, I like it. Makes you an easy target. But sometimes you need a little balance."

"Balance? That's rich coming from the man who divides his time between various entertaining activities without a spare moment left over for actual work."

A pang of guilt shot through the center of his chest. In all the time they'd known each other, Simon hadn't thought twice about the secret he was keeping from Marcy. He'd ignored her, dismissed her and outright lied to her without blinking an eye.

And he'd had good reasons.

Now they didn't seem so important. Part of him wanted to tell her the truth, but he couldn't do that. The tiny voice in his head told him he could trust Marcy. But then, he'd thought the same thing about Courtney.

He wouldn't make the same mistake twice. Not even because of stellar sex.

Truthfully, the stellar sex made him question the urge even more. Until right now, he'd never felt the need to tell her. So he'd keep his mouth shut…at least until he was sure any decision he made wasn't clouded by some misplaced afterglow effects.

Besides, he knew Marcy well enough to realize she would not appreciate learning he'd been lying to her for two years. And he wasn't ready to put that wedge between them.

Not when she was going to leave anyway. Yet another reason to keep his secret to himself.

"Sounds like I'm the perfect person to teach you something about being wild and irresponsible."

Scooping her up into his arms, Simon barely paused before stepping off the edge of the pool and plunging them both into the water. They were near the center, so the water only came to his waist. However, it completely soaked his pants, plastering the thin fabric to his body.

In her cradled position against his chest, Marcy barely got wet. In fact, only the back of his T-shirt was damp, water soaking slowly up from the bottom hem.

"Hold your breath," he warned right before opening his arms and letting her drop.

Aside from the sharp intake of breath, she didn't make a sound. Her body splashed into the water…and slowly sank.

He'd expected her to flail, or pop up quickly. He watched for several seconds, the navy cloud of shirt billowing around her until she settled on the bottom near his feet. Her body collapsed in slow motion, her hair floating around her head.

Simon panicked. What the hell? Bending his knees, he sank down and grasped a handful of shirt so that he could jerk her back up again.

Later, when he looked back on the moment, he

couldn't be sure exactly how it all happened. One minute he was hauling Marcy out of the water, afraid she was drowning, not understanding how that could happen since the water was shallow enough for her to stand.

The next, his feet had been swept out from under him. Already off balance, he went completely under. Water poured into his open mouth, but instinct had him spitting it out and holding his breath.

He opened his eyes beneath the water, trying to find his bearings and figure out what was going on. And Marcy was there, bubbles escaping slowly to drift around her face. Her eyes were open, too. Staring at him, a taunting smile curling her lips.

Before he could reach out and grab her, she darted away through the water, sleek as a seal.

The peal of her laughter hit him hard as he broke through the surface. The wet, clinging fabric of his pants slowed him down. Taking a few precious seconds, Simon jerked them off, leaving them to settle on the bottom of the pool in a gray blob.

The water was pleasant against his skin as he shot after her. She dived again, disappearing into the deep end. Although the trailing dark blue tail of his shirt was as good as a red flag.

She surfaced for air and he caught her. Beneath the water, his fingers slid over her soft skin. The force of her rocketing ascent piled his shirt high on her torso. It was nothing for him to grab it and pull it off her. He dropped it back into the water, and they watched together as it sank to the bottom.

His mouth latched onto the curve of her shoulder. Her skin tasted of chlorine and lavender. The broken surface of the water lapped gently around the curve of her breasts. The soft pink center of her nipples jutted temptingly.

She kicked her legs lazily, churning the water around them. The currents were like a caress.

"See, the wild side's not so bad, is it?" he whispered as he lapped droplets from the line of her collarbone.

She sighed, the soft gust of breath tickling his ear. "Too early to tell."

He wrapped his hands around her waist, holding her still as he ducked under the water. His eyes opened so that he could see her, the sting of chlorine worth every second. He took the distended bud of her nipple into his mouth. Her gasp was muffled, but he could feel the vibration of it against his fingers still splayed over her rib cage.

He rolled his tongue lazily around the hard nub before switching to the other side. Her skin was silky smooth and cool, unlike the heat building inside him. His lungs burned with the need for oxygen, but he wasn't ready to let her go. He wanted to stay there forever, lavishing her breasts with attention. Beneath the water, everything was muted and it felt as if there was nothing else in the world but the two of them.

Eventually he had to come up.

And when he did Marcy was there to meet him. Pushing her fingers into his wet hair, she dragged him up to her mouth and devoured him. The taste of her desire exploded against his lips. She didn't even let him wipe the water from his face, instead letting it rain down over both of them.

Droplets clung to her eyelashes, tiny glittering diamonds in the moonlight. Her legs floated up around him, bringing their bodies tight together. The heat of her center slid against his pounding erection.

Reaching down, he spread her open wider. His fingers slipped through the evidence of her desire, thicker than the water that tried to wash it away. She gasped, jerking tighter against him when he found and teased the swollen button of her clit.

He'd meant to bring them closer together, to tease them both, but he couldn't do it. Not now that he'd touched her. Sliding his fingers into her white-hot depths was inevitable.

He pushed one inside, and then another. Her muscles pulsed around his invasion. The same rhythm echoed deep inside, hammering through his blood. This need for her had somehow become a part of him, melding with the pieces that fit together to make him the man he was. Something that had never happened with another woman.

Marcy's head flew back. She clung to him, the water holding them both up. Her breath was fast. She trembled. He worked her, letting his fingers move in and out.

She was wild. So slippery that without her arms and legs clinging to him it would have been difficult to hold on.

Raising her head, she speared him with her gaze. Her eyes smoldered, hotter than her body wrapped so tightly around him. She licked her lips and said, "Please tell me you have a condom stashed somewhere."

Simon stilled. And groaned, a sound that had almost nothing to do with the fist she'd just wrapped around his cock.

"In my pants."

"Thank you," she breathed, looking up to the sky. Her fingers drifted lower, began to caress the heavy orbs hanging from his body. He really hated to stop her, but…

"At the bottom of the pool."

This time they both stilled. He could count her pulse by the throbbing beat at the center of her body where his hand was still buried deep. Her grip on him tightened somewhere just this side of painful. Together, they slowly turned their heads toward the shallow end.

Marcy laughed, a low, aching, sexy sound that rolled through him. Pushing away, she disentangled their bodies. He realized she was putting space between them to thwart temptation. But the primitive animal that had somehow inhabited his body wanted to howl a protest and haul her back to him.

"Which one of us is going down after it?"

"What you really mean is you're the idiot who let the condom sink to the bottom of the pool, so get your ass down there."

Her eyes glowed. It was different from the smoldering desire that had been there moments before. Although that glitter was still there, too. But now there was more. An…ease that had never been between them before.

"Since you put it that way."

Taking a deep breath, Simon dived, then pulled the soft cotton back up behind him. Slipping his hand into the pocket, he retrieved one of the tiny, important foil packets. Holding it up triumphantly, he turned to Marcy. Water dripped, landing noisily on the surface of the pool.

She frowned. It wasn't exactly the response he'd been hoping for.

"What's wrong?" he asked.

"Nothing." She shook her head. "I'm just trying to

remember everything I've read about water and condoms. Does a good soaking weaken the integrity?"

He stared at her. Seriously. "Weaken the integrity? Jesus, Marcy, who talks like that?" Were they really having this conversation? In the middle of the pool. Naked.

While his body burned with a need for her.

Even floating in the deep end, with her feet nowhere close to a solid surface, she somehow managed to place her hands on her hips, cock her head to the side and give him that "Marcy stance." He'd long ago realized fighting her in this mood was like bashing his head against a brick wall—he was the only one who ended up in pain.

Ripping into it, he held up the perfectly dry condom. "Dry as the desert."

Her eyes flashed and she crossed her arms over her chest. He was absolutely sure she had no idea of the effect. The edge of the water lapped tantalizingly against her protruding nipples. His stomach muscles clenched hard and beneath the surface his cock jerked painfully toward her.

"Yeah, but for how long?"

"Huh?" he asked, unable to follow the conversation. Not while fantasizing about what he was going to do to her. Glancing behind him, he imagined her stretched out beneath him across the gleaming white steps leading out of the pool.

"Dry. How long is it going to stay dry? In the pool." She gestured offhandedly to his completely submerged groin.

Surging toward her, he grasped her around the waist and pulled her hard against him. "I don't care," he growled. "All I know is if I don't get inside you now I'm going to explode."

She looked up at him. Innocence mixed with mischief, a complicated combination that set him off-kilter. "Isn't that kinda the point?"

Had she just made a joke? He didn't think he'd ever heard Marcy do that.

Picking her up, he fought the pressure of the water, walking to the steps where he'd envisioned her just moments before. She didn't protest. Instead, when he laid her out on the wide ledge several steps up she stretched, undulating her body.

The shrewd look in her eyes told him she knew exactly what she was doing. And that was sexy as hell. He'd always been a sucker for a powerful, self-confident woman. And there was no one more confident in her own skin than Marcy.

Water lapped softly against her body, submerging her legs from the knee down. The waves they'd created in the empty pool teased against her hair, swirling it around her head one minute and leaving wet fingers of it trailing down the stairs the next.

The water reached just above his knees, but left the rest of him blessedly free. Somehow the condom had miraculously remained dry and he rolled it quickly down his pounding erection.

She watched his every move, those intelligent eyes missing nothing. Reaching out, she trailed a single fingertip down the latex-covered length. A strangled sound erupted from him, the combination of constricting latex and throbbing desire almost too much to bear.

"Satisfied?" he asked.

Marcy spread her thighs before him. Water caressed

the swollen pink slit of her sex. He wanted to be there. Doing that to her instead.

"If you mean am I satisfied that the condom is dry and not going to break, yes. If you mean am I satisfied with *you*—" her eyes flicked up to his before settling back on his erection "—I never thought you were the kind of man who fished for compliments. Does your ego need stroking?"

He growled deep in his throat. "No, but I damn sure know something that does."

She laughed, the tinkle of the sound settling somewhere in the middle of his chest and burrowing there. It itched and pinched and warmed him with a pleasant ache that had nothing to do with the fact that she was naked in front of him.

Reaching for him, she pulled him down on top of her. For a minute he worried about grinding her into the edge of the stairs, but the moment she wrapped her hand around him and guided him to the entrance of her body he forgot all about it. She didn't seem to mind.

He slid home inside her in one easy stroke. She arched beneath him, pushing their bodies tighter together and taking all of him.

Wrapping her arms around his neck, she held on tight. Each time he pushed high and hard against her, tiny bursts of air tickled his ear. They urged him on.

And so did her words. "You feel perfect inside me," she groaned as he pushed them both relentlessly to the edge. His body strained. His muscles shook. And she was with him every step of the way.

Her teeth latched onto his shoulder, holding on. Her labored breaths puffed against his skin. Every muscle in her body drew tight beneath him, a taut bow just waiting to snap. He relentlessly pushed them both, driving into her over and over.

Their bodies slapped together. Water rocked violently around them.

Marcy let go of him, falling back against the stair. With her eyes closed in ecstasy, her mouth opened wide on a silent cry that didn't, couldn't last.

She fell apart in his arms, bucking, writhing, a scream finally rolling up through her body, erupting at the top of her lungs.

Seeing her wild was an experience he'd never forget.

And he let himself fall behind her. A fiery ball of heat built at the center of his spine, exploding out to engulf all of him. His hips surged. The ravenous need that had built inside him spilled out and into her, his own guttural cry mixing with her scream.

He couldn't breathe. It felt as if he was down in the deep end again, his lungs straining, drowning in her. And just like then, he didn't care.

He might have stayed there forever, their legs and arms tangled together and his body buried deep inside her.

Except a voice interrupted the moment.

"What the heck was that?"

He recognized Paul's deep voice.

And Christine's higher one. "Don't you mean who? Sounded like sex to me."

"Maybe it was a jaguar?"

"That was no jaguar."

Marcy stirred beneath him. Still connected, their hips ground together and her breasts brushed his chest. Her body was tense, not from unspent desire but from the realization that their privacy was about to be invaded. And he had no doubt she did not want to be found stretched out naked on the stairs of the pool. With him.

Some perverse voice in his head suggested he should stay right where he was, let Paul and Christine find them like this so everyone on the island would know she was his. But that would be stupid. And definitely not what she'd want.

Simon gathered his spent body beneath him, meaning to roll away from her and provide a distraction if necessary so she could escape.

He was surprised when she reached up and stopped him. Her eyes hot and intense, she looked him straight in the eye and whispered, "Hell, yes, I'm satisfied."

He knew she didn't mean anything other than the face value of the words. But that didn't stop male pride from mixing with the buzz of satisfaction in his blood.

Scooping her up, he paid no attention to the water that rained down both of their bodies. Striding across the complex, he didn't stop until the door to the main building closed behind them. Everything was dark and silent. Marcy squirmed in his arms, silently ordering him to let her down.

He ignored her. He dragged his finger over her swollen bottom lip and said, "Of course you are. Your satisfaction almost got us caught."

10

SHE WAS MORTIFIED. Although she fought the urge to cover her tingling cheeks with her hands. She twisted harder against Simon's hold and he eventually put her feet to the floor. It was cool against her skin and for the first time she realized she was completely naked.

Yes, it seemed like a silly revelation considering what they'd just done. Twice. But she couldn't help it. She wasn't in the habit of running around public places without a stitch of clothing on.

Even if the guy she was with owned the place. Or maybe especially since the guy who owned it was with her.

She watched Simon. His blond hair was dark, flopping into his eyes. Where was the lazy man she'd worked with for the past two years? Somewhere over the past two days he'd disappeared, to be replaced by the man before her. Even the line of his jaw somehow seemed tighter, stronger.

Droplets of water rolled lazily down his chest to pool on the floor at his feet. She really should clean that up.

She'd thought she knew Simon. Apparently she was wrong. She'd believed the same thing about her old boss, as well. Dread twisted in the pit of her stomach. Marcy pushed it away. She didn't work for him anymore. She was not making the same mistake. Simon wasn't married. Was he?

"You don't have a wife tucked away somewhere, do you?"

Simon's eyes widened with shock, before narrowing slightly. He studied her for several silent seconds before finally answering. Or not answering. "I think that's the stupidest thing you've ever said to me."

Yeah, she knew she was being an idiot. But she couldn't help herself. Spinning to hide the embarrassed flush on her cheeks, Marcy disappeared behind the check-in desk and returned with several towels. She'd stopped long enough to wrap one around her sarong-style.

Silently she handed one to Simon. He rubbed it over his hair before slinging it haphazardly around his neck.

Shaking her head, Marcy crouched down and began mopping up the mess they'd left on the wooden floor. It would be ruined if they didn't get rid of the water.

She didn't get far. Simon reached beneath her arms and pulled her back up. Spinning her to face him, he drilled into her with his gaze and she thought maybe he saw more than she'd realized. It definitely felt as if he could see straight into her soul. She didn't like that at all. She had plenty of secrets she wanted to keep.

"What was that about?"

She opened her mouth, but closed it again before actually saying anything.

He waited. Not pushing her. Not wheedling for an answer that she was obviously reluctant to give. He didn't try to charm her or belittle the seriousness of the situation. He just calmly stood there, waiting.

And that's why she told him. "I dated a married man."

This time it was her turn to wait for the condemnation that usually came…that she deserved. But it didn't come.

"I didn't know he was married."

Simon nodded his head once, succinctly, as if that was all there was to say about the situation. As if her lack of knowledge was a given.

"It, um…" She cleared her throat nervously and hated herself for the show of weakness. "He was my boss."

Simon's jaw clenched. "He took advantage of you."

She laughed, a broken sound that gurgled up from deep inside her chest. "Hardly. Do I look like the kind of woman who'd let herself be taken advantage of?"

"At the moment?" His hand cupped the back of her head and his thumb skimmed softly down the side of her neck. The caress was different from the rest. Oh, the sizzle was there, but it was muted, overlaid by an understanding that surprised and humbled her.

She shook her head, not wanting him to say anything else that could make her care about him more than she already did. It was bad enough as it was, this connection she was suddenly allowed to explore.

"You look like a woman who's been hurt. And that makes you more human and accessible than all of your skill and competence and order."

A lump rose in her throat. She swallowed it, conscious of the way his thumb continued to stroke her skin.

"Accessible is overrated."

"So is being alone."

He pressed his lips to hers, a soft brush of skin to skin. And asked, "Do you think you're the only person who's ever been hurt?" against her mouth.

She tried to look at him, but he changed the angle of their kiss so that she couldn't see his eyes. She wanted to see the honesty there. To know the truth.

When he wouldn't give it to her, she pulled back again and asked him point-blank. "You've been hurt?"

She found the idea laughable. Simon Reeves, charming, sexy, roguish. He epitomized one-night stand. Although she had to admit that she'd never actually seen him take a lover from the many guests who'd thrown themselves at him during her time here.

But that didn't mean he'd had no meaningless affairs. It just meant he didn't poach from his own back yard.

She tried to imagine the man standing before her, unapologetically naked, going two years without a lover and almost laughed out loud.

He must have seen the suppressed flicker in her eyes. "What's so funny?"

"Nothing."

While she tried desperately not to dissolve into fits of laughter, his eyebrows slammed together.

"Fine, I was trying to remember the last time I'd seen you with a woman and couldn't come up with one since I've been here. And then I wondered if maybe you've been without one for the past two years. And that thought was funny as hell."

"I'm glad my dry spell in the bedroom could entertain you."

"Please," she said, finally giving in to the bubble floating through her chest.

He wrapped his hands around her waist and jerked her hard against him. His mouth settled roughly over hers. Heat suffused her, only this time it had nothing to do with embarrassment. She went under easily, dragged there by Simon's overwhelming need for her.

It felt as if his fingers burned through the cotton to brand her skin beneath. He let her go. She gasped. Her towel dropped heedlessly to the floor.

"That's exactly what I'm telling you. I haven't slept with a single woman since you stepped foot on this island."

She stared at him, dumbfounded. Her mouth went dry. She searched his face for some sign that he was lying. Or joking. Or playing one of his games.

But he wasn't. He was serious as a heart attack.

Something pinched sharply in the center of her chest.

He reached for her again, pulling her back into his arms, and she let him.

This time when his mouth claimed hers the aggression of a moment before was gone. Replaced by something else, something softer and more persuasive.

"Not laughing now, are you?"

SIMON STARED at the ceiling. It was still dark out, probably somewhere between two and three in the morning if he had to guess. And he couldn't sleep.

Beside him, Marcy breathed softly and evenly. She'd been out for at least two hours. And he couldn't blame her. He couldn't remember a time in his life when he'd come so many times. Not even during his wild college days. His reputation had been legendary, all of his partners more than satisfied. But one or two rounds a night had been his limit.

Not with Marcy. With her, it didn't matter if he'd had her three hours or three minutes before, he wanted her again. Immediately. He couldn't get enough of her.

Which was part of the reason he was still awake.

His mind was going in circles. She was leaving. Maybe not tomorrow, but soon. A few days ago he'd wanted her to stay because the resort couldn't function without her. Now his need for her had nothing to do with her job as his manager and everything to do with wanting her in his bed. Today, tomorrow, three months from now.

And that made him restless.

He hadn't let anyone in since Courtney. He hadn't trusted anyone. He hadn't even trusted himself or his ability to judge character.

The ones on the page, the ones he created, were easy to read. He knew them inside and out. Even his villains, sadistic and evil as they were, did only what he wanted them to. Outside that comfort zone, anything could happen. And he couldn't manipulate the situation to his preference.

His eyes strayed to Marcy. She'd pulled the covers up to her nose, her crown of blond hair the only thing sticking out. Reaching over, he pulled a lock between his fingers, the silky texture of it a caress.

Even if he wanted her to stay, she was leaving. The only reason they'd let this happen was that she wasn't working for him anymore. And after hearing her confession downstairs, he understood now why that was so important to her.

He fought a surge of pointless anger when he thought of the bastard who had hurt and used her.

He wasn't going to solve anything lying here, staring at the ceiling. And he wasn't going to sleep. It wouldn't be the first time in his life he'd pulled an all-nighter. Hell, it wouldn't be the first time this week.

Pushing quietly from the bed, he tried not to jostle Marcy. His office was to the right of his bedroom. It was actually bigger, with a better view and several large windows open to the Caribbean Sea. Most people might have made it the master, since the bathroom actually connected to both rooms, but he'd saved the best room for where he spent most of his time.

Sleeping was an annoying necessity. And since he hadn't taken a lover lately, that was the only thing his bed had been used for. Closing the door behind him, he settled into the soft leather chair behind his desk. He reached automatically for the button on his computer, only to remember there wasn't any power.

Today he was firing that crew. He'd fly another one in from Jamaica if he had to. Of course, that meant he'd have to call the ferry back to the island. He wondered briefly if Marcy would take the opportunity to leave, and then decided he'd find some way to convince her to stay. Even if it meant keeping her naked and occupied until the boat was gone.

His lips twitched at the thought. It definitely had potential. He wondered if he could convince her to experiment with handcuffs. Maybe that was taking it a little too far, though.

He was in a much better mood when he pulled out the printed copy of his latest manuscript, lit a candle his decorator had probably intended to be only for show and settled onto the couch. He might not be able to work forward, but he could take the opportunity to go over what he already had.

MARCY WOKE ALONE. She knew it without even opening her eyes. She reached across the bed, the cool sheets telling her she wasn't wrong. Cracking her eyelids open, she rolled her head so she could see the other side of the bed. It barely looked rumpled.

How could he already be awake?

After the day and night they'd had, she'd been so exhausted she'd felt drugged.

Groaning, she pushed herself up out of the warm cocoon of covers, searching for an alarm clock. There wasn't one. What kind of person didn't have a clock beside the bed?

Frowning, she realized who she was talking about. Simon didn't care anything about business hours. He surfaced whenever he wanted to. *Must be nice.*

There was definitely sunlight coming through the window. Judging from the brightness, it was probably late morning. Ten, she guessed, climbing from the bed.

Her brain felt stuffed with cotton. She desperately needed coffee, but without power or water that wasn't going to happen. Marcy found a robe hanging on the back of the bathroom door and wrapped it around herself. It smelled like him. Clean, warm and male. It was soft, well-worn, and she pulled it tighter around her, letting the material hug her body.

Walking into the kitchen, she opened the small refrigerator and settled for caffeine in the form of a warmish coke. Not her first choice, but better than nothing. Leaning her hips back against the counter, she took several slow sips.

The fuzziness began to clear. She frowned, sweeping her gaze across the kitchen. She'd bet it hadn't been used in days. Possibly weeks. She ran a finger over the top of the backsplash and came away with a glob of dust.

She needed to get housekeeping in here stat.

It was a knee-jerk reaction, one she immediately countered. No, that wasn't her job anymore.

Where was he?

She wondered if maybe he'd gone outside. But surely the door closing would have woken her. She wasn't a heavy sleeper normally—the hazard of living where you worked meant you were on call twenty-four hours.

But she'd been so exhausted that maybe she could have missed him leaving.

Since she'd been standing there, she hadn't heard any noise from the rest of the apartment. But before she went tromping across the resort in Simon's bathrobe, she decided to check to make sure.

The door to his office was closed, but she was used to seeing it that way. Although when she thought about it she realized it had been open when they'd come in last night.

She'd long ago gotten out of the habit of knocking on Simon's door. He never answered when she did, choosing to see a knock as more of a suggestion than a request—one he usually ignored.

The familiar exasperation that accompanied her trips up to Simon's office filled her, an ingrained habit two years in the making. But the minute she stepped inside, it disappeared.

He was slumped on the sofa that stretched along the far wall. A pile of papers was stacked haphazardly on the floor beside him, upside down, the blank side up. Another stack fanned out across his chest. They rose and fell in a steady rhythm with his deep, even breaths. So far, none of them had slid off, but she didn't think that could last very much longer.

The sunlight streaming through the windows at the end of the room didn't reach him, probably the only reason the light hadn't woken him. His hair, dry and lighter now, brushed across his forehead, the ends falling to hide one closed eyelid. His face was relaxed. It was a surprise to see, because she'd always thought that was his normal, everyday expression. Only now, when she truly saw him without anything pulling his face taut, did she realize that wasn't true.

It was an act.

When had she begun to realize that? When he'd sprinted down the path to take charge of the chaos? Or maybe when he'd walked into the fire to rescue a man he didn't know. Or perhaps it was the moment he'd touched her and something hot had sizzled down her skin.

Or maybe she'd known it for a very long time and just hadn't wanted to admit it to herself. It was easier to hold him at arm's length when she convinced herself she didn't like the man he was. But she did like him. Maybe too much.

Shaking her head, Marcy realized it didn't matter when. Her opinion of Simon had changed.

But her course of action hadn't. Hopefully in a few weeks she'd be leaving for a new position in the city. It was where she belonged. And all this would end.

She reached for the papers on Simon's chest, easing them softly out from under his folded hand. He was so peaceful. She didn't want to disturb him. He'd been through just as much as she had yesterday and from the looks of things hadn't been able to drop immediately off to sleep as she had.

Snagging the pile on the floor, she walked across to the desk. She meant to scrape them into neat, even stacks and leave them sitting on the top. But something caught her eye and stopped her as she was shuffling the papers together.

At first it was more a realization of what they were—pages and pages of words—than specifics. *What in heaven's name is he doing?* Why would Simon have a document like this? There had to be hundreds of pages between the two stacks.

Sinking into the leather chair that he normally occupied, she cringed when it creaked, and her heartbeat sped up. Why did she suddenly feel like a burglar trespassing on private property?

Frowning, she looked over at Simon, realized he hadn't moved and chastised herself. She wasn't prying. Okay, maybe she was, but she hadn't started off to do it.

Flipping over the pile from the floor, she immediately saw the words *Chapter One* in bold letters halfway down the first page.

It was a book.

Her gaze flew across to Simon. What was he doing with a manuscript? Reading it for a friend, maybe?

She didn't mean to read it. But her eyes started moving across the page, devouring the words as fast as she could. She was only a few in when it hit her. This was a Cooper Simmens book.

How had he gotten hold of it? The story was one she'd never read—and she'd read everything of his— so she could only assume it was the newest book, one not yet released. A spurt of jealousy ran through her.

Logically, she realized she should probably put it down. But she couldn't stop herself. She kept promising herself she'd stop after this scene or at the end of this chapter. But it never happened.

She had no idea how long she sat there, the sun moving in a slow arch behind her. However long it took to read through 120 pages. Because that's where she was when a quietly menacing voice asked, "What do you think you're doing?"

11

ANGER, IRRATIONAL AND BLINDING, rolled through Simon. Waking up and finding his manuscript gone was his worst nightmare come to life. Again.

When Courtney had left him he'd been blindsided, confused and upset. But when he'd realized leaving hadn't been enough for her, helplessness, anger and panic had quickly taken precedence. His work was gone. Not just copied, but every single file on his computer erased. His backup hard drive smashed to bits.

Not only had he lost months of work, but he'd also lost every shred of evidence that could be used to prove the manuscript she'd begun shopping was his. It was a new project, something different from the series he'd been working on previously. There were no common characters he could even lay claim to.

His agent and editor had been aware of the project, but he'd convinced them to let him work on it in secret, since it was a departure from his tried-and-true. He hadn't even given them a synopsis they could use to help him. He hadn't trusted his instincts or his talent enough to let anyone see it until it was done. All he had was a contract for an unnamed book that was due. A book he was unable to produce.

He'd been devastated. He'd lost not only the woman he'd thought had loved him, but also months of work. His reputation suffered. His publisher didn't appreciate the upheaval or the media storm that followed. The saying that any publicity is good publicity was a crock.

The betrayal was almost worse the second time around. Although he had no idea why.

Waking up to see Marcy sitting at his desk reading his manuscript had been like a knife to the gut, reopening a wound he'd long thought healed.

Apparently he'd been wrong.

She jerked her head up when he spoke, guilt clearly stamped across every feature of her face.

"I...I..." she sputtered, a hot flush tingeing her throat and face.

He reached across the desk and snatched the paper out of her hand. Breath hissed through her teeth, shock crossing her face. She turned her hand over, and he watched as a thin line of blood welled across her palm.

For a second he felt guilty. Fought against the urge to kiss it and make it better. No, it wasn't his fault she'd gotten a paper cut.

She looked down at it for a second, as if she wasn't exactly sure what to do. Slowly she brought her hand up to her mouth and sucked.

Mumbling around her palm, she said, "What the hell is wrong with you?"

What was wrong with him? "Nothing. Absolutely nothing. Why would anything be wrong when you're sitting in my own damn office violating my trust? Reading my manuscript."

His voice escalated with each word. He heard himself, but couldn't seem to stop the outburst.

"I'm not violating anything, you big idiot. You fell asleep with these—" she picked up the papers and waved them in the air "—spread all over the place. I was just…" Her words trailed off and her eyes went round.

Simon didn't understand what had happened. One minute she'd been yelling at him, fighting verbal jab for verbal jab. The next she was looking at him as if he'd grown a second head.

The heat that had spilled through his body eased, burned out by the explosion of his initial reaction.

"Wait," she said slowly. "This…" She swallowed. "These—" she gestured again to the papers sitting in neat stacks on the desk "—are yours?"

"Yes."

"This book is yours?"

"Yes."

"You wrote it?"

He didn't know how many different ways she could ask the same question. Was she expecting a different answer? "What did you think?"

"That you were reading it for a friend."

Well, hell. That would have been a great cover story if he'd stopped long enough to think about it instead of flying off the handle.

"Ohmygod." She dropped her head into her hands, covering her face. The back of her neck flushed a deep, dark red.

Simon tilted his head sideways, trying to figure out what was going on. Had he woken up in an alternative universe? He looked around his office. Nope, everything looked the same. But Marcy was definitely not acting the same.

"I just slept with Cooper Simmens," she mumbled into her hands.

With a deep breath and a frown, Simon sank back onto the couch behind him. "Don't tell me you're going to turn into a fan girl." He sighed.

Dropping her hands just far enough to reveal her eyes, she speared him with a sharp gaze. "You know me better than that."

Well, he thought he did, but then he'd thought he'd known Courtney, too, so that seemed like a really bad measuring stick. His only answer was a shrug.

"But apparently I don't know anything about you." She groaned, letting her head rest back against his desk chair. Her eyes closed and without opening them she said, "That's what you're always doing in here, isn't it? Writing."

"Obviously."

"Jeez, Simon. You could have told me."

She jumped up from her chair. Simon watched as she paced across his office and ran her fingers through her hair, ruffling the blond strands into a floating cloud around her face. It was incredibly sexy, the agitated way she moved and the intelligence as the wheels in her brain spun.

Settling back, Simon decided to let her work it all out. And while she did, he worked a few things out himself. She hadn't known the manuscript was his until he opened his big mouth. His mind replayed the vision of waking up and finding her sitting behind the desk reading.

The look on her face had been pure absorption. His exclamation had startled her and it had taken several seconds for her to refocus on the world around her. That was a good thing, right?

It was entirely possible his initial reaction had been a little much. Obviously, she wasn't Courtney and hadn't been in the process of stealing everything he'd worked hard to produce. She wouldn't have been sitting in his chair if she had been, would she?

Relief mixed with the awareness that never seemed to leave when Marcy was anywhere nearby. It was a heady combination that was difficult to ignore. Especially with a hard-on throbbing relentlessly against his fly.

She finally stopped pacing, spinning on her heel to face him. It was what he'd been waiting for, her undivided attention.

"I have my reasons for keeping this a secret."

"But you could have told *me*. I was your manager, Simon. You trusted me with sensitive details about the resort, the finances, everything. If you had told me from the first moment it might have changed our entire relationship."

"And we would have ended up in bed together months ago."

"Yes. No." She blinked. "One has nothing to do with the other."

"Oh, I think it does. All those arguments were just a safe outlet for the passion sizzling between us."

"That's not true. I genuinely didn't like you."

"Keep telling yourself that. You wanted me from the moment you stepped onto this island. Why not admit it? I sure as hell wanted you."

Her mouth dropped open. Slowly she shut it.

"Why do you think my actions and attitude pissed you off so much?"

She crossed her arms beneath her breasts, pushing them high and tight against the opening of his robe. The hem trailed higher up her thigh, drawing his attention. He couldn't stop his eyes from trailing up and down her body.

And she noticed, her lips parting softly and the black of her pupils pushing against the bright blue of her eyes.

"Because you're damn frustrating," she said, but her voice had gone soft and airy.

"Oh, absolutely. I didn't know you from Adam when you first got here. I don't trust blindly, Marcy, and wasn't willing to take the risk of bringing you in. Only a handful of people know who I am."

"Zane!" she exclaimed. "He knows, doesn't he? Son of a bitch. He told me there was more to you than I realized, but he wouldn't explain further."

She was quick. It was one of the traits that made her great at her job, but it was also very sexy.

"Yes, Zane and I were frat brothers in college. He knew me before I sold my first manuscript." He also knew all the details surrounding the theft of his manuscript, because he'd consulted his buddy in the CIA to see if there was anything he could do. Or any way he could retrieve the data from his computer.

"By the time I might have considered telling you the truth, you'd already been here for months. I didn't think you'd appreciate learning I hadn't told you the entire truth."

"Oh, so it was better to keep lying to me?"

"Lying is such a nasty little word."

"Then what would you call it?"

Simon shifted uncomfortably against the leather of

the sofa. "Letting you keep your own assumptions. I don't believe I ever told you I wasn't a writer."

She growled, low in her throat. "No, but you let me rail at you like a shrew on more than one occasion when simply explaining why you were preoccupied or busy could have prevented a lot of frustration."

Surging up, Simon grasped Marcy's wrist and pulled her down beside him. She collapsed onto the sofa in a pile of arms and legs, a huff blasting through her lips. She tried to get up, but he tugged again, keeping her there.

He leaned against her body, bringing his lips to her ear. "Maybe I like it when you're a bit of a shrew. It actually turns me on."

Her breath caught in her lungs. But it didn't take her long to start pulling at her wrist again. "You're laughing at me."

"Not on your life. I'm serious. I like it when you get upset. Your skin flushes and your eyes darken and flash." His lips trailed down the soft curve of her neck. Her pulse beat there, steadily increasing beneath the heat of his caress. "It was the closest thing I could get to seeing you go wild in my arms."

"You should have told me, Simon."

"Maybe, but you know now."

She frowned, tilting her head sideways out of his range. She turned, slowly, to look at him. "Not because you told me. You probably never would have if I hadn't found that manuscript on the floor."

Her eyes searched his face. He knew exactly what she was looking for, some sign that he was going to try to lie to her. But he wouldn't do that. At least, not now.

"Probably not. Don't take it personally, Marcy. I don't let anyone in that far. Not anymore."

She brushed a single finger over his lips. Darting out his tongue, he tried to suck it deep inside his mouth. She wouldn't let him, instead pulling back.

"And you aren't going to elaborate on that and tell me why, are you?"

He shook his head, sadness rolling unexpectedly through him.

Simon had no idea what Marcy might have said, what she might have done, because before she could do anything a loud knock echoed through his apartment. Part of him wanted to ignore it, to push her and see where this went. But most of him just wanted out of the conversation before he did or said something he'd regret—like spilling his guts at her feet.

He opened the door to Xavier. Realizing he couldn't ignore the man, Simon swept his arm toward the office door, inviting him in.

Marcy had pulled her bare feet up onto the couch beside her, burying them beneath the edge of his robe. She self-consciously tucked a strand of hair behind her ear, but other than that gave no sign of her discomfort at being caught in his office practically naked.

Xavier didn't pause more than a heartbeat before nodding and saying, "Marcy."

Leaning back against the edge of the desk, he addressed them both. Smart man. Marcy might have told him several times that she wasn't in charge anymore, but Xavier obviously wasn't going to burn any bridges just yet.

"I'm taking everyone off fire rotation. Things look fine and I don't expect any problems. I'll keep an eye on the area from the Crow's Nest, though, just in case. Obviously the shed is a total loss, but we can deal with that later."

Simon nodded.

"We need to talk about the construction crew. They'd like to leave to see to their friend."

"But we have a contract," Marcy protested.

"That I really have no desire to enforce," Simon countered, the right side of his lips twitching upward. She couldn't stop herself. She might not want to step in, but her work ethic was just too strong to resist.

Throwing her hands in the air, she pushed herself up from the sofa. He was certain it wasn't intentional, just a tactic she'd learned over the years to compensate for her stature. The power position was never sitting lower than your opponent. "How are we going to finish the repairs and renovations in time if you fire the only crew we've got? Not to mention now we have debris to clear away. They might not be the best, but surely they can handle the simple jobs while we look for someone else."

He liked the way she used the word *we,* but he knew better than to let it mean anything. "What about their friend?" he asked.

"I'm not an unfeeling bitch, Simon. I'll call the launch myself and have them taken to the hospital right now. Losing one day is better than three or four."

"I never said you were."

She grimaced.

Turning back to Xavier, he said, "Arrange for them to be transported to the main island. Please tell them to concentrate on their friend, that I won't need them back again, but I'll compensate them for the lost time."

Marcy scoffed and turned away.

He ignored her. Xavier, apparently happy with his marching orders, turned to leave. Halfway across the room, he stopped short. He continued to face the door for several seconds, as if considering whether or not to mention whatever he'd just remembered.

Finally he spun slowly on his heel, a move that was definitely military precision.

"Apparently Paul and Christine heard some noises last night."

Simon cut his eyes toward Marcy just in time to see the flush that touched her skin. Clamping onto the inside of his cheek, he fought hard not to grin.

"What kind of noises?"

Xavier's eyes studied him, missing nothing. "Sex noises."

Simon raised a single eyebrow. "Imagine that." The sarcasm wasn't lost on his head of security.

"A shirt and pair of pants were found on the bottom of the pool."

Marcy's spine stiffened. No doubt Xavier had known immediately that the clothes were theirs. He'd seen them wearing those exact items last night in the lobby. However, he was smart enough not to point that out.

Simon forced a noncommittal sound through his throat, afraid if he did more he'd burst out laughing. He shouldn't find her discomfort funny, but he did.

"What would you like me to do with them?"

"Leave them on the pool deck. I'm certain the owners will come back for them eventually."

Simon saw the sharp mirth that lurked deep in Xavier's eyes. "Would you like me to pull up the surveillance footage?"

He had to admit he kinda liked this guy. Xavier had a wicked sense of humor paired with a competency that Simon knew he could trust. He was glad. After Zane had left, he wasn't sure he'd find a head of security he'd feel 100 percent comfortable with.

"No!" Marcy exclaimed.

"Not necessary," Simon said a little more slowly.

Xavier shrugged in acquiescence. "Between the fire and being short staffed, no one was watching last night." He dragged his eyes slowly back to Marcy. "Good thing."

She gave him a tight smile. "Isn't it, though?" she agreed, leveling a daggered glare at Simon's chest. He was definitely going to pay for this.

And something told him he would enjoy every minute of it.

12

SHE'D NEVER BEEN so relieved to see someone leave as she was when Xavier finally walked out the door.

The security system hadn't even entered her mind when Simon had pulled her outside. How could she have forgotten that huge detail? Mortification rolled through her. She'd never been one for public displays of affection. She'd never understood the allure of sex in public places.

At least not until last night. She supposed the fear of being caught might have possibly added a layer of danger to the entire experience. But that was as far as she was going. And while some of their guests seemed to delight in their exhibitionist tendencies, she was not about to join their ranks.

Yes, she realized, the moment Simon had scooped her up into his arms and carried her off with the staff watching, everyone had probably known they were headed for his bed. The heated purpose in his eyes had been hard to miss. But that didn't mean she wanted herself on display.

Sagging against the edge of Simon's desk, she let it take the weight of her embarrassment.

"That was interesting," Simon said from across the room.

"What was?"

"Watching you squirm," he said, sliding in front of her. He wrapped his arms around her waist, pulling her into the cradle of his body.

"I do not squirm."

"Like an inchworm searching for the next leaf."

She rolled her eyes. "How could I not have known you were a writer? Only someone who makes their living using words would say something like that."

His eyes, bright and playful a moment before, became suddenly sharp and serious. "Because you saw what you expected to see. What you wanted to see."

"What you wanted me to see."

"Are we going to cover this ground again?"

She twisted her lips into a crooked line. He had a point. It wouldn't do any good to rehash what was already done. But she wasn't completely ready to let it all go. There was more he wasn't telling her. And that bothered her. She didn't like secrets. Especially her lover's secrets. They'd come back to bite her in the ass before and she really didn't want that to happen again.

"I suppose not. For now. But don't think the conversation is over."

Heat seeped into her skin where his hands spanned her hips. Her body tried to convince her to give in to it, to drag him back to the still-rumpled bed and forget everything else for a little while. But that wasn't going to work. Not right now.

Shoving against him, she slipped out from beneath his arms.

"I'm going to make you a deal."

"Does it involve letting me see what's under my robe?"

"Not right now."

"Then I'm not interested." He reached for her, trying to pull her back to him, but she resisted.

"Oh, I think you will be." She scooted away, putting the desk between them as a barrier. Without it, she didn't trust herself to stay on course. "Why did you need me here?"

His eyes were shrewd as they roamed her face. She watched as he measured the distance across the desk, calculating whether he could reach her before she was out of range.

Rolling the chair in front of her, she added another layer of defense.

"I'm serious, Simon. Why was it so important to keep me here that you canceled the ferry and practically kidnapped me?"

"The book's late and I needed these two weeks to get it finished. If I don't, my editor and agent are going to draw straws to see who gets to murder me."

Jeez, even now he joked.

"And I knew I couldn't handle everything here and finish without you."

Marcy ground her teeth together. Idiotic man. She wanted in on the straw draw, but she'd worry about that later.

"I'm going to ignore that you chose kidnapping me rather than telling me the truth. For now." The flash of guilt that crossed his face was almost enough to make her forgive him. But not quite.

"I will take care of the resort so that you can concentrate on finishing your book—on two conditions."

He looked at her warily but asked, "And what are those?"

"First, you understand that I will be leaving. Soon. I want this job in New York, and even if it doesn't work out the next one will."

She knew he was probably going to have the most trouble with this first one, which was why she'd led with it. And she wasn't wrong. The muscles in his jaw worked as he fought against his initial instinct to argue with her. She had to give him credit for the restraint.

"Fine," he conceded reluctantly. "As long as you leave open the option that you might want to stay."

"Because we slept together?" She tried not to scoff. "Simon, I'm not stupid. You aren't the kind of man who does long-term. And I'm not looking for a relationship."

His face was stony, but he didn't argue. "Second?"

"You can't question any decision I make. If I'm back in charge, I'm back in charge. And now that I know you have other things to concentrate on, I want you to butt out."

Simon rolled his eyes heavenward. "Now she wants me to butt out. I've been telling you for months that I don't care what you do."

"Bullshit. But that's neither here nor there. I promise I'll have power and water back up and running within twenty-four hours."

"All right, but I have a condition of my own."

Marcy eyed him warily. "What is it?"

He shook his head. "Uh-huh. I'm not telling you until you stop acting like I'm an animal about to pounce on you and come out from behind that desk."

Marcy raked her eyes up and down his body. She realized it was probably a trap. But considering he was naked from the waist up, she'd done well to resist him as long as she had.

"Behave," she admonished as she scooted slowly to the right.

He flashed her a smile, full of fake innocence. The minute he could reach her, he wrapped his hands around her body and pulled her against him.

"No going back to the way things were before," he growled against her mouth as he crushed her lips with his. "I don't care if you are working for me again. I need you in my bed. I can't concentrate anymore. All I think about is you."

Her knees went weak. Man, he was good. He knew exactly what to say to devastate her.

"You give me more credit than I deserve," she whispered. "I couldn't resist you to save my soul."

"Thank God for small favors."

His hands roamed restlessly up and down her body. They had no specific destination, touching, caressing, teasing wherever they landed. He pushed his knee between her thighs, pressing them open.

"One more thing," she said, completely breathless from desire.

"Anything."

"Be careful what you promise."

A grunt was his only acknowledgment of her warning.

"I want to read it."

He stilled. And pulled back far enough that she could see his eyes. He was surprised, she realized, and that surprised *her*.

"Why?"

"Because it's damn good. And I want to know how it ends. And because I'm a huge fan."

He laughed, the warm, rich sound rolling through her chest. "Of course you are."

This time she was the one reaching for him, pulling him against her body. She sucked gently at the pulse thudding beneath his jaw.

"Don't let it go to your head."

MARCY SAT IN HER OFFICE. She had to admit it felt good being back behind the desk. She'd handled the problem of the construction crew. The group they usually used would arrive tomorrow. After contacting several plumbers and electricians and explaining the situation, she'd found two who had promised to have the problem fixed within the twenty-four-hour time frame she'd foolishly promised Simon.

They'd exceeded her expectations. The power had been restored the night before. And while part of her had been looking forward to sex with Simon by candlelight, air-conditioning and coffee had been much more important.

And when the plumber had water restored early that morning, Marcy had almost kissed the man's feet. She would never underestimate the importance of a hot shower again in her life. Unfortunately, the reservoir system had been depleted and wouldn't be restored again until it rained, but in the meantime everyone on that system had been moved to vacant hotel rooms.

And considering it was hurricane season, Marcy expected the reservoir to be refilled in no time.

Things were shaping up nicely.

The desk chair creaked as she sank farther back into it. For the first time in a very long time she didn't feel stressed at work. She was…happy. And while it felt a little weird, it was also good.

Looking around her, she realized there wasn't anything else for her to do. She got up and was just about to flip off the light switch and leave for the afternoon when her direct line rang.

Picking it up from the opposite side of her desk, she hoped the call wouldn't take long. She had the sudden urge to spend some serious time on the beach. She wondered if Simon had finished his work for the day and might be persuaded to join her.

"Marcy McKinney, how can I help you?"

"Ms. McKinney, this is Richard Bledsoe from Rock Island Hotels."

She knew perfectly well who he was. "Mr. Bledsoe, wonderful to hear from you."

"I wanted to let you know you're at the top of our list of candidates for the general manager position. Everyone enjoyed speaking with you the other day and we're very excited about your ideas for expanding the hotel and filling our vacant spaces. We were impressed with the marketing campaign you put together for Escape, and the results."

"I'm so glad to hear that." Marcy's heart fluttered uncomfortably inside her chest. She hoped he couldn't hear the pounding tattoo through the phone.

"There are a few people on our hiring committee who raised concerns, since we weren't able to meet with you in person."

Marcy frowned. Damn it!

"However, I think I've convinced them that combined with a letter of recommendation from your current employer, the video conference should suffice as your final interview. If you can provide that for me by the end of the week, I can guarantee the position will be yours."

Euphoria bubbled inside Marcy's chest. Somehow, and she had no idea how, she managed to keep it down. In a calm, professional voice, she said, "I don't think that will be a problem, Mr. Bledsoe. I'll have Simon, um, Mr. Reeves fax it to you as soon as possible."

She took down his fax number, handled the niceties and the minute the phone was on the cradle let out a huge whoop.

"Well, you're certainly happy about something. Can't be our miraculous return to civilization, since that happened this morning."

Marcy whirled around. Simon lounged in her open doorway, his right shoulder pressed against the jamb, his hands shoved haphazardly into his pockets and a wide smile on his face.

It was hard to keep the excited expression from her own face.

"I got it."

The light dimmed just a little in his eyes, but she hardly noticed.

"That was Mr. Bledsoe. He said I got the job. Well, actually what he said was that if you faxed him a letter of recommendation by the end of the week I'd have the job."

She reached for his hands, pulling him along with her as she spun around her office. Everything she'd worked so hard for was falling into place. In a few short weeks she'd be back in New York, in the thick of things, managing a world-renowned hotel.

Her old boss could eat his heart out. Actually, she'd love to be a fly on the wall when he heard she was coming back. And to such a powerful position. No longer someone's lackey, running errands, taking orders, being the scapegoat when things went wrong and getting no credit when everything went right because of her hard work. She was going to be the one in charge.

It took her a few minutes to realize Simon was far from as excited as she was. He moved with her around the room, but only halfheartedly.

She stopped, finally focusing on him. He wasn't happy. But then, she really hadn't expected him to be. The man had kidnapped her rather than let her leave the island. And, yes, she now knew the real impetus behind that move. She had to assume he still wouldn't be thrilled when she left.

"I'm pleased for you. I know this is what you want."

"I'm sorry, Simon. I didn't think. Of course I won't leave you in the lurch."

"I know that, Marcy."

She licked nervously at her lips. "You'll send the letter, right?"

"Of course."

She started to smile, but it just wouldn't form completely on her lips.

"We both knew this wasn't going to last." She moved her hand through the space separating them.

Simon nodded. "Yes, but that doesn't mean I have to be happy about you leaving. I need you, Marcy. I can't finish my book without you here. I don't have time to deal with anyone new right now."

She tried not to be hurt, but it was a difficult thing. Of course his reluctance had nothing to do with her personally or the affair they'd begun. She'd been an idiot to even consider it for the few minutes she had. They'd both been clear from the beginning that it wasn't going anywhere permanent.

It still stung to hear him say her value to him was in

keeping the complications of running the resort from disturbing him.

"You don't have much more, do you?" she asked.

"No. I should be able to finish by the end of next week."

"Well, I promise not to leave before you're done."

"What about Mr. Bledsoe?"

"Surely he'll appreciate integrity in a future employee. I'll just tell him I can't leave you high and dry."

Simon's fingers brushed softly against her cheek. Her first instinct was to lean into the caress, but something stopped her. The ease and comfort they'd found together over the past couple days had been marred by his reaction.

She shouldn't let it bother her, but she couldn't help it.

"Thank you," he said, the corners of his lips lifting for a moment before going flat again.

Shaking his head, he flashed her another smile, but this one didn't go all the way up to his eyes. An ache settled in the center of her chest.

"We need to celebrate. I'll call Chef and ask him to prepare a special meal. Go home, put on something beautiful and meet me in the dining room in an hour. We'll have the place to ourselves."

A shiver snaked down Marcy's spine. A romantic dinner sounded perfect. She knew it wasn't, but she wanted desperately for the special celebratory feeling to be real.

How long had it been since she'd planned that romantic welcome dinner for Lena and Colt, the couple who were supposed to pose for their advertising campaign? At the time she'd been so wrapped up in the details and worried about something going wrong—

which it had—that she hadn't really thought about what she was doing.

Afterward, when everything had fallen apart, Colt refusing to let her use the photographs and threatening to get an injunction against them, she'd looked at the pictures from that night and felt this bone-deep longing for what Lena and Colt had.

Sure, it had taken them longer than it should have to realize they loved each other and belonged together, but their love had been obvious to anyone who'd seen those photographs. She'd definitely recognized it.

Tonight she wanted that. And she wanted it with Simon. The problem was, she knew she shouldn't. Because even if tonight was perfect…it wouldn't be enough.

13

WITH THE POWER FINALLY restored, the restaurant no longer looked like a creepy, deserted building harboring serial killers around every corner. Instead, soft candlelight flickered over the empty tables, glinting off crystal and expensive silverware.

Simon could probably count on one hand the times he'd ventured inside the room. At least, once everything had been set up and the resort opened. After that, he'd left things to the talented chef and maître d' he'd hired. Rarely did he feel the need to sit at a romantic table by himself, especially when the kitchen would deliver to his apartments.

Now Marcy sat across from him and he realized he should have done this much sooner.

Although she probably wouldn't have agreed to it then.

She was beautiful, an intriguing mix of soft and hard. Wispy blond hair curled around her shoulders. The sloping line of her jaw begged him to lean across the table and take a bite of *her* instead of the food sitting in front of him. But the sharp, direct, intense eyes

that strayed over to him again and again made a mix
of emotions tumble through his body. Awe, desire…
and if pressed he'd admit a little bit of fear.

Marcy was a force to be reckoned with. He'd seen
her in action plenty of times, and while going toe-to-
toe with her always brought on a delicious burst of
adrenaline, it also challenged him.

He didn't want her to leave.

And that made this night bittersweet. They were
here to celebrate a job offer that would eventually take
her away from the resort. Away from him. And the
thought made him crazy. He wanted to yell at her, to
forbid her to leave, to force her to stay.

And that had worked so well before. Acrid sarcasm
curled in the pit of his stomach. He put his fork down
on the edge of his plate, unable to eat any more. Chef
was not going to be happy.

Simon couldn't ask Marcy to stay. The expression
of sheer joy on her face when she'd hung up that phone
had punched him in the gut. Leaving was what she
wanted. And he'd known that.

Falling in love with her was his fault. His problem
to deal with.

The thought formed, at once surprising but also
completely easy and somehow right. Of course he
loved her. Who wouldn't? She was intelligent, sexy,
strong and confident.

In the time they had left, he was going to put on the
best game face he could find and pretend a happiness
he didn't really feel. The one thing he couldn't handle
would be seeing pity in her eyes before she walked
away from him.

"The replacement construction crew will be here in

the morning," she said, glancing up at him through the shield of her lashes.

Simon shook his head. "I don't want to talk about the resort, Marcy."

She mimicked his move from earlier and precisely laid her fork on the edge of her plate. He noticed she'd eaten only about half of her food. He was going to have to smooth some ruffled feathers in the kitchen for sure. But that was a problem for later.

Pushing her plate away, she folded her arms on the table in front of her and leaned forward. "Then what do you want to talk about?"

He'd spent the past two years with Marcy. They'd fought. They'd loved. A warm river of desire melted into his blood along with the hope that he'd have her again in a few short hours.

But all he knew about her was what she'd put on her résumé. And what he'd picked up here and there as they'd interacted. He had no idea if she had sisters or brothers or if running a resort had always been her life's goal. He might know what college she graduated from, but not if she'd enjoyed the experience and reveled in the freedom as he had.

And that made him feel a little sheepish. He knew the color her skin turned when she was frustrated, the way her breath caught in her chest when he touched her, the warm sound of her laugh. But he hadn't taken the time to *know* her before he'd set out to seduce her.

And while that had never bothered him in the past— what difference did it make if he knew those kinds of details about a woman he had no intention of seeing again?—he found with Marcy it did. She was so much more to him.

"How did you get into hotel management?" he

asked, settling back into his chair. He needed to put some distance between them so that he could concentrate on her answers.

"My dad," was her succinct answer.

He waited for her to elaborate, and when it became obvious she wasn't going to, he prompted, "And…"

"And he was a hotel manager. My mom died when I was young." He watched as she played absentmindedly with the gold ring on her right finger. "It was just the two of us."

Okay, so no siblings. He could relate.

"With him, life was always an adventure. We lived in big cities with museums and gardens and theaters. Hotels were my playground."

"Like Eloise."

She smiled. "Now, that's something I never would have imagined."

"What?"

"Cooper Simmens, fan of little-girl storybooks."

"Hey, it's all market research. Besides, I have friends with small children."

She laughed, the sound tingling down his spine.

"You're close to your father." It was a statement, not a question. He could see the happiness and connection she had with her father shining from her eyes. "How come he's never been to visit you?"

The brightness dimmed, clouding with a sadness that he wanted to kick himself for causing.

"He died five years ago."

"I'm sorry."

She gave him a slow, sad smile. "Thanks. I try to remember the good times instead of the bad. He was sick for a while at the end."

Simon wanted to see that brightness again, so he asked, "Tell me about one of the good times."

She considered him for several seconds. Her fingers fluttered atop the table, a "thinking" gesture that he'd noticed she had. She couldn't sit still, even when her mind was whirling.

"I think you'll like this one. Dad was always a reader. One of my earliest memories of him involved the two of us cuddling up on the couch before bedtime, Dad reading me a story. As I got older we'd each have our own book.

"I remember the first time I picked up his, wondering what kind of story interested him. I think I was probably twelve or thirteen. I can't even remember what it was now, but I do vividly recall him telling me that it would scare me and that I couldn't read it until I was a little older.

"I pestered him relentlessly until he finally gave in. I don't doubt he started me out on something easy, a psychological thriller that kept me up half the night turning pages. I quickly progressed to Stephen King, which he regretted when it kept me up worrying about evil clowns and rabid dogs.

"Even when I'd made friends and was spreading my wings, Dad and I always came back to reading. It was something we shared."

Simon watched as she reached for her wineglass. She'd barely touched it, but now it seemed to be the most interesting thing in front of her. She ran her fingers up and down the stem, staring into the clear glass instead of at him.

"We read your first book together." She darted a glance at him through her lashes before jerking her gaze back down to the mesmerizing wineglass. "Actually, I read it out loud to him during his first stay in the hospital. He was too weak to hold up the book himself at first."

She laughed and he couldn't help the soft smile that tugged at his lips.

"Your books got him through three more trips to the hospital and hospice care." She looked up at him, unshed tears making her blue eyes glisten. "Thank you for giving him a little peace."

Simon swallowed. He'd gotten those types of letters during his career and they always meant something to him. But this was so much more. This was Marcy sitting in front of him, sharing pieces of her life, telling him how his work had given her hurting father a few moments away from the pain.

It was more than he'd expected. And he didn't know what to say. He used words to make his living and for the first time in his life couldn't find the right ones.

Dropping her head into her hands, she rubbed at her eyes for a moment. Her voice was muffled behind the curtain of her palms, but he heard her anyway. "God, how depressing. I'm sorry."

"No." He reached for her hand, pulling it away from her face so that he could see her eyes. "Thank you. I think that's the best compliment I've ever gotten. I'm just sad you had to go through that."

Marcy sighed and waved her hands as if to clear the air of the whole thing. "I had lots of great years with my dad. We were really close. Not everyone has that. I'm lucky and I know it. And I wouldn't trade a single minute of the time we had together. He taught me to appreciate what I've got, and the best way I can honor him is by remembering that."

God, she was strong. If he hadn't known it before,

he would after hearing her say that. He admired her for that strength and integrity and wished he could be more like her.

"Enough about me. How's your book coming? Has Francesca figured out who's trying to kill her yet?"

If he'd known talking about his book would be the thing that put fire, excitement and a happy glitter back in her eyes he would have started there rather than making her recall something difficult. They sat in the restaurant for hours, picking at every single dessert on the menu, talking about not just his work but other books they'd both read and loved.

It was something he hadn't done for a very long time, and until that moment Simon hadn't realized how much he'd missed it. The freedom to talk with someone about the story, how it was going, where it was wrong, what questions had cropped up during his creative process... It was exhilarating.

And when she left he'd lose that, too.

Once again he'd be locked alone with his secret. When he'd moved to the island without telling anyone three years ago, it had felt like the right decision. Sitting across from Marcy, he was no longer certain that was the case. He was afraid that without her, it wouldn't be the same.

"Marcy."

The voice startled her and she jerked her head up from the computer screen she'd been staring at for the past few hours. Realizing if she didn't leave Simon's apartments he'd never get any work done, she'd come downstairs to her office. She'd needed to begin the long process of finding him a replacement manager and preparing a detailed accounting of the responsibilities she handled for whomever he ended up hiring.

She tugged self-consciously at the red striped T-shirt she'd grabbed out of her drawer when she'd visited her bungalow this morning. She couldn't believe it had been days since she'd slept there, and that she wasn't missing the sanctuary she'd always found in her small home one single bit. She'd discovered something better—Simon.

For about three seconds she'd tried to talk herself into putting on one of her trademark suits, but that hadn't gone very well. She was on vacation, sort of. The resort had no guests and she was the only person who worked in the front office and was still on the island.

She looked up at Nicole, one of their massage therapists, and tried to work up the guilt she would have felt last week at being caught behind her desk without all her professional armor in place. But it just didn't come.

"What can I do for you?" Marcy smiled at the petite brunette. Marcy had never taken the time to indulge, but guests raved about Nicole's magic fingers.

"Not a thing." Nicole smiled back. "But I can do something for you."

Marcy raised a single brow. "Oh?"

"Simon told me to take you to the massage hut and give you an hour."

She started to protest. "That's very nice, but not necessary. You're on vacation. Simon shouldn't be asking you to work."

"I don't mind. Really, my fingers need a workout or they're going to get lazy. Simon said you'd try to refuse, though, and he told me I couldn't take no for an answer."

Marcy felt a flutter of anger brush through her body. "Well, Simon doesn't get to dictate what I do."

Nicole laughed softly. "He said to tell you he wouldn't let you see what he's been working on if you refused."

Bastard, Marcy thought, but she had to give him credit for the maneuver. The sneaky man knew she was dying to read his latest pages. It was blackmail, pure and simple, but he was, after all, trying to do something nice.

She was making a mountain out of a molehill, but old habits died hard.

"All right," she said reluctantly. "Let me finish up here. I'll meet you at the massage hut in about fifteen minutes, okay?"

"You won't regret it," Nicole promised.

"I'm sure I won't. I have a file almost an inch thick of guest feedback singing your praises."

She shrugged. "I'm good, what can I say?"

Several minutes later, Marcy was heading down the path toward the beach. Massage hut was probably not the best name they could have given the place. Hut didn't do it justice at all. The structure was impressive. Large and round, built high on stilts, it jutted out over the tempting blue depths of the Caribbean Sea.

Deep-colored panels of polished local wood ran around the room, but went only halfway up. The top half of the room was completely open, providing the soothing lap of water against sand and a calming view of the sea. A tall thatched roof rose in the center, the rustle of the straw only adding to the atmosphere of relaxation.

The structure was high enough that no one could look in, so no guests ever felt worried about their modesty. In fact, the beach area for twenty feet in either direction was blocked off so no rowdy beach play could intrude.

Marcy had to admit that she'd always wanted to schedule an appointment, but it just never seemed to happen. She was a little excited as she walked through the open doorway to find Nicole waiting for her. She was fiddling with a line of bottles that ran the length of a low shelf.

"I'm going to step out and let you get undressed," she said, indicating the privacy screen at the far end of the room. "Lie facedown under the blanket and relax. I'll be back in a few."

Marcy tried not to be self-conscious as she folded her clothes into a neat pile. The screen was strategically placed so that she had only three or four steps to the massage table Nicole had indicated. She realized no one could see her, but she couldn't help feeling as if she was doing something naughty by walking naked across a public place in broad daylight.

An unexpected thrill rushed through her, sending goose bumps down her spine. Jerking up the blanket, she dived beneath the soft surface and situated herself. Apparently "sexy rebel" was not one of her characteristics.

Her heartbeat evened out as she took several steadying breaths. When she put her face into the face cradle, a sweet and relaxing smell filled her lungs. Vanilla maybe, although she couldn't be sure. She'd have to remember to ask Nicole. Her eyes closed and after a few moments she realized her lungs had synchronized with the ebb and flow of the water washing beneath them.

The floorboards creaked behind her, but she didn't

turn to look at Nicole as she entered. Instead she asked, "What's that scent. Vanilla?"

A quiet affirmative hum was her only response. Marcy wondered if maybe she wasn't supposed to talk. It wasn't as if she'd ever done this before. Were there rules? Maybe she should have asked that before she got naked.

Nicole's warm hands pressed lightly into the blanket against her back. They rubbed slowly up and down. Marcy inhaled deeply, held her breath and let it out slowly, releasing the tension she hadn't even been aware she was holding inside her body. A low hum of pleasure rolled through her and for a minute she was embarrassed at her reaction.

But Nicole didn't seem to notice or care. After a few moments she felt the soft breeze of sea air against her naked back as the blanket was folded down to her waist. It went lower than she'd expected, stopping just at the top swell of her rear end.

But as soon as Nicole's hands touched her skin she didn't care anymore. Her muscles warmed with a deep heat as insistent fingers dug into her back, worked along her shoulder blades and kneaded her spine. Nicole was stronger than she'd expected. And her hands were larger, spanning halfway across Marcy's back without even trying. Marcy had never really noticed that about the other woman, but maybe that's why she was so damn good.

Thumbs dug into the dip at the base of her spine, rubbing against the abused bundle of nerves that rested there. Another gasp of pleasure and relief leaked through her lips as the muscles on either side pulled tight and then released.

Unexpected fingers of arousal arrowed out from that

spot to settle between her thighs. Marcy tried to tell herself it was a biological reaction. Normal. But she fought against the urge to bring her legs tighter together to find some relief.

Before she had a chance to catch her breath, the blanket was replaced over her back and disappeared around her left leg. A draft gusted up beneath the blanket, touching her exposed sex and making her ache. The edges of the cloth were tucked around her hip, leaving the bottom swell of her ass bare.

Marcy tried to shift around, but a hand at the top of her spine stopped her. This time when the hands touched her, she was aware enough to realize something wasn't right. Calluses ran across the top of each one where fingers met palm. Why would a massage therapist who made her living with her hands let them get in that kind of condition?

Strong fingers worked her calf, moving steadily up to her thigh. She could feel the muscles relax just as those along her back had. But there was more. Her body began to throb, to respond with a need for that hand to go higher.

A gasp blasted through her when the fingers slipped, brushing across the outer folds of her sex. Her body jerked at the caress, silently asking for more.

Marcy wasn't sure exactly when she became aware that Nicole was not the one touching her…not that it mattered. She tried to raise her head to confirm—she was the sort of girl who enjoyed fact-checking—but a solid weight at the nape of her neck prevented her from moving.

"Simon," she warned, although the single word lost all its power, directed toward the wooden floor and muffled by the headrest of the massage table.

He didn't say anything. Suddenly the entire blanket that had been covering her body was yanked away. A shiver rocked her and she tried again. "Simon!"

But he was already running his hands up and down her body, pressing her harder into the soft padding of the table.

He continued to stroke her, mixing what probably should have been relaxing movements with stolen caresses. She tried to close her thighs, to restrict his access to her, but she couldn't keep them that way. A few minutes later she'd find herself squirming against the table, opening again and begging him to touch her where she ached.

His lips pressed against her back and his teeth nipped at the low indent of her spine. Her brain told her the person touching her was Simon, but her eyes hadn't seen him and a single finger of doubt kept trying to creep in.

She was fully aware that he'd done it on purpose. Her senses were heightened. Arousal mixed with adrenaline, driving her higher and making her writhe. Her breasts ached, the tight point of her nipples under constant torture as she rubbed against the cotton-covered table. Heat blasted through her.

And when he finally ran his fingers full tilt up the greedy opening of her sex, she nearly flew apart. "Simon," she said again, but this time there was no reproach, only begging.

The pressure of his hands on her body disappeared. Taking the opportunity, Marcy flipped over onto her back. Simon loomed above her, his eyes hot and heavy as they dragged down her body.

"Simon," she breathed again, part relief and part benediction.

Leaning up onto an elbow, she wrapped her hand in the cotton of his shirt and pulled him down with her. She claimed his mouth as expertly as he'd just played her body.

She just hoped the massage table could hold them both.

14

THE TABLE CREAKED and swayed beneath them. Simon didn't care if it collapsed to the ground. He'd buy a new one and it would be damn well worth every penny.

Touching Marcy had been pure torture. It had been difficult to hold himself back. He let her take control, enjoying the frenzy he'd built inside her.

He relished the way her hands moved restlessly over his body, seeking something she couldn't quite find. When her fingers slid beneath his shirt to run up his back her soft puff of satisfaction made the muscles in his stomach twist.

His cock throbbed painfully. It wouldn't take much to have him exploding. And when he did, he wanted to be deep inside her.

He wanted to ruin her for every man that she'd ever meet once she left him.

Marcy pulled his shirt off over his head and flung it away. He was afraid it might have gone straight out the opening in the wall above her head. At this rate he wasn't going to have any clothes left.

Her nails scraped down the planes of his chest,

flicking his stiff nipples and forcing a hiss through his teeth. She didn't bother taking her time, arrowing straight to the waistband of his shorts. She made quick work of the fly. Simon tried to stop her, to slow her down, but she was a force to be reckoned with.

And he had to admit that he liked it.

Diving her hand into his back pocket, she smiled up at him, sultry and promising when she pulled out a condom. Her eyelids lowered over glittering blue eyes. She pushed his shorts down over his hips. They fell to his knees and stopped there. She moved on, leaving him hobbled.

His foot was a half inch off the floor still trying to get rid of the shorts when she rolled the condom down over his erection. The combination of cool latex and warm hands was thrilling. The thing constricted around him. He could hear his pulse pounding heavy and hard in his own ears, could count each beat in the throbbing erection she fisted.

Marcy's tongue licked across her open lips. She spread her thighs wide and guided him exactly where he wanted to be. With her. Buried deep.

In one swift motion he brought them together, her warmth enveloping him and swelling up through his whole body. Simon grasped her head, silky strands of hair weaving in and out of his fingers. He took her mouth, bringing them together in every way possible. They worked together, hip to hip, breast to chest, mouth to mouth. Pushing, pulling, coaxing, grasping for one second more.

He breathed her in, lavender and vanilla. Sucked her tongue deep into his mouth, taking her in just as she was ensnaring him. The tremors that signaled his release began deep inside his belly. Simon clamped them down, refusing to let go just yet. Even with their lips locked, she panted against him, her body bowing up tight beneath him. He could feel the trembling pulse of her orgasm just on the edge.

He stroked in and out of her, reveling in the feel of their joined bodies.

Something hot and brittle expanded inside his chest. It hurt even as it felt good. A tightness that had his eyes closing and his hands clenching tighter around her so he could be sure she was still there.

Emotion overwhelmed him, something that had never happened before. He gasped, his eyes springing open. He found her, staring deep into him.

They came together, both giving in at the exact same moment. Marcy threw back her head, screaming his name at the top of her lungs. He couldn't find the breath to utter a single sound. Instead, he leaned over and drank the words from her lips, letting them fuel him when nothing else could.

They stayed there wrapped together in a tangle of limbs, shallow breaths and sweat-slicked skin. Her racing heartbeat eventually slowed. The steady drum of it against his chest was the only thing that seemed solid.

After a few minutes she mumbled weakly, "At least we didn't break the table."

The ghost of a laugh tried to roll through his chest, but he just didn't have the energy for the full thing. She got the idea, though, shaking her head in helpless agreement.

Tightening her arms around his body, she brushed her lips across his shoulder and said, "You're going to have to tell me where you learned to do that."

"What? Make you scream?" he asked, a satisfied

smirk on his lips. What could he say? He was a smug son of a bitch.

Marcy smacked at his chest, breathless laughter bursting through her slightly swollen lips. "No. Give massages."

"The same place I learned how to make you scream," he said with a completely straight face.

She pushed against him, but a smile glinted deep in her eyes.

"That was a dirty trick."

"What? Making you scream?"

"No," she said, exasperation mixing with laughter. "Pulling a switcheroo. Do you know for about five minutes I wondered whether I was attracted to Nicole."

"Liar. You knew it was me the minute I touched you."

"Maybe," she admitted reluctantly.

"Besides, I hadn't exactly planned on doing it. I set up the appointment with good intentions."

She scoffed. Simon gazed at her innocently. She raised her brows in a silent challenge.

"Really. I wanted to give you a treat. You've more than earned it."

"Well, isn't that sweet. And about two years late."

Simon tried to ignore the guilt her words induced. "True. But better late than never has always been my motto."

"No joke. Perhaps you should look at changing that. Maybe to something old and Latin. *Carpe diem* usually works for me. Seize the day."

"Have you been paying attention? The only thing I want to seize is you." To demonstrate his point, Simon began kissing up the side of her neck.

She tilted her head, giving him better access, but

offered a halfhearted protest. "You are the most insatiable man I've ever met."

Simon pulled back and looked into her eyes. "Only with you." There was no trace of the humor and comfortable banter that they'd been batting back and forth. He was damn serious and it was suddenly important that she knew that.

He couldn't tell her that he loved her, not when she was leaving. But she should at least know she was different. Unique.

She stared at him for several seconds, her bright blue eyes wide with surprise. An uncomfortable buzz zinged between them. She finally broke it by saying, "You sure do know how to make a girl feel special."

"All morning the only thing I've been able to think about was you down here, naked on this table. Do you know how difficult it is to concentrate with a permanent hard-on?"

"Yes."

Simon shook his head.

"I mean, no. But I know what it's like to be so distracted that if you don't find an outlet for the desire running through you, you're either going to explode or go mad."

A smile on his lips, he reached down and claimed hers in a quick caress. "Yes, that," he said against her mouth. "You're not so bad at making a guy feel sexy and powerful."

"Who said I was talking about you?"

Simon jerked back, ready to break some other man's bones. Until he saw the humor she couldn't hide lurking in her eyes.

"Minx."

Pushing up from the table, he grasped her hand and pulled her with him. With a little nudge toward the privacy screen, he said, "Get dressed."

Glancing over her shoulder, she exaggerated the sway of her hips as she walked away. "I think that's the first time you've ever said that to me."

"How about we try for another. Get dressed so you can find the shirt you threw out of this hut."

Sticking just her head around the screen, she countered, "I don't think so. Consider it payment for the shirt you tore."

"You're never going to let me forget that, are you?"

"Not on your life." She smiled, the expression sharp and wicked as she ducked away.

Raising her voice to be heard around the barrier, she said, "Besides, I'm covered in oil. Do you know how hard it's going to be to get the sand off my skin if I go out on that beach right now?"

He pulled on his shorts and crossed the room. Leaning against the pillar closest to the privacy screen, Simon shoved both hands deep into his pockets and watched as she dressed. Her back was to him, so she didn't realize he was there until he whispered, "Not hard at all, especially if I help."

She whirled around, her shirt pressed against her chest.

"You haven't seen my shower yet, have you?" Simon let his eyes travel slowly down her body. All he could think about was grabbing that shirt from her hands and taking her again. However, he refrained. "It's pretty big. Definitely room enough for two."

They never did find his shirt. When they went back several hours later, it had disappeared, probably taken out to sea with the receding tide.

OVER THE NEXT few days they settled into a routine. The new construction crew had arrived and were working hard to complete the repair list before reopening. Marcy spent most of the day at her desk, handling whatever resort business came up. Simon locked himself inside his office and she tried very hard to make sure no one disturbed him. At night they'd come together. She'd give him a rundown and he'd tell her what he'd written.

Marcy basically moved into his apartment, using the small kitchen there for probably the first time since Simon had renovated the place.

It was easy and scared the shit out of her.

She knew it couldn't last, but the longer she stayed the more she wanted it to. A sense of dread began to turn her stomach at odd times. She was waiting for something to go wrong, for Simon to turn back into the antagonistic, self-absorbed, infuriating man he'd been before. Or for another disaster to befall the hotel.

She'd even taken to checking the National Hurricane Center website several times a day for forecasts. No storm was heading their way…yet…but she just knew the ease and happiness couldn't last.

And she was right.

Late Tuesday afternoon she was sitting in her office, looking at the track of a storm that had just formed off the coast of Africa, when her phone rang. Picking it up absently, she answered, keeping her focus on the chart she was studying. It didn't look as if it was heading for them, but if living in the Caribbean had taught her anything it was that storms could veer at any moment.

"Ms. McKinney."

Mr. Bledsoe's voice got her attention, though. She'd

called this morning to make sure everything was progressing smoothly.

"I was surprised to get your message this morning," he said, confusing her.

"I'm sorry? Why is that?"

"Well, when we didn't receive your letter of recommendation we assumed you'd changed your mind about accepting the position. I really wish you'd called me and told me in person, but I respect your decision."

Marcy propelled herself out of her chair, sending it rolling backward to collide with the wall. "What are you talking about? Of course I still want the job."

Marcy's skin flushed hot with anger and then cold with self-disgust.

Simon hadn't sent her letter. And yes, she was pissed off at him for that. But she hadn't followed up on it, either. She knew what Simon was like—easily distracted. She'd reminded him once on Thursday night and he'd promised her it would be taken care of. She hadn't bothered him again, and hadn't actually thought about it herself until now.

She'd been distracted. By him.

Once again she'd let lust cloud her judgment and ruin her career.

Damn it! She wanted to scream. She wanted to storm through the resort and find Simon so she could yell at him.

A sense of betrayal welled up inside her. Had he really not sent the letter because he was distracted, or because he hadn't wanted her to get the job? She was talking about the man who'd practically kidnapped her to keep her on the island. But that was before she'd known his secret and understood why he needed her here.

She'd promised him she would stay until his book was done.

But maybe that wasn't enough for him.

God, she was an idiot.

Mr. Bledsoe cleared his throat and Marcy realized she'd begun to breathe heavily.

"I'm sorry, Mr. Bledsoe. I was just working through some anger. Apparently my current boss didn't send my letter, if I understand correctly."

"Yes."

"Well, I was under the impression that it had been sent." She fought against the small kernel of guilt buried deep in her chest. This was not her fault. But she wondered if Mr. Bledsoe would want to hire a manager who couldn't follow up on the smallest details.

"Oh, my," he blustered. "Well, that is unfortunate. We've already begun to interview new candidates."

Marcy sucked in a steadying breath and then blew it out in a silent stream, trying to find some calm and get her mind in order.

"Perfect. Perhaps I can be part of that group. I could be on a plane to the States in a matter of hours. I know not interviewing me in person was your selection committee's main concern."

A thoughtful hum drifted out of the receiver. "I couldn't promise you anything, Ms. McKinney. I'm not sure the selection committee will reconsider."

"I'll take whatever chance you can give me."

"Very well, if nothing else, they might be impressed with your tenacious attitude. But you'll need to be here by tomorrow at noon—it's the only appointment time I have left."

She'd paddle a boat to St. Lucia herself if she had

to. "No problem. I'll call you as soon as I arrive in the city."

"I look forward to meeting you in person, then."

They hung up. Marcy stared blindly down at her desk for a moment. Then she sprang into action. After her assurance that she wouldn't leave until his book was finished, Simon had reinstated the ferry service. Turning her wrist, Marcy looked at the slender gold watch her father had given her as a college graduation present. She had exactly one hour and twenty-seven minutes before the ferry arrived and she had a lot to do—make plane and hotel reservations, pack…

What she wouldn't be doing was saying goodbye to Simon.

Not only did the man not deserve the courtesy, but she was afraid the sight of him might make her resolve cave. Right now she was angry with him. But if he touched her…she wasn't sure she'd be able to leave.

And leaving was exactly what she needed to do. She refused to let another man derail her career.

Even if he convinced her to stay, how long would he want her around? He hadn't talked about anything permanent. And when he got tired of her, she'd find herself out on her ass yet again.

No, this was the right thing.

And if leaving without telling him goodbye made her seem catty, then that's what she was.

15

It was late when Simon finally looked up from his computer. He'd been sitting in front of it for ten straight hours, bothering to get up only for coffee and bathroom breaks.

But he was finished. At least with the rough draft. The end was always easier for him, the threads finally coming together in a rush sort of like a snowball rolling downhill.

And he was damn happy with it. He only hoped his agent and editor would be as pleased. Although the one person he really wanted to celebrate with was Marcy. Everyone else could wait until tomorrow.

Getting up from the desk, he listened to the whirr of the printer as it spit out the last fifty pages. He walked over to the windows, placing his hands at the small of his back and leaning into a stretch. His spine popped, a mixture of pleasure and pain as his abused muscles finally relaxed.

When had it gotten so dark? And why wasn't Marcy here? Lately she'd been showing up late in the afternoon. And even if she quietly opened his door to check on him and silently walked back out, he always knew she was home. Her presence registered in the back of his brain.

He'd become accustomed to hearing the soft sounds of her feet as she walked through his apartments. Enjoyed the scent of whatever she was cooking for dinner as it filled the space. Sometimes knowing she was there had been so distracting that he couldn't concentrate and soon joined her, hoping they had time for a quick reunion while something simmered. Other times he'd continued working, the comfort of knowing she was there enough to keep him relaxed and in the story.

Where was she?

Strolling through the hotel, he realized that he actually missed the hustle and bustle of when it was full. While running the place was definitely a distraction, hearing laughter and happy voices did something pleasant for his soul. He liked knowing other people were enjoying the island he'd brought back to life. Sure, there was some pride of ownership in there, too, but who could blame him?

With his book finished—ahead of when he'd expected, thanks to Marcy—he was actually looking forward to a few weeks off once everyone returned. Although it wouldn't be long, because the first book in the series was coming out in three months and his publisher had arranged a five-city tour, ending in New York.

He wondered if he could convince Marcy to go with him, pulling up short when he realized she'd probably already be there at her new job.

A frown was pulling at the edges of his mouth when he stopped at her office. Before he even poked his head through the doorway he knew the office would be empty—there was no light shining through the door. Maybe she'd run to her bungalow to pick up a few things.

Setting out across the resort, he made it there in record time. The flutter of unease that had begun to pick up speed inside his chest diminished when he saw the light shining from her place. Maybe she hadn't wanted to disturb him. She'd known he was close to the end.

Without knocking, he opened the door and went in. The minute he stepped inside he knew it was all wrong. There was definitely no one home. The first time he'd visited, he'd thought there was nothing of her here. He'd been wrong.

The kitchen cupboards stood wide open, bare of the handmade dishes she'd brought with her. Through the open bathroom, he could see the perfect row of bottles was missing. The rug that had been stretched across the floor, curtains, a metal lamp curved into an abstract form   all rolled, folded and stacked together in the corner.

What the hell?

Stalking through, he yanked open the closet door. The rattle of empty hangers was all that greeted him.

Gone, gone, gone.

Without even saying anything.

Anger mixed with pain, a sharp knife that was lodged in the center of his chest. He reached up and rubbed at the spot, hoping it would help. It didn't.

He was about to storm out when a single white envelope propped against the back of the stove caught his eye. His name was scrawled across the surface in neat, precise letters.

His heart plummeted to his toes, knocking against

several organs on the way down and leaving him bruised and battered from the inside.

His hands did not shake as he reached for it. They didn't. He wouldn't let them.

But his knees definitely wavered as he broke the seal and pulled out the single piece of white paper inside. She hadn't even left him a handwritten note, instead typing it out on her computer as if it was nothing more than a resignation.

He walked unsteadily to the sofa and sank onto it. It was either that or sit on the floor in the middle of the kitchen, and he refused to be that pathetic.

Damn it!

Betrayal, a familiar and unpleasant sensation, welled up inside him. How could she leave without saying goodbye? And he wouldn't even think about the promise she'd made to stay until he was finished. It obviously hadn't meant as much to her as he'd thought.

Why did he have to fall for women who were unscrupulous and self-centered?

Even as he thought the words, he knew they weren't true. Marcy was neither of those things. Courtney definitely deserved the label, but not Marcy. Although knowing that didn't ease the sharp pain.

Smoothing the paper out on his knee, Simon read the letter she'd left him. There was no salutation, not even his name, just a few lines. Short, sweet, with no real emotion at all.

Mr. Bledsoe called and said they never received your letter.

Shit! How could he have forgotten to send that? His entire body sagged back against the cushions.

I convinced them to give me another chance to interview in person, since that was their concern. I had to leave immediately to make the appointment. I left a document titled Marcy's Job Description on my computer. My replacement should find it useful.

Marcy

The paper crumpled in his fist. The corners pinched his palm, but he didn't care. What had he done? Obviously he hadn't done what he'd promised her he would.

He'd been preoccupied. Wrapped up in finishing his book and spending every spare second with Marcy, milking every moment he could, knowing she'd be leaving soon.

But he'd thought he'd have time to prepare. That he wouldn't be blindsided when she simply walked away.

And maybe that's exactly what would have happened if he'd followed through, but he hadn't. He'd screwed up, big-time.

But there was something he could do to fix it.

MARCY WAS BLEARY-EYED and sleep deprived when she walked into the corporate offices of Rock Island Hotels. A pleasant receptionist greeted her and directed her back to Mr. Bledsoe's office. She'd expected to be sent to a conference room full of people staring at her across a long, empty table as they drilled her with questions.

Instead, Mr. Bledsoe stood and welcomed her, asking her to sit in the chair opposite his desk. She'd seen him once on the video conference, but she had to admit he was a little more intimidating in person. He was tall—but then wasn't everyone compared to her?—

with broad shoulders, silver-and-black hair and tanned skin that helped camouflage the lines running across his face.

But his smile was genuine and friendly.

"Ms. McKinney, wonderful to finally meet you in person."

"Marcy. Please call me Marcy," she insisted, grasping his offered hand and shaking. "Is the interview delayed?" she asked, looking out into the hallway trying to see who else she might be speaking with.

"No, it's actually been canceled."

Marcy's heart fluttered uncomfortably in her chest. "I'm sorry. I don't understand."

Mr. Bledsoe sank back into his chair. Marcy followed his lead and did the same. He studied her for several seconds, his eyes quick and intelligent. Marcy shifted nervously under the scrutiny.

"I had an interesting phone call this morning at six o'clock."

"Oh," she said, feigning interest. What did an early call have to do with her and her interview, or lack thereof?

"It seems Mr. Reeves takes full responsibility for not sending your letter. And while I have to admit to some concern that my potential manager wouldn't follow up on such an important detail, he assured me that you were under the impression it had been sent."

"I'm sorry, that's not—" Marcy tried to correct the lie that Simon had obviously told Mr. Bledsoe. All the while, her brain spun faster and faster with the realization that Simon had called this man at the crack of dawn.

Mr. Bledsoe waved his hand as if he already knew what she was going to say and didn't care. "I'm quite impressed with the level of support and loyalty you seem to have earned from your last employer. Mr. Reeves went so far as to intimate he might have not sent the letter on purpose in a misguided attempt to keep you in your current position."

"No, Simon would never do something like that. He's absentminded and gets distracted easily, but he has good reason for that."

He raised a single eyebrow and asked, "Oh?"

Marcy felt a flush move up her skin, but she refused to acknowledge it. Or elaborate. She'd already gotten close enough to Simon's secret and no matter what else might have happened between them, she wasn't about to betray that trust.

It was her turn to dismiss an entire topic of conversation with the flick of her wrist. "It doesn't matter. Simon didn't do it on purpose and you're right, I should have followed up."

Reaching down, she gathered the straps of the briefcase she'd brought with her and started to stand up. "I wish you had called to tell me I was no longer being considered for the position before I came all the way down here, but I suppose I understand your reasoning. I appreciate you explaining to me in person."

She was half in and half out of her chair when Mr. Bledsoe's words stopped her. "You're right, you aren't being considered for the position. It's already yours. I canceled all the other interviews first thing this morning. I'm assuming you'll need a few days to settle in, but I hope you can start next Monday."

Marcy collapsed back into the chair, not caring that her posture was hardly ladylike or professional.

She stared at Mr. Bledsoe, trying to make the wheels

in her brain turn again so she could process what he'd just said.

"I have the job?"

He smiled. "You have the job."

She didn't know what to say. She should be filled with excitement.

But she wasn't.

Sure, she was looking forward to the challenge, to moving back to the city of her heart.

But there was something missing.

"You don't appear pleased," Mr. Bledsoe said in a soft, worried voice.

"No, no, I am. A little shocked is all. And terribly jet-lagged. It was a long trip."

Marcy gathered her wits and managed to have a coherent, relatively professional conversation about the details of her new position. An hour later, she was walking back out the door. This time when she left the receptionist addressed her by name. "Welcome aboard, Ms. McKinney. We're all looking forward to working with you."

Marcy sent her a smile, but she knew it didn't come anywhere close to being real.

MARCY HIT THE GROUND running. Finding a new apartment, settling into a new job... Before she knew it several months had passed. And while she was certainly busy, it wasn't exactly what she'd expected.

Running the flagship hotel for the entire Rock Island Corporation was definitely challenging. And she enjoyed the moments that tested her skills and kept her on her toes.

The job wasn't the problem. It was the hours afterward. She'd lived on her own for almost twelve years. Being alone had never bothered her. But it did now.

She missed Simon. And the resort.

More than she ever would have thought possible.

Considering she'd never really gotten attached to any particular place growing up, feeling homesick was a new experience for her. One she really didn't know how to handle. And the bone-deep loss that accompanied it didn't help.

It had probably taken her two weeks to realize why she was so upset. She'd let herself do the unthinkable and fall in love with Simon.

God, she was an idiot. The problem was she didn't know what to do about it.

She couldn't go back, not after the way she'd left. Simon would never forgive her. Besides, she might love him but she was still a little pissed off at him. True, he'd fixed the problem, but the reality was he'd made her a promise and hadn't followed through.

Although she had to admit, if he were standing in front of her right now, she'd probably forget all that and leap into his arms.

But the main issue was still there. What would she do if she went back to Île du Coeur? She refused to work for Simon while they were lovers. She'd been there before and she wouldn't do it again. Relationships were hard enough without throwing in business to complicate things.

And even if she didn't have a personal history to draw from, her experiences with Simon would have been enough to make her hesitate. The last couple of weeks they'd been together might have been fairly smooth, but she had no doubt that, given time, their tempers, strong personalities and different views on how to run the resort, would have clashed again.

Her choices were to have Simon and lose her job—a huge chunk of her identity—or to lose Simon and keep her job. She respected herself and her business abilities and refused to sacrifice a job she enjoyed and was good at. Especially for a relationship that wasn't a sure thing.

Who knew if Simon would even be interested in picking up where they'd left off? Not once had he given her any indication that he wanted more than the short time she had left on the island.

All of these arguments and insecurities combined to keep her tied to her job in New York, despite feeling unhappy and dissatisfied.

A few weeks turned into three months and as winter set in with a vengeance, she couldn't help but miss the welcoming heat of the island. Before she realized what she was doing, Marcy found herself searching websites hoping to find another Caribbean resort in need of a general manager.

When had her idea of the perfect life changed so much?

She knew the answer to that, but couldn't bring herself to admit it.

16

The second Simon walked out of La Guardia he missed his island. Not only was New York cold as hell, it was also crowded, dirty, loud and almost made him claustrophobic.

However, the fact that his heart was pounding hard in his chest had nothing to do with this new aversion to crushing crowds and everything to do with the fear that Marcy wouldn't show up.

He was in town for the last stop of a whirlwind book tour. He'd started in L.A., continued through Chicago, Dallas and Atlanta. Being in a different city every day was wearing on him big-time.

But it was almost over. In a couple more days he'd be back home, on the soft sand beaches of his island. It was hard not to hope that Marcy would be standing there with him, but he just didn't know. It had been three months since she'd walked away. He hoped a little space might have given her enough time to forgive him. Or at least made her willing to listen as he groveled and begged her to come back.

Of course, that assumed she'd actually accept the invitation to attend his book signing. He'd had a copy of the book hand delivered by courier two weeks earlier, so he knew she'd received it, the information about the signing and his handwritten note asking her to come.

If she didn't, that would tell him everything he needed to know. Which, if he was honest, just meant he'd have to hustle up her home address and track her down there. He wanted her to come to him on her own terms because that's what she deserved. But, at the very least, he wouldn't leave the city without apologizing to her and telling her that he loved her and wanted her in his life. On whatever terms she dictated.

A car deposited him in front of the bookstore. The crowd that waited for him no longer surprised him. Apparently the rumors from several years ago had done nothing but increase his notoriety. Thanks to his fading from the spotlight and recent reclusive tendencies, his first appearance in years had become something of a media frenzy—at least, that was his agent's take on things. Personally, he just figured this tour had coincided with a slow media week. Everywhere.

He'd always been successful—enough to buy a Caribbean island, for heaven's sake—but this was more attention than he'd ever had before.

His publisher was certainly happy, and he knew the marketing team had been quick to spin the story to the best advantage. He didn't care. Whatever sold books.

He just hoped the crush of people didn't deter Marcy. His eyes scanned the group staring back at him. It took him less than thirty seconds to realize she wasn't there. Even with her short stature, he would have known.

Trying to hide a frown, Simon sat down at the table the store had set up. Stacks of books sat on either side of him. But he'd agreed to a short reading followed by a question-and-answer session before he started signing books. And after four of these things, he already knew what everyone was going to ask him.

And he wasn't wrong.

Eventually they'd get around to their curiosity about his career, this book. Some hard-core fan would probably even ask about the rumors and scandal from three years ago.

But first, they all wanted to know "Who's Marcy?"

"Is she with you?"

"Where did you meet?"

Yeah, the dedication he'd written had gotten even more fan attention than his past, his secrecy and the book itself combined. He tried not to let that bother him, considering he'd also written the dedication. Although that hadn't been for them, but for her.

Who would have guessed people would care so much?

He was about to give the standard answer he'd developed after being blindsided by these same questions in L.A.

But the words died on his lips when someone in the back shifted and he saw her standing there. Her blond hair was pulled back into the same tight ponytail she'd always worn before their precious two weeks. Her cheeks were pink from the cold. A scarf was wrapped around her neck, the ends tucked beneath the heavy folds of her winter coat.

She was thinner, the bones of her face pushing slightly against her taut, chilly skin. She stared at him, her teeth worrying her bottom lip. He wanted to reach out to her, but a crowd of people stood between them.

Her eyes were hesitant. They watched him almost

warily, as if she was ready to sprint away at the first sign of…something. Her mouth stayed straight, unsmiling, although she did raise a single hand in a sort of pseudo wave.

The crowd began to turn to see what had caught his attention and struck him mute. First one, then five and before he knew it hundreds of heads had swiveled to focus on Marcy. He hadn't thought her skin could get any pinker—but he'd been wrong.

But she didn't back down, not his Marcy. Instead, she stared at them all, raising a single eyebrow and daring them to say anything to her. Jeez, she was something to watch.

Clearing his throat, he stood and gestured for her to come up with him. She shook her head. Simon narrowed his eyes and, with nothing more than a cock of his head, challenged her. They didn't need words for him to tell her that she had two choices—come up with him or be mobbed by the crowd between them when he finally opened his mouth and told them who she was.

She might not have fully understood, but she got enough of the gist that she began pushing through the people, trying to find the path of least resistance. Which wasn't hard, considering that they all parted to let her pass.

Everyone in the room realized there was an undercurrent flowing between them, and they all wanted front-row seats to watch it play out.

Marcy halted in front of him. He tried to reach across the table and draw her around to his side, but she sidestepped out of range. His heart did a little stutter. He had to admit the minute he'd seen her standing back there, he'd assumed everything was going to be okay. Why else would she be there?

Especially if she'd read the dedication.

But maybe she just wanted to hear the words. Wanted him to grovel in person.

And he was willing to do that. With an audience, no less.

Marcy was worth it.

Shrugging, he turned to the crowd and said, "This is Marcy."

The deafening roar that went up nearly shattered his eardrums.

The crowd surged forward. Panic and surprise shot across Marcy's face. Several people from the store and Simon's team jumped in front of Marcy to protect her from the people now yelling questions at her.

In the confusion, he reached around, grasped her beneath the arms and bodily pulled her to the other side of the table with him. At least it offered a little barrier.

He wrapped her in his arms, pressing her against him. Everything came flooding back, overwhelming him. He'd forgotten how fragile and perfect she was, and how unbelievably arousing it felt to have her in his arms. The scent of lavender washed over him and he drew a heavy breath just so he could hold it inside him again.

She didn't fight him, but melted against him as she always had.

"What just happened?" She looked up at him with dazed eyes. He wanted to crush his mouth to hers, but realized it probably wasn't the right time.

But it was touch and go there for a minute. Three months had never felt so long in his entire life.

"You started a moment of hysteria."

She blinked slowly. "How did I do that?"

"Just by being you."

She nodded as if she understood, but he could still see the confusion in her eyes. "That makes no sense."

He shrugged. "What can I say? They like the dedication."

Her bright blue eyes stared up at him. Around them people peppered them with questions. He heard the words, but let them bounce off him.

"What dedication?"

"You didn't read it? You didn't read the book I sent?"

Slowly she shook her head again. Guilt, pain and something he seriously prayed was hope flitted across her face. She licked her lips and then said quietly, "It hurt too much. I couldn't read it without thinking about us."

Something thick and heavy churned in the pit of his stomach. And yet, despite it, he knew exactly what he had to do.

He let out a loud whistle, and was amazed how quickly the crowd fell silent. Every single eye in the place focused on him, including Marcy's.

Reluctantly he let her go to reach for one of the books stacked high on the table. Facing the crowd, he said, "She hasn't read the dedication." Soft murmurs rippled through the group, but everyone quickly became silent. They all knew what he was about to do. Everyone except Marcy.

She stood there staring at him as if he'd just grown feathers.

Turning to face her, he opened the book and flipped over the first several pages.

"First, I want you to know how many hoops I had to jump through to get my publisher to change this at the last minute. I think I owe them my firstborn child."

A soft twitter from the crowd sounded beside them.

His eyes dropped to the page, but they didn't stay there long. He didn't need to read the words to know what it said. He had them memorized, had agonized over just what he should and could say to her. He didn't want to see ink on paper.

He wanted to watch her. To see the expression in her eyes.

"'Marcy, I might have been able to write this book without you, but it wouldn't have been worth the effort. Nothing matters without you in my life. I know I don't deserve a second chance, but I'm hoping you'll give me one anyway. I love you.'"

Every woman in the crowd sighed in unison. Every woman except the only one who mattered—Marcy.

She just stared at him, her eyes wide.

"Say something," he whispered, although everyone in the place could hear, since they were all holding their breath.

"I love you, too," she said, her voice scratchy.

Another loud roar filled the room, covering up Marcy's next words. "But how are we going to make this work? Simon, you lied to me, broke promises, didn't trust me enough to let me in. I can't go back to the resort and work for you—I refuse to mix business and pleasure. And I won't play Russian roulette with my career again. It's too important and I'm too good."

"I trust you now. With my life. My heart. The resort. Whatever you want. Everything I have, everything I am is yours, Marcy. I promise never to lie to you again. And while I can't promise never to get wrapped up in my head and forget something again, I can promise you I'll try."

Simon glanced quickly at the rapt faces of the audience, realizing he was about to spill his secret to them and the reporters loitering at the back of the room. But if it meant convincing Marcy to come home it would be so worth it.

"Someone I once cared about betrayed me in the worst possible way."

The crowd murmured darkly, knowing exactly what he was talking about.

"My fiancé. After that it was just easier to shut everyone out. To cut myself off from everyone and everything. To hide."

He would have gone on, giving her as many details as she needed, but she stopped him. With a single finger to his lips, she said, "You don't have to explain. I understand."

Of course she did. She'd experienced the same kind of betrayal.

"That doesn't fix our employee, boss, lover problem, though, Si— Cooper."

"I trust you. Now, my question is do you trust me?"

Marcy closed her eyes for several seconds. He knew this was hard for her. She was such a strong, independent person. Putting her faith and future in someone else's hands was difficult. But he really needed to know if she would do that for him.

He'd learned over the past few months that trust had to run both ways. Looking back on his relationship with Courtney, he could admit that he'd known there was something wrong with it, something missing. It hadn't bothered him, though. The sex had been good. She'd been a beautiful hostess and trophy he could show off, along with his expensive apartment and career accolades.

But they hadn't loved each other and had never put

the other first. Not the way they should have if they'd really cared about one another.

The way he cared about Marcy.

Given her history, he understood her hesitation. And, yes, time would prove to her that her fears were unfounded. He had no intention of ever letting her go again, but he also understood her need to work, to feel that she was using her skills. There was a part of her that would always judge her own value by the job she could do.

And her drive was one of the reasons he loved her.

"Absolutely."

"Well then, leave everything to me," he said with a smile. Then he bent her backward over his arm and kissed them both senseless.

17

SIMON'S HANDS SPREAD WIDE over her face, blocking her eyes. Marcy could hear the sound of the waves as they washed against the sand. A soft breeze carried music and laughter.

She'd been back on the island for less than a week and already it was hard to remember the months she'd been gone. They seemed more like a cold dream than reality.

Mr. Bledsoe hadn't exactly been thrilled when she'd told him she was leaving. But she'd stayed on for a month—a lonely month, considering Simon had returned to Escape—to assist in the transition.

A few things had changed in the four months she'd been gone. For one, someone else now occupied her old office. At first she'd been surprised to learn that Simon didn't intend to let the new manager go. Although, considering she'd told him she couldn't work for him, she shouldn't have been. It was just difficult to stand by while someone else did her job. Or what used to be her job.

But once again, he'd asked if she trusted him. He'd

told her a few things were taking longer than he'd anticipated and that she'd just have to wait a couple more days to find out his solution to the entire problem.

Apparently she was going to find out now. Although what it had to do with walking her outside blindfolded, Marcy didn't know.

"If this is just an excuse to get your hands on me, you realize it isn't necessary," Marcy said.

She thought she heard a sound, almost like smothered laughter.

"Trust me, I have every intention of touching you plenty later," he whispered into her ear. His breath tickled, sending a shiver of anticipation racing down her spine.

The new manager had also taken over her bungalow, but Marcy hadn't minded moving into Simon's apartments. After being separated from him for so long, she really hadn't wanted to be anywhere but in his bed anyway.

And they'd definitely made up for lost time. In fact, she'd barely had a chance to be bored or worried in the past week. He'd kept her too occupied—either aroused or exhausted.

"Where are you taking me?" she asked, trying to concentrate on something other than the desire lashing through her. She had to admit, with his hands over her face, the scent of him was filling her lungs and making concentration extremely difficult.

"Almost there. Just a few more steps."

Small sounds began to filter into her brain. The soft shuffle of shoes against concrete. The low hum of whispered voices. Someone saying rather loudly, "Shhhh."

Before she could ask Simon again what was going

on, he dropped his hands from her face to settle softly on her shoulders. Most of the staff stood in front of her, crowded around the garden Simon had built beside the main hotel building to hide the scars from the fire.

He'd done a great job, and she wished she could have seen him in action. From what she'd heard, he'd planted some of the bushes and flowers with his own hands. Now, that she would have paid money to see— Simon with his arms elbow-deep in dirt.

Looking at him now, with his ruffled golden hair, a bright blue Hawaiian shirt that matched his eyes and a deep tan across his skin, he didn't look like the kind of guy who believed in manual labor.

But then, it had taken her more than two years to figure out that the image he showed the world was not a true reflection of the man beneath the surface.

"What is going on?" She turned to look at Simon, her eyes widening. "Who's running the resort?"

"Don't worry. Enough of the staff stayed at their posts. The guests won't even notice the difference."

Marcy hummed deep in her throat, but it was no longer her job to direct the staff. A sharp pain lanced through her chest, but she ignored it. She'd told Simon she trusted him, and she did.

"Okay, anyone want to tell me what's going on?"

"I thought the staff should meet the new owner of Escape."

Marcy just shook her head. "Simon, don't you think you should have done this a long time ago?"

"I did. I wasn't talking about me."

She was confused. Seriously. "What *are* you talking about?"

Xavier handed Simon a sheaf of papers bound in a blue cover. She'd seen enough legal documents to realize they were important, whatever they were. Reaching down, Simon pulled up her hand and set the papers against her palm.

"These documents detail the transfer of ownership for the resort, from me to you."

Marcy blinked at him, certain she'd heard him wrong.

"Excuse me?"

"You own Escape."

Her fingers curled around the pages in her hand. In the back of her mind she heard the rustling sound as the top few crumpled, but somewhere between her brain and hand the signal to relax got lost.

"No." She shook her head. "This is too much."

She tried to grab Simon's hand so that she could shove the papers back at him. Panic and disbelief mixed heavily inside her chest. What had he done?

Simon clasped his hands behind his back. That didn't stop her. She smacked the bundle against his chest, her fingers splayed wide, and held them there.

"It isn't too much, Marcy. This place belongs to you. You care about it. And you're good at running it, unlike me."

"You handled it all just fine while I was gone."

"Maybe," he conceded, but that was as far as he was going.

"But...but..." she sputtered. "What happens if we break up? If you get pissed at me or I get pissed at you or the entire thing falls apart?"

He smiled at her, that charming, mischievous, wicked smile that had always driven her crazy. And it still did, but it also made her heart flutter inside her chest.

"First, I fully expect that both of us will get angry at

some point. We'll yell. Disagree. And then we'll make up. That doesn't mean either of us is going anywhere. Second, I have no intention of ever letting you off this island again."

"Simon," she said in a warning tone.

"I kidnapped you once, do you think I won't do it again?"

His arms came out from behind his back, but instead of taking the papers, he wrapped them around her and pulled her tight against him. Uncaring that the legal documents governing his entire resort were now crushed between their bodies and getting more destroyed by the second.

He wrapped his hands around the nape of her neck, angling her head so that he could stare down into her face. Gone was the playful glint that always seemed to lurk in the back of his tempting blue eyes. In its place, she saw sincerity, love and an intensity that had her bones melting.

"Everything I have is yours, Marcy, because none of it is worth a damn without you. I know this is important to you. You gave up your dream to come back to Escape with me. And I want to show you how much that sacrifice means to me."

Guilt suffused her. "Actually, leaving New York wasn't hard at all." She pressed her forehead to his, bringing them closer together. "I forgot how cold it is there."

The staff laughed and Simon's lips quirked into a smile.

"But mostly, you weren't there. My dream doesn't matter to me anymore if you're not there to share it with."

"So now we're both happy," Simon said. "Besides,

this way I don't have to deal with the headaches anymore. The resort is yours." He raised his head from hers and turned to look at the people beaming back at them. "You hear that? Problems go to Marcy. I don't want to hear about anything. Not even the thread counts on the sheets."

Marcy smacked at him. "Now I understand. This was all an elaborate scheme to get out of working. I should have known."

This time his little-boy smile couldn't hide the hint of guilt that lurked in his eyes. "Hey, think of it as effective management. I know my own shortcomings and I'd be an idiot not to take advantage of your skills. You're so damn good at running this place."

"Flattery will get you everywhere," she said, her heart swelling inside her chest.

Before she knew what was going on, Simon was slipping out of her arms. At first she thought something was wrong, since he was heading for the ground. But the startled expression on her face didn't last long when she realized he hadn't fallen over, just dropped onto one knee.

"Oh, my god," she breathed out. "What are you doing?" That seemed to be her favorite phrase today.

"I'd think that was obvious," Simon said, mock frowning up at her from his position at her feet. She tried to pull him up off the ground, but he wouldn't budge.

"Marcy, I told the entire world that I loved you in the most public way I could think of because I want everyone to know how I feel about you."

A hard lump formed in Marcy's throat and her eyes glazed over with tears.

Who would have thought almost two and a half

years ago when she'd walked onto this island that she'd end up here with Simon Reeves kneeling in the dirt, about to propose to her? Definitely not her. She'd come here looking for an escape. An opportunity to prove her worth—to herself and the world.

And instead she'd found all of that and more. A man she loved who loved her in return. The kind of person she could see spending the rest of her life with, having children, growing old.

Maybe there was more to that little legend about the island than any of them had ever realized. She'd certainly found her heart's desire and it was nothing like what she'd expected.

"But I wanted to share this moment with the people who've come to mean something to us both," Simon continued. "Some people think of this place as paradise. Some might see it as isolated. But I just see it as home and I want you to stay here with me forever. To build a life together."

"Yes," she whispered, the tears she was desperately trying not to shed choking off the word. "Yes," she said again, stronger and more sure.

A happy whoop from the crowd accompanied her answer.

Simon picked her up and spun her around, bringing their mouths together. The familiar heat spilled into her body, the buzz of it delicious and comforting.

They were definitely going to have some fun adventures together. With Simon, there was no telling what was coming around the corner.

A breathless laugh burst from her body. She was dizzy with happiness. Finally Simon put her down, the world still spinning gently around her.

She gazed unsteadily at the people gathered around them. Friends…no, family.

Marcy wanted every single person who visited Île du Coeur to find the same happiness she had found.

Colt and Lena, Zane and Elle, she and Simon… Marcy really hoped they were part of a long line of couples who would find love here. Which gave her an idea….

"Simon, I'm going to hire a wedding planner."

"Fine." He shrugged. "I would have expected you to be too ana—" Marcy's glare had Simon choking back his words. "Um…organized…to want to let that go."

"Not for us. For the resort."

Simon's eyes went wide with fear before he apparently remembered that whatever she was planning, it was no longer his worry. "Whatever makes you happy."

March had visions of sunset ceremonies on the beach and grand parties in the ballroom. It would be perfect.

Reaching up on tiptoe, she wrapped her arms around Simon and pulled his mouth down to hers, whispering against his warm lips, "*You* make me happy."

Simon swept her up into his arms again and carried her away, completely uncaring that he was leaving behind the crowd of people who'd come to congratulate them. She'd apologize later. His mouth nuzzled at her neck. *Much later.* The corner of his lips curled in a smile full of devilment and charm and his eyes flashed with heat as he mock growled, "Happy's good. But naked's so much better."

* * * * *

MILLS & BOON®

Regency Vows Collection!

If you enjoyed this book, get the full Regency Vows Collection today and receive two free books.

2 BOOKS FREE!

Order your complete collection today at
www.millsandboon.co.uk/regencyvows

0615_MB512

MILLS & BOON®

The Thirty List

At thirty, Rachel has slid down every ladder she has ever climbed. Jobless, broke and ditched by her husband, she has to move in with grumpy Patrick and his four-year-old son.

Patrick is also getting divorced, so to cheer themselves up the two decide to draw up bucket lists. Soon they are learning to tango, abseiling, trying stand-up comedy and more. But, as she gets closer to Patrick, Rachel wonders if their relationship is too good to be true…

Order yours today at
www.millsandboon.co.uk/Thethirtylist

0515_ST_13

MILLS & BOON®

The Chatsfield Collection!

2 BOOKS FREE!

Style, spectacle, scandal…!

With the eight Chatsfield siblings happily married and settling down, it's time for a new generation of Chatsfields to shine, in this brand-new 8-book collection! The prospect of a merger with the Harrington family's boutique hotels will shape the future forever. But who will come out on top?

**Find out at
www.millsandboon.co.uk/TheChatsfield2**

CHATSFIELD_PROMO_BK

MILLS & BOON®

The Sharon Kendrick Collection!

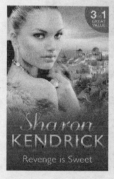

Passion and seduction....

If you love a Greek tycoon, an Italian billionaire or a
Spanish hero, then this collection is perfect for you.
Get your hands on the six 3-in-1 romances from the
outstanding Sharon Kendrick. Plus, with one book
free, this offer is too good to miss!

Order yours today at
www.millsandboon.co.uk/Kendrickcollection

0415_ST_10

MILLS & BOON®

Why not subscribe?
Never miss a title and save money too!

Here's what's available to you if you join the exclusive **Mills & Boon Book Club** today:

✦ *Titles up to a month ahead of the shops*
✦ *Amazing discounts*
✦ *Free P&P*
✦ *Earn Bonus Book points that can be redeemed against other titles and gifts*
✦ *Choose from monthly or pre-paid plans*

Still want more?
Well, if you join today we'll even give you
50% OFF your first parcel!

So visit **www.millsandboon.co.uk/subs**
or call **Customer Relations** on **020 8288 2888**
to be a part of this exclusive Book Club!

SUBS_2014